VOICES OF REDEMPTION

A NOVEL

by

Byron Rivers

Published in the United States of America by
Pathlight Stories., Atlanta, Georgia.
ISBN 978-0-615-19199-7 a trade paperback book.

For book orders, author appearance inquiries and interviews,
contact us via the publisher at: pathlightstories@yahoo.com
or visit my web @ www.byronrivers.com

Library of Congress Cataloging In Publication Data

Graphic Designs by Richardjr@reldezignsolutions.com

VOICES OF REDEMPTION

A NOVEL

by

Byron Rivers

In memory of Mom and Dad

ACKNOWLEDGMENTS

I am very thankful for the inspiration to write Voices of Redemption, my debut novel. Many people were placed along my path throughout this long journey. Though they are far too many to mention, I am extremely delighted that they already know how special they are. Foremost, I'm thankful that my mother, Katherine Rivers, had the opportunity to enjoy it before recently going to glory. She flatly told me the first draft wasn't really about anything, prompting me to raise the bar and do four rewrites until she ultimately smiled with joy. Thank her if you smile too. I also thank the late Dr. Frederick Sampson, former Pastor of Tabernacle Baptist Church in Detroit. His message regarding the value in inspiring others stayed in my heart and changed my life. A special dedication extends to all men and women who enjoy singing for our Savior in every Choir U.S.A. and the Music Ministers who artistically lead them like Jerese M. This story is for that deep down feeling derived from putting your heart and soul in the song, and the resonance that remains long after taking your seat. To the many book clubs across the country I've yet to meet, I'm looking forward to your invitation. I may even sing you a song if you feed me, but be careful what you ask for—the story is far better than my singing voice. Last but not least, to my daughter Brittany. Your faith in me has been awesome, and the joy of being your father has made me a better man. Let's persevere and climb that next mountain now big girl! Agape love extends to all of you.

Byron Rivers

PROLOGUE

Just east of the city limits of Atlanta, Georgia in what used to be a small town called Stone Mountain, there still can be found a narrow gravel road lined on both sides with a beautiful assortment of pine, magnolia and dogwood trees. Its metropolitan surroundings now bustle with the urban sprawl of other cities, yet little has physically changed in this pocket of paradise where blue jays commonly nest on the trees elongated branches. The branches and their leaves are thicker and more numerous now than in times past, yet they remain poked with just enough sun rays to offer all who pass the chance to look up and catch birds and squirrels dancing. The road was cut first as a swath in 1866 by newly emancipated slaves. By day they labored hard, making their living under the Georgia sun by carving huge granite blocks of white rock out of Stone Mountain. This rock was used for the construction of magnificent ornate monuments both locally and across the U.S. By night they prayed and sang spiritual songs on weary legs with happy hearts. As time passed these men not only gained knowledge of how to cut this massive rock expertly, but also how to build structures for themselves. Through much dedication, faith and skill they built a solid granite structure of worship in 1884. They named it Mt. Tabernacle, just like the gravel road that precedes it, and their tombs nestled in back of the church today still speak of their spiritual reverence. Come see the landscapes beauty and you'll sense its rich history. Listen carefully, and you can still hear their songs.

ONE

Peachtree Stadium, Atlanta, Georgia

Like a mild mannered man, suddenly transformed into a werewolf at the stroke of midnight, my Christian persona disappeared when I wore uniform number 44. Teammates and close friends who really knew me swore that my body was only leased to this All American safety at Northwest Georgia University, but that wasn't surprising, you should have seen their first impressions. As a kid playing Little League Football, I can vividly recall looking up to my parents for approval after aggressively tackling opponents. My proud Dad merely winced from time to time, while Mom hastily covered her mouth and looked terrified instead of clapping for me like the other Moms did. By the time I started playing high school football, I'd concluded that they just refused to accept my tenacity and that maybe a lifetime of spirituality may have made them soft. I soon discovered there was more to it than that. One evening after practice they sat me down and told me they feared for me, and prayed I wasn't inspired by the devil. I was shocked, but I assured them that it wasn't the devil, but God Almighty, and we'd go back and forth with these arguments regularly with neither side proving their point. One thing is sure. It was me then, and it's definitely me now. I'm Kyle Medley, College Football All American. Now standing 6'3 and weighing 255 pounds, I'm strong, extremely fast, and a mean enough hitter to make a junkyard dog cringe, walk and testify.

On the bus ride to the stadium this afternoon, I reminded my teammates that we were playing this special game for our Creator, and that we should thank him for this beautiful autumn Saturday. I led them in prayer too, just like I did before each game. As game time approached I became more animated, jumping up and down constantly while getting my blood warmed up for what the sporting nation called judgment day.

Over 90,000 fans excitedly filled the stadium as an approaching nightfall signaled to them that game time was finally near. "Hey Kyle, we love you," read several huge signs held tirelessly by a dozen beautiful girls to prove it. "Bring us blood assassin," read others held by the more macho segment of loyal 'Colts' fans. Most would bask in this attention, but not me. It was time for business, so I ignored the distraction as I lined up on special teams to cover the opening kick. Everyone in football nation felt I was really covering Reggie Pittman —Tennessee A&M speedster and fellow All American—and they were right. Off the football field I knew of him since our opposing high school games in metro Atlanta. I even begrudgingly respected him, since his team usually won. Respect was the furthest thing from my mind now as blood rushed through my veins like hot, volcanic lava. It always did shortly after I suited up, but I can't blame the uniform or the devil. If the football field was really a jungle as they say, then I was truly the jungles king. Just like lions in a jungle, the fans, coaching staff, and pro scouts who came to see me never minded watching an animal like me feast, either. For them, it was like going to the zoo on Saturday afternoon, only this Saturday, the stakes were higher. The winner of this game would win the Southeastern Collegiate Championship. It's just a game, some will say. Maybe so, but for me, the approaching nightfall meant it was time for this lion to feed.

The opening kickoff incited me, but that was no surprise. What was surprising was the fact that the football went right into Reggie's hands. Our kicker knew better, or should have done a better job of keeping the ball away from Reggie, so said the sportscasters. As for me, I liked the challenge, and I wouldn't have planned it differently if I could. Reggie had a reputation for running fast and running pretty, and fielding the ball from the five yard line he immediately proved he didn't come to disappoint.

I ran swiftly downfield after the punt, fueled by an unknown rage brewing inside of me with every yard I sprinted. I slowed down just enough to watch him cut right and elude two tacklers. He then cut left and eluded three more before making his biggest mistake by running straight up the middle of the field. I was waiting to intercept him, but not waiting still, like one would for the mailman. I was now moving like a freight train in the night.

He felt my presence, the last man between him and the goal line, even before he saw me. Instinctively, Reggie spun around in an attempt to change direction and elude me too. The move almost worked, but it was too late. I unleashed a furious hit to his lower back as he turned, making sure I tackled him and prevented him from beating us on the return and scoring. His body fell hard to the emerald green artificial turf below that was more solid than the hit, but I hadn't fully made my point. I picked his mangled body up again, only to violently throw it back down to the turf once more. While walking away with that euphoric feeling of victory, I cynically looked back and noticed Reggie still laying flat on his back. I could never forget how he talked trash for years—ever since Little League—in victory over me. There couldn't have been a more fitting time to deliver back to him some of his own medicine and talk some trash of my own, either.

"Go ahead, get up. Get up and face the music Reggie, because it's my turn now," I yelled. "That's right! Your day might have been yesterday, but the whole world will know who the winner is today, understand?"

I knew I'd unloaded a vicious hit on him without even noticing the unnecessary roughness flags which spiraled across the field like huge pieces of yellow hail. Unfortunately, I'd grown too used to them. I fully expected him to take a few seconds to recover before he got up and told me how weak the hit was also, but my intuition hinted that this scenario would be much, much different. Frantically, I ran back to him, arriving before his teammates eventually came to form a circle around us.

"Hey Reggie, for goodness sake, get up, alright?" I begged him over and over, but his body would remain limp long after the stretcher arrived. Reggie Pittman never walked again. We'd won the game, yet there really was no point in tallying scores for me. Why did I really do it? How could a so called man of God be so violent? Was this what Mom and Dad meant? Searching myself and finding no answers to what was truly inside of me, I vowed to never play football again. That day, the lion returned to his den, and guilt has followed me every day since. I turned down pro football offers. Two months later, I turned off the news. I went to small, reclusive place of my fore fathers. I went back to church.

TWO

Mt. Tabernacle Full Gospel Church
(7 years later)

> *"Lord you made a difference in my life,*
> *helped me to overcome all the pain and strife.*
> *Gave me the sunshine and the rain, taught*
> *me faith when born again.*
> *Lord you made a difference in my life."*

Music Minister Roberts just shook his head from side to side. "Brothers, that's a nice effort, but we have to project our voices better in the Baritone section. Bring it up from the gut Brother Lewis, praise the Lord, from right here," he said as he pointed to his mid-section.

"I probably could do a much better job if I had half the gut you do," Brother Lewis whispered.

"And Brother Sherman, let me remind you that you are singing, and not reciting Shakespeare for the school play. Therefore you pronounce it 'diff-rence,' with two syllables, not diff-err-rence in my life, with three, got it?"

"Yeah, I got it," Sherman replied, "but what 'difference' does it really make," he muttered?

"And who on earth is that in the first tenor section that's singing second tenor?" Minister Roberts asked.

Most of us stared hopelessly at each other before looking back to him in a curious fashion. Truth was, half of us didn't know the difference between the two tones of singing, and the other half who knew couldn't vocally articulate where one harmonically ended and the other began. Thus, nobody replied, until suddenly brother Humphries pointed his finger and nodded his head toward me, Kyle

Medley. Music Minister Roberts frowned while shaking his head back and forth with an exasperated gasp. The culprit could have been most of us, yet I was fare enough game for the mystery to be solved. "I see, so it's Kyle huh? I should have known," he replied, then shook his head.

"Alright men, lets go through it once more from the top."

I was sinking deep in sin,
until I found you and you took me in
How could I make it so very hard for you for so long?
But you washed my sins away, gave
me new meaning to this new day

The very reason why I gladly sing your song
So I'm telling you the Lord—
you made a difference in my life
Gave me the victory from
this worlds madness and its strife
Gave me sunshine and the rain,
taught me faith when born again
I say Lord you made a difference in my life…

Minister Roberts loudly pounded the last note on the piano before rising up and slowly walking over to us. Like Pavlov's dogs, we'd become overly conditioned to what followed after hearing the last key struck in that manner.

"Brothers, our Men's Day Celebration is in four months, and as faithful and optimistic as I try to be, I can't fathom the men of Mt. Tabernacle bringing this low level of vocal stamina to the forefront of our church in its honor. If we do, gentlemen, it certainly won't be Kingdom quality. In fact, if there was a gospel version of American Idol, I think all of you would be sent packing." There was an eerie silence among us all. It was an odd silence, considering that until recently we were accustomed to being the loudest and most unrestrained voices in the sanctuary every week. Our horrible voices were a subtle testament to

Pastor Adams, the church's spiritual leader. He'd long remained sincere in his commitment to allow all men, regardless of vocal talent, to sing for the Lord as long as the spirit moved them. Pastor Adams noticed that some of us appeared uninspired, while others were down right ticked off, and spoke up.

"Quality of the spirit is respected a whole lot mo' around here than the quality of your voice, Minister Roberts. Besides, everyone knows that this kind of singing displays our brand of ole' time religion."

"But pastor, truth be told, this kind of gospel singing barely masks the fact that the vocal chords of these men just can't do any better."

Pastor Adams eyeballed the brother from Boston with his glib tongue and high expectations before responding.

"If that's the truth Minister Roberts, then it sounds like the church will get a two for one deal-ole time religious singin' without knowin' that the men singin' to em' can't even sing, now how bout' that?" Most of us erupted in laughter and nodded in approval. We loved Adams heartfelt support, and instantly we were comforted with poor note bliss. Deep down we all felt that a higher power, working through Pastor Adams, knew our hearts and souls were in the right place, so why not sing boldly—or indeed terribly?

Time proved that no matter how free spirited we felt, the tension still brewed. Roberts had been with us for six months and the honeymoon was officially over. He took gospel to a level nobody ever dreamed while romancing Atlanta's gospel radio. His ears thirsted for more while he marveled at the big, mega-church choirs he visited across town. Some nights, he'd listen to the 'Voices of Praise' radio station before falling asleep. Other nights, he'd merely watch gospel singers on cable channels until they watched him. Through it all, he found himself comparing their vast commercial appeal with us, a bunch of humble and dedicated men who weren't quite sure what had really hit them.

Initially, Roberts probably disliked himself for it, but as gospel crazed and fanatical as he may have been, he knew it was unfair. Yet, as rehearsals progressed—if you could call us progress—Roberts seemed to dislike us even more. It was safe to say that he wanted to take things in another direction, and nothing less than kingdom quality sound from us was going to do. This made things awfully uncomfortable for most of the men, but not me, Kyle Medley. Somehow, they've elected me, a man running from his past, to lead them as their President. As awkward as it first seemed, it became a fitting distinction for me to lead a group of vocally challenged men. Sure, I was their worst singer, but history was on my side.

My great-great grandfather, Lazarus Medley built this church and served as its first pastor. His tomb out back with the Medley name on it reminds me that strong leadership is in my genes. Sometimes I even feel a higher calling to lead this church the way my ancestors did, at least until painful memories from 'the hit' convicts my conscious. That hit on Reggie Pittman has kept me in spiritual limbo for the last seven years. It's an awkward place to be with the men looking to me to solve the new challenge brought in the form of Minister Roberts, but I think I can handle that. Indeed, his graceless approach inspires me to want to. Most of us in the Manpower Choir agreed, but out of respect for Pastor Adams appointing Roberts to lead the Music Ministry, we would never voice it. It only became an issue during the nights we'd practice and Pastor Adams didn't show up, and lately, this was pretty often. On these dreadful nights Minister Roberts would berate us while insisting we stand up the entire evening to sing. Then we would again re-sing a stanza over and over again until we either got it right—or even more wrong. More often than not those evenings culminated with our raspy voices coming to a screeching howl while Roberts shook his head in pure disgust. Tonight was especially brutal, yet unique in that Pastor Adams was present. After rehearsing another song, Minister Roberts again banged the last note on the piano's ivory keys and turned to me.

"Kyle, I want you to take this song from the top now, by yourself, with nobody joining in to help you."

"Okay Minister Roberts," I responded. Fifteen minutes of hard vocal labor hadn't passed before he was at it again.

"Kyle, what is your choir doing? You should hear yourselves. Do you ever listen to yourselves by the way, any of you? That's what I thought," he muttered at about the same time I'd pretty much had it.

"What do you want from us Minister Roberts?" I asked in my best attempt to break the onslaught.

"What do I want from you?" he repeated, as if the question had mystical origins.

"That's right. You're trying to squeeze blood from a turnip if you're asking us to sing like professional Gospel singers, and if so, I wouldn't hold my breath."

"Professional Gospel singers you say? Why, that's awfully ambitious of you don't you think?" he asked sarcastically.

"Wait a minute now." We're showing up every Thursday night trying to bring good spirits and proper attitudes after working hard jobs all week, and all we've accomplished lately is hearing your constant criticism,".

"Criticism?" he incredulously replied. "What a small view of my role here. Let me remind you of something Brother Medley—or should I just refer to you as "The Assassin?"

"Brother Medley will do fine, but do know that you are pushing it."

"I'm sure everyone knows that I don't want to do that, don't they? Anyway, do recognize that I am the man Pastor Adams has commissioned to lead this Music Ministry into Men's Day and beyond. You should be thankful that he—no God, has sent me here to make you all better, and not view this as criticism."

"While you make up your mind who it was that sent you Minister Roberts," I replied, "I only want to know one thing."

"Go on."

"What would you say if we told you that you've made us better, and this is as good as we're going to get?"

"I'd say you're suggesting this choir can't do better, and that's nonsense. It also sounds like you're telling me that my job lacks purpose."

"I'm not exactly going that far," I assured him.

"Oh yes you are, buts it's okay, forget about it.

"Forget about it?" I asked. "Forget about what?"

"I think that's something they say back east, Kyle," Brother Sherman said. "Don't ask me why."

"Yeah, forget about it," Roberts repeated. I'm not angry about your ignorance of good gospel—just highly annoyed. Rest assured though, because from what I'm hearing, this is only the beginning of my work here."

"No, Minister Roberts, I don't think you understand," I cautioned. "The men are getting restless and running out of patience. Three have come to me this week threatening to quit, and a couple others may be following suit." I'd hoped he'd be remorseful by the news, but instead, Roberts face lit up.

"Now that's the best news yet. Let them quit. It'll be the finest thing to ever happen to Mt. Tabernacle. You see, nowhere in the Bible does it say a man has to sing in the choir. Psalms says praise him with just about every kind of instrument and voice, but it doesn't say he has to be in the choir, now does it? Let them quit for Christ sake." He smiled with contentment while scanning his beady eyes about. He even changed his tone.

"You'll all have my blessings if you quit gentlemen. Trust me... they'll be no hard feelings on my part. I say quit *and* forget about it. God will forgive you I'm sure. Heck, he may even love you more," he confirmed.

"I hate to disappoint you Minister Roberts, but quitting is not the answer for any of us, I can tell you that right now."

"Huh? Then tell me Brother Medley, what do you think might be the answer?" Roberts asked, visibly annoyed.

"That depends on the question. Let's see, do we quit because you want us to, or sing on because we love this choir? Hmm...Maybe we can call ourselves "The Forget about Its" if we stay. It's a nice option. We can promise everyone a fast track to heaven if they come to our performances to hear us sing— following your logic."

"Are you being cute Kyle?"

"Only as cute as the issue is absurd Roberts, because I don't see what makes this whole thing so difficult, really."

"You don't see, huh? Let me spell it out for you then, given you *all* probably think it's cute. We have this," he mockingly stated as he pointed his finger at the lot of us, "and we have four months to prepare for Men's Day. We also have the bigger question of how we will prepare. No, we have a state of emergency, because all the preparation in the world makes no difference. Now how do you suggest we solve it?" How do we prepare for a grand Men's Day with Elgin Roberts name on it as the Minister of Music?" Everyone grew quiet upon hearing the awkward question that had never been posed.

"I'm listening," he added.

"Minister Roberts," I said, breaking the silence. "Nothing's broke here, and since nothings broke, nothing needs fixing, plain and simple."

"That's right," "that's what I'm talking bout," "alright now," were the men's varied responses.

"Right. Somehow I knew you'd all say that," Roberts retorted. I knew you all would bring me nothing but resistance. You see, only in choirs where the vocal talent is so low does a Music Minister get this kind of 'bucking resistance'."

"Did he say what I thought he said?" asked Brother Humphries.

"No I didn't Humphries!" Roberts assured. "I said bucking—bucking resistance. But I think I have an idea, one that might please everyone," he suggested, still cutting his eyes at Humphries.

I raised an eyebrow in honest suspicion while three of us stepped forward to listen. We were all skeptical, realizing Roberts bright ideas could spell trouble.

"Why don't we see if we can call more men up from the congregation to join the Manpower practice session next week? After all, there is strength in numbers, and if each one of us were to ask two men, then who knows what kind of sound we could inspire here in his Kingdom. What do you think?" I'd braced myself for far worse, but his words were unusually conciliatory for once. Somewhat relieved, I thought it better to give in to an appeasing suggestion before blowing my top and responding with the "NIGROE PLEEZE!" refrain resting firmly on my lips.

"It might be worth a try," I conceded. Minister Roberts wasn't even listening. He ignored me completely and instead looked to Pastor Adams for approval, but in his haughtiness he must have forgotton this was Thursday night. Any other night of the week our pastor made his opinions known. He was too much of a natural leader not to, but not nearly so much as on a Thursday night. On this night Pastor Adams would retreat into being one of the most unassuming brothers—one whose main priority was to simply show up, strap on his bass, and pluck that guitar nearly as horrendously as we sang. Yes, it was good on Thursday nights, when you felt blessed to know your pastor—when you knew that the small town guy who seemingly overnight turned into a big city spiritual leader simply missed being one of us. Being one of us made it no surprise that Pastor Adams ignored Minister Roberts question the way Roberts ignored me too. Without saying a word, Pastor Adams aimed his head down and began plucking each string. His body language indicated he was more interested in hitting the right line in the song than in the outcome of any decision. Add that to the fact that the sky wasn't falling, and there you had him—a poster child for worry free living for just one evening out of the week.

Minister Roberts again glanced at Pastor Adams, unable to ascertain whether his unspoken words suggested he should proceed or just as well jump in the river. Thus, Roberts responded ever so cautiously, like a carpenter seeking to reinvent the wheel, only now discovering how daunting the task really is.

"Mt. Tabernacle has been blessed," he sheepishly began. "We have gained over 500 new members since I arrived from Boston just months ago. Not only have we grown numerically, but we've grown spiritually as well. We don't have the infighting among our Deacon board, our choir, **Amen**, or any other area of our blessed congregation **"Amen, Amen."** "What we do have is tunnel vision though," **"Well"**, "because the Manpower Choir of Mt. Tabernacle has simply existed unto itself for the last several years. We should exist more like my old church in Boston..."**What?"** "Like a salt shaker, we should spread the invitation to join our fabulous choir to all men. That's right! We should invite more men to our table to share in this smorgasbord of blessings, instead of behaving like a fraternal order of men, inviting only a few to our ranks."

"There he goes again," remarked Brother Sherman. "The man can't even make a good comparison to anything without putting food in it!"

"I know that's right," I said to Sherman before loudly proclaiming to the brothers. "Alright, we'll take Minister Roberts suggestion and invite more men every week to join the Mt. Tabernacle Manpower Choir."

"Amen, Amen, 'Ah-men'," responded all the men of Manpower. It was 8:45p.m., and Pastor Adams modestly stood up to speak. "Well brothers, unless any of you have anything more to add, I'd like for us to join hands in prayer before we bring an end to our evening." The brothers gathered around in a circle and held hands.

"Anyone have a special prayer?" There was a brief pause until Brother Lange broke the silence.

"Yes brothers, I'd like you all to pray for me and my wife. You see, I thought that marriage would be easy since we loved each other so much. But I have been agonizing over the last six months or so because I don't know how to please her. I just don't know what to do, and driving over the road in my tractor trailer after I leave her on a sour note just grieves me even more."

"Man, you been crying about that girl since the day you married her," barked Brother Humphries. "As much as you do for her, I would pretend she was the road kill the next time you run over a squirrel or deer, move on in your truck, and leave her by the side of the road."

Stephen Humphries reached out to get five from one of the brothers before Pastor Adams sternly spoke.

"Brother Humphries, we will pray for your spiritual maturity first, for we all love this grieving brother and feel his pain, and your antidote is from a single man's perspective, and not a holy one at that."

"Brothers, let us bow our heads. Brother Lange," the pastor continued, "we will all pray that the Creator will enlighten your wife enough to see and appreciate your efforts. Yet, if her expectations are reasonable, we will also pray that you gain the wisdom to recognize what they are and act accordingly. We pray for her virtue, and that she willingly follows you as you follow Him, Amen, therefore allowing you the peace of mind that you need—that He wants you to have—when you are at home and also while traveling these dangerous highways away from home.

"**Amen... Amen,**" the men responded.

"Now are there any more prayer requests?" Pastor Adams asked while glancing about us. I could have remained silent and let things proceed, but something was gnawing at me. Sometimes words are better left unsaid, yet other words stay on your chest so long that you have to let them go, and this one-this one had to fly.

"Yeah, I answered. I'd like for you all to pray for me, especially you Pastor Adams." The brothers lowered their heads as I continued.

"Because—you know the two watermelons you had growing in your watermelon patch? Well, I...I...well I'm the one who took them!" Pastor Adams abruptly lifted his head and opened his eyes, as did everyone else.

"I wondered what dirty and low down negro..." he remarked in clear disdain by the deed. The men lifted their heads up slowly and glanced around at each other. Upon meeting equally blank stares, they all looked at me in a curious fashion before bursting with laughter.

THREE

D & B's Soul Creation
Detroit, Michigan

Donald hurried to add the day's receipts while hoping Bianca didn't come out of the guest room too quickly. Like most late evenings, she was one of only two or three patrons inside the restaurant. Still, there was no reason to put it in her face. No reason for her to witness just how meager those receipts had become lately, at least.

"Goodnight Anita, you've had a full day. It's time to go home," Donald expressed in his most concerned bedside manner possible. The last of only three employees of D & B's Soul Creation took the bonnet off her head and untied her apron.

"Don't worry Don, five minutes and I'm out of here anyway," she said.

Bianca Kincaid, his lovely fiancée, was anxiously waiting for this moment after contenting herself for the last two hours by writing her haiku style of poetry. She'd become quite good at it lately, transcribing words and images of love and spiritual upheaval onto pages so beautifully they now reflected the essence of her very soul. She often smiled when she wrote because she knew that the true secret in giving someone wings—especially an artist—was love. Dressed in the $1,000 dollar designer dress and wearing the $10,000 engagement ring Donald recently purchased, she thumbed it back and forth on her finger while desperately searching for that one right word that would artistically convey her thoughts. She'd ignited the crowd at her first open mike night reading, but little did they know she had so much more. She smiled to herself again, secretly affirming that she had every reason to be cheerful. It wasn't because of the material trinkets or the cloths he showered her with either—at least that's what she told herself—but the man she'd fallen in love with and soon planned to marry. But enough of romancing words on the page for now. She was living love, she reasoned, and could therefore afford to make beauty leap off the pages later. She strolled toward the front of the restaurant, just to say hello to him.

"Donald, you know you work too hard."

"You are so right, baby."

"Are you almost done?"

"Almost. I was just telling Anita that we may have to close on Sundays to honor the Lord." Anita tried to contain the look of shock on her face, but finding it too difficult she turned to make her exit sooner than planned.

"Goodnight, you two."

"Goodnight," they both responded back to her. Bianca paid no attention to her abrupt departure, and only waited for the door to shut before speaking.

"Is there anything I can do to help sweetheart? It's getting late you know."

"I've got everything…well, almost everything," he confirmed.

"What more do you need?" she asked.

"If you'll bring me another food inventory log, that'll be of help. It's located in the left hand drawer of the desk in my office."

"Sure thing," she replied.

Bianca walked back to Donald's office to search the same desk she just hurriedly left moments ago. Pulling the left drawer open, she didn't see anything resembling the log he mentioned. *Maybe he meant the right drawer.* Sure, he must have meant the right drawer. She pulled on the drawer, only to quickly discover it was locked. Looking around the office, she noticed a small set of keys dangling on the wall and removed them. Opening the drawer was easy now, but what covered the logs jolted her senses and would prove to change her life forever. Print outs of at least seventy-five credit card numbers with various names on them filled the drawer. With a voice laced with tension she called out to him.

"Donald. Donald," she repeated.

"Yeah baby, what is it?"

"Come here please."

"What's wrong?" Donald shouted from the other room. Upon hearing his footsteps entering the room she tossed the keys down on the desk and turned to face him.

Bianca wasn't street wise, but she was a quick thinker. She'd received her Masters degree from a Big Ten University but her cultured persona came by way of the tutelage of her widowed mother, a former Miss Tennessee beauty queen who strived to amply prepare her daughter for society at every turn. In spite of all of this, Bianca felt ill equipped, because nothing she'd encountered in life helped her understand Donald's world until now. Stepping back as though in a trance, her body shook from an epiphany of how their illustrious lifestyle was financed for the first time.

"What's wrong, Bianca?" he asked again, but still, she didn't answer. She only stared at him like the new stranger he was before speaking.

"Who do these credit card numbers belong to?" she asked.

"That's not the drawer you were asked to look in!" Donald shot back. "Going through my personal things already I see, huh?" His retort was meant to make her feel guilty and throw her off balance, but only sadness roared through her heart. She pressed on anyway, faithful in her resilience and reasoning she'd gain her composure at whatever point it came.

"It was an honest mistake, but tell me anyway. Who do these credit card numbers belong to?"

"Don't be silly, Bianca. They belong to customers, just every day people, alright?"

"I see. People who'll get excessive charges billed to them!" Her voice now rose in nervous confirmation. On principle, Bianca took no prisoners and she continued pressing him to the ropes like a relentless boxer on a mission while he stood mute.

"People you say, right? Lot's of people who'll become caught in a financial bind out of the blue one day, and many who may never even realize what's going on, isn't that right?" Don appeared completely dumbfounded as she pressed on. He knew he could no longer hide the truth, yet his words and demeanor proved far from apologetic.

"Yeah, that's right, college girl. Let's put it like this. They won't get them back any quicker than you can take the dresses, the jewelry, the vacations and the cruises back, alright? They'll get them back when you tell me you haven't enjoyed the five star hotels, the concerts, and the expensive restaurants we always go to. When you're ready, I'll be listening, but so far, I don't hear you." More sadly surprised than before, she quietly sobbed at the sight of his overt defiance. Before she could fully grapple with her tears though, he grabbed her arms so tightly her circulation waned.

"How did you think we paid for all this, huh? Be for real, you have eyes. Do you really see that many customers coming around this restaurant? Don't stand there acting innocent, like you have no idea. Tell me, do you?" Her emotions were fast moving beyond hurt, and had now reached the stage of 'proud' which meant not even acknowledging the crude way in which Donald now handled her. Waiting until the physical and mental pain sank in deeply enough to reawaken herself to this new reality, she decided to answer him first before begging for her own comfort.

"Actually, I don't count your customers, so no...I have no idea. I do know that I wouldn't have enjoyed all of this if I knew," she coolly responded. "I trusted you. You've been telling me that business was good, so...now you're really hurting me," she finally conceded. "Get your hands off of me now!" she ordered. Donald released his grip on her, stepped away, and remorsefully turned his back around. In a fit of anguish, he put his hand to his forehead, but remained smoothly relentless in his counter attack as he turned again to face her.

"So you mean to tell me you're really that naïve? I don't believe that. You've had to notice something."

"Then you tell me," came her slow and measured reply. "What things should I have been looking for?" Donald had no immediate answer, and Bianca had no hesitation about pressing the issue on.

"Maybe you're right," she conceded. "Maybe I am a bit naive, because how do you love and trust someone and still know what to look for?" Donald shook his head as if the question was too impossible to answer, but he knew deep down that a street life— one she'd never led—could prepare you to do that very thing.

"No, you can't tell me, because you're too good...good at deception, that is, but it doesn't matter, because I've seen enough, now. Some things I can't—I won't just stand by and look at."

"What are you talking about?" he asked. "Just what can't you look at?"

"What do you think? This way of life, Donald...I won't live this kind of life with you."

"Listen baby. I'm sorry for handling you like that. I overreacted."

"Don't worry, the bruises will go away in time," she confirmed. His eyes opened wide with her response. "Hey, it's only natural that you feel this way. I understand you, because I know you. You're a good woman, and a good woman only see's what they think they should see—a world that's all good—but calm down, alright? This is simply the real world. Trust me, you'll get used to it."

"Oh, I'm calm, but you're *still* not listening to me, are you? I won't live or watch you live this lifestyle." Donald paused, and through his silence he embraced the prospect of a new approach.

"Oh yes you will. You'll just close your eyes to it, that's all."

"Really," Bianca replied? "And if I don't? What if I don't want to close my eyes?" He looked at her sternly before responding.

"Then I'll have someone close them for you," he said coldly.

Bianca stood paralyzed. Her heart was now pumping wildly as he moved closer to her. Slowly, gently, he caressed his fingers through her hair before softly placing one hand on each cheek. With the tip of his fingers, he wiped the white lines of freshly dried tear drops that had fallen from her saddened eyes around the slopes of her ebony cheeks.

"Tell me you're not serious Donald," she asked, hoping to sound unafraid while inwardly begging for his confirmation. Instead of comforting her, however, he gave her a look so sinister that it frightened her even more. She now wanted to scream and run. Hitting him with the electric pencil sharpener to her left was a thought, but she ruled it as an option she'd use only if he left her no way out. She was determined to play it safe and let him slowly perish with his own sword, his own advice. Let him see what he wants to see, but when the time is right, she'd get as far away from Donald Morton as she possibly could.

"Donald?"

"Yes."

"I'm sorry, but this is just all so sudden. Maybe I'm acting too spoiled and unappreciative. Maybe I need some time to allow this to sink in, that's all."

"I understand. Trust me, it will," he assured her. "I've got everything covered baby, and we'll be fine, you'll see."

"I'm sure I'll be. You've always taken care of me. Forgive me. I'm the one who overreacted, okay?"

"Sure thing Bianca, believe me baby, all is forgiven."

FOUR

From all outward appearances, Sunday's 8:00 o'clock service was just another church service at any church U.S.A, with only a few major exceptions. This happened to be Mt. Tabernacle, not one of the two or three mega-churches across town that garnered all the publicity among the socially elite. It also was a church that was literally and spiritually built on the rock. A church that just so happened to be under the leadership of Pastor Troy Adams, the country boy whose powerful sermons brought a huge, uncanny stature to his razor thin build. Most believed he cared three times as much for your soul than your money, and everyone who experienced his leadership knew he was the best kept secret in Atlanta—maybe this whole side of the Mississippi river. Longtime members boasted that like the Mississippi, Mt. Tabernacle held an undercurrent of love and goodwill that ran swift and deep, too.

This Sunday the men sat infused with a bit more pride and purpose than usual. All of them felt like meaningful forces of those same undercurrents and rivers flowing within the church, and so they listened intently to Pastor Adams preach while occasionally glancing about the crowd.

"Y'all forgive me," Pastor Adams began. "Pray, and forgive me people if at times I don't get that excited when you tell me you are getting married."

"Well."

"That's right, for I look around this congregation and see too many casualties of war, instead of fruits of love. Too many ill advised union's are dissolved, and I see too many unequally yoked couples who are seeking me to marry them instead of seeking to find out what God wants you to do first."

"Lord, have Mercy!"

"Many of you are looking like a reindeer in the road when you shine your headlights on them, just waiting to get hit!"

Brother Lange made a deliberate effort to not look at his wife seated next to him.

Yeah, he's preaching the word firm and hearty as usual, but he's not referring to me and my woman. Or is he? Well, even if he is I know I've got plenty of company, Lange thought.

Pastor Adams concluded his sermon amid the customary shouts of **"Amen" "You tel-lit,"** and the unrelenting rounds of applause from our church family.

"In closing," he said, "I'd like to ask that men who are not presently active in a church auxiliary receive the calling to join the Manpower Choir."

A majority of the men sitting in the congregation seemed to look bewildered. Maybe they couldn't believe they were being extended the invitation, while some weren't so sure they wanted it. Who knows how many of them felt embarrassed, feeling they really didn't deserve it. The only thing for certain was that most of them weren't ready to jump out of their seats and embrace it.

"Now don't run like roaches in the night when they have been hit by a light," Pastor Adams cautioned. "You all can at least greet these men of Manpower on your way out and listen to what they have to say. Am I forgetting anything, Lauren?" The pastor glanced over to his trusted and poised announcer for any messages that might have been overlooked during his fervent sermon. The petite young lady briefly whispered below the microphone into the pastor's ear, smiled, and walked away from the podium.

"Y'all have to excuse me," Pastor Adam's continued, "for sometimes the urgency of one message makes me forget the importance of another, Amen. Another important announcement that I want to share with you all is the fact that Mt. Tabernacle will be sponsoring a new member's class that you can now complete in one Saturday session from 9:30 to 5:00, instead of our nine weekly sessions. I do hope this works for your schedules, Amen. In the meantime, allow the sweet Voices of Angels to take us home."

At least thirty women, all clad in beautiful purple and gold robes, stood up and launched a sweet rendition of 'The Lord Changed Me.'

"Their voices are heaven sent," said Brother Akins, the oldest member of Manpower and the only one who didn't waste many words.

"Why don't us men have as many good musicians as the women do?" whispered Brother Sherman to Brother Akins.

"I'm not sure, but I think it's because more women turn out to practice and sing in bigger numbers than the men, I guess," Brother Akins replied.

"Why don't we sing those progressive gospel songs like the women do, instead of those low flavor, old, negro spirituals like we sing?" whispered Brother Humphries to Brother Baker to his right.

"Because we're men," Brother Baker retorted—as was his way, "and maybe our low numbers and rusty voices can't carry that jazzy kind of gospel."

"Really, Humphries asked?"

"Of course not...what...do you think any of us sound like the Mighty Male Sounds of Standard or something?"

"I wouldn't even know who those guys are, 'tell the truth, but I have another question if y'all don't mind," said Humphries.

"Go ahead young brother," Baker said.

"Well, is it me, or doesn't our new music minister have a sweet kind of swagger about him?" quipped Brother Humphries to Brother Wakefield.

"Might be you and him!" was Wakefield's witty response. Humphries looked surprised.

"What'd you say?"

"You know what they say," Wakefield continued.

"Naw man, what do *they* say?"

"Looks like a duck, quacks like a duck, it's probably a duck." Wakefield confirmed.

"You mean looks like a gay dude, acts like a gay dude, it's probably a gay dude, I understand, but what's up with the might be you and him part?" Humphries asked suspiciously.

"Well, don't forget, you are in Atlanta," said Brother Baker.

"Well, don't you forget, you are in church, in Atlanta!" I shot back to Baker. Brother Lange had been listening to our conversation, and obviously wanted to add his two cents.

"So what are you saying—that gay people should not be in the church? If so, then I think you guys are a little late to stop it," Lange advised.

"Speaking of late," Humphries said, "I just finished a nine week Bible study course, and now they announce that you can just add water and stir you a Christian man in a one day study session?" I had heard enough and decided to intercede.

"Let's hush down brothers," I said. "The Angels are singing, so let's give them our undivided attention. Oh, and by the way, the new music minister is a very educated man from the east coast."

"Which means what?" asked Wakefield.

"Which means, he's probably used to those Ivy League types of mannerisms, but that doesn't make him gay." I then stood up and clapped for the Angels. Eight of the Manpower members followed suit, standing up and clasping their hands in unison with the Angels, leaving Brother Humphries as the last one to slowly rise.

"Why should I follow the path of a watermelon thief, and how did he become the Manpower President?" Humphries muttered.

"Just leave it alone, at least he had the guts to admit it!" Brother Akins shouted back to Brother Humphries above the noise of the singing.

"Yeah, that took a lot of guts. Still, if I were that fool, I wouldn't have come close to admitting it just like that," Humphries countered.

"Just stick around a while and see how real men of the spirit behave. One day you'll have the guts to admit worse."

"Don't hold your breath waiting," he cautioned. "I can sing all day and night with you all, but that doesn't mean you're going to be all up in my business, alright?"

Uneasy stares from the brothers proved therapeutic, for little else other than time could make Humphries realize that he had a long way to grow before learning the ways of a spiritual man. He quieted down and started clapping while staring at me and Brother Akins. As the song ended, the Brothers of Manpower dispersed among the crowd, shaking hands and reintroducing themselves with the men and women as they always do. All of them posed the same question to men familiar and unfamiliar.

"Why don't you come out and join us this Thursday?"

"What are you doing this Thursday?"

Of course, Humphries still kept things as real as he knew it. Upon greeting them he clasped their hands firmly and looked them squarely in their eyes. Pulling them closer to him, he then leaned over and whispered, as if he were planning a military rescue mission.

"Brother, the Men of Manpower Choir would like you to join us this Thursday at 7:30 p.m. for practice. We are getting ready for our Men's Day Celebration in a few months. Come on out and don't even worry how you sound, because most of us can't sing anyway!"

FIVE

Peachtree Motors:
Atlanta, Ga.

It wasn't always this way for Kyle Medley, the head service manager of Atlanta's largest black owned auto dealership. Co-workers still laugh while reminiscing how I used to conduct Bible study meetings at lunch time. Starting with only myself in attendance, I'd bring the smallest radio I could find to the break room in the hopes that it wouldn't appear staged. After settling in, I'd turn the volume up as music blared with the latest tunes from all of the Gospel greats. It was interesting as people took notice, yet the calling to minister to my fellow workers bore fruit when I least expected it—the day I realized I was alienating them by singing along with the music. For well over two weeks now I sang the lyrics of gospel hits more frequently, especially with the comings and goings of co-workers to and from the snack machines. On this particular occasion I hurried and gulped my food faster as I heard the footsteps of Tony approaching. I quickly adjusted the volume as well as the direction of the CD player to project to him, while synchronizing my voice to the music.

"You're everything, dear Lord," I blared, even closing my eyes to denote the fact that I was truly "feeling" God's message. I then heard Tony's sandwich hit the bottom of the machine and my eyes opened wide—just in time to notice him squeezing his big hand inside the small flap and grabbing his sandwich. He then hurried off without offering to sing along or anything, displaying the same urgency of a passenger securing a life vest before exiting a sinking Titanic.

After reflecting for a moment, I stood up from my chair and slowly walked over to the break room window. Staring up to the dark clouds on this stormy afternoon, it dawned on me that God had little to do with anything coming from my vocal chords. Was this a revelation? As my better judgment kicked in, I quickly remembered that although a great revelation was received on a mountain top by Moses in biblical history, I was not Moses. I'm just Kyle Medley, ex-All American football player—now receiving the brutal revelation that I can't sing while standing on the 2nd floor of a car dealership.

The revelation was again confirmed when out of nowhere, Bianca Kincaid, the new customer service representative, appeared. Bianca was all of 6 feet tall with an ebony hue to her pretty, dark chocolate skin. Strikingly beautiful in her classy mauve dress, she was truly built like a car that hadn't even been designed yet. Men still discussed how they'd never seen her before, although she'd worked for Peach City Motors for over four months now and her presence should no longer be news. Most of the sales reps referred to her as the new B3-Black Beautiful Bianca. They treated her like an object, as if she just rolled off a Detroit assembly line or something. She resented the commercially flirtatious approach from all of them, especially Ed Tyson. Ed epitomized a smooth talking womanizer with a glib tongue. He was handsome, tall, and lean, and being the selling machine that he was he'd proven countless times that he could sell ice to an Eskimo and sand to a desert man in the lowest of gears. He dressed impeccably too, but what separated him from most wolves was the fact he was nearly rich after being named car salesman of the month over two dozen times. That kind of status entitled him to serve as the well respected leader of the pack, but that didn't matter either. Bianca consistently let the pack know that she wasn't for sale. With Ed, she merely conveyed it with everything but a bull horn. She liked and trusted me however. Maybe it was because I was single, low keyed, and more interested in spreading the gospel than eying her curves. I deserved the Nobel Peace Prize for restraint *and* a slap upside my head for letting her go unspoken to for so long.

Whatever the case, Bianca happened to be seated just a few feet apart from my table, fully witnessing the chain of events. After watching Tony leave the break room she'd noticed the look on my face. That's when she quietly stood up and slowly walked over to my side while I stood near the window.

"Do you mind if I join you?" she asked.

"No…I don't mind at all," I replied, wondering how I missed noticing she was even in the room.

She clasped my hand gently and began to speak.

"Kyle, stop trying so hard to sing your message to these people, and just continue on to be an example of how a man should conduct himself when church is in him, and not simply when he is in church."

Now I stand tall at 6'3. With smooth brown colored skin just a couple shades lighter than my African forefathers, I'm also built as tightly as the shackles with which they began their first journey on American soil. Some say my eyes are big and deep enough to look right through you while still maintaining their innocence. But did she say 'continue on'? I was shocked that Bianca had paid any attention to me. After all, I'm no longer the gridiron star of yesterday, but I'd never confuse physical assets or past stardom with my spiritual inventory anyway. Maybe she sensed this, but even if she didn't I was struck that the first words she uttered to me would be of this nature.

"I'm simply praising His Holiness through song B3. Why, does it look like I'm trying that hard?"

"First of all, you can call me Bianca, Bianca Kincaid is my name, not B3, and secondly, yes—a blind man can see that you are going just a bit overboard with your daily gospel music, but your ministry is an uplifting change for this place."

"Then you already know that singing is not all I do, right?"

"Sure I do. I see you're always up here reading or preaching from your Bible most every day too," she said. "You've probably been too immersed to notice me, but I could really use a little brushing up on the Word. I somehow feel like I've been going away from it lately, especially after what I've been through."

"Is that right? Well, the Word is spiritual food, and spiritual food is good nourishment no matter what is happening in your life. Before we start, why don't you share with me what it is that you've been going through?"

Bianca looked at me as if she wished her eyes could tell me her story so she wouldn't have to. All I could gather was that they were big and beautiful eyes, possibly the kind of eyes that were not meant to tell anything as sad as the story which they visibly conveyed. She hesitated before speaking, as though in pain.

"I'm trying to free myself. I almost feel like I've been running with the devil. Now I feel like I'm finally coming close to understanding what my Savior wants of me. It's the key to shaking the devil off of me."

"I understand. Believe me. I'm trying to shake him too. Sometimes you think you have all the right moves, and you still can't shake him. I'll be happy to pray and share with you what I'm learning about redemption though."

"That's nice of you, but I don't think you understand. How could you? Kyle, I'm trying to free myself of the memory of what I thought was a healthy and promising relationship, an engagement I had with a man. I loved him, but later I discovered that all he wanted to do was perpetrate his way to my affection, shower me with gifts, and then treat me like he owned me, not to mention the way he made his money. "

"Is he out of your life now?" I asked.

"He lives in Detroit."

"Okay, but is he out of your life?"

"Kyle, Detroit is my home. I miss it, but I came here with no family for a fresh start, so what does that tell you?"

"It tells me you've traveled a fair distance," I said.

"I have, but I get your point. I don't know. You see, instead of confronting this situation bravely, I chose to run away from him and hide. Now, I feel like a coward."

"Why would you say that?"

"Because I didn't resolve it, that's why." She grew quiet and solemn. I felt it was time to change the subject, and I was about to before she continued.

"I'm sure our Father has a plan for how to best handle it," she said. "Hopefully it's over, and if not... I just hope he shows me."

"He will. I know he will. This may even be the time that he does."

"It may be. Tell me Kyle, can I join you sometimes for prayer and Bible study," she asked?

"Sure you can Bianca, I'd be happy to have you. *Why couldn't I have said that another way?* I mean, anytime."

"I want the things we discuss to stay between, you, me and The Almighty?" she said.

"I've got no need to mention anything about it," I assured.

"Good, then all we've talked about today as far as anybody is concerned is the fact that you can't sing, okay?"

"Right," I blindly agreed.

"And that you shouldn't sing, at least up here to everybody."

"Now I don't know about that."

"Okay, let's rephrase. That you shouldn't sing as much as you should minister The Master's word through your deeds and actions then, how about that?"

"Agreed," I replied. She then extended her hand in friendship for me to shake and I grasped the silky smoothness of it while we gazed at each other. I'd like to say that moment ignited a spark of electricity that existed between us, but the truth was that it was only me feeling shock waves for sure.

Taking her advice was easy, since I was already desperately trying to live Our Savior's will as a Christian man in the new millennium. But most notably, somehow the pact made with this beautiful woman reminded me of the similar pact I'd made with another beautiful black woman, my dying mother. Instantly, I briefly reminisced over nineteen years to her bedside...

"Come here Kyle. You're going to be a very brave young man one day son, so don't be scared." The nine year old boy walked slowly toward his mother—his eyes welling with tears but yet refusing to cry. *"Here, take my hand and listen carefully. Momma's going to be leaving you soon, but remember I'm going to be watching you up in heaven, okay?"*

"Yes Momma, I know."

"That's good. See you're a leader, and I see in you a vision. Your father, bless his heart, got derailed from the calling to Pastor. It's not for everyone, you see. But if you ever hear the voice of God calling you to that pulpit, not man, then I hope you heed it."

"I understand Momma, I will."

A friendship commenced that day between the two of us, as Bianca and I would talk, laugh, and pray about everything. I couldn't figure out what occurred between her and this man that would make her run. I trusted her when she told me it didn't involve her owing him money. Was he physically abusive? Maybe, I thought, although I hated to suggest it—partly because of the royalty and class she carried herself with. Besides, as spiritually mature and innately sophisticated as Bianca was, who on earth would be naïve enough to think they could keep this sister down? Sales reps at the dealership had gone from harassing her, to flirting with her, to genuinely appreciating most anything she had to say to them. Either way she could certainly hold her own with the best and worst of them.

Who knows? Maybe the salesmen were right, and she did roll off the Detroit assembly line as the only B3 model in her class. It really didn't matter how she got here, though. Bianca had relatively low mileage on her for a 28 year old woman. Her thoughts were too positive, her heart and soul too pure, and her smile was too bright to be a bitter victim of too many love battles lost. I placed her at roughly 9,000 miles, and why not? It was part of my job to know such things.

The following two months evolved in heavenly fashion, as both of us met routinely for lunch and Bible study. On a casual walk to the sandwich shop one day I asked her to respect her temple and to never again cast her pearls to such a swine as she acknowledged she did with this man named Donald. She looked at me strangely, and subtly reminded me that she had the utmost respect for her pearls. Feeling awkward, I decided I'd take my time before going there again, but she did make me think. I initially thought I was helping her, but it wasn't long before I realized Bianca was an even bigger inspiration to me. She complemented my Biblical understanding enough to help me ferment the notion of spreading the gospel in spite of myself. As time passed, we'd begun to connect spiritually and socially, and one day she invited me to hear her recite poetry at Atlanta's Spoken Word Cafe. Until then, she'd never shared the fact that her passion was in her writing before, but I was hardly offended. Seeing her take the stage was magnificent. Her words were soulful, thought provoking, and uniquely her as she gave a stirring oratory of The Creator's plan for our life through his love. Quietly, I added 'culturally beautiful' to a list that had room for much more.

****

While Bianca was swiftly gaining recognition with her spiritual brand of poetry, I was affectionately becoming known as a bonafide Bible school teacher among my co-workers at Peach City Motors. Six of the service technicians soon began to appear regularly at Bible study as well. One day, Ed Tyson even appeared. Now I know I'm not God and therefore I shouldn't judge, but I am a heck of a fruit inspector. When Ed used to sell used cars, he would sell lemons to little old ladies and young couples with children. Rarely did he ever warn them about the car's defects. A blind man could see a mile away that Ed just wasn't right. Yeah, it would have been nice to think Ed's presence was all due to my spiritual charisma. But every time I heard that sandwich drop from the machine down to the slot when Ed used it, unlike when Tony did, I got closer to the reality that where there was honey in Bianca, Ed and others were sure to follow. No small wonder that the very week she planned to come visit Mt. Tabernacle was also the week I didn't need to invite hardly anybody else, again.

"Why don't you come on out and visit us one Sunday at Mt. Tabernacle" I asked Bianca.

"I will, but first you'll have to give me directions," she replied.

"Well from downtown you can take I-20 East until you get to I-285, then…"

"Slow down", Ed said from out of nowhere, "I can't write that fast."

"Yeah, that's right," said two other guys from the service department who pulled out pens and paper just as quickly. I recalled asking all of them to join us at least four or five times with no luck.

SIX

Thursday, March 28

I checked my watch to insure I was on target to arrive at least twenty minutes early to choir practice. Just like football practice years ago, I always felt a sense of serenity by arriving before anyone. The peace of the church sanctuary was a virtual prescription for my guilt. Without realizing it, that sanctuary was gradually becoming my new football field, too. The devil was now the opposition, and I was inheriting the whole world as teammates. It was much more meaningful than a game, for sure, and the struggle for good over evil was always in season. Moving along at no rush I slowly parked my pick up truck on the side of the church lot. Breathing a sigh of relief that the day was over, I reached for my Bible before getting out of the car. Exiting my truck, I glanced up at the sky, like I knew the clear crisp night full of stars was ordained for me. Striding toward the church my arms and legs exerted a gait and swagger that I hadn't employed since my football days.

"I got sunshine on a cloudy day, when it's cold outside, I got... Bianca, Bianca, Bianca, talking bout," I liked the way my R&B voice resonated while singing the song in the low pitched crooning fashion, and wondered why I didn't try that pitch more often. Might make a difference, you think?

Swinging open the big wooden doors of Mt. Tabernacle and making my way down the carpeted isle toward the sanctuary, I couldn't help but notice the last pew on the left. The back pew was where I've sat for years since the infamous 'hit'. Guilt does that, you know. What? You thought the back rows were only for late arrivals and those who left the service early to beat traffic? Nope. They're also for sinners. Like new swimmers, they can only stick their spiritual toe in the water, so they sit in the back. After a seven year 'marriage' to guilt and shame I was happy to find myself moving up to the front pews of worship. Occasionally I'd wonder if I was worthy enough to serve as President of the Men's Choir without being branded as an imposter. It wasn't like I courted thoughts of slamming opponents down to the turf again and again, but they often took up a nightmarish residence inside me anyway. Yet, on a good day, and lately there seemed to be many, I could still hear fans roaring and calling my name. I came to equate them with the angels, now reaffirming I might be doing something right.

Striding onward without a care I was suddenly startled, and briefly stopped in my tracks to look up. Music Minister Roberts appeared to be lecturing as usual. A closer look revealed him just bragging to two brand new members of Manpower who were coming for their first night of practice.

"I'm telling you that this tofu diet coupled with the diet pills I'm selling makes for the best weight loss plan that you brothers have ever been introduced to," Roberts carried on. "If you believe in respecting The Redeemer's temple then you have to know that we as spiritual folks of the church eat way too much. We're eating before church, right after church, after the wedding, right after the funeral, and every other occasion we're filling our faces. Then we're dutifully announcing on Sunday morning how we should pray for our sick and shut in. We never stop to think how we're helping to kill each other by throwing all of this rich food in with our praise and worship.

"Yeah brother, that's right," responded one of the new brothers. **"Word"** replied the other. *'Word?'* I absorbed the conversation while walking up the isle to meet and join them. *"There he goes again, the fattest guy in the church has the nerve to give pointers on weight loss methods. At least his rhetoric made a little sense, but by God he's gotta know he's talking about him self more than any of us."*

"Well, well, well, if it isn't Brother Medley. Brother Medley, meet these two new brothers who have stated that they wish to be a part of Manpower."

I reached out my hand to them without waiting for an introduction from Minister Roberts.

"I'm Kyle Medley, Choir President, pleased to meet you."

"I'm Clifford Daniels, good to meet you."

"Jonathan Williams is my name, pleasure meeting you too." I greeted them both with hearty handshakes before my curiosity got the best of me.

"Brother Williams, I've seen you around the church for three or four years. What made you finally decide to join us?"

"Well, I've just been coming out to church most every Sunday, watching the service, enjoying the preaching, and just going home. To be honest with you, I've just been a Christian couch potato of sorts, and I've just gotten tired of having what I feel like is a shallow Christian experience, you know?" Brother Williams replied.

I was satisfied with his answer, but Minister Roberts would have no part in leaving well enough alone.

"I see, and you like the sounds of the Manpower Choir and knew that it's the best place for you to start, huh?" Roberts quipped.

"Well, of all the auxiliary groups I could join, I thought you all probably could use me the most," Williams replied.

"Are you implying that we can't sing?" I asked with a smile.

"No, I'm not implying, but I'll say straight up that y'all can't sing, but regardless, here I am."

"Then I'll trust you will help make us better," said Minister Roberts.

"I'd rather play it safe, and let you know that I think I'll fit in perfectly with what you've got." Smiling, I subtly confirmed to Roberts, "I think he'll fit in just fine," but Roberts didn't find it funny and cast a stern look back in return.

"I don't need to remind you that the last thing Mt. Tabernacle needs is another voice that resonates with a mere half note, do I Kyle?" While raising my hands as if I weren't sure the doors to the sanctuary could be heard opening and closing. Brothers Lange, Humphries, Sherman, and Akins cheerfully walked in amid the fiasco.

"I found one at the unemployment line, one at the nightclub, and the other one getting his ankle bracelet put back on by his probation officer," Humphries chuckled. "And the worst part about it is that they all agree that the biggest sinner is the one who was in the unemployment line—broke with no money, hah!" Humphries walked up the isle toward the gathering of men with a gait in his stride more akin to a bop while slapping five from us all. Pastor Adams entered from the side door as usual, along with Brothers Wakefield, Keats, Richards and Gonzalez, the only Hispanic member among us. The pastor had caught the tail end of Brother Humphries remark and smiled broadly. Brother Humphries was the one brother who gained immunity from open judgment from any of us. His charisma and boldness cast an innocent shadow over his obvious lack of spiritual maturity, and we loved him for it. Most assumed that Stephen Humphries reminded Pastor Adams of himself before he got truly saved—a misguided young man imbued with more vinegar and urine than the Holy Spirit. Whatever the case, nobody lit up a room the way he did.

"Good evening Brothers of Manpower," Pastor Adams greeted before shaking the hands of all the men. Let us gather around in a circle and hold hands as we pray.

"Dear Lord, as we stand before you grasping hands, please edify our voices along with our souls as we begin to praise you through song. Please enable us to learn to live these words that we are about to sing about, not to simply serve as an empty vessel that helps to deliver your message through a hollow shell. As you fortify our voices, please renew these worn and withered hands with the wisdom to recognize the sinful burden that they have carried for so long. Free our hearts and hands from jealousy, contempt, drugs, violence, gambling, greed, and the sexual predation which threatens to stand in our way while seeking your glory. Amen."

"Amen, Amen, Amen," the brothers responded. Most of the

men weighed in with heavy hearts that spoke randomly on any given night. Tonight, Brother Sherman's heart was particularly heavy.

"God bless you for that prayer Brother Medley, you hit it right on the nose.

SEVEN

Now brothers, lets sing! I need everyone to stand in their proper order of first, second, and third tenors among the three pews," Roberts commanded.

The brothers shuffled about briefly before dutifully taking their respective places three or four each in the sparsely populated pews. There we stood. Ten men fortified with the blood. Ten proud Christian men of color! Seven men who couldn't sing a lick, one who barely could, and two who feel they'll fit right in regardless. Exactly who we were was open to many interpretations.

"Let's begin with 'They Both Prayed,'" cited Minister Roberts.

Everyone knew that this was my signature song, and I boldly stepped out of the pack and grabbed the microphone with authority in case they forgot. I began to, well, sing along with the music.

> *"A lady prayed for me, she had so much to do.*
> *Before her day was through,*
> *but still, she took the time and she prayed for me."*
> *And I'm the one who is glad, see he joined, and*
> *prayed for me while sad*
> *Fervently did, with closed eyelids she prayed for me.*
> *"Yeah, both prayed for me..."*

Minister Roberts face cringed while his body slightly riveted. He'd decided he could no longer pretend to miss what his eardrums had come to expect.

"Brothers," he began. "I, nor any individual in this house, would ever doubt that the spirit is moving in our presence.

"Amen, 'Ah-man,' they all responded.

"And knowing this we should be grateful about it, and move on to other pressing matters at hand."

"You feel a curve ball coming?" Humphries asked.

"Sshhh, I think it's a fastball, Brother Humphries."

"There has come to mind a couple of things that I'd like to bring to Manpower's attention," Roberts continued. "First off, I'd like all of you to keep in mind that we are scheduled to sing at the 11:00 o'clock service next week, and we will all wear gray suits and red ties for the occasion. Secondly, as the Minister of Music, I have decided that as of next week the Manpower Choir will begin to hold auditions to determine entry for all of its members."

"Auditions...Auditions...what...did he say auditions?" they asked. Most stared in disbelief at what they were hearing.

"I told you it was a curve ball too," Brother Sherman lamented back to Brother Humphries. I was partially shocked as well, and subtly cast a stern look of betrayal from my wary eyes towards the ambitious Music Minister, then over to Pastor Adams. *Hmm, so now he's trying to kick me and half of these Brother's out to replace us with a few "just add water" Gospel singers. What gives him the right, and how could Pastor Adams co-sign such a move.*

"Let me get this straight. Do you mean to tell me that each one of these men—who probably average three years or more of singing in this choir—are going to have to audition for you like we never met or something?" I asked.

"Well, what I was thinking," replied Minister Roberts, until I quickly cut him off.

"Whatever happened to quality of spirit over quantity?" I continued.

"That's right, you tell 'em' Kyle," barked Humphries.

"Better yet, whatever happened to the "we need to invite more men to the ranks of Manpower and do that salt shaker 'thang' you was talking about, remember? Instead, Minister Roberts, you've been acting more and more like you're one of those uppity Simon folks, riding us about our singing like you're hosting a version of Gospel Idol!"

From the looks on the men's faces it appeared they were in full agreement. Humphries nodded back to Brother Sherman, acknowledging it was a curve ball indeed before blurting to Roberts.

"You start holding auditions for us, and one day you'll regret turning the Manpower Choir into what will look like an empty parking lot..." The majority of the brothers remained stone faced but took solace in the message being given to Minister Roberts by the two of us. After all, none of these men were desperate or remotely desirous of "belonging" to an exclusive membership denoting anything commercial.

Indeed, half of them already belonged to popular fraternities, lodges, or civic groups, and had long ago pledged their time to praising their Savior through song. Brother Akins was seasoned and wise at age fifty-eight. He was a devout family man and one of the wealthiest entrepreneurs in Atlanta, though you'd never know it unless someone told you.

"I'm here because I've been called here to do this," Akins began. "Not, Mister Roberts... not because you think I'm vocally good enough to belong. I wasn't called to the ministry like, well, Pastor Adams for instance, but when I heard the voice to join the Manpower Choir I didn't hesitate." Tommy Sherman—one of the only men in the group who could sing—decided to share his thoughts as well.

"I was never one for commercialism, and I don't like the notion of belonging to a 'select' group of our creator's children," he proclaimed. "I'm just singing because it's in my heart to do it, man. Just singing because I'm blessed and free, you know?"

"Brothers, replied Minister Roberts, your comments are admirable, but lately I've agonized how unfair it is of me to allow the vocal standards for Manpower to be so low. The Holy Spirit itself has got to be running away from your voices, and we cannot risk being abandoned this way."

"Did he really just go there?" someone asked, but Roberts ignored him to further make his case.

"No, the bar needs to be set some where, and right now it's simply way too low."

"That's real nice of you to agonize like that, but for goodness sake, we've invited every Tom, Dick, and Harry we could find to the choir already, so what's the problem now?" I asked.

"Things are about to change brothers. I hope somebody has told you all sometimes change is good?"

"Minister Roberts, it's late and we're tired. Would you please cut through the chase and tell us what you've done now?"

"Alright, I will. Listen up, brothers. I believe our Savior, the church, and everybody else will like the new men who have contacted me recently. Most of them are really excited about auditioning in practice next week." All of the men turned their heads in shock.

"Who said anything about auditioning," I asked. "These men were supposed to join us, not compete with us!"

"Calm down Kyle. I understand your apprehension particularly, but look at it like this. You all talk and act pretty tough sometimes— tougher than most men I've ever led in music in fact—like you're made of iron really.

"Amen...True to that, Well...I know that's right...Nothing soft here," were their varied responses." As Roberts continued talking one of my eyebrows went up while Humphries head turned to the side like a curious puppy. "There's one passage that's surer than death and taxes gentlemen, and it's the fact that only iron can sharpen iron. Ultimately, all I see is us having more iron to work with, your voices improving, and everything being okay in our future," he concluded.

At least it sounded better than the first time he sold it, but the packaging still made me uneasy. Looking around I confirmed I wasn't alone.

"As long as Manpower won't suffer spiritually, and you can manage to extend a little dignity about this whole thing, we may be alright," I agreed.

"Trust me brothers," Roberts assured. "In time everyone will see that what we're doing here will glorify The Almighty even more. Now who would like to lead us in prayer or recite their favorite scripture reading to conclude our session here tonight?"
To the surprise of many Brother Humphries responded.

"Brothers, please join me in the reading of Psalms 51:10. This has been a favorite passage of mine as of late." *Amen...Amen*

We gathered around in a circle and commenced to flipping pages in our Bibles. Most of us were in rare elation and anticipation of Brother Humphries—the spiritual neophytes offering. As he spoke we all began to read along in unison.

"Create in me a clean heart, O God; and renew a right spirit within me.

Cast me not away from thy presence; and take not thy holy spirit from me.

Restore unto me the joy of thy salvation; and uphold me *with thy* free spirit.

"Amen." "And Lord *please* don't let Minister Roberts mess up this choir," Humphries begged..."because it's the only thing that's keeping me out of the nightclubs these days!"

EIGHT

The men slowly strode out of the church and waited around before going to their cars. Most had more to say. You could feel it in the night wind like an approaching storm. Brother Humphries didn't wait for the door to shut behind him before ranting on.

"Minister Roberts is up to something, I can feel it," he warned. "I wonder where Pastor Adams stands on this issue. Why doesn't he speak up? There's only so much rope even a gospel fanatic deserves isn't it?" I'd overheard him long before the big wooden doors closed behind me.

"Brother Humphries, I think you're going to be just fine," I said. "You're pretty much right, too. Although Roberts has gone completely commercial, I think the only reason Pastor Adams doesn't call time out on him is because he's talented, committed, and lets face it…he's one of the few men who have stepped up lately and at least communicated an ounce of leadership. I've thought about it. Pastor Adams isn't shy. Lately, it seems that leadership is all he wants to see in us for some reason."

"You're at least half way right about that Kyle," Brother Sherman said. Minister Roberts is stepping up, but real leadership isn't what he's showing. He's proving he's bold enough to plot a vision, for sure, but that's not true leadership. And the irony of it all Kyle, is that you, more than any of us, are the one who has any real spiritual vision."

"There it is," Humphries blurted. For some reason you're acting like a retired gunfighter, one who's got it in him but won't any longer strap on his holster and lead us. *Ouch!*

"Maybe Pastor Adams may not mind playing this quiet pastor role out a bit until he sees who's going to step up and where this will all go," added Brother Keats.

"Well, I think this is the end of the gospel line for me, and I'm going," said Brother Wakefield. "What do you mean, you're not quitting are you?" I asked.

"Listen, I joined a Men's Choir, not Gospel Idol," Wakefield said flatly.

"Brothers, it's been nice you see, but I ain't going to audition for 'nan-nobody' next week either, just so I can take more of this abuse!, 'No mas—No me gusta." said Brother Gonzalez.

"Pastor Adams—he's never been this quiet about anything like this," said Akins.

"You're right, maybe Pastor Adams is testing us, okay? You guys need to just hold on to your horses and not rush to leave the choir."

"It's one thing to be faithful, Kyle. But on the other hand it's quite another to ignore the writing on the wall," said Brother Keats.

"What do you mean by that?" I asked.

"I mean, what if? What if Pastor Adams takes the reigns off of Minister Roberts and lets him have his way?"

"I won't like it, but life will go on."

"Kyle," beckoned Brother Akins. "If Roberts has his way, who is going to console **you** after **you** audition next week?"

"Oh, so that's where you're going. I'll be alright brothers. They're going to have to physically kick my butt out of here before I leave. Even if they do, they still can't stop me from singing for the Lord. You brothers go home and at least think about it."

"We'll do it on one condition big 'fella," Humphries stated. "We'll do it if you lead us the way you were meant to. See, if you don't then maybe I will, and everyone knows I'm too new to the God Squad to take the reigns."

Brother Gonzalez nodded and shook my hand. Many suspected that he joined Manpower a few years ago only to see how much spiritual soul he could muster after marrying a black woman. If that were true then it worked, because his Spanish tongue now exuded a hip combination of salsa and black slang whenever he spoke.

"Me gusta,' my brother. Congratulations. We look forward to you stepping up." My attention then turned to Brother Lange, who was talking on his cell phone as desperately as a convict would to a probation officer.

"Just relax, okay? Of course, I'll get the Cranberry-Pineapple juice this time. I know, I know, I only got Cranberry the last time but calm down...Look, I'll see you in a few minutes and we'll talk about it," he said in an anguished tone before hanging up and joining the rest of the men as they walked to their cars.

"I heard everything y'all said, man. True enough my wife gives me the blues, but Brother Humphries wanted me to treat my woman like road kill, and that's not the answer. Go ahead and step up, Kyle. You have to."

"I hear all of you talking brothers. I can't answer you now, but I hear you, and I'm sorry if I'm letting you down."

"You should be," somebody said. I didn't bother to see who because it could have been most any of them.

Driving home, I found myself wondering how to keep the brothers motivated, but one thing was for sure, they deserved more. Whether or not they were right to look to me to expect it was another issue. I've got to get back on that horse, I told myself, but how? Surely everybody will throw up my past if I step forward. With no immediate answers, my thoughts suddenly turned to Bianca. *I wonder what kind of man she was used to having, or maybe still has. I'm probably a little too square for her,* maybe a bit too country for a city girl like her. I glanced over at the passenger seat of my pickup and tried to visualize her sitting there next to me. *If me and my truck ain't her kinda scene, then she's just gonna have to tell me, yeah, I think I'll just let her tell me. After all, just because I'm a man of God and have never been as close to anything as fine as she doesn't mean I don't deserve her.*

I'd grown tired from the long day, but not at all as tired as I pondered the possibilities—that I should call her at home sometimes, invite her to dinner instead of the usual lunches we'd shared in the dealership break room. Upon walking through the door of my neat modest home I decided to do just that.

"Hello," was the sweet young voice on the other end.

"Hello Bianca," *I suddenly liked my newfound Baritone voice upon hearing her speak.*

"This is Kyle, Kyle Medley…How are you tonight?"

"I'm fine, who is this?" Bianca asked.

"This is Kyle, err-um, Brother Kyle Medley from Peach City Motors."

"What do you mean, calling my home at 10:30 at night and calling yourself 'Brother' Kyle Medley?"

Uh oh, this really isn't going along the way I planned.

"I know who you are Kyle, and I know where you work. Why are you calling people late at night? Are you going to pray for them if their cars don't work?"

"Well no, not really…"

I then heard Bianca chuckle before exploding into laughter. It was a beautiful, sweet laugh, a laugh that embarrassed me while also relieving me to hear.

"Okay, I'll come once again. This is Kyle, and I'll just get to the point." A bit of silence passed, and Bianca spoke up.

"And your point is Kyle?" she said sincerely, sensing my awkwardness while trying to contain her laughter.

"I'd really like to get to know you just a little better Bianca."

"We're already getting to know each other better, Kyle."

"That's true, and I like it, but I'm talking about a lot 'mo better than regular better, you see. I want to know you best. I was wondering if you would join me this Sunday afternoon after church. Maybe we can go for a walk at Stone Mountain Park."

"Kyle, that sounds very nice, but before you continue I have to let you know that I don't date my co-workers…" My heart almost hit the floor. What was I thinking?

"Sorry," she offered humbly.

"Yeah," was my dismal reply.

"But if you're looking at the park as an extension of his holy house, and in friendship, then that's another story."

"That's great, because that park is definitely Our Father's back yard. You'll see what I mean. After our walk, maybe we can have dinner?" I must have lit up like the night of the 4th of July.

"Slow down. Now that sounds like a date!" Bianca countered.

"In the spirit of friendship," I retorted.

"In the spirit of friendship, I'd love to see you. I just don't want you to have any false expectations."

"My only expectation right now is for us to spend Sunday together, and unless I'm reaching too far, I expect us both to enjoy it." It sounded as if she put the telephone down and muttered, *"Would you just listen to the fire in this sweet country boy!"*

"I told you now, that I don't date co-workers, but considering the fact that you work in the service department and me in billing, we may not technically qualify as co-workers."
I smiled broadly, hoping it was the start of the 'better' I was referring to.

"It's time you lightened up a little. I'll pick you up at 10:00."

"That works just fine for me," Bianca replied, "I'll see you Sunday." Before I could hang up the phone and savor the pleasure of Bianca's acceptance, the line beeped to signal an incoming call. Clicking over I announced my name with nearly the same off key vigor that I sang.

"God bless you, this is the Medley residence."

"Good evening Brother Medley, this is Pastor Adams. I was about to ask how you're doing tonight, but your greeting confirms that you are quite immersed in the spirit."

"Yes I'm blessed Pastor Adams, so blessed and highly favored, and you yourself?"

"Equally blessed and highly favored," the pastor responded. "Listen Kyle, Pastor Jackson was supposed to teach that day long new member's class tomorrow, but he called this morning saying he's caught the flu. I think the years might just be catching up with him a bit you know?"

"I understand pastor."

"Well, in looking for his replacement the main criteria I'm using are someone who is spiritually mature, loves the Lord, and doesn't mind spreading the gospel, like I hear you're doing over there at Peach City Motors."
How in the world did you hear about that?

"I see pastor, I try," I replied.

"Well, if you will, I'd like you to teach the classes. The lesson plans spanning Genesis to Revelation are already laid out for you. That is, if you'll be accepting this request. Do you accept Kyle?"

The phone grew silent. "Kyle," he repeated?

It was too late. The image of that football hit on Reggie was as vivid as yesterday. The only redeeming thing is that Momma wasn't alive to see it. I've relived that nightmare over and over. Finally, I could hear Pastor Adam's voice again.

"Kyle, I know what's bothering you. Let it go son. Give it to God. You'll have to sooner or later or that guilt is going to kill you. You've asked for forgiveness, now let it go! I'll understand if you're not ready, but it's just one class—one day," he emphasized. I was too humbled to refuse the pastors offer, and almost stuttered in my response.

"Why certainly pastor. I'll accept, but only to teach new members class for just one day. I'm quite honored that you asked me too."

"Well, you're committed Kyle. I know you're ready deep down no matter what you tell me—given what I see in you."

"Just hold on pastor..." I said before he cut me off.

"You're walking in some great footsteps whether you like it or not. Starting with your father, Deacon Fredrick Medley, and his father, Pastor Fredrick Medley Senior, and your great grandfather, Lazarus Medley, who helped build this church."

"Thank you pastor, but please, don't."

"No I will. See the apple don't usually fall too far from the tree either, so it's well deserved. But like I said, it's just for one day, anyway. Nobody's exactly crowning you yet, so there's no need to get too jittery. It's just a shame that we can't get your father to come back to the church. How's he doing by the way?"

"Well, since he had the leg amputated last year he's gotten pretty cranky, but his faith is unshaken as usual."

"That's wonderful. You just tell him we're still praying for him, that we still love him, and our doors are always open should he choose to come back."

"I do, pastor, all the time. Dad hasn't lost his relationship Our Father you know, in spite of the fact that he no longer comes to church.

"I wouldn't doubt 'yo' Daddy still loves the 'Lawd'. Everybody who knows him knows that, but he still needs the spiritual coverage through fellowship. You know that from scripture, and believe me, no matter how much he might tell you otherwise; in his heart he knows it too. Anyway, listen, we normally pay our full time ministers, but since you are not a full time staff member I'm sure you expect to do this for the church."

"Most certainly Pastor Adams, I'm here to offer my time, tithes, or talents. Whatever is needed, alright?"

"I thought you would say that Kyle. I may stop in to lend my support, but even if I don't, don't forget to bring about $30.00 for the watermelons you stole from me, alright?"
Whatever nobility I felt quickly diminished as I remembered how the pastor never failed to keep things real.

"I don't know what I was thinking pastor... those melons were just looking so fresh and green, like they belonged more to the earth than to anyone else."

"I understand Kyle. Since the beginning of time when Our Creator made heaven and earth, he gave man nearly free reign over its fruits."

"Amen to that Pastor."

"But things have changed, son, and though I'm an earthly pastor, but just go to the supermarket or plant your own next time, okay? Now have a blessed night."

I hung up the phone feeling pleased he'd called while feeling even guiltier still. Above all else, I knew I still hadn't made the one call that mattered most. It was the call I dreaded, yet it was also the call that was the only hope and catalyst to turning me back into the leader that I was meant to be. Picking up the receiver I pulled the small, wrinkled piece of paper that displayed the number from under the lamp. I dialed the first five numbers, but as usual, I found it too difficult to find the words to say. Grappling with the awkwardness of the situation I suddenly heard a familiar voice from down the hall.

"Kyle, Kyle, you in there? Come here...right now."
I'd grown accustomed to responding to Dad's emergencies and pompous whims alike, but lately I sensed a macho fear within him as he valiantly sought to handle a diabetic disease that he knew might slowly get the best of him. Either way I didn't need a better

reason to hang up the phone, and after putting the receiver down I marched swiftly down the hallway to his bedroom. I appeared at his door to hear his first words.

"Are you still taking me to the doctor in the morning, he asked?"

"Good evening, Daddy, and how are you?"

"I'm fine son, just fine, and yourself?"

"I'm blessed and highly favored."

"Very well…listen, are you still going to take me to the doctor," he repeated?

"Of course I'm going to take you, I always do, don't I?"

"I guess you do," Papa Medley conceded.

"Right, now you listen. Pastor Adams wanted me to tell you that he and the rest of the congregation miss you, and they'd like to see you come back to the church."

"Is that so?" Daddy replied.

"Yes, that is so," I confirmed, "and needless to say, I'd love it too."

"Pastor Adams is a good man, but don't either one of y'all need to get your hopes up," Daddy cautioned. "Those church folks have gotten too political and back stabbing for me over the years. You know it used to be a spiritual place, a holy place. Now it's gotten to be no more than one great, big fashion show. And the days they're not modeling they're staging a political convention. Now you can quit asking me about going back to anybody's church." Papa Medley paused, squinted his left eye, and cautioned, "You keep fooling with those so called Christian folks and you'll see what I mean."
They say to whom much is given, much is asked, but I think I have enough jobs to not be Jamaican.

NINE

Saturday, March 3
Detroit, Michigan

The building committee meeting was nearly over for the Greater Hope Church of Detroit, Michigan. Their dedicated members had tirelessly worked out details for the new church building, including all the architectural and landscaping specifications to insure it achieved kingdom quality elegance. Don Morton knew he didn't have the time nor interest in reviewing schematic plans and the like. He had made a promise to the church's spiritual leader, Bishop Cameron Searcy, and he was determined to at least do his part. The tires on his white Cadillac Escalade glided in to the church parking lot and the vehicle came to a smooth stop. The wheels continued to spin round and round, reflecting the sparkling white snow covering the grass like a never ending ocean tide. Don Morton was on a schedule. He stepped out of the vehicle and marched up the steps toward the church business office. One by one, the men leaving all greeted him by name. As respectful as it seemed, it was only a half empty acknowledgement since it was only his name and not him that they knew.

"Good morning Brother Morton," said one deacon. "Young man, you missed a fine meeting," said another. Don nodded towards them as he reached the door, ever intended on keeping the wall up that had shielded the 'real' him for the latter half of his thirty three years. As the wheels were slowing down outside on Don's wheels, so did his guard. He cracked open the door to see Bishop Searcy ending the conference with the last visible deacon.

"Hello Donald, how's my boy?" Bishop Searcy beamed. "Come on in and have a seat." Don smiled and took a seat across from the closest thing to a father he had ever known. As he looked on, the busy Bishop politely ushered the last deacon out of the door.

"Sounds to me like we've got a handle on it, and now we just have to let go and let God," Bishop Searcy told the deacon.

"Amen, Bishop. I'll see you tomorrow," the deacon replied as he shut the door behind him. Bishop Searcy took a seat across from Donald, staring intently at him before speaking.

"Boy, if you haven't got your mother's eyes, and even her smile, 'umph.' But you wanted to meet with me today, and here we are. Now tell me, what's on your mind son? Oh, and while you're at it, tell me how that new soul food restaurant—D&B'S Soul Creation, is going?"

"Well Bishop Searcy, the restaurant is coming along slowly but surely. The Grand Opening was just four months ago, and they're still streaming on in. Hate to say it, but being downtown in the same block as the Casino has been a big benefit for me."

"I can imagine. Well, I'm glad the devils den is paying dividends for somebody. You know, had you picked another location, I would have steered half the church to your Grand Opening. But the devil is tempting our flock enough without my inviting them to his own back yard."

Yeah, well, from what I've seen you can blindfold them and trust they'll still find a way to the devil's den, Donald thought.

"I understand. I know you would have Bishop Searcy, and that's why I came. I just wanted to give a little pledge for the new church building without all the fanfare, you know?"

Don reached for his wallet and pulled out a check already made out to Greater Hope Gospel Church.

"Hopefully we can keep this between you, me and God. I believe my mother would have wanted me to do this," he said before handing the check over to him.

Bishop Searcy looked at the check with the calmness of a spiritual man who was not obsessed with money, but surprised none the less.

"Ten thousand dollars! Good God Almighty, is business that good son?"

"Yes it is sir," Don replied.

"I can't accept this Donald. You go put this back in your business."

"Business will be fine Bishop. Take it."

"Alright, but you never know when that rainy day is coming, and the roof goes caving in, you know? Are you sure you don't need it?"

"Bishop Searcy, now you know I've seen you receive donations bigger than this, so what's wrong with mine?" Bishop Searcy let out a mild sigh that still surprised Donald.

"The truth is Donald; I've always felt a sense that the church... or better yet me ...I should have been there for you years ago, a lot more than I was, anyway. In spite of the fact that I wasn't, you come walking in here with a gift like this, and it's humbling, almost embarrassing, that's all."

"Maybe so. That would have been nice, very nice, but it's bigger than that. I feel my Mom would want this. I know she would. It would make her proud, you see. So here, take it anyway."

"If you insist, son. but God will bless you Donald, even if he somehow does it through me. And I won't mention your contribution, if that's your wish. Where is Bianca, by the way? I thought you both would be walking in here before now, telling me that you all have set a wedding date after six months of counseling sessions. Instead, I haven't seen you or her in church for quite some time." The room got quiet for a moment before Donald spoke up.

"She left me Bishop Searcy." Bishop Searcy's eyes widened at the news.

"You don't say?" he replied.

"I guess the women of today get cold feet just as much as the guys used to, you know?"

"That's what I understand, son. That's what I understand. You know the Spirit has always led me to believe that 'Women's Lib' should have come with some spiritual counseling. If it did, then maybe a woman wouldn't be so quick to leave a man, especially a good man." Bishop Searcy paused and waited for Donald to offer further explanation, but it never came.

"Well, I'm sorry," he said.

"That's okay. I'll just have to work my way through it somehow, I guess."

Bishop Searcy rose up from his desk and walked around to Donald's chair. As Donald stood, the Bishop grasped him in a bear hug of love.

"I'll keep you in my prayers son. In the mean time, stay strong in your faith, and remember. He promised never to leave you alone."

"I know, I know. I'm hurting Bishop, but I'll be okay," Don assured the Bishop as he shook his hand and turned to leave.

"Hopefully, I'll see you in church tomorrow, Donald."

"I'll try Bishop Searcy," Don said as he turned around briefly while heading toward the door. "You know that Sunday is a busy day at the restaurant."

"I know son, the Bishop replied, still don't stake your fortune on working on a Sunday, because you'll never really prosper."

Donald heard the words pass through one ear and out of the other as he nodded to Bishop Searcy, turned, and exited the door. Despite how touched he was to receive such a generous gift, Bishop Searcy could sense that only a small piece of the little boy who clung to his mother, Casey Morton, every Sunday morning remained.

Her job at the car assembly plant had afforded them a comfortable home with ample food, clothes, and two weeks of YMCA camp every summer. Casey made every attempt to compensate for the father who lived across town on Detroit's East side, yet never bothered to leave his new family to come see Donald. She had done the best she could and then some — working her petite fingers to the bone while tithing every Sunday, until an aneurism carried her to glory at the age of thirty eight. Donald was twelve years old when his world caved in. His twenty-nine year old aunt took him in and tried to pick up the pieces of his life. Helping to cushion the blow, Bishop Searcy visited him regularly and made sure he had a ride to church. It only worked for so long, though, because loneliness would set in. When it did, Donald felt the world had forgotten about him. It was usually then that Bishop Searcy would reappear and surprise him with tickets to the baseball games, where the fresh crack of a baseball bat would invigorate his senses and offer temporary hope. In the end it was Donald's new found freedom — courtesy of the same young aunt who proved too young to govern him. Coupled with the trappings of their drug infested neighborhood, it sealed a fate that the Bishop had hoped Donald could avoid.

Bishop Searcy peered through the window at Donald as he walked toward his SUV. *"What on earth was all the secrecy for concerning this gift?" he asked himself. Dear God, please keep him resting safely in your hands...and please... forgive me,"* he whispered.

Donald started the engine feeling a deeper and more profound connection of love and devotion to his deceased mother. It was the kind of feeling he'd hoped his gift would evoke. The gesture was bittersweet though, as he reflected how sad it was that she wasn't there to see him. Making matters worse, he'd envisioned Bianca joining him the next time he met with Bishop Searcy, and the remorse gripped him even more. Bianca was the closest person that he'd had loving, intimate feelings for over those years.

Without her, he silently feared he'd become heartless and cold. He reached for his cell phone, and after scrolling to her name, punched in the number to Bianca's mother. She answered the phone with a voice far from welcoming.

"No, I don't know where Bianca went and please don't ask me any more Donald!"

Those same words blared from her voice three weeks ago, but today caused a pounding echo in his ears like never before. He knew the call was fruitless the moment he made it, yet the pain since her disappearance had graduated from arrogant indifference to shock, from shock to feelings of betrayal, and from betrayal to a sense of sorrow that threatened to implode within him. In desperation, every gesture and initiative to locate her now made perfect sense. He pressed the end call button during the second ring.

I'll just have to find out on my own, he reasoned. *I don't know where to start, but I'll find her. After all I've done for her, and all I've built for her, I can't believe she'd have the audacity to up and leave Don Morton, especially over this?*

Donald put the car in gear and headed north on Woodward Ave. As much as he tried to refrain from doing it, he found himself glancing to his right at the beautiful Fox Theatre. It was painful. He and Bianca had seen numerous plays and concerts at the Fox. Bianca had always insisted his life lacked culture, but instead of deriding him, she introduced him to upscale, contemporary plays, far and above the usual 'chitlin' circuit, as they say. At first, he'd merely patronized with her by quietly sitting through those first few plays. As time passed, she'd explain their rich, story structures and ignite him further by marveling at their characters—so much that after a while he surprised himself by not only enjoying them, but recommending plays to her.

Maybe it was the sweet, sensual way Bianca reacted to life when they dressed up and stepped out. In that setting she was so feminine—a far cry from the rowdy, tomboy persona she displayed whenever they went to football games. Donald liked this dichotomy, and loved her for her strangeness. Eventually over time, while still processing her beauty, he now understood what people meant when they spoke of the ambiance of love.

Approaching downtown Detroit, he turned onto Jefferson Avenue and headed east, toward Bell Isle. Like most Detroiters, the beautiful island was always a special place to him. It held a charming view of the Detroit skyline across the river on one side and the view of Windsor, Canada on the other, enticing all lovers both young and old to the realization that the mood was perfect to be just that. Bianca loved it too. She lavished every opportunity to jog along the edge of the river. It was there, by the river, where they met one day as she finished a five mile run.

She'd run the last several minutes at a furious pace, and had approached the last sixty yards with a wind sprint that propelled her even faster before finding herself staggering along the shore, punch drunk from exhaustion. Panting for breath she'd inadvertently approached Donald with his back turned. In a most sportsmanlike fashion, he'd pretended to be flinging his fishing rod back to once again unleash it into the water. Instead, the hook of his fishing rod caught her in the arm of her sweat suit before she could pass by. Thus, the relationship began with him smiling sheepishly and doing his best to feign it as an accident before persuading her to seek comfort in his folding chair. He'd done everything possible to hook her ever since.

He now rolled his SUV along with his memories onto the Belle Isle bridge as the spinning wheels now reflected both the sparkling river below and the confusion in his mind of where she could be and how he would find her. After circling the south corner of the island he slowed down and brought the vehicle to rest at the curb near the site of that first meeting. *"Just think, think a little harder, there has to be a way."*

TEN

"Hal-le-lu-jah, Hal-le-lu-jah....
"King of Kings, Hal-le-lu-juh, , and Lord of Lords...

Basking in the rich gospel melodies that filled his white sedan, Minister Roberts began his Saturday morning in customary fashion. The cool March morning in Atlanta didn't normally warrant air conditioning. The beads of sweat popping from his forehead after the 'All-You-Can-Eat Breakfast Buffet' he'd just left, did. Frantically, he turned the A/C up a notch while reaffirming his allegiance to the music. Burping madly, he also reaffirmed his allegiance to rich food. Satisfied, he abruptly passed gas while sitting atop the fine leather car seats.

'Rip-Rip-Rip' "Good Lord!" he moaned. 'R...iiii...ppp' again went the seat.

"Have Mercy," he exclaimed.

The Music Minister turned the A/C dial up even further, and suddenly felt convicted. Once again, he had committed the sin of gluttony! Guilt came over him, as it so often did, and he hit the auto button on all four car windows. Subconsciously, he cleansed himself of sin; the fresh air seeping in while malodorous fumes rushing out. As the odor left he repented. Instead of heading back home, he decided to pull over by the side of the road and pray, so he negotiated the white sedan to the nearest curb. The color white was chosen for its purity, and he once hoped to fill its seats with a family, but as 38 years whisked by, his self righteousness dictated that no woman was ever good enough or spiritual enough for him. His insatiable quest for gospel elegance, his food, and the occasional company of an uncultured female friend from the other side of the tracks were the only things that really mattered to him now. Stopping the car and lowering his head he began to pray for them.

"Dear Lord, please forgive my gluttonous ways and allow me to serve as a vessel for your word, and lead me and guide me to where you want me to be...and...and....." Suddenly he remembered the fact that today was the first day of the day long new member's class session at Mt. Tabernacle, and turned his prayer to ponder.

"Hmm. Everyone must complete the new member's orientation class before they could join the auxiliary groups. And if there are going to be many men, then they too might join an auxiliary group. And if they were going to join an auxiliary group, then maybe they will join Manpower. And if they can sing, surely you don't mind if they can sing—I mean *really sing Lord*. Good gracious, what a glorified Gospel Fest we're going to have for our Men's Day Weekend Celebration. So that's it Lord, you're speaking to my heart Lord you're speaking to my heart this morning, just like I knew you would. You want me to check on the new flock of members today in hopes that we can find better singers to glorify your name. Yes Lord, I will do your will, yes Lord."

His excitement was uncontrollable as he popped in his next favorite CD, featuring 'Speak To My Heart.' As the song began to play he forged a U-turn. Heading back to Mt. Tabernacle its lyrics alone seemed to glide his machine throughout the ten minute journey. Trying to contain the exuberance of a child at Christmas time, he strolled past the church sanctuary and came upon the huge auxiliary room. The Music Minister scanned the room like a computer, trying to gain a quick profile without looking conspicuous.

Now most people might be surprised to find who they'll see in heaven, assuming they ever make it. If that's a given, the next biggest shock on this earth, judging from the look in the Music Minister's eyes when he peered in, was who they'll see teaching the new members class one day in their home church. Minister Robert's had just finished tallying the new members when he looked past them and saw me. Y'all pray for me, really pray for me, because I would have given anything to freeze frame the way his eyes bucked and that jaw dropped when he realized it was me about to teach that new members class.

"Well good morning to you too, Minister Roberts. You don't have to be a stranger to us today you know. Would you like to come on in and join us?" I asked.

"Uh no! No thanks. I just thought I'd check in to say hello," he replied.

"Two, four, six, eight, nine, eleven, twelve, fifteen new members," he whispered while counting with his finger. "Six men and nine women, all eagerly anticipating a new Christian experience at Mt. Tabernacle," Minister Robert's eyes were still scanning and counting as he spoke.

"I'd like you men to come on out to the Manpower Choir practice session this Thursday night," he began. "Brother Medley will be sure to remind you about it when you're finished today, won't you Kyle?"

"Of course I will," I replied. "In fact, I'll be letting them know about all the auxiliary groups." And since you're leaving now, I'd like us all to join in and wish you a blessed day, Minister Roberts. Everybody, that's our Minister of Music, Minister Roberts, and unfortunately he was just leaving. Have a fine and blessed day."

All of us joined in to tell the Music Minister goodbye. As much as I loved it, I prayed for my own cynicism, and hoped enlisting the new members to send him off didn't appear too obvious. It must have been his destiny though, as another catalyst showed up moments later that routinely encourages men to stay.

"Excuse me please," came a sweet and familiar voice from the side of the minister's girth that blocked half the doorway. As Minister Roberts stepped aside, Bianca Kincaid walked in, and it was my eye's turn to buck. Her aura was begging for attention, so resoundingly that all of the men present, and half the women, launched radar stares before looking away to not draw attention. They drew it anyway. Our eyes met as she glanced up to the front of the room as she walked like a self assured winner of a beauty pageant to her seat. I smiled at her broadly and unabashedly. I'd just spoken with her last night, and she gave me no clue she was coming to join the church today. She returned a nod to acknowledge me yet kept her game face on, informing me she came here for a purpose. Behind her came Charles Nix. Not everyone recognized him, but I did. That face. I'd seen it for over two months now as he quietly sat in the sanctuary during Sunday services. I couldn't place it before, but now it hit me. Charles was an ex-con who used to be called the 'Gentleman Bandit'. His secret was safe with me, though. Just after him 'Car Salesman of the Month' Ed Tyson (the shark) followed. *Now that just takes the cake, chasing skirts and writing bad deals all the way from the job to the sanctuary!* I somehow thought about that sandwich dropping to the bottom slot again. *Who am I to judge?, no sir. I'm not God, yet maybe it's okay to just inspect the fruit today a little more.*

I checked my watch and noticed it was 8:55A.M. There might be something I can do for the Lord without Minster Robert's interfering ego after all. As I gathered my notes together, Keith Terry walked in the door. I'd seen Keith bring his car in to get serviced from time to time over at Peach City Motors. Gossip had it among some of the mechanics that Keith was one of the biggest gamblers in Georgia, Florida, and Tunica Mississippi. At 36 years old, he never met a bet he didn't like. All through college he never smoked, drank, and rarely uttered a curse word. He had married his college sweetheart, and together they had a son and a beautiful daughter. Keith worked hard to become a highly successful C.P.A. He had taken his first trip to Las Vegas over two years ago, and that was the beginning of the end for the monthly mortgage and thus the marriage. The solemn look I noticed in his eyes formed a window to his soul. It was an understatement to say he, like all of us, needed Jesus.

"Good morning new prospective members, I'm Kyle Medley, and I'll be prayerfully leading you from Genesis to Revelation today. We will not be judging anyone's level of spiritual maturity, so don't hesitate to share what you know about scripture. Likewise, don't hesitate to ask questions about that which you don't understand. I don't have all the answers, but with your help, I'll try. Let us all introduce ourselves, and then we'll say a prayer."

Looking over the sea of eighteen souls I felt humbled to be there, just like a fruit inspector with an understanding of where precious fruit comes from.

ELEVEN

It happened to be dress down day, and Pastor Adams looked every bit his African heritage wearing his black and gold dashiki. While he preached, the members who normally shouted **"Amen"** and **"You tell it Pastor"** after every sentence didn't pick today to differ. The passive shouted, and even the spiritually nonchalant were even motivated to move a leg or two.

"You see," Adams began, "there's a big difference between "Holy" Christians who are naturally filled with the Holy Spirit and "Wholly" Christians, who are much more filled with themselves. You see, a Holy Christian will…, while a wholly Christian will…" he continued on, drawing analogies that you'd think nobody would think of.

His sermon was electrifying enough to make many stand up and testify right there on the spot. Unfortunately, that's just what the virtually unknown gentleman who sat in the middle section of the pew decided to get up and do.

"Excuse me, pastor." The unknown voice abruptly came from the middle of the congregation so loud and deep in its tone that it bubbled up like a volcano. Pastor Adams stopped his sermon while half of the congregation turned every angle in search of its whereabouts since nobody but nobody ever interrupted Pastor Adams sermon. Suddenly a tall, slender, black man rose up from the midst of the middle pew while his wife sat motionless and completely embarrassed to his side.

"Excuse me y'all, but I've just got to tell y'all how wonderful it's been since I've given my life to the Lord," he said.

"Well that's wonderful," Pastor Adams replied with the kind of heartfelt sincerity that would normally have been plenty for most impromptu testimonials, except this man continued.

"You see, I was a drug dealer for most of the last ten years. I sold drugs so much that I got myself arrested and put in jail. I sold drugs to my brother and I sold drugs to my sister. I even sold drugs to little kids on their way to school. I started doing drugs at home and even at work until the day that I lost my job. I even made drugs in my home and sold them on the street." Many of the older women in the congregation were gasping with enough **"have mercy Jesus"** and **"you don't say's"** to fill up a weeks worth of witnessing. One of the deacons even called him a rotten dog not very far below his breath. His standing up and testifying was interrupting a perfectly good sermon, and we were more than annoyed.

Looking over to my left I noticed some of the choir members—like the congregation—looking angrier than me. Glancing still further I met the eyes of Brother Humphries. It was obvious that if his eyes could talk they were waiting on my signal authorizing him to pick that fool up and bounce him out of the church the same way it's done at the nightclub. I raised my hand up, signaling to all that we must be patient. Upon seeing my gesture, Humphries laid his head back on the back pew support as if he were in defeat. Pastor Adam's demeanor, on the other hand, displayed the patience of Job. You could still sense there was once a time in his life when he would have called on us to throw this man out of the place, and at any most time in ours we gladly would have.

"I think what you are trying to tell us is that you were once a drug dealer and a drug user and you basically lived a life of sin, is that right young man?" Pastor Adams asked.

"Yes sir pastor, that's what I'm saying," he replied.

"And now you would like to seek Your Saviors forgiveness by dedicating your life to him and becoming reborn in the spirit and washed with the blood, is that about right?"

"How did you know Pastor? How did you know that?" the man asked.

"I think you gave us a subtle hint," Pastor Adams replied with a smile amongst the snickers. "I will send a minister over to you after service to pray with you and for you," and if you can hold your testimony until then, I'd like to dismiss the congregation now."

The drug dealer's testimony ended as abruptly as it began after everybody followed the pastor's lead and patiently heard him out. Pastor Adams had that way of making his point in the most diplomatic way possible. After prayer he dismissed us, and I rose up only to walk slowly towards the front door. I glanced over at Bianca and motioned to her with a nod of my head as I smiled. I had no intention of leaving church today without her.

A beautiful March afternoon sun met everyone as they filed out of the church to their cars. Brother Akins walked out of the doors with his wife, and was soon followed by Brothers Humphries and Wakefield.

"Say brothers, I called out. Why don't you all come out and join me at the Gospel Network this afternoon?"

"You'll have to excuse me," Brother Akins replied, as he came closer to me and extended his hand, "though my faith is high, my gospel spirits right now are a little low."

"I figured that," I replied. "That's why we need to go over there anyway."

"Just what are we going to represent?" Brother Humphries said.

"We'll represent the Manpower Choir of Mt. Tabernacle, just like we always do!"
The brothers stood there first looking at me and then each other for a moment. I hoped their quiet faces reflected the prospect that the suggestion had merit.

"Look, why don't you guys tell all the brothers that we'll meet over there at 2:00 o'clock, alright?"

"Alright, we'll tell 'em', but don't expect everybody to be too enthusiastic," responded Humphries.

"Just get them over there, and we'll trust God to fill their spirit up later." I turned around to face the door in just enough time to see Bianca Kincaid come out. She was smartly dressed in a mauve dress with her hair spiraled down her back in a style very carefree and natural. Her black skin seemed to glisten with the sun in a manner I had never seen before.

"Good afternoon Mzzz B3—If you aren't a sight for sore eyes."

"You look very handsome yourself Kyle, and your eyes don't look too sore either, at least not as sore as your head will be if you call me B3 again." Why don't you just call me B4 the next time you want to call me B3? You'll probably think another B is appropriate when you see my reaction, then maybe you'll stop saying it once and for all!"

"What would another B stand for? Somehow I feel you don't mean blessed," I replied.

She smiled in a way that reminded me how her pearly teeth contrasted with her black skin. The smile also let me know that some things need not be said.

"Never mind, you don't have to say it, I think I know. I sort of like the name B-3 though, and I always thought it was a rather flattering one."

"That's just it. I'm tired of always being flattered. It gets real old, real quick. I'd much more prefer to see a guy just being real with me, you know? It shows more substance and far less game."

"Careful, you're about to lose your game face, and I know you don't want to do that," I said. She blushed ever so sweetly, and gazed at me.

"You don't know me all that well, so stop pretending like you do. Anyway, where are we going?"

"Did you bring your walking shoes?" I asked.

"I did, they're in my car," she replied.

"Well I'll go walk you to your car to get them. If you don't mind riding with me we'll go to Stone Mountain Park for a walk. But first I'd like to take you to the Gospel Network."

"I've heard about the Gospel Network, but I'm not sure what that's all about. Tell me, what's it like?"

"I'll walk with you to get your shoes and explain." I held out my hand to guide her. Without hesitating she grasped it and held it firmly as we descended down the steps towards her car.

"The Gospel Network is where Christians go on Sunday afternoon to unwind and share in fellowship. See, back in the day our parents and grandparents used to go to church, and then come back home and cook. But now that church membership has skyrocketed, there's come a recognized need to not just let everyone go home on Sunday, but to gather with our church and other church families."

"So you all gather and do what?" she asked after opening her car trunk and bringing out a pair of track shoes. She then followed me to my truck without breaking our conversation.

"Well, lots of stuff. We share each other's church newsletters while making announcements about the most exciting things happening in each other's church every three months. Or we eat fabulous meals as we sip non-alcoholic drinks and play cards. Or go to the game room and play checkers, chess, shoot pool, or simply watch a basketball or football game on T.V. There's even a personal and group prayer room. "

"It sounds innocent enough, but maybe just a tad bit boring. What about the music? Is there music?" she asked, as we turned to walk toward my pick up truck.

"Of course there's music. That's the best part. First Sunday of the month there's a nationally known gospel artist or group over there. The other three Sundays are where the best church gospel groups around Atlanta come in and perform live gospel."

"Now that sounds nice. Even nicer if you all really manage to have all that without any liquor over there."

"Well, nothings perfect. Occasionally you'll smell the ones who just can't help getting juiced up on the way over. They usually swallow a gallon of Listerine to try and cover it up before smelling like a liquor and Listerine sandwich—running around sweating it out their pores on the low. But that's life."
Bianca stopped at a new, high end vehicle assuming it was mine.

"I'm over here," I said, while motioning toward the small pick up truck next to it. "Would you like to get in?"

"Sure."

"Wait a minute. It's our first date, and I should open the door for you."

"I've asked you not to use the word *date*. You mean it's the first time I ever rode in your car on a Sunday afternoon. Whatever the case, don't call it a date, because I'm not ready for that. And if you don't normally open doors then…"

"Excuse me Bianca," I interrupted, after circling around to her door, "but I've never been out with anyone as beautiful as you, to go anywhere. I don't even know what I normally do. And secondly, if you don't like the word date, I don't have to use it. As long as we can have a few more of whatever this is, then I'm okay with the vocabulary."

"You know you're silly, and a bit country," she chided before stepping into the pickup truck. I got in to start the engine, then looked over at her and smiled. Where I once couldn't conceive it, my thoughts now confirmed that her riding along beside me were as natural as anything.

"Yeah, I may be a little country," I went on, "but I know it. You, you're just one Detroit assembly line or two removed from where I'm from, though. So tell me, what part of the country are your folks from anyway? Alabama? Mississippi? New Orleans?"

"Actually, my Mom *is* from S. Carolina and my Dad *was* from Georgia, but they are Southern folks, and not country folks. There is a difference, you know."

"Really? Well there's not a lot of difference to me. The only difference I see is the number of verbs and nouns they split while eating their soul food. Most Northerner's don't do it as much because they're not used to eating that good to begin with."

"Hmm...that's one interesting perspective. It's outlandish, very outlandish...but interesting. And what makes you say a thing like that," she asked?

"Cause of the way that I've seen northerners eyes get buck wide when they get a hold of some good southern cooking. Now take country folks..."

"Like you?"

"Like me, yeah. We may break our English from time to time, but that's only because we like to stay as casual as we can while we eat our soul food. And in doing so, we just let our verbal guard down a bit from time to time."

"So eating is the only time you do that?"

"Okay, I see where you're going with that. As a representative of the country, do allow me to explain something. We country people feel "y'all Yankees" have already lowered the standards by coming down here dressed in all those loud colors. That's right! Don't even look like you're surprised to hear that cause you're not. Then you're always talking bout how y'all don't like this and that about the south, running around in those bright orange and lime green colors, looking like a peacock with those alligator shoes on too. You know its country. But we're real folks who just want to make y'all feel good, so we split a verb or a noun sometimes, so what? We do it just so y'all don't feel too self conscious, that's all."

Bianca looked at me and tried to maintain a serious face, but it was no use. Her smirk soon turned to laughter as I joined her, at least until she wiped her smile off and put her 'game face' back on.

"Now you just back up off of my Motor City Brothers and sisters. I think much of it is stylish, and if it *is* country, then we learned it here first."

"And that's my point. You're just a couple of assembly lines removed from where I'm from girl, now welcome back home."

"Thanks for the entertaining history lesson. Now at the expense of sounding like a child, are we there yet?" I veered to park near the odd looking structure on the right. In the midst of the brick buildings that surrounded it stood the Gospel Network. Boasting 12 rooms, the massive structure stood three stories high. Its huge windows and colonial style porch gave it a unique historical look that was reminiscent of one of the precious things spared during General Sherman's infamous march on Atlanta years ago. Two wooden columns on both sides of the porch extended its inviting welcome even more.

Exiting the truck I noticed how Bianca's eyes gazed at the building and marveled at its beauty. She gently nudged me in my side as we walked towards it.

"Just who have you seen from Detroit that eats their soul food with bucked eyes anyway?" she asked. "And now that you mentioned it, slaves originally cooked chitterlings—if that's soul food. It was the only part of the pig that their masters left for them. Beyond that, unless it's cooked by the restaurants I know of up north, your version of soul food has much to be desired. You really reached out on the deep end with that one, Kyle."

"Sure I did, especially since those bright colors look so good on you girl. I like that mauve you're wearing especially, to tell the truth." Bianca smirked before cutting her eyes at me to let me know she liked the compliment but wasn't going to get carried away with it. She then changed the subject.

"This place is very quaint. It has lots of character, but it's different."

"Different how?"

"I guess because I've been invited out to a nightclub, a motorcycle club, and a yacht club before, but never a gospel club. That's a little different."

"Not really. Not when you consider that Gospel music has come a long way in the last twenty years or so. For over 100 years blacks sang Ole Negro Spirituals inspired largely by pain and faith. Most of it began without music—just raw emotion, and the black church made it their cornerstone. Then, along came a revved up version of what we call gospel music. It maintained a consistent style for decades before taking off with new vocal styles and sophisticated instruments, tapping a real pulse among believers and waking up non believers too. The only down side was as they shook their heads to it, they wondered if it had become too secular, or too rhythmic, to be Christian. That's a big reason why most of the R&B singers of the 60's and 70's crossed over after coming out of the church." They needed a forum for their voices that had become too restrictive for the church."

"I know. Several of them came from Detroit, right?"

"That's right, they did. Anyway, things started changing much faster about 20 years ago in the gospel community. Along came a lot of bold and innovative gospel singers who took chances with the music."

"Uh, still from Detroit."

"That's very true, but we'll just give that a rest now." Bianca chuckled and grabbed my hand as we approached the front porch.

"Look at the big, old fashioned wooden swing on the front porch. Let's go and sit down on it before we go inside." Her enthusiasm was refreshingly contagious, and we remained hand in hand while climbing the steps toward the swing built for two. She sat down first and then patted the empty space next to her, motioning for me to join her.

I sat down next to her and shoved my feet off the floor until the swing took off with a good sway. Smiling like children at one another we failed to notice an elderly couple walking arm in arm up the steps. After navigating their way to the top they both paused. Staring at us for a moment they each smiled broadly.

"Look at the young love birds Josephine," he said while pointing to us as if we were deer in a forest.

"I see them Barry," she responded. "They remind you of us about fifty years ago, don't they?" she asked. "You bet," but I was far more handsome than this young man," he boastfully whispered back.

"We're celebrating our 50 year anniversary young folks."

"That's awfully special," I acknowledged.

"Thanks for sharing that with us. So what's your secret, Bianca asked?"

"It's more of a recipe than a secret babe," Barry instructed. We've always tried to do it God's way," Josephine replied. "That's all."

"That's beautiful," Bianca replied. "We'll remember that," I promised. Have a great day and may God bless you both," Bianca added. "That really was special," she repeated as they walked away. Now tell me what stirs this special passion you have for Gospel music, Kyle."

"Well, gospel singers are still being raised in the church. But a vast amount of them are putting awesome lyrics and beats to this music, which is taking it through the roof. Instead of crossing over to R&B, Jazz, or Hip-Hop, they're showcasing their creativity to the world by singing gospel through all these forms. People in turn want to hear more of it. That's why so many churches' today strive for really nice choirs. People who love the music don't want to wait until Sunday morning to enjoy it. They're singing it everyday, and everywhere!"

"I know, she said, and it sounds good. I hear a lot of choirs. Some of them sound so good that I sometimes wonder what they do with the people who want to join them, but can't even sing?" There was a brief silence as Bianca looked to me.

"Kyle, Kyle why are you so quiet? What's wrong? Wait a minute, don't tell me. I know you aren't going around that church singing the way you used to at work, are you? Are you in the choir Kyle? You must be, or you would have said something by now."

"I'll do one of your numbers, and just tell you to quit acting like know me so well," I replied in light hearted fashion, but she had become serious.

"At work I see how you treat people," she began. "And last week at church I saw how well you teach. You know, you might even be anointed enough to one day preach. But Kyle, your singing...and you were doing so well."

"And I was doing so well? You make it sound like I was a hospital patient whose condition was suddenly downgraded, or a sprinter who suddenly broke his leg."

"You know I don't mean it like that. You're just an exceptional Bible teacher, that's all. But really, are you trying to sing in the choir Kyle?"

"Alright Bianca, here's my testimony. I've been in the Men's Gospel Choir of Mt. Tabernacle for over six years, and it's President, the Manpower President that is, for over two." Bianca tried to contain her smirk of laughter, as she must have thought this was cute. I admired her sensitivity.

"The book of Psalm's says to praise him with every instrument and every breath, you know."

"I know, and I'm sure you should. But it doesn't say you have to do it in the choir Kyle, *(Lets see, where have I heard this before)* or at work, or especially around me while we are on one of our un-dates." She looked at me sweetly and sincerely in an attempt to get me to smile.

"The Manpower President huh, well, you just *go* then boy!"

Even though I wasn't in the mood to smile she made me feel darn good. Our eyes met suddenly like a magnet while our faces drew closer toward one another. She was being real with me while not wanting to hurt my feelings. Little did she know that between God's grace, and my desire for her that I was already long over it. The sweet sound of the Gospel hit "Whatever It Is," began reverberating from inside the Network. Before we exchanged more silence—and I got caught up in the foolish flesh of wanting to kiss her on our first date—three cars approached. Bianca's face and mine remained frozen on each others like a frame frozen to protect a portraits beauty from the world, yet there was no voice that could bring me closer to the reality of the world like Minister Roberts. I had no intention of allowing him to make the picture shatter as he arrived with the men.

"Yes brothers, we've got to see ourselves. God wants us to see ourselves, not as we are but what we can be. And we can one day be a great choir, showcasing ourselves here at the Gospel Network, on the radio, and just about anywhere we want."

Minster Roberts was speaking to Brother's Humphries, Akins, and Wakefield as they walked alongside. It was obvious they were patronizing with him while trying to contain their resentment. *Just how do you try to inspire men after telling them they now have to audition for their place in the choir? They were more inspired before you told em that, you know.* As they approached the stairs I stood up to greet them. "Good afternoon brothers, I'm glad you all decided to make it on over."

"Hey Kyle, we didn't see you up here," said Akins.

"That's okay. Did you all tell all the brothers to come on by?" I asked.

"I tried," Akins confirmed. "Some said they'll come, while some of the others feel that the devil is trying to kill their joy and just weren't motivated." I looked and noticed the brothers glancing at Bianca and realized it was time for an introduction.

"Brothers, I'd like you to meet a good friend and new member of Mt. Tabernacle, Bianca Kincaid."

"Bianca, these are my fellow choir brothers; Humphries, Akins, and Wakefield." Bianca stood up in a lady like manner and shook all of their hands, then glanced over at Minister Roberts. His eyes seem to salivate at the prospect of meeting a beautiful woman like her, albeit by chance, in the only atmosphere that would afford it.

"And this is our Music Minister, Elgin Roberts."

"Pleased to meet you Bianca, yes, yes, indeed it is," he said excitedly. "So tell me dear, have you been inside the Network before?"

"No I haven't, but Kyle was just about to escort me in, weren't you Kyle?"

"That's right. Why don't we all go in and grab a table together, but first I'd like to give Bianca a quick tour before we join back up with you guys, alright?" Beautiful music engulfed us all as I opened the door for them. Walking in I noticed eight of the twenty neatly decorated tables below the stage were full, with members of two mega-churches comprising most of them. It was about 2:30 and the "New World Voices" Gospel Tabernacle Choir wasn't set to perform until 4:00.

Minister Roberts grabbed a choir schedule from the news rack as the men took their chairs. He was sharing the itinerary of church groups due to perform as I waved 'so long' to them. It didn't seem quite fair to leave the guys to Minister Roberts, but the guys were grown and could handle worse. Besides, I wanted to devote some personal attention to Bianca.

"You think you could cut that tension between you and Minister Roberts with a knife," she asked?

"A dull blade or a butter knife could work just fine too, but in an ideal world you weren't supposed to notice that."

"Then thank God I live in the real world. Hey, this is a nice place, but where is the kitchen? I'm a little hungry, and I have to order dinner."

"If that's your wish," I replied. "But allow me to treat you to it."

"That's okay, Kyle," she said as we walked through the oval opening doorway of the adjoining room. "Oh, and I'd like to see the prayer room also, is it over here?"

She pointed to the royal burgundy curtains that contained the 'unoccupied' sign right next to its velvety smooth exterior. Peeking inside, she observed the large, immaculate room with fresh burgundy carpet, two benches, and a big wooden cross on the center wall with a full picture of His Son nailed to it. She closed the drapes upon seeing the "no shoes allowed" sign and shed her camel leather boots. Reaching in her purse she grabbed a twenty dollar bill and through an opening in the drapes extended it to me.

"Thanks for bringing me here. Now, would you order me a plate of collard greens, string beans, and macaroni and cheese, and whatever I can treat you to please? I'll only be about fifteen minutes. And by the way, I'll try to keep my eyes from bucking too much when I eat it, okay?"

"Sure thing," I replied, "but your money is no good here."

Just as I walked off, Bianca overheard Josephine speaking to her husband Barry as they sat on the couch with their backs turned.

"You've been a good husband Barry, and I'm blessed to have you all these years. But sweetie you've asked me what I wanted for our anniversary more than once now."

"And you've never told me. Why is that?"

"Because I know we don't really have the money to get it, that's why."

"Maybe, maybe not, but tell me anyway pumpkin?"

"Alright, Barry, just for once…"

"For once what sugar pie," he asked?

"Well, for once, I'd like to have a really nice ring, that's all."

"You telling me you don't like our wedding bands?"

"No, I love our bands. Oh Barry, just forget it. You'd never understand. I've never owned just one really nice ring, and I thought it would be nice, that's all. But more than anything I'm happy, and…" Instinctively Bianca went to her purse to grab the engagement ring she'd removed after Donald threatened her. She would have gladly given it back to him had she not left the restaurant so hastily, but it didn't matter. Donald would never accept it back, and she couldn't see herself ever wearing it again. She walked over to Barry with the ring lodged inside her hand just as he'd started reluctantly reciting their needed home repairs in the manner Josephine knew he would. After gently tapping him on the shoulder Bianca brandished the ring and placed it in his hand as he turned around.

"God told me to give you this," she told them. Josephine's mouth gaped open and Barry appeared startled, yet Bianca continued. "Happy Anniversary! This ring was meant for Josephine, so please accept it and don't keep her waiting, okay?" Barry was surprised and he was proud, and he didn't hesitate to take it.

"Happy Anniversary Josey," Barry said, and while he slipped the ring on her finger Bianca smiled to her self.

"It's beautiful, but what can we do for you young lady," Josephine asked?

"You two can pray that I myself will one day find the man that was meant for me, so we can wind up just like the two of you, that's all."

"Of course we'll pray for you, and you will," they confirmed.

Bianca then humbly turned and walked back into the room. Still shoeless, she relished the smooth and tender feel of the carpet beneath her feet. Noticing the wooden rack on the wall held a Bible, and walked over to grab it. Closing her eyes, she held it snugly to her heart. She still felt far from home, yet now safer and secure in her new atmosphere than at any time since she'd arrived. Walking over to the prayer bench she placed the Bible upon it. Slowly, she knelt down on her knees before opening it to her favorite scripture. As she prayed and thanked The Almighty for keeping her, I returned and placed the twenty dollar bill back in one of her boots.

TWELVE

My enthusiasm for choir rehearsal tonight was somewhat tainted by the pompous way Minister Roberts had earlier told us to prepare for tonight's audition. All week I had spent rallying the troops, who'd grown increasingly reluctant and offended. I'd been careful hoping to not convey the remorse in my own eyes too. I opened the big wooden doors, which lead to the foyer, and noticed the word Manpower on the bright orange leaflets on the table. Upon picking one up it read, **"Calling All Men of Mt. Tabernacle! Come Audition for The Manpower Gospel Choir this Thursday night at 7:30 P.M. Singing experience preferred."** As I read it Brother Akins walked through the door.

"What do ya know Kyle?" he said somberly.

"Things are changing around here, that's all I know," I replied. "Here, take a look at this." I handed him the flyer as he instantly remarked "I've seen it already, haven't you?"

"Nope."

"You didn't see Minister Roberts passing them out after church on Sunday? I thought he gave one to every man twice! Where were you? Wait, you were with that beautiful girl after the service, that's why you missed it."

"Maybe so, but my point is....can you believe this? Singing experience preferred. Just eight years ago this church had what, maybe fifty members?"

"You know I remember," Akins replied. "They used to ask me to play the organ for the church even when I told the pastor I had never graduated beyond 'Mary had a Little Lamb."

"And don't forget about the eleven year old drummer we had back then, Deacon Chaney's boy Michael. Remember the time he just stood up and cried right during a song?"

"Do I ever," Akins replied, and everybody shouted—thinking

he'd caught the Holy Ghost or something, not realizing 'till' later that he'd been wetting on himself since the start of the song?" Both of us laughed for a moment, until I lamented what was heaviest on our hearts.

"And most important, you could sing for the Lord as much as you liked, as long as the spirit moved you." Quietly, we reflected while staring at each other. We then turned our attention on the big wooden doors behind us, squeaking loudly to inform us that Brothers Humphries and Lang were walking in.

"What's this, a Men's Choir rehearsal or a funeral going on here?" Brother Humphries blurted. Brother Akins cast a look of stately wisdom at him before speaking.

"Might be a little bit of both, Stephen," I answered.

"Well, it just might be, but if you ask me I'd say maybe it's time to sing one of our favorites, like…"

"I don't know what you came to do"

"I don't know what you came to do"

"I come to praise the Lord," Humphries crooned, *"and I say we…"*

Suddenly the sound of music started playing in the sanctuary. It began with the organ and quickly followed with the sound of drums, instantly drowning our singing party out. An electric guitar even joined in with a progressive upbeat rhythm that never graced the sanctuary before.

"Who ever played an electric guitar here?" asked Brother Akins. "And listen, that bass guitar sure doesn't sound like Pastor Adams." Brother Humphries seemed to muse at the suggestion before responding.

"It can't be Pastor Adams, sounds too good, besides, the pastor told everybody in the congregation last week that he was headed to Haiti today for three weeks of mission work," I reminded them. I checked my watch and then peered at the men like a ship captain whose boat has gone astray.

"It's only 7:25, and the music's beginning before we've even prayed together, what in heavens is going on?" The robust sound of a man's voice blared through the speaker, drowning out my words.

"Who is that? That sounds like a professional gospel singer. Y'all sure we're in the right place," Brother Lange asked? We all cast a puzzled look at each other.

"Well its high time we found out," I answered. I opened the next set of doors as the decibel of the music radically increased. Together, we walked briskly into the sanctuary as four more of the brothers entered the foyer to instinctively follow behind. What we saw upon our first few entry steps froze all eight of us. Five new members were standing in the same spots where we formerly stood, and along with the help of three new band members, including the bassist, singing a song that was not in our repertoire. To be more accurate, it was well beyond it.

> *"What do you do, when your spirits are low*
> *You're broke, she's gone,*
> *and it seems you can't make it through*
> *Tell me how do you cope with the pains of the world?*
> *You just pray, and then to yourself, simply say..."*

It wasn't even a polished version of one of our favorite songs, yet it was as beautiful as it was alarming to us that we weren't singing it. As beautiful as it was alarming that upon further glance Ed Tyson, a.k.a. "The Shark" was singing lead. As beautiful as it was riveting that Roberts must have told the new Manpower members to arrive at 6:30, so he could hear them sing like sparrows—without us—until we arrived at 7:30. Glancing across them I noticed Charles Nix and Keith Terry were in the middle position of two other men outside the direct scope of the microphone. The best singers always stood center to one microphone, and upon a good listen to the background voices the reason rang clear, they could flat out S.A.N.G.!

"You know these guys?" Brother Humphries asked me.

"I can't hear what you said, speak up, the music's too loud, what did you say?"

"DO-YOU-KNOW–WHO-THESE-DUDES-ARE," he loudly shouted?

"Let's all go back out in the foyer where we can talk." I replied. As we turned around to leave I noticed Minister Roberts glance our way with a look of indifference while still playing the piano. *The nerve of that swine, he couldn't care less if we stayed or left for good.* I motioned for the men to follow me back in to the foyer, and after the door swung closed behind the last man to join us I began to speak.

"I know a few of them, probably better than ya'll, and have seen the others. Look, you recognize a couple of them don't you? That's Clifford Daniels and Jonathan Williams, the two who just joined up with us for the first time just two weeks ago. Singing lead is Ed Tyson, former New Yorker and car salesman at Peach City Motors. He gave himself to the Lord just last week." *Who until then had to be the most crooked car dealer and whoremonger in Atlanta.* "Another one of them is Keith Terry. He's a prominent C.P.A. here in Atlanta who also just finished new member's class last week too." *And a man who could account for everything except for how many bets it would take him to lose his family, help me Jesus, I'm judging.* Another one is Charles Nix, a Brother who joined the church a month ago and finished new members class also last week."

"Y'all really don't want to know his past," said Brother Wakefield.

"Charles Nix, Charles Nix, Chuck Nix, wait a minute, I remember that name and have seen that face. Don't nobody take this wrong, but wasn't he the bank robber they used to call 'The Gentleman Bandit,' Humphries asked?

"That's right. Always robbed a bank in a three piece suit and tie, politely asking the teller to hand over all the money while warning her not to throw the die in the bag, or else he'd blow the place up," said Brother Akins.

"Had a plastic hand grenade in one suit pocket and a fresh bottle of cologne in the other when they caught him walking down Peachtree Street with a briefcase full of fresh stolen money."

"I also heard he..." said another before I cut him off.

"Alright, enough already," I insisted. "That brother just finished doing seven years in prison, and he's paid his debt to society, now the rest is between him and God. So let him make his retribution for his sins just like the rest of us must do for ours. If anything, we should all thank God that we're given another day to do it. Now I'm just as shocked at how this audition has started as the rest of you, but I have a strange feeling that if we truly want to sing for the Almighty, then no matter what we just saw, we've got to get over it. Now if you will, ya'll can follow me back in there. We're going to wait until they finish so we can audition."

"But you heard how good those guys sound. We can't hold a match to them. How are we going to look auditioning with our voices, trying to get next to that? I think it's silly," said Brother Gonzalez.

"Down right embarrassing," said another.

"That's the way Minister Roberts thought we'd feel. He probably hoped we'd walk in on them this way, knowing we were going to get frustrated and just turn around," I replied.

"Well it worked because we just did," said Brother Wakefield.

"Sure did," said Brother Lange, "I walked out right behind you!"

"Is that right? Well, we're going to turn around and walk right back in," I said. "I don't believe you all. Already he's making you think that you have to sound beautiful to lift up his name, right?"

All the brothers stood mute.

"Come on," I pleaded. You mean he's already convinced you?"

"I think so, because here we are," Brother Lange said.

"So, is that how all of you feel," I asked.

Most of the men seemed frozen, but thinking about the question gradually thawed them out. Slowly they began to echo 'no sir', 'no way', and 'impossible', with the kind of conviction I was looking for. Brothers Akins and Gonzalez didn't seem to need a gut check. Of course, neither did Brother Humphries, who treated our meeting as a mere formality that he couldn't wait to end before going back in.

"Well alright then brothers. You all say you want my leadership, and I say let's go," I said, as the brothers followed proudly behind the most 'non-sing-ingest' men's choir leader this side of the Mississippi. Walking back in I noticed Minister Roberts appearing surprised that we'd returned. They were well into their next song, a song as equally outstanding as the first, while we folded our arms and stood patiently for it to end.

When it did end, Brother Humphries blurted out to Minister

Roberts; "I think that I should sing lead on that one. Would you like me to give it a try, Minister Roberts?" I loved it so much I decided to let convention go and joined in.

"You can use me for the lead singer role on the first one. Yeah I'm a first tenor, let y'all tell it, but I don't mind trying it in second tenor."

"And we'll be the primary back ups. After all, everybody knows we can hold a microphone with the best of them I'm sure, now don't they?" Brother Akins exclaimed," referring to the remaining cast of brothers.

Minister Roberts cast a look of disbelief, which quickly turned to disdain. Slowly, he dismounted his piano chair and walked over to us.

"How dare you men come into my practice session with this kind of chaotic, sacrilegious disrespect? You wouldn't attempt this mockery in the presence of Pastor Adams, so why do you choose to do it now," he asked?

"Do you want to tell him why Kyle, or do you want me to," asked Humphries? I motioned a halting gesture with my hand raised to Humphries.

"Hold on Stephen, I'll handle it. Listen, Minister Roberts," I said, "you're right about one thing. We probably wouldn't have stormed in here like this if Pastor Adams was here, but then again, it wouldn't be so obvious that you've lost all respect for us if pastor were here either."

"That's ridiculous. You're jumping to conclusions much too quick," Roberts responded.

"I don't think so. If I am, I'm jumping way too late. Something told me to ask Pastor Adams to put you and your glorified choir dreams on a leash long before he left town."

"As I was saying," Minister Roberts continued, "You jump to conclusions quicker than you can hold a note."

"Keep punching below the belt if you like, but admit it," I said. "There's no way you would have begun this practice session early— without us at that—if Pastor Adams were here. And speaking of a mockery, the Men's Chorus has prayed before every Assembly since my great-grandfather worshiped here over 100 years ago. It is a blessed ritual that we've all cherished to this day.

By sidestepping it, just to slide these men in our place, you're acting like a spiritual hypocrite." Minister Roberts stepped back in his piety and looked me up and down.

"Who do you think you're calling a hypocrite?"

"I didn't call you a hypocrite. I called you a spiritual hypocrite!"

"Just as well," Roberts shouted. "I've been charged with the responsibility for uplifting this choir and making it one of the best, and I've been overly patient for nearly a year, listening and directing a group of men who can't even hold their own. Like I've asked you before, just listen to yourselves sometimes. You think we could ever perform at the Gospel Network? Wait...forget about the Gospel Network for a minute. Do you believe you can even inspire a decent Men's Day Celebration here at Mt. Tabernacle? I think not, and it's just one month away now, you know."

"That's sad, real sad," I said.

"No, the sad part is that most of you men have no pride, Roberts responded.

"No pride? We have plenty of pride," I countered. "It's sad because you'd notice more of it if you had a genuine spirit. Listen, Minister Roberts! Can't you see what I'm trying to tell you?"

"Make your point Medley," Roberts said.

"Okay. Here we all are," I continued. "We are the lips of the wise, even though some even may sound like the lips of the fool ish when we sing. It doesn't matter. What matters is that we can all sing like songbirds if you really listen to another quality within our voices."

The brothers, both old and new, looked astonished as we spoke, and were speechless as we volleyed our points back and forth.

"Enough. I'll hear no more of this," Roberts commanded. "Now, I'm the Minister of Music, and if you want to continue to sing for Manpower, I hereby implore Brothers Wakefield, Gonzalez, Lange, Lewis, and Akins, to get up there in the third row in the Alto section. Hmm, let me see. Brothers, Sherman, Humphries, Baker, and myself, will sing behind them in a new fourth row we'll create. All the rest of you men stay right where you are."

"But Minister Roberts, there aren't even any microphones up here, who in the world is going to hear us?" Brother Humphries asked.

"I know. We'll just have to soon correct that, now won't we," Minister Roberts responded.

The men looked on skeptically as we slowly marched to the third and fourth rows to take our assigned positions.

"We won't worry about it right now, Stephen," I said as I walked toward the last row, keeping my head turned towards Minister Roberts, "for in the Bible it also says that obedience is better than sacrifice!"

All fourteen of us stood in position, as Minister Robert's dispensed copies of the words to the song 'Stand' and 'Rest Upon My Heart'.

"Now I know that most of you haven't had enough time to meet, but they'll be enough time for introductions and idle chatter later. We've wasted enough time tonight, and I need the new members to become familiar with two of our old songs and the old members to become familiar with a couple of the new. Now let's take 'Stand' from the top, and I only want to hear brothers Nix, Terry, Tyson, and Williams singing lead while everybody else backs them up in Chorus section, understand?"

The musicians revved up their instruments as the new brothers stepped to the microphones. Ed Tyson eloquently carried the song again while we sang an occasional word or two in the back up. Without microphones we knew we had to project our voices loudly, even though to me it didn't sound like we'd be heard either way. After it was over, Minister Roberts smiled and asked us to start the song again, and then once more before moving on to 'Resting On My Heart.' Brothers Nix and Terry carried the song almost single handedly while we rehearsed it again and again. It was as beautiful as it was fatiguing. We sucked up feeling the agony-of-de-feet as our watches rolled past 10:45, and raspy voices greeted us upon finishing the last note. Minister Roberts then stopped and finally smiled while looking us over like his newly branded cattle.

THIRTEEN

"That was a little better I guess. Okay. You all can take your seats now." We plopped down like tired soldiers. "Now this sounds like the makings of a gospel Choir, and though we still have much work to be done, you all should take solace in your efforts tonight. Do you guys feel you're ready to sing this Sunday at the 11:00 o'clock service? It might be the warm up you need for the Men's Day Celebration, you know."

"Sure, why not, I'm ready, okay!" All of us responded in the affirmative, and it wasn't surprising. Never before had we sounded nearly this good. Most of all, Men's Day was fast approaching, and since we wanted to represent it well, a good tune up didn't hurt us a bit. Of course Minister Robert's didn't mind having his day in the sun by showing us off, either. As for me, I thought it would be a nice surprise for Pastor Adams to witness this vocal delight upon his anticipated return, so showcasing our improvement for Men's Day would be perfect.

"Alright, it's decided. We'll all wear our red sports coats with white shirts, red ties and black pants, understood?" Minister Roberts said.

"I don't have a red sports coat, or a red tie," said Brother Humphries.

"I don't either," said Brother Wakefield.

"Neither do I, nor most of us original members here," I pointed out. "Why can't we all just wear our usual black suits, white shirts and black or blue ties? It's all worked for us before."

"Because a lot of what we feel was working before was actually laying down on the job, Brother Medley. We are now a new, progressive and contemporary choir, and it's time we purchased at least three or four outfits to represent it. Start saving your pennies gentlemen!"

I looked at the proud faces of some of our original Manpower members who could afford it, and they didn't look much different from the ones who couldn't. The economic realities of life had hit many of us pretty hard. Singing for the Lord was a luxury that until now everyone took for granted they could afford. Even Brother Akins, who had the money to dress us all if he had to, didn't like the idea. All of us knew Brother Gonzales was unemployed and a diabetic without medical insurance. Brother Lange openly prayed for the resources to keep his truck repaired and on the road. Even Brother Humphries, who could have been the black poster child for a 'What, Me Worry?' campaign, was known to be struggling while trying to get a new overnight courier service off the ground.

"I think we ought to just take this just a little slower, gentlemen," I said, not wanting to acknowledge the few who couldn't financially handle it. Nobody spoke for a few seconds until a few unfamiliar voices were heard.

"I think it's a great idea," Ed said.

"I can get it by Sunday," said Keith.

"Not a problem," and "sounds fine to me," echoed Charles Nix and Brother Williams. All the new members were supportive of the idea, and Minister Roberts couldn't wait to take credit and steer it further.

"Brother Medley, that's been my point all along. You brothers just move too slow, but we'll compromise. Let the new Manpower members come dressed in their red blazer outfits on Sunday while the old, I mean, established Manpower members wear their black suits."

"We've never dreamt of dressing differently and you know it, Minister Roberts," I said.

"Well its now time to think outside the box, gentlemen. And come to think of it, it will be time to elect a new Manpower President sometime next month. Let's all think about that while Kyle thinks about taking things slow."

I casually absorbed his comment and moved on to my agenda, not wanting to openly convey that his words carried any more weight than they deserved.

"Brothers," I said, "we need prayer. For all of you new members,

do understand that this ritual shall not ever again be sacrificed for any reason, especially now. Would you all come join me down here on the stage to hold hands?"
The men all gathered around in a big circle as I began to lead them in prayer.

"Does anyone else have a special prayer" I asked? It was now past 11:00 p.m. and the men were tired. The silence was calming until Brother Baker spoke up—his voice nearly breaking.

"Brothers, many of you don't know this, but my son, Joshua—after spending the last few months of marine duty in a relatively safe zone, has now been called to serve in the most dangerous area of Iraq. I ask that you pray along with me for his safety." We all fell silent to allow Brother Baker's pain, anguish, and hope to transmit among us.

"Lord, we ask that you extend a spiritual shield and increase the protective armor of Joshua Baker. No matter what our personal feelings are about the war we ask that you cover him Lord, and thousands of other young men like him, so he will soon return to us and be given the opportunity to serve his family and his community one day, just as valiantly as he is serving our country Lord, Amen."

"Amen, Amen," echoed the thunderous shouts amongst the brothers as Brother Baker fought desperately to hold back a tear before yelling "the power in prayer!"

I said goodnight to all of the brothers as Minister Roberts just beamed with a look of pride and anticipation as they departed for their cars. He then cast a big frown toward me, one I'd like to say I wasn't accustomed to. Ignoring him, I walked out into the night. Instinctively, I turned toward the rear side of the church, walked about ten yards, and came upon nineteen seldom-viewed tombstones, all made of smooth white granite. I passed my grandparents tombs before coming upon the tombstone of William Medley, my great grandfather and one of the founding fathers of the church. Kneeling down I whispered praise and blessings aloud while thinking about the quality of their spirits. Like their African ancestors, how untainted, pure, and happy their souls must have been to not be exposed to the commercialism of today.

****

The idea came to Donald shortly after turning to Bianca's favorite gospel station. He'd conceptualized it completely after pulling over to the side of the road and waiting for the wheels on the tires to stop. As they did, he slid the cell phone off of his hip and hit the speed dial number of her old job, Motown Motors. The phone rang three times as he checked his watch and turned the gospel music up. *It's 5:00 o'clock on a Saturday afternoon, somebody has to pick up*, he thought.

"Motown Motors, this is Yvonne speaking," echoed the friendly voice.

"Hello Yvonne. This is Raymond Tate of Gospel Inspirations 106.9. I'm calling to congratulate Miss Bianca Kincaid on winning two praise pass tickets to see the Gospel Explosion Tour at any major city in the United States. This includes dinner for two at select five star restaurants in Detroit and twelve other major cities..."

"I'm sorry but I better stop you right now," Yvonne interrupted; "Ms. Kincaid is no longer employed by our company."

"I see, well that's too bad. I guess we'll just have to move to the next caller."

"Wait just a minute," Yvonne exclaimed before briefly pausing. "Let me transfer you to her old department. I'll let you speak to someone there who might be able to help you, okay?" The line clicked over to Bianca's former department, but Donald knew his voice was too recognizable to her old co-workers and quickly terminated the call. He calmly waited three minutes and redialed the number.

"Motown Motors, this is Yvonne, how can I assist you?"

"Nobody picked up the line when you transferred me back Yvonne, but I'll tell you what...the devil is always busy when the Lord is trying to do great things. This is Raymond Tate from Gospel Inspirations calling back..."

"Oh, I'm so sorry Mr. Tate."

"That's alright. Listen, I got a couple of messages that Bianca Kincaid had called the station trying to get these tickets, so I figured I'd go way out of my way and call back this one last time."

"Nobody picked up back there, she asked with surprise?"

"Not a soul," Donald confirmed.

"They must be away from their desk or gone home early this Saturday. Look, our policy is to not give out any personal information about our employees—past or present."

"I see," Donald replied.

"Well, Bianca is a dear friend of mine and this will be a great surprise for her while she's away down there."

"Down where," Donald asked, trying to sound indifferent and not convey the anxious curiosity that now arose within him?

"Well does the tour go down to Bug-tussell, Alabama ," she asked?

"Now wait a minute Sister Yvonne, have mercy. There has to be a few people in the town to have a concert, have mercy. We're talking about a major Gospel festival. Bug-Tussell? I've heard of some small towns in Alabama, but that takes the cake sister."

I'm just testing him, she thought to herself, *but I guess he passed.* What the heck, I'll just go ahead and tell this man the truth. I don't think Bianca would mind me giving her number to Detroit's foremost gospel radio station, anyway.

"Bianca is in Atlanta, Georgia working for our sister dealer, Peach City Motors. Do you want her work telephone number?"

"You can give me her work number, but I'll have to warn you. If she's not there I'm going to have to move on to the next lucky contestant because I've wasted enough time."

"Okay, okay, I understand," Yvonne anxiously replied. "Her work number is easy to remember. Just dial area code (770) PEACHES. Tell her Yvonne says hello."

"May he bless you, Yvonne, I will."

FOURTEEN

Peach City Motors was hitting on all cylinders this Friday morning. The corporate office had been authorized to offer customers a two thousand dollar cash rebate plus a 36 inch flat screen color T.V., effective today on all new car purchases. Instead of the sales department opening at 10:00 a.m., the doors opened at 8:30, and the new car salesmen like Ed Tyson were happily salivating after rebounding from a tough fiscal quarter. With the push on to sell cars it created a brisk environment for me and my crew of men in the service department as well. We hurried to evaluate the condition of several lemons and legitimate trade-ins, along with making our customary repairs. Most of our car evaluations were for proposed deals for Ed, so it was customary to see him back here from time to time checking on the valued condition of the cars.

"Good morning Brother Medley, how is my main man today?" The Bronx, New York accent was familiar, though it took a minute to match it with the friendly words that came from behind the tire of the raised car I was inspecting. I stooped to look around it and noticed the smooth Ed Tyson. As usual, he was immaculately dressed, sporting a deep blue blazer, black slacks and square toed leather shoes. He peered at himself in the shiny wheels of the overhead sedan while brushing his instant-wave curls toward the back.

"I'm fine Brother Tyson, blessed and highly favored, actually. I see you've come a long way in just a couple of weeks since joining the church and the Manpower Choir and all."

"Yeah, the spirit is moving rather fast within me," he said while bothering to stop the rhythms of his brush strokes.

"That can happen too. I never knew you could sing like that, and it's good to see you come out of the starting blocks like this." *Now if only you can stay in the race with your devilish self,* I thought. "Tell me, what made you decide to join the choir?"

"The reason is simple," Ed replied. "I love the Lord, and I hear him talking to me, asking me to change my ways more and more, and besides, I can hold a note with the best of them."

"I understand. It's good to have you with us."

In near record breaking time we had both run out of things to talk about. Fortunately, Bianca walked into the service area toward us anyway, finalizing any point either of us wanted to make if we did.

"Good morning Kyle, good morning Ed. Ed, the sales department has been trying to reach you. There is a woman asking for you up front."

"Thank you Bianca," Ed replied. "I'll come right up. Actually, I'd like the both of you to walk up front with me. I have somebody I'd like you two to meet."

"Sure, who?" I asked.

As the three of us walked toward the sales department door Ed tugged at our elbows and stopped. "Kyle, I want to thank you for bringing me closer to the spirit and introducing me to Mt. Tabernacle and the choir."

"You're welcome Ed. Don't mention it."

"And Bianca, I apologize for all the times I called you B3 and hit on you, especially when I knew you weren't even interested in me. I'm sorry..."

"That's quite alright Edward, I understand," Bianca replied, blushing at his newfound humility.

"After all, everybody can clearly tell that you and Kyle have got something pretty hot going on already!"

Bianca rolled her eyes at Ed like she wanted to slap him, so I quickly intervened. "No smooth Eddie, what we have here is a friendship going on. One day I hope you grasp the weight of that with a woman."

"Okay, okay. I'm just testing the waters here man, chill out," Ed offered.

I didn't have a problem letting it go, but Bianca had no intention of dismissing it that easily.

"Temperature check, Ed. The waters were warming up a bit, but now they're as cold as Arctic ice. And you're just a small rowboat traveling through them going nowhere," she snapped. "Now exactly who is it that you want us to meet?"

"Ouch," Ed replied, and sheepishly opened the door for the both of us before pointing at a slender, caramel skinned woman. She stood about 5'7 inches tall, and had long, golden pig tail braids of hair that matched her butterscotch and caramel colored complexion without fail. She was staring inside one of the new floor model vehicles when we approached.

"Come on over here with me you two, I'd like you both to meet my version of the Hollywood of the South," he said. We were both annoyed enough with Ed to turn back around and leave him standing there, but after coming this far we decided to finish the charade.

"Hey Nora," Ed said, these are the two I told you about, Bianca Kincaid and Kyle Medley. I want you to meet my new lady friend, Nora Johnson. That's Minister Nora Johnson of Faith Hill Christian Church." Nora turned around and stared at us with wonderfully bright and apologetic eyes. Her smooth hands appeared equally baked by the sun as she held one out and smiled. Her smile radiated two dimples in her cheeks while quietly showcasing the honesty of a razor thin gap between the whiteness of her front teeth. Wearing no makeup or jewelry except for the small silver watch and gold cross that hung around her neck, her beauty and spiritual aura could not have been more stunning. Bianca shook her hand first, and after I did the same she lightly whispered *"What in the world is she doing here with Ed?"* in my ear.

"So are you doing business with us today Nora?" Bianca asked.

"Well, my father's church is considering purchasing three new vans for our Transportation Ministry. Its time we serve our sick and shut in more comfortably. I might be purchasing a car for my personal use as well. I've heard about your dealership for some time now and figured it was time to stop in. I was told to ask for someone here but forgot who it was, and when I called the other day Ed insisted that the somebody was him." Ed grew quite animated after that and unfortunately we were hardly surprised.

"That's right," Ed said before offering up his spill.

"Some people are chosen to help with your Christian walk,
   But I've been chosen to help with your Christian drive.
   Some people are real good with the Christian talk,

But it's me they thank when they leave work round five."
I'll admit I was shocked, but Bianca almost went into labor. Nora helped out by speaking up again and breaking the awkward silence.

"I believe Ed has offered to let me test drive this model here before taking me to lunch, isn't that right Ed?"

"It most certainly is, Ed responded. "Now please excuse us Kyle and Bianca, we're running a little late for our plans."

"Very nice meeting you," Bianca said before I offered a warning for Nora.

"Ed, you be careful with this nice woman now."

"Don't worry, she's in good hands," Ed replied.

"That's what we're concerned about," Bianca said as we waved goodbye. As soon as the door closed behind them Bianca looked at me and began, like I knew she would.

"What do you make of that, Kyle? And please don't sugarcoat it with one of your 'ultra positive', 'look at the bright side' kind of phrases, either."

"Nice sister. Maybe he just wants to sell her and her church some new vans. That won't be a bad commission check for him you know."

"Oh, I'll believe he'll make his money. Guys like him always make their money," she assured, "but you know what I mean."

"No, I don't know what you mean."

"Well, we know he just joined the church, and you told me he's even in the choir now, but do you really trust Ed Tyson?"

"You mean the new and improved, saved, sealed, and delivered from sin Ed Tyson?"

"Keep going," Bianca said, "that's exactly who I'm talking about,"

"I trust he'll get her back here safely. Beyond that, how much do I need to trust him? I think what you're really asking me is if I judge Ed Tyson, and the answer is no. I'm going to let God do that."

"I know you're right, but she seems too innocent and sweet to be going to lunch and getting chummy with…"

"Alright, listen, I've got to get back to work, and you do too. Let's talk about it later."

"But I'm not working tomorrow," Bianca replied. "And neither are you... are you?"

"Nope, but I wasn't thinking about us working, but more like us going for a run. I saw those 'designer looking' track shoes in the back of your car last week. Maybe you bought them to just to profile in, or maybe you don't mind joining me for a five mile run around Stone Mountain Park in the morning."

"Actually, I do like profiling in them, as you say. Fact is however, I can also run a country boy silly and still looking good in them! Now what time in the morning?"

"Let me see, all things being equal, the Lord willing, and the creek don't rise, I'll see you at, say, 9:00 o'clock. Will that work for you?"

"Well the time works for me, but I'm not sure about the country prelude to your answer," Bianca said with a sweet smirk. "I'll see you then," she said, and as she turned to walk toward her desk, she thought about his answer. "All things what?" she muttered. It really didn't matter, she thought, because she'd already confirmed what a vast difference there was in a man like me in comparison to Donald Morton anyway.

"Okay, I'll see you later sweet thing," I said. As she walked away I noticed for maybe the 25th time how lovely and well defined her calf muscles were. Heaven help me!"

FIFTEEN

I drove to Bianca's apartment complex on a beautiful Saturday morning dressed in my yellow 'Southern Colts' football suit. Though eager to get a good workout, seeing her was the real source of my anticipation. I rang the buzzer to her entry gate to hear her sweet reply. "Kyle, is that you, she asked? We briefly chatted between the intercom clicks at the gate.

"Good morning Bianca, yes it is. Will you let me in the gate?"

"I'm not sure. Let's see, are all things equal?"

"What? Yes they are."

"Is the Lord willing?"

"Yes, the Lord is willing," I answered with a broad smile.

"And did the creek rise this morning?"

"No Bianca, the creek did not rise today, and I'm here, now let me in please," I said while pressing down on the talk button.

"One more question before I let you in."

"Alright, what is it?"

"Is this a date?" she asked. I must have paused for a few seconds before responding. I felt her gauging my intentions and showing a vulnerable side that that I'd never seen. Truth be told, I didn't want to turn Bianca off any sooner than I wanted to lie.

"I'd rather enjoy it far better than try to define it, but Ed was hopefully *halfway right* yesterday wasn't he?"

"You are so blowing it Kyle."

"I was kidding Bianca. It was a joke, now there are three cars pulling up behind me and waiting to come in..."

"We'll have to talk about that one. You were doing great before you put Ed's name in it, you know. Now remember, just hang a quick right and the next two lefts, go past the tennis court and come to building 7000, and I'm 7361." She was right about one thing.

I wasn't identifying with Ed Tyson, that's for sure. As the gate lifted up I drove around the sprawling complex to her building. I was prepared to come up when I saw Bianca racing down from the top of three flights of stairs. She wore a green and white Great Lakes State sweat suit and green head band. She was moving like the wind and her hair bounced with each step, signaling a soul determined to prove she was coming to work out first and worry about her perm second. It was consistent with her natural, earthy self and I found it most impressive. After gazing intently at the agile way she hit the steps and rounded the landing turns, I found myself lucky to get out and open the passenger door in time for her as she approached.

"Hi Kyle, you could have stayed in your car and just popped the latch without getting out," she said.

"I know, and if you were just one of the fellows I would have, but it makes me feel more like a man to treat a lady like a lady, so here you are," I said. I was sincere *and* amused at myself for making such a chivalrous comment. After shutting her door I walked back around to get in, and while driving out of the complex I noticed her smiling to herself. The smile made me realize maybe she knew something I didn't...that maybe I wasn't so clever after all, but just a newly discovered lonely, single man, rounding out about a years worth of weekends with little more than my church, my choir, and my ailing grumpy father.

"So *this* is how you look on a Saturday morning," I asked.

"How do I look," she asked?

"Lovely and relaxed—a little more comfortable then you are at work."

"I hope so. I appreciate the compliment because I am. But do believe that I'm prepared to run your socks off, either way."

"We'll just have to see about that, now won't we. Hey, did you actually go to Great Lakes State," I asked?

"I sure did. All four years on a track scholarship."

"A track scholarship, whoa, I see...in that case, a simple walk around the water fountain today sounds fine with me." She smirked while shaking her head as I stayed mindful to take us through the most scenic route available en route to Stone Mountain Park.

"They say that a man should never start doing anything for a woman that he doesn't plan to continue doing. Now, do you always open doors for a lady, Kyle?"

"I sure do...well, most of the time, anyway."

"Why do you do it? Is it to score points?"

"Nope, I like being a gentleman."

"Are you always a gentleman?"

"I try to be, but I'll admit that the more inspiration a woman gives me, the more of a gentleman I become. And when a man like me is inspired, he'll...he'll..."

"Just tell me," she interrupted, "do you open doors for large, unattractive women too?"

"Of course I do, all the time," I responded. "A lady is a lady. I just don't have a habit of dating too many of them. Therefore, it might tend to be a church door more often than a car door I'm opening, that's all."

"Excuse me for interrupting you earlier, but what will you do when you're inspired," she asked?

We drove a bit further, until the scenery became filled with green trees, rock formations, and flowers, and then drove further still—until I thought up an answer for her. We approached the West Gate of the park, and I gave her the answer I hoped she'd coyly awaited.

"Oh, I got it. This must be the hot seat, I see, but I'll tell you. When Kyle Medley is inspired, he'll move mountains—that's what he'll do, okay? And speaking of mountains, here we are, Stone Mountain Park. That huge piece of granite is Stone Mountain itself." Looking over at Bianca, I observed her quietly engulfing herself in the landscapes scenic beauty. It was as if the sight took her breath away, and she glanced back at me to signal she wasn't through.

"Thanks for finally answering the first question. Now, Mr. Big Shot, you think you could move that mountain for a girl like me?"

"Maybe," I answered, "maybe when we come back on another day."

"I must be getting large and unattractive these days," she sarcastically lamented. "I hope you realize how mean that sounds Kyle." She was right, but I stared at her unashamed, just secure in the knowledge that she was everything but that. Changing the subject, I spoke of the sights we passed as a tour guide would. After all, being a regular visitor for years, I knew almost every yard of the 1600 acres it boasted. It was my personal invitation to God's country. I stopped short and fought the temptation to speak further, once again, after glancing at her lovely eyes. Those eyes, and the subtle spirit they conveyed within them as they perused the grounds, were a special tour for me also. Like her, I wanted to quietly enjoy the tour. It took all of five minutes into the park for the silence to break, however.

"Why are you looking at me like that?"

"What?" I ignorantly countered.

"I'd like you to tell me more about this place, instead of gapping your eyes about me and trying to size me up."

"Well, over the last 200 years, Stone Mountain Park has been many things to many people. First, the mountain you see over there happens to be one of the biggest granite formations in the United States."

"Interesting, but who are those soldiers carved into the rock back there? And why are there so many confederate flags around here, hanging from places called the plantation?"

"It's to honor those who died fighting for the South during the Civil War. That's why you have confederate this and confederate that all around, too."

"But I don't get it," she said. "In my history classes we learned that the Confederacy *lost* the Civil War."

"I know, and they did, but there are a lot of folks who just want to commemorate this time as a sort of wealth of the South. And of course you have others, like hate groups that held Labor Day rallies right up on top of Stone Mountain's peak until the 1980's. They revere the Confederacy too for entirely different reasons. Here, I'll park the truck and we can get out and get a better view of it." As we parked in front of the mountain I walked around to open her door and let her out.

Stepping out of the vehicle she took a few steps before halting to glance about. As she did, her face maintained an expression that denoted beauty and an appreciation of wonderment as her eyes fully digested what they now saw. Men and women, boys and girls, Blacks, Whites, Latinos, Asians, and other representatives of

Gods children were hurriedly walking up the mountain trail above us. Behind us were bicyclist sporting rainbow colored garb as they whizzed by leaning over ever so gracefully to one side. Joggers and a few roller skaters soon followed to join the melting pot of athletic and multi racial personalities converging about us.

"What a lovely sight," Bianca said before sighing. "Wait a minute; that is the top of Stone Mountain. Martin Luther King exclaimed 'Let freedom ring from Stone Mountain's mountain top' in his famous 'I have a dream' speech."

"He sure did," I confirmed.

"It's hard to imagine all the crosses being burned and all the hate that spewed up there once before, especially when you look around now. It must have just been the devil, working through the withered hands of man."

"What did you just say Bianca?"

"I said it's just the devil working through man's withered hands." I paused for a moment to absorb the gravity of her words.

"That's what I thought you said. You're right. I want you to come take a walk with me. Two miles down this road lays a little known piece of African American history. It's the kind of a place that you won't find in a history book, though, at least the kind that's read to us," I said.

We strolled several yards toward the joggers trail. Bianca picked up her pace, and I soon found myself at the point where I had to slowly run to keep up with her. A few yards later she abruptly slowed down and tugged at my sweater.

"Enough. Tell me Kyle. What on earth is Ed Tyson up to?"

"What do you mean?"

"Hate to sound so cynical, but Nora seems too genuine to do any thing more than buy a car from somebody like Ed, and even then she should probably wash her hands real good "

"I see, and now that Ed has joined the choir I'm supposed to know what's on his mind, huh? For God's sake Bianca, he was just inviting her out for a business lunch. That is part of the man's job, you know."

"Kyle I know how intuitive you are. You had that discerning look on your face at the new member's class recently. It was as though you were trying to look right through each and every one of us. Now I can tell how much you really love that choir. It's one of the most sincere things about you and I respect you completely for it, but..."

"But what?"

"But maybe you're turning a blind eye to some of the things going on with that brother. Or maybe you've got such an idealistic view of that choir that you tend to sugarcoat everything bad that you see. My guess is yes, Kyle, you do see Ed almost the same way I see him, a self serving money hungry hound. And if you don't, then I'm willing to bet that you've at least thought about it."

"Whoa, just hold up now. I don't know what's on Ed's mind any more than you do, but yeah, I've thought about it. So many things are changing lately, I've thought about a lot."

"So, what's on your mind?" Bianca asked.

"Among a lot of other things I think about you, and I'm puzzled."

"Puzzled? Puzzled about what?"

"Puzzled about why you are so concerned about Ed and Nora, for starters? What about that wall of yours that you have up?" I asked. "That's a lot more important, I think."

"What wall, she asked?"

"You know what wall. Let's call it, The Great Wall of Bianca. The wall that will only allow me to see you as long as I don't show my desire to treat you like anything more than..."

"Than what?"

"Than somebody somewhere between one of the deacon's wives or the high school bully's girlfriend...That same wall that your eyes seem to ask me to climb sometimes, and when I do, they invite me to step on a loose brick that makes me fall to the wayside. That's the wall. I do feel a tad better than the guys at the dealership, but I only get the benefit of being put in check on a more personal basis, that's all."

"Hmmm, you must have put some thought into that one didn't you? Well guess what?"

"What?"

"That sounds like a crock of real crap, and don't think you'll get any sympathy from me after saying it, because that's not me at all... or is it?"

"I'm just calling it as I see it," I said.

"Kyle, I really don't mean to put up any barriers to our friendship. Actually, I thought if anybody knew who I was warming up to, it would be you. Ed reminds me of the worst in my ex, Donald, that's all. He's a slick hustler with very few morals, and if I had to sum him up I'd call him a fraud. Can your choir impeach him?"

"Hold on now. Ed's no boy scout indeed, but a fraud might be going a bit far. Incidentally, choirs don't impeach people, you know that."

"You told me yours holds auditions, didn't you?

"Yeah but that's different," I said before pausing. "Alright, your points well taken," I conceded, "but it hasn't gotten that bad yet. Your experience with him sounds like it was worse than I thought though. What exactly did this "Donald" do?"

"He made me feel like a queen, that's what he did," she began. "For three years he wined and dined me at four and five star restaurants. He also took me on lavish trips to Spain, the Bahamas, and Maui. And no matter where we went, he was always mindful to mail in his tides to Bishop Searcy if we missed a Sunday, and we rarely missed a Sunday. He then proposed to me, and I said yes. We went to marriage counseling and even set a date to marry on April 17 in Detroit."

"That lifestyle sounds like the average woman's dream. Wait a minute. That's only a month from now. Are you still thinking about it?"

"We'll, take our hat off to your average woman Kyle, but unfortunately I'm not her."

"I know you're not, but..."

"Then why do you ask? You know if I were thinking about it, I sure wouldn't be walking around this redneck park with you today, now would I? Do you realize I'm miles away from all my family and friends?" She was becoming emotional, and I silently chastised myself for causing her to be.

"I'm sorry Bianca, but I thought it was a fair question, and I kind of like this park. I didn't think you'd take it so hard."

"Well now you know."

"Okay, I do. Now what is it that you're not telling me? What happened?"

"Donald was an entrepreneur—seemingly a good one—who went from owning a dog grooming business to purchasing a soul food restaurant in Downtown Detroit. He named it D& B's— Donald & Bianca's Soul Food Creation—after us."

"But what made him a fraud?" I asked.

"One day he asked me to locate a manila envelope in his office while he sat in another room going over his taxes. While looking for it, I accidentally discovered an envelope full of credit card numbers. There had to be over seventy, all with different names. When I asked him about them he instantly freaked out. At first, he made excuses for how they got there. When he sensed I didn't believe him he asked me to really think about the lifestyle we lived. He claimed I had to know he was doing something illegal to justify the money he spent on me. Just imagine, he tried to make me feel like the guilty one, can you believe that? Then he threatened to hurt me if I didn't close my eyes to it, telling me the marriage was still going to go on regardless, that is, if I enjoyed life itself." Bianca's eyes began to well up with tears. I slowed down our walk even more and gently grabbed her arm to stop our stride.

"Come here Bianca, don't be scared," I said, reaching out to hug her as I spoke. "It wasn't long ago I see, but it's still the past. God didn't grant us the spirit of fear, and he will protect you, even if he has to use me to do it."

I hoped my words consoled her, though deep down I sensed the gravity of her life and how much it had physically and emotionally changed, all in a few months. Suddenly she pushed out of my arms almost as fast as she fell into them. Wiping her eyes with her hands, she proceeded to walk on again at a brisk pace, grabbing my arm to follow.

"So maybe now you see what I mean. Because I've been there, and I've experienced what it feels like for a naïve woman to get involved with a man who's nothing like what he pretends to be. And that's what I sense in Edward Tyson." She was panting from exertion as she spoke.

"In that case you might be able to relax. If that sister, Nora, is as immersed in the spirit like I think she is, then Ed better watch out before she puts something on him. I don't think he's that scandalous though. And if he is, there's nothing like a so called player getting captured by spiritual game anyway. But the bigger question is what about you?"

"What about me?"

"Are you going to continue running from this man? Or do you kind of like your new home and think you might want to stay?" I tried to act nonchalant, and refrain from sounding like so much of my hopes rested on her answer.

"I like Detroit and I miss it a lot. I miss my Mom, my friends, and my family. But I've got to put some time and distance between Donald and myself for a while. Hopefully it will squash his feelings for me and keep me safer in the mean time."

"But here. Do you like it here?" I said, unconcerned of how anxious I must have appeared to know her answer.

"It's too early to really tell, but I think I really like Atlanta too. I like my job for now, but my degree and passion is in journalism. Since it doesn't look like I'll be marrying anytime soon I thought that maybe I'll get a chance to become a broadcaster for the National News Network one day."

"If you do, you won't be remaining incognito too long, but that's good, because you've got to come out of the woodwork sooner or later." Bianca waited for a moment before she continued.

"I'm hoping and praying that I'll feel like this is behind me soon. Anyway, I really like Mt. Tabernacle and its unique feel. And yes Kyle, I like you too, and though I'm not ready to give you a green light to me, I'm not putting up any walls either, if that's what you want to know. I just need time to pray and a little time to heal. Besides, everyone giving directions here tells you to stop at the red light, or turn at the red light, or go one or two red lights up before turning at the red light, so you're probably used to a red light anyway, right?"

"Well that's how we give directions in the south," I said, but...

"But surely by now you've noticed street lights are also green, and even yellow? I'm just looking for one good reason why the light always has to be red. Are you all eternal pessimists or something?" *She moves from joy to pain to introspection and now down right sarcasm, almost like a moody cat.*

"Well no, but..."

"Come here Kyle," Bianca commanded. Pulling my chin close to hers she put the palm of her hand in my face. "Do you see that Mister? That's a red light, and it means stop in most languages and cultures." She then took one step backwards and placed the tip of her index finger on the tip of my nose. "That's a yellow light, and it means..."

"It means caution, alright, so what's the big secret here," I asked?

"Patience Kyle, I was just getting to that." She then came towards me and planted the most delicious kiss on my lips. It felt succulent, moist, and very sweet, although in reality it registered only slightly above a peck. I easily became a willing victim to the sin of the flesh by languishing in it and attempted to kiss her back.

"Now that's a green light there," she said, pulling away from me before I confirmed to myself whether I had the strength to hold back or not—I didn't.

"Now, do you see the difference?"

"I do, I do, I replied. The light doesn't have to be red any more. It's green, it's green. When giving directions in Atlanta one must use the green light!"

We laughed heartily for a while, and before either of us realized it we were holding each other by the waist, gazing at each other as if we'd both longed for this closer view.

"Now it's your turn to tell me some things about you," Bianca said, bringing me out of my trance.

"Okay, what is it that you want to know?" She released her hands from me and we began to walk slowly.

"You can start at the beginning if you like, or at the end and work back. Either way there is something different about you that I can't put my finger on. I don't think I've ever known anybody like you. You don't seem to care about material things. You are one of the most humble men I've ever seen. And at a time in their lives when most guys are thinking about money, cars and women, you seem to be obsessed with that choir—not like it's a bad thing or anything."

"I understand. Well, I do love what strong men who sing for the Lord represent far more than I love material things. I love the camaraderie too, but I'd be lying if I told you that my values were always that simple, or I was even always this kind of person."

"Really," Bianca replied. "Just who did you used to be?"

"Bianca there's really no need to go there, let it just be a closed chapter."

"Okay now, let me get this straight. Not only are you the only man at Peachtree City Motors that I've opened up to, but I just spilled my guts to you and told you one of the most innermost and painful parts of my past. Now, in return you tell me your life has chapters I don't need to know about, well guess what?"

"What?"

"You can have your chapters. My God doesn't want me to have a new friend who has hidden chapters in his life. After all, I've already got an ex who hid a whole book."

"You're wrong, wait a minute. I didn't mean it that way," I replied.

"It's really okay. I'm out of my element anyway."

"How are you out of your element?"

"Well first, I'm in a park, one that you've brought me to, that has buildings called the plantation. Then you're talking about closed chapters while you're trying to get to know me, while I prefer a man who opens the whole book."

"It's not that way at all. Okay, listen, all I'm saying is that — you've really never heard of me before now?"

"I can't say that I have, unless of course your real name is Elvis or Tupac? In that case I have, otherwise, Kyle Medley? Sorry, it just doesn't grab me."

"I happened to be the college football player of the year just seven years ago. I played for Southern. I was playing in my last game, a Conference Championship game I wanted to win badly, when I recklessly tackled a man and paralyzed him. Well, not only did I tackle him but I picked him back off the turf after tackling him and slammed him back down again." Bianca looked surprised, but attempted to comfort me.

"Did you know he was hurt?" she asked in a tone now full of sensitivity.

"No, I didn't He was probably a vegetable after the first time I hit him, but I did it anyway."

"Kyle, I'm so sorry, I really wasn't expecting anything like that."

"Yeah, from your reaction, I imagine you weren't. Do understand Bianca; I'm not carrying 'those' types of skeletons you're thinking about. Sure, it was an obvious tragedy for him, but it was an unsuspecting tragedy for me too."

"I'm sure you've asked God for forgiveness, haven't you?"

"I've worn my kneecaps out with prayer, but the guilt is still there. The guilt has paralyzed me as badly as the injury immobilized him. On top of that, I've got some worldly forces to overcome as well."

"Let me guess, its Minister Roberts. I bet that whatever it is, somewhere he's got something to do with it."

"You know, at first I thought he was annoyed with me just because I don't sing as well as most everybody else."

"Well that's one way of saying it," she said, trying not to snicker.

"But somehow I'm beginning to think there may be even more to it than that."

"Pastor Adams asked you to teach the class instead of them, didn't he?"

"He did."

"So do you think he might be a little jealous because he wasn't asked?"

"Could be, I just don't want to believe that a Minister of a blessed and formidable church like ours would be that insecure."

"You know it's a good thing that you call it like you see it, but the problem with you is that sometimes..."

"Sometimes what...?"

"Sometimes you just don't see it," she said. "Pastor Adams sees something special in you Kyle, just like nearly everyone else does, including me. Judging from the way Minister Roberts looked at you at the Gospel Network, I'd say there's some jealousy going on, some spiritual hate if you will. Pastor Adams probably didn't even consider asking Minister Roberts to teach the class. If he did he wouldn't have been hanging around the door entrance that day— looking like a schoolboy who'd lost his little red wagon."

"You may be right, but either way I'm going to have to try and deal with it. We'll all have to, at least until Pastor Adams returns from Haiti. Now, here we are," I said. This is the Stone Mountain Quarry Exhibit." I led her through a small opening that formed a trail not far off the beaten path of our walk. As we approached it, I stopped to show her a picture of nine black men, all of whom held heavy hammers up in the air over the huge granite rock to simulate the hard labor that lay before them.

"These are the pictures of the men, many of whom were freed slaves, who in 1845 hammered wooden wedges into cracks in the huge stone by hand and forcing them to split. The granite they cut was first used to meet the high demand for monuments and gravestones during the civil war. After the war, they worked to cut stone to meet the heavy demands for this preferred granite to rebuild war torn cities. A couple of these men are my ancestors, and the founding fathers of Mt. Tabernacle."

"Hmm, interesting," Bianca said as she read aloud the excerpt about their hard work quarrying the mountain.

"Stone Mountain formed deep underground during the creation of the Appalachian Mountains over 300 million years ago, and was eventually exposed as the miles of land on top of the dome washed away with time."

"Like a man."

"Huh? How do you compare a mountain to a man?"

"Easy. Like this mountain, men are all exposed over time—good or bad."

"That's one way of looking at it," I countered.

"So if you are here to really make a difference Kyle," she continued, "then let your light shine before men, that they may see your good deeds and praise your father in heaven." I nodded towards her, quietly thinking about the gravity of her words along with the old southern adage 'Your woman is your wisdom'. It now made perfect sense. Suddenly the sky turned black and a rainy mist filled the landscape. I took my jacket off to lend to Bianca's head and shoulders. I then escorted her to a nearby bench where we sat under the added protection of huge, generous green leaves. I then wrapped my arms around her in a tender and loving fashion.

"Your hands feel good Kyle. Thanks for realizing my desire to be just held."

"Thanks for realizing my desire to just hold you," I responded, before doing my best to insure that not a drop of rain fell on her.

SIXTEEN

It started out as a harmless Saturday afternoon drive for Keith. His first stop was Piedmont Park, where he was to pray and contemplate life's possibilities. Of utmost importance was replacing the habit of gambling with that of reading scriptures. He sat on a nearby bench and opened up his seldom read Bible. Somebody in a casino once told him to reference Proverbs 28:20 and Matthew 6:24 after he lost over $10,000 one night, but he never did. His experience as a C.P.A. had trained him to record numbers that mattered, but it required incalculable discipline to translate an urge to the bottom line. That took wisdom and patience he thought he didn't have. Consequently, his time was spent flipping pages of scriptures randomly, but it was a start.

The introspective afternoon was ending. Dark clouds now filled the sky and rain began to softly trickle down. He'd already grown bored, and now the 'itch' was getting worse. What would be the harm in just passing by the newly renovated underground Atlanta district next, he thought? After all, it's just a drive, nothing more than a few buildings to see. His soul and his hands were both getting restless after holding a Bible for nearly two hours, two hours on a Saturday at that. It had been four months and counting. No blackjack, no slot machines, no greyhound dog races, no lottery, not even a dollar toward the basketball pool at work. Four months. Today would be different though, because today he felt like challenging the devil toe to toe with his own arsenal—luck. He placed the Bible in the back seat and started the car engine while clasping both hands and fingers together. Quickly he cracked his knuckles before placing the car in gear.

Forget the devil. After all, with luck on your side, what's his battle for? He drove by the new casino twice before parking his car. I've got the luck to go anywhere, he reasoned, and in no time he'd found a parking space and was heading inside the casino.

"Hey Keith, Keith Terry, is that you?" Keith heard the voice and agonized to himself before slowly turning around. Lord, please don't let it be anybody from church, even though they've got some explaining to do if it is. He turned to notice a short, prematurely balding man wearing sunglasses and smiling broadly.

"Keith, it's me, Rodney. Come on, don't act like you remember. I'm Rodney Alexander, from graduate school."

"Hello Rodney, how've you been?"

"Great man, I'm doing just great. It's been over ten years since I've seen you. How's Evelyn, did you two get married after we graduated?"

"We did."

"That's what I'm talking about. Everybody knew that you two were the campus couple anyway," he beamed. And how many kids?"

"Two. I've got a 19 year old son and a 16 year old daughter."

"Wonderful man," Rodney said before pausing, "but you said 'I', you do mean 'we' don't you?"

"Well we do, but....we are now divorced." Rodney looked on in disbelief, and as he did Keith noticed, and figured he'd just as well explain.

"Two years ago like she asked me to give her another baby— saying it would bring more purpose into her life, and when I refused, she filed for divorce."

"What? Keith, I'm so sorry man."

"It's okay Rod. I still see her name on the back of my checks, so she's alright. Look, I've got to meet someone. Sorry to rush, but its good to see you too. Take care of yourself, and maybe I'll see you at this years alumni reunion, okay?"

Rodney looked perplexed as Keith turned to walk away. Everyone thought it was a pity for Evelyn to end their marriage and break up their home, especially due to Keith not wanting to have a third child. But this was yesterdays lie. Little did they know that Evelyn was merely co-dependent and at the mercy of Keith's expensive habit. If anybody wanted to bring a third child into the relationship, it was Keith, and it happened to be a monkey!

It started slowly with Keith telling Evelyn they just couldn't afford the family vacations they took once a year. From there it escalated to account for why Keith's half of the house note often went unpaid, until graduating after they divorced and Keith was twice thrown in jail for lack of child support. The tears were suspended as he bid farewell to Rodney. Caressing his wallet he stepped onto the escalator to get even closer to the sounds of the slot machines. Restraint was still a word he could pronounce as he circled the $1.00 and $5.00 slots twice. His was now removed from trusting God with his finances and beyond walking away, now feeling that he could play and win against all odds. His swagger happened upon the $100.00 per hand blackjack table. It was currently full of players who sat in the green circle and battled the dealer for riches, or at least whatever they felt they could afford to lose. Keith instantly rekindled that old feeling with make believe. Standing along side the men, he envisioned himself in his old role—another comrade in the gambling war against the dealer. But this wasn't a spectator sport, as a man who'd lost several hands reminded him by becoming frustrated and leaving. The itch was now a sore of monkey size proportions. Keith looked at the chair intensely before balling his hands up and placing them in his pocket—*four months*. Wisdom, patience and discipline were now after thoughts. Keith knew that if he took that seat, God had nothing to do with the outcome.

SEVENTEEN

That same afternoon drizzle that romantically nurtured Bianca and me had also signaled an end to Keith Terry's Bible study. Across town, Charles Nix watched it from the balcony of his one bedroom apartment and interpreted it with a far different meaning still. Gazing up to the sky he took note of the mixture of sun and clouds before removing the neatly folded towel off his left wrist. Like his life, he mulled, the sun was desperately trying to shine through despite the tears of his past. He proceeded to take the top off of the smoking grill, and—growing accustomed to using tongues again—tossed the chicken and flipped the salmon. He then seasoned the food ever so lightly to achieve a healthy taste. *A 36 year old man on the cusp of approaching 'older man' status should eat properly,* he thought. Indeed, eating healthy and spending time with his son and two daughters were the joys he missed and craved the most.

Newly released from the Atlanta Penitentiary, he found it ironic that it was easier to form a relationship with Christ while locked up than it was as a free man with a career as a pharmacist. Shaking his head, he vowed never again to allow imposed discipline to be the catalyst that insured he'd take better care of his temple, or uplift his worship.

Looking over his right shoulder he noticed a newly formed rainbow that stretched over the nearby hills and seemingly ended twenty yards from his balcony. He was educated enough to know the workings of this wondrous phenomena, yet spiritual enough to recognize it as none other than a true act of God. Casting scientific facts aside he fixed his eyes back to the rainbow, and in its beauty he became lost in its possibilities. *Could it be that he and his family were now like the rainbow's beautiful colors,* he thought? If so, then like the rainbow, maybe they too were meant to rise up and travel over vast terrains of this mad, unpredictable world before reaching a destination of true happiness. Hmm, what color would I be if I were immersed in that rainbow? The purest color maybe? The widest and darkest color? Surely, since only God knew I would end up here, alone...like this then... I would have to be... the blue color.

A sigh now came over his face. Charles never thought he would end up like this, but here he was. He'd spent seven years incarcerated. The first two were spent drying out and kicking the crack cocaine habit that started with recreational cocaine use. It got more frequent and more expensive, but the middle class professional with the equally educated wife felt he could afford it. He soon indulged in crack cocaine regularly after finding a new sub circle, away from the wife and friends who considered themselves recreational users. Always a gentleman, Charles was known to complement and tip everybody who crossed his path and served him, yet he had a knack for changing cloths and catching metro Atlanta banks by surprise from time to time.

The media offered bold news headlines advertising his new profession. All everyone beckoned for in return was his real identity.

'Gentleman Bandit Strikes Again'

'The Gentleman Bandit compliments teller's dress, apologizes for the inconvenience, and then orders them all of them to donate to a charitable cause...'

'Best Dressed Bandit'

'The Gentleman Bandit wore a black tuxedo today.' "He robbed and told them to hurry, he had to rush off for an engagement. He complemented his black suit with white shoes. Dan believed to be a well educated dark skinned male. His take after six robberies believed to be $200,000. Why does he do it?"

He knew why. Recreational use had now become a very expensive habit. The plan for supporting it had worked quite well for a while—much better than even he imagined. It worked so well and he stayed so high that subconsciously he wanted to get caught, so he became more brazen. He'd always been considered by many to be a decent and upstanding kind of guy. Goodwill came from his heart. That's why he had to get caught. His conscience was gnawing at him. Now, years later—his debt to society paid, he faced a new dilemma. He owed Francine and the kids much more. He owed them his word after promising her he would stay drug free forever. If so—if he proved to last this first year, she would consider reuniting with him for the sake of their marriage, and family. When released six months ago, Charles knew he didn't want to face the stigma he felt from his college educated peers. More so, he knew he had to go straight to the Lord and not pass go. Thus, joining Mt. Tabernacle and the Manpower Choir was an excellent start. It brought to him a sense of normalcy, a sanctity and peace that, ironically, he'd last discovered in the Atlanta Prison Choir.

He covered up the meat on the grill and went to his closet. Once, there was a fleet of suits and over ten pairs of shoes in the walk in closet of his huge, luxurious home. Now, there stood four pairs of slacks, one pair of work and dress shoes, and one black suit next to the red blazer he'd purchased today—all in the tiny closet that in one step you'd walk by if you weren't looking for it. Charles confirmed he had all he needed for tomorrow, especially since this was his biggest engagement in over seven years. The phone rang once, then twice. Who could be calling me now? He wondered.

"Hello, this is Charles."

"Charles Nix? Good evening brother. This is Kyle Medley from Mt. Tabernacle. How are you?"

"I'm doing well, and yourself?"

"Blessed and highly favored brother. I just wanted to let you know that we are looking forward to you singing with us tomorrow."

"Same here Brother Medley, but..." Charles paused a moment before going on.

"But what, Brother Nix?"

"There seems to be an issue with the colors we're wearing, and frankly I didn't want to get into an off sides sparring match between you and Minister Roberts. I've got a new red blazer I just bought today, but should I wear a black one?"

"I'm glad you asked brother. As you know, the original members are wearing black, and we do like to be unified."

"Then it's settled, Brother Medley, I'm wearing black, and I'll encourage the new men of Manpower to do the same by calling them tonight myself."

"Very good."

"You know, I like the way you fellowship."

"Well thank you Brother Nix. You said the key word, fellowship, because after all, we're just a bunch of fellows in the same ship."

"Yeah, it doesn't seem like you can tell Minister Roberts that though."

"Even in the church, it is what it is, Brother Nix. But it's still a fellowship brother, remember that, and have yourself a good night."

"You do the same Brother Medley." As soon as I hung up my phone rang again.

"Hello, and God bless," I answered.

"Man, how is he going to try and play you? I'm trying to hold back and do this Christian experience thing right, but Minister Roberts is making me want to say a couple of things to him of the world that may not just sit so right, know what I mean?"

"Now calm down, who is this anyway? Wait a minute, Brother Humphries?"

"You know it, and I'm gonna burst if I gotta keep holding my tongue."

The brothers were solidly behind me, and it felt good. It also felt right, because now— more than ever—I was starting to believe that God might be too.

****

"I think we better hurry up and get back to the car before the rain gets worse, Bianca."

"Hmm" she purred, as if not wanting to be disturbed, "If you insist. You know you were literally saved by mother natures rain today Kyle." Bianca then stood up and leaned into my side. She then playfully nudged me as we started walking.

"And just how do you figure that?"

"Well, just before you set me down to look at our ancestors back there I was ready to challenge you to a sprint. I figured since you bought that college jogging suit you're wearing, you might have been in store for the run of your life."

"Bianca I hate to disappoint you. Remember, I was an All American Safety. NFL scouts were drooling to have me..."

"Yeah, yeah, yeah," she responded in dismissive fashion.

"What did you..."I began, in total disbelief that she'd challenge me.

"See that lake up there on the right," she asked?

"Yeah, I see it, what about it?"

"Well I'll race you to the yellow marker in front of it at count of three. One, two," she counted, before smacking me on my rear as hard as she could before flying off like a rocket and screaming, "three!"

Her head start wasn't needed as her legs moved with the quick and elegant strides of a gazelle. I took a mental snapshot of her grace for a few seconds before I raced off too. I quickly noticed plain ole speed wasn't going to catch her in time, so I imagined I was chasing down an opponent headed toward the goal line before he scored. It was enough to get dead even with her, but as soon as she got used to me being right along side of her—which was nearly the moment I did—she gave me a stiff arm to the shoulder. I let her take it home after that, and laughed aloud at the clever and rambunctious nature I was coming to expect from her. Bianca tapped the yellow marker before turning back around. Smiling and panting wildly she then gave me a huge hug.

"I hope you're not mad at me for getting just a little head start," she said coyly, making her best attempt at innocence.

"I'm sure you're feeling bad about it," I replied, knowing all the while she could have sold me on her innocence ten times over.

"Let's go Bianca. If it starts raining any heavier I'll have to build us an ark. You won't complain, because we can have a bunch of pretty babies and start the world back over again." We walked to my truck and had a nice chat during the drive back to her place.

"I enjoyed my afternoon with you Kyle, thanks for showing me Stone Mountain and sharing all that history with me. It is a beautiful park, in spite of those plantation landmarks. And by the way, you're not a bad runner to not be from the Big 10."

"That's merely because I'm a better runner from the S.C.C. By the way, I almost forgot to tell you. We're singing tomorrow."

"That's wonderful."

"Will you be coming?"

"Of course I'll be coming, and I'll look forward to making it by to support you and your beloved choir. Will you be singing lead?"

"No, not tomorrow—and there's no need to get cute, you know." I stopped the truck when we arrived at her apartment and leaned over to kiss her on the cheek.

"Good night," she said, before planting a similar kiss on my cheek and exiting the car. After waving, she then pranced up the steps casually and serenely, not attempting half the rate of speed in which she earlier ran down. While reaching for the keys inside her pouch Bianca heard the telephone ring once, then twice. Still in no hurry, she again waved good bye before entering the apartment. The phone was on ring number four when she walked in. In no hurry to answer, she felt serene listening as the rain gently tap-danced against her window neatly in rhythm with the song playing in her heart. Her voice message had started playing when she finally picked up after the fifth ring. "Praise God, you have reached..." "Hello," she spoke, as if she were in a dream while leaning down on her sofa.

"Hello Bianca, this is Donald—I've missed you," echoed the deep and familiar voice on the other end of the line. "And please, don't hang up the phone." Bianca instantly sat up at attention as the rain stopped. She grimaced while coming to grips with the reality of his voice, agonizing further on just how she would respond to it.

"Hello Donald, how did you get this number? I know my mother didn't give it to you."

"No she didn't, but you still have old friends who were obviously concerned about your being in a new city. You know, you should call them more often to let them know you are alright. They trusted your number would be in safe hands with me though, and their right."

"Is that so, she said, while fuming inside at whatever ploy he must have used to get her ex co-workers to divulge her whereabouts.

"So how's the weather in Atlanta," he asked?

"It's been very nice lately, especially without the northern cold front coming down here this winter," Bianca responded.

"Listen baby, I was hoping we could talk about us."

"What us? Donald, my being here alone should signal to you that there no longer is an 'us'. Besides, if you wanted an 'us' you would have been living right with your lifestyle and putting God in your business. But you go and threaten my life instead of cleaning up your act with God. It just goes to show what kind of man you really are, and how you don't even know God."

"I'm sorry Bianca, I was wrong. I just panicked at the thought of losing you, saying things I had no business saying."

"I'll say. Well, maybe in your next relationship you'll know better Donald."

"That's just it, I don't want another relationship with anyone else but you."

"Donald its over and you know it, so please. Please don't call me any more."

"You're mistaken, it's not over. It's not over until I say it's over. Now I know where you work, and I'm coming down there soon, just to talk. You'll change your mind."

"Donald, please don't come here."

"I still love you Bianca, good night," Donald said as he hung up.

Bianca placed the phone down, and methodically paced about the room. Feeling shocked that her new world had suddenly been shaken up; she contemplated—looking for answers. As she did, the returning sound of raindrops on her windows was now a distraction. She thought about calling the police, but knew that wasn't the best response, at least not now. A restraining order, maybe? Would it work? Would that really serve to protect her, or just make him angrier? Her first instinct was to call Kyle to talk about it, but thought it selfish to bring her personal drama into their new friendship and ruled against it. Finally, she reasoned that Donald's restaurant, along with his other 'businesses,' made too much money for him to waste his time coming down here for her anyway. After all, he liked power and control so much that a long distance empty bluff was indeed more typical of him than simply fading quietly out of the picture. It would be too much like right if he didn't, she thought, and anything less would somehow spell defeat for him. Initial fears that sought to grip her slowly receded while her inner resolve demanded she find a way to deal with it. Trusting her Savior to show her, she knelt down on her knees to pray.

EIGHTEEN

"Daddy, I made you breakfast. Are you hungry?"

"Did you fry me those two pork chops I had in the refrigerator?"

"Of course I didn't. You know that stuff isn't any good for you."

"Then you didn't make *me* breakfast then, now did you?"

"Listen, I left five strips of turkey bacon and two hard boiled eggs for you. The doctor said you better start eating right before you lose the other leg, now I suggest you give it a try."

"Lose the other leg? I don't know what you mean by "lose the other leg." I can still feel my so called amputated leg tingling and itching."

"You don't say Daddy, really?"

"Really son, in fact it's itching down here...right here at the foot," he said while motioning his cane where his foot used to be.

"Daddy, I hate to keep telling you this, but you no longer have a foot on that leg you don't have."

"I do have a foot. Y'all just can't see it, that's all. You see, it's like faith. You know its there, because you can feel it, and when it's going strong it doesn't matter what anyone else says. By the way, there isn't a 'thang' wrong with my diet either, so where are the pork chops?"

"Yeah... right, whatever you say. I was feeling the faith analogy, but sorry, the pork chops I threw out. Now, I'm going to Sunday service. You know Manpower's singing today, and we've got a few new members too. You need to come hear us sometimes Daddy, I think we're going to be pretty good."

"How many new members y'all got, three or four?"

"Nope. Try five, not counting the new Music Minister we got about six months ago.

"Is that right? That sure is a lot of folks all of a sudden, at least for a small church. Well just who are these new men, anyway?"

"What do you mean, who are they?"

"I mean, you know just what I mean, who are they? Are they some kin to the deacons, or Pastor Adams family, some of y'all, what?"

"Oh, that's what you mean. Well let's see. One is a car salesman from the job."

"Yeah, I bet you can really trust him?"

"And another is an accountant."

"I see, probably on the run from a corporate scam."

"Two of them, well, I don't remember what they both do, but I think one is a policeman."

"How nice, donuts at choir practice now."

"One is or used to be a pharmacist I think. He's sort of starting life over again."

"Correction, donuts and drugs at choir practice, that is."

"I think one is an anesthesiologist—they put people to sleep."

"I know what they do, smart aleck. It's the same thing you do to people when you start singing. Folks probably run first, if the pews aren't full. If they stay, their head hurts so bad they gotta stop—then just go to sleep. The difference is, an anesthesiologist puts you to sleep on purpose, and gets you comfortable before they do it."

"Very funny Daddy, but we're becoming a very progressive church, with a progressive choir, while you're laughing."

"You know one sign of a progressive black church—and choir, is when you have other races in it, like Whites and Hispanics too.

"We have one Hispanic member."

"What about white folks?"

"Actually we've talked about it, but it seems nobody really knows any white folks—at least knows them well enough to ask them to come out and sing with black people."

"Whether we have a black President or not, the dream across America is only slowly coming true. On Sunday morning we are still as segregated as they come in this country."

"You're right," I acknowledged.

"I know I'm right," was his macho reply. "I bet that Hispanic fellow hooked up with a black women before he joined, now didn't he? Just tell me I'm wrong."

"Okay, okay. Come to think of it he does have a black wife, but can't you for once stop being so cynical about everything Dad?"

"Uh-huh," he replied.

"You were always a great counselor," I continued, "a great leader, especially years ago when Momma was still living. Now, I hate to say it, but you're acting like a bitter old man who's lost his spirit and his religion."

Papa Medley sat quietly for a moment looking almost childlike. I peeked inside his eyes, hoping they revealed a heart that absorbed the weight of my words while not hurting too much. He then just shook his one leg back and forth, then side to side before speaking. As he spoke, I once again heard a glimpse of the man who'd not only led his family to Jesus, but himself to the pulpit of Mt. Tabernacle before succumbing to church politics.

"Son, I've never lost my spirit for Jesus. But, you're right about one thing. Maybe I've lost interest in religion, for not fooling with church folks anymore, but never my spirit. Now it's nice that you feel that 'y'all' have more than pretty voices singing, but you better be careful. The book of Psalms may tell you to praise God with everything you have, your voice, the harp, and the strings. But when the church gets too many pretty voices, the next thing you know, they're going to want to make some of you audition for your spots, especially somebody like you. Then, they'll want to dress y'all up and like a fashion show and display a bunch of shiny cars every Sunday that hardly anybody can really afford. See, everything is getting so commercial. Everything, or nearly everything, man puts his hands on just turns to sin. Just keep on living; you'll see what I'm talking about." Staring at this wise man with barely a high school education, I wondered why people place so much emphasis on degrees alone to gauge a smart man.

"I see it already, but the bad never outweighs the good, you know that. Maybe during Men's Day Celebration you'll make it out, huh Dad?"

"Maybe you'll find you a wife to take to church one day and stop harassing me. I hear you singing all over the place and on the phone a lot more lately. Something of the world's got you inspired like that. Now who is she? Is she a spiritual woman? Or is she lying most every time her lips are moving?"

"You're getting so nosey I can sometimes hear you listening, but I think she's special Daddy. Time will tell more, but I think she's real special."

"Really? Well, if she's half the woman your mother was, I wouldn't waste too much time son."

"I know," I said as I turned my head and stared at the large picture of April Medley perched on the coffee table in the living room. As I looked at her, I heard her voice speaking to me somehow, just as it did years ago. I never forgot that message, how could I? Maybe she'd been speaking to me often lately, and until now I didn't hear, I'm not really sure. Whatever the case, her words now rang out to me in the purest pitch of clarity, with her image more vivid than ever. Unaware of it, I returned to the little nine year old boy at her bedside.

"Kyle, I see in you a calling to preach. You're a vessel from Heaven, and you were meant to spread the gospel, save souls and change people's lives. But it doesn't matter what I see. You've got to see it, and until you do I want you to live your life praising Him for everything. And if the calling comes to you from The Creator, don't run from it. Embrace it son. Now give me Momma your hand."

I did so bravely and unafraid, and she caressed it gently, smiling faintly at me before slipping away to eternity.

"Are you alright there, boy?" Papa Medley interrupted, and just like that I shouted, "Praise God, praise God, I'm blessed and highly favored Daddy."

"Alright son, very well," Papa Medley replied. I looked back at my father, more intent than ever before continuing.

"Put it this way. You're really too wise to not go to church anymore. You know the Lord too well to not respect the fellowship, too." Daddy's eyes widened as he listened.

"And you know yourself that there isn't anything happening in church now that pretty much wasn't going on during biblical days, when Paul spoke about divisions in..." Papa Medley began to recite as I frantically searched for my Bible about the room before stopping in my tracks. The words came to me as if I'd written them myself. With newfound God given authority I nearly shouted the text verbatim as Papa Medley read along in a low pitched voice while aided with the bottom of his bifocals.

"First Corinthian, verse 10 and 11. Now beseech you, brethren, by the name of our Lord Jesus Christ, that ye all speak the same thing, and that there be no divisions among you; but that ye be perfectly joined together in the same mind and in the same judgment."

"For it hath been declared unto me of you, my brethren, we both continued, by them which are of the house of Chloe, that there are contentions among you."

A look of surprise appeared on his face as he ended the verse and stared into space, then back over to me. I knew just what it meant.

"See, I knew you haven't forgotten—especially as much as Granddaddy used to tell me this verse long before I knew what it meant." Papa Medley shrugged.

"Yeah he did, didn't he? No I haven't forgotten son. I see you not only been reading but you starting to know the Bible. That's good. I also haven't forgot another Medley favorite that's been passed way down, and don't you."

"Oh yeah, Daddy, which one is that?"

"You can go to college, you can go to any school, but if you ain't been saved, you're just an educated fool. You just go on now boy, and give Mt. Tabernacle my love. Maybe you can put my Bible up before you leave, just right over there in the den."

"Alright Daddy, but I wish you can bury your differences with the church and move on. Either way, I want you to know something."

"What's that son?"

"I've been called by God to preach, Halleluiah."

"Is that right son?" Papa Medley asked as he looking on at his only son. Slowly, tears filled his eyes, and he said nothing else.

NINETEEN

Some measured commitment by the amount of tithes brought forward. Others witnessed spirit, while still others noted the plain ole' ability of so many to get up early Sunday and go to the house they love. The 8:00 o'clock service was said to be filled with the most committed members of any church. Many said the preaching was better too, but there was no telling when Pastor Adams would light a fire to your soul. It could be at the 8 or 11 o'clock service, Wednesdays hump night service, or even the times he'd join you in the church foyer when you came late and the doors were shut. He'd often touch you on the shoulder and pray for you, usually when you hit an all time low in your spiritual walk. I know, because it took me two years of being convicted by the tackle I put on Reggie before his prayers for me freed me to join Manpower, and I wish I didn't wait. I never even discussed it with Pastor Adams, but I was certain he knew my pain before he'd mentioned it upon my Bible study invitation.

It was now 7:40 as we gathered in the foyer to meet. It was strange and disappointing that Pastor Adams wasn't present as we did. True enough, we all knew that Our Creator's star was a star much brighter than the pastor's. You just couldn't catch those who knew him well bragging about it, that's all. All fourteen of us flowed through the doors present and accounted for. We even smelled good, but the real kicker was seeing everyone dressed in black suits, white shirts and dark ties. They subtle smiles we sported further conveyed our contentment to appear as strong and unified men, and everyone knew it was a nice touch without even saying so.

I garnered their attention and we proceeded inside to the front of the sanctuary. The room erupted with smiles and clapping from the congregation the very moment we entered it. Their enthusiastic reaction was fairly humbling, especially considering that the better portion of us still were the most non-singing men in any choir, in any church in the U.S.A. Yet, at the same token why not rave about us? We were indeed God's rock stars if nobody else's.

Taking our positions in the front stage pews Brother Humphries turned around to give me a high five. He had to reach up, as I stood in the back row of an inclined floor with no microphone—a quite different perspective than what I was accustomed to. There was no time or place for humiliation however, as I hastily directed the men who had forgotten their seating arrangements. Minister Roberts rose from his piano stool and beamed with excitement. He was beyond caring whether the new men wore red now, as long as I was in the back and couldn't be heard. He walked to the front of the sanctuary and directed us to sing "Would I Trade?" on the musical queue we'd rehearsed. We stood listening to the music and preparing for our queue to begin and thus...

I've heard of people making all kinds of deals
Cars, Boats, Money and superficial thrills
But I'll trade nothing to live without my God
With Jesus I'd rather swim an ocean, going against the
tide Or cross a battlefield alone, knowing he's by my side
But without Jesus they can't take me for a simple ride
Trials are too much, and the costs are too great to
bear No way, no way I can live without you, here.

I thought we sounded good in rehearsal, but nobody could have told me I would one day sing a nearly mute role to a great gospel-fest like this. It was fantastic, to say the least. We weren't even half way through the song when most of the women and a third of the men began to stand, smile, and clap along with us. Even Sister Simmons—who normally only caught the holy ghost during a sermon from Pastor Adams—began to dance, shout, and move about the floor as if she knew she was going to glory today. Our deacons, who usually supported us in merely sympathetic and dutiful fashion, were all on their feet with an earnest joy and excitement that I'd never seen before. Their wives, like most of the women that comprised the highly regarded Unity Choir, were likewise shouting with praise and jubilation. One could safely say there was a feeling that we had finally 'arrived'. Scanning the faces of the pews from left to right

I noticed somebody in the congregation glowing at me that special way. She wore an all black suit, white shirt and a white carnation; colors I'd like to think were chosen to complement me. But my dream was short lived since I never mentioned to her what we were wearing. At lest there was nothing vague about the look she gave me, though. That look can't be bought, sold, or misinterpreted in any language anywhere. She raised her two fingers up in the air and then bent them forward in an E.T. call home sort of fashion. I reasoned it conveyed a huge down payment on the promise of tomorrow, and smiled back at her in gratitude before focusing my attention back to Minister Roberts. A choir director, like an Army captain, deserves your full attention. I gave it to him, despite my voice being unnoticeable and the microphone so out of reach it could have been a country mile away. Counting my blessings anyway, I looked around at everyone.

To my right front stood Brothers Humphries, Lange, and Sherman. These men exuded an unmatched passion for Christ and the gospel they sang, regardless of how well they sang it. To my left stood Brothers Williams, Baker, Gonzales, and Daniels, who with the aid of others seemed to bring out the Alto section like nobody else could. To my right down in the Tenor section stood Brothers Nix, Baker and Lewis, who were obviously feeling the song quite passionately as well. Only the devil made me wonder if Charles Nix was any more passionate when he used to politely ask the bank tellers to fill those bags up with all that money. My conscience then begged me to consider that after all, the brother did get the new members to wear all black instead of red today so shoo, devil, shoo, I thought. Next to him stood Brothers Terry and Akins, who seemed to be a sure bet to enjoy the experience as well. I realized that I was indeed human as I grappled with the worldly cynicism that suddenly came over me. Was it from going from the front to the back of the choir?' Maybe. Was it from being displaced by virtual strangers? Possibly. Or did I feel resentment that regardless of my love of singing for the Lord I should have considered myself lucky simply to be here, courtesy of Minister Roberts? Definitely. Since God knew their hearts and had his own plan, I decided I'd continue to be bigger than all of it and just savor this experience.

The song was coming to a close as the church clapped loudly. Minister Roberts stood up from his piano with the broadest smile of them all. He looked like he'd either gone to heaven or just recently left a 'see-food' buffet. That smile dimmed to a frown as he walked over to us. At that point he nearly scowled, looking very much like some angry football coach who didn't want to see his team too caught up in celebration before the game is won. I think he was a little envious of all the attention not being strictly on him for a change, but then again—I'm just a fruit inspector. He leaned into us and whispered ever so softly "Speak To My Heart."

With the help of two new saxophonists and a lead guitar player we could instantly sense the musical justice that this interlude deserved. A gospel connoisseur could make a case of the injustice we used to do to the song, but no more. As the interlude progressed, Ed Tyson walked deliberately to the front and grabbed a microphone. We all then joined in to sing the song together.

Now I don't know if it's spiritually correct to call two back to back gospel songs a one-two punch in church, but until I see the rule book why not? Scanning the congregation I easily noticed most everyone not simply smiling, but indeed crying. Sister Simmons head rocked back and forth so much that it wouldn't have been a surprise to see her in a neck brace for a week. The majority of the men finally stood with their fist balled to possibly conceal the fact that they too were crying, or on the verge of tears. I know, because I was one of them. I believe Ed just considered it a personal victory that his face was now known to the congregation. He might have been given a bonus blessing due to the fact that his hair wasn't quite dripping on his shirt before the song's end. Looking up on the stage I saw the guest speaker of the day, Pastor Bradford holding his head down in solemn appreciation for us.

If the only thing worse than following our new choir voices was following with our old choir voices, then it's equivalent had to be Pastor Bradford following in the footsteps of Pastor Adams as the guest pastor today. Oh sure, most liked him, and genuinely appreciated his coming all the way from Brunswick, Georgia. Still, you had to wonder after hearing the bland effect of Pastor Branford's sermons, what it must be like to try and fill the shoes of Pastor Adams for an hour—let alone a day. Bradford was a small town preacher with only a limited vocabulary and a mere trace of charisma, but he was so brave and pure of heart that I took my hat off to him. Why not? The man would preach just as quickly as I would sing. I brought him a glass of water out as he stood and walked up to the podium microphone. Speaking in slow and measured words he began.

"Good morning Mt. Tabernacle, it's a blessing to be here with you today. God Bless these strong men y'all got 'sangin' in this Manpower Choir here today boy I'll tell you!" The church again let out another round of applause before slowly quieting down.

"When Pastor Adams called and asked me to come before you and preach today, I told him it was an honor to do it, that's why I'm here."

"Amen, Amen, alright," many echoed, while a few members turned to each other to denote that this simple logic made good sense to them.

"Before I begin though, I want to enlist yawl's support to pray for 'yawls' Pastor, Pastor Adams. He has informed me that he's taken sick while down in Haiti on that mission of his." The mood among the congregation changed dramatically.

"Oh no, oh my, you don't say—say what?" came their echoes, followed by the hushes of other members waiting to hear the full gist of his message.

"Yeah, your pastor and my dear friend, my brother, has unfortunately come down with a case of malaria, and has been ordered to stay rested in a Haitian hospital until he's well enough to travel back home. He wanted me to tell y'all not to worry though, and to pray for him, and with enough prayers everything is going to turn out alright."

Most of the congregation continued to display the kind of shock expected after hearing the terrible news about a revered family leader. It was indeed far from typical, and caused a special sadness to permeate the church. Though Pastor Adams was not reported to be lost, the mere threat of his loss beckoned many to remember his prophecy about needing other leaders to step forward and assume a share of the leadership. Mt. Tabernacle had a Music Minister in

Minister Roberts to step forward and assume responsibility for the music of the church in the pastor's absence. Unlike an effective church, however, there was nobody there to assume leadership of the pastoral duties during the Pastors absence. Sure, there was a once able Assistant Pastor in Pastor Jackson, but at 78 years of age, he had reached elderly status. Hard of hearing and cantankerous, his most exuberant days were now well behind him. Thus, Pastor Adams earlier words, beckoning for new leaders to step up, came crashing home upon reflecting on the sorrowful news from Pastor Bradford.

"Let us bow our heads and say a special prayer for your pastor. Since your church is blessed with such strong men of God, let us afterwards devote this entire service to praise and worship with the voices of the Manpower Choir. Heads bowed please;
Dear Lord, we pray that your hands will bring a special healing to Troy Adams this morning and that his return home will be swift. We know that the power is in your hands dear Lord and our faith is in you...Amen." Many among the congregations most faithful were seen crying openly. The mere thought of losing Pastor Adams was daunting. Who would take his place? Who could take his place? Surely someone would but.... The thought took a backseat upon the request from Pastor Bradford's further request.

"Now can we get a few songs from our men?"

The faces of the church were glued on Manpower as we sat, with their eyes beckoning for leadership they felt only strong men of God can deliver. By now most had given up any real hope of hearing us reach harmonic heights, but seeing the swelling of our ranks was more than enough to ignite them. Resounding quiet overtook the church as Minister Roberts again rose slowly from behind the white designer piano. Standing motionless he cast his eyes upon us for several moments, surveying us as if he were Caesar judging Rome. He began to walk toward us, and as he neared, he cupped his hand and gave the much anticipated signal. We stood up in valiant fashion, each like baseball batters stepping up simultaneously to a diamond plate. As we did, Charles Nix calmly walked forward to the front and grabbed the microphone from its stand.

In this one life you are going through
And you don't really know what to do
Just call on Jesus, He will see you through
The son of God knows, yes Jesus he knows

If there is a path or a trail that comes your way
Or two or three roads you've searched for a brighter day
Just call on Jesus, he will show you the way
For He Knows, Jesus He knows
And he'll never, no, no, no, never lead you astray.

He was superb, and as long as our voices mixed in softly among the new voices that really mattered, so were we. The congregation was soon on its feet again, moved by the spiritual message which the power of the song exuded. After singing "Jesus is on the Main Line," we moved quickly to the third song, and the roars of jubilation so stirred the congregation that Sister Simmons smiled broadly before weeping. By the fourth stanza she was wailing uncontrollably. Stares from many of the new members, especially those with all the protocol, appeared to suggest she was fanatic. The old guard among us dismissed that notion however, citing how Sister Simmons was always the first one to boldly stand and eagerly clap, despite the many years we vocally stunk up the place. Maybe her tears were partly tears of joy, a rejoicing, glorified joy that signaled our self inflicted misery was coming to an end, and she no longer had to be the sole lender of support. Either way, she and half the deacons walked briskly toward us to congratulate us before nearly everyone else in the congregation did. They smiled broadly from ear to ear while shaking our hands. No sooner had it all began when Minister Roberts abruptly interceded.

"Men, that was okay, but I think we all should go over to the Gospel Network after the service for a little more practice. I reserved a slot already for us to sing. What do you say gentlemen?" The men were all smiles at the notion of going to sing at the Network and why not? Up until now the very notion of performing there would have been deemed anywhere from daunting to laughable. We all agreed to come, and half the congregation announced they'd follow. Bianca assured me she was going to come early, so she could sit ringside to see us.

TWENTY

Conversation was at an all time high when we approached the entrance to the Gospel Network. One woman stood outside talking on her cell phone with her back turned as we approached. She carried on about our earlier church performance as if we had just come from another planet.

"Girl, you have to come by to see and hear the big strong men that they got in Mt. Tabernacle's Manpower Choir now. Honey they can really sing, and they fine too. Yeah, yeah, they got about five or six new members, but the rest of them are the same, you know. They weren't singing those old Negro spirituals like they used to either, we talking about some progressive gospel kind of stuff. And those new musicians, you better just come on—they already announced that they were getting over here at 2:30 to perform, so hurry if you want a seat."

Three men from one of the local mega-churches were sitting at the table chatting when I and a few other members of Manpower entered the room.

"Yeah man, I checked with the staff here earlier, and guess who they said was going to perform today?"

"Peachtree Memorial Gospel Choir's is supposed to. At least they're on the schedule."

"No brother they're not. They had to cancel due to half their musicians and members having the flu."

"Then, who?"

"Would you believe Mt. Tabernacle my brother?"

"Mt. Tabernacle? Come on now. You mean that little church over there in Stone Mountain?"

"You're half right. Mt. Tabernacle used to be that small church over there in Stone Mountain, but it's blown all the way up now.

"You don't say. They've never sang here before, or anywhere I know of. I hope they're good."

"I hope so too brother, because the last time I checked, that church wasn't even big as a minute you know." The oldest and most silent among them had been listening quietly, but chose to now offer his take on the situation.

"For years they've been small. My grandfather told me ex-slaves founded and built it, and they're still practicing that 'ole time religion' over there. Whatever they've got, you rest assured the spirit is moving over there with every step they take."

****

You could always find the formal church news in the available bulletins, but if you wanted to hear the latest gossip you had to meet and mingle with the church folks at the tables of the Gospel Network. We strolled past at least twenty-five of them before taking our seats near the front stage. Brother Humphries sat next to me at the table as half of the original Manpower members joined us. The rest of Manpower sat at the adjoining table.

"So this is how the other half lives? Humphries asked. You know I could get used to traveling around like a big gospel star, couldn't you Kyle?"

"I don't know, man."

"What do you mean, you don't know?"

"I mean, it just might take me some getting used to again, that's all."

"Again?"

"That's right. It's kind of funny actually. I used to crave a lot of attention, and when I got it, it never came from standing around and singing, but moving around on a football field with onlookers noticing every move I made. Now that I'm at a point in my life where I don't need attention, I find strangers looking me right in my eyes."

"Is that right?" Humphries asked.

"That's the truth," I confirmed.

"That's too bad. I don't mind the attention," Humphries stated. "I believe a man has to come out of the bathroom shower with his voice sooner or later, and I'm cool with it. As for you though, well, it's a flat stage."

"What's that got to do with anything?" I asked.

"Let's face it," Humphries continued, "Roberts has got you so far in the back that once we line up on a flat stage, you won't be too worried about many people looking at you, so relax," he said before roaring with laughter, slapping my shoulder and finally nudging me.

"You can keep on laughing, but they got a third row of microphones up on that stage, and the day when Roberts turns them on will be the day they'll hear from me for sure. Then the jokes will be on the both of you, okay?" Humphries smiled broadly before looking at me with a straight face before speaking again.

"But seriously Kyle, I admire the way you have kept your cool about being placed back there by Roberts. I mean, with no microphones or nothing, and you're just rolling with it like nothing ever happened. I probably would have gone berserk, but you...you must know you're still the man."

"I know I'm still blessed Stephen," I humbly responded, "if that's what you mean. Being blessed is better than being the man. Just look at Pastor Adams all the way down in Haiti with malaria. It's a lot easier for me to roll with it than it is him." Minister Roberts abruptly walked through the doors with a big grin on his face.

"Get ready men, we're setting up, which means we'll be on in less than twenty minutes. Remember gentlemen that this is the kind of opportunity we've been waiting for, so lets give it our best," he said.

"You have a good point," Stephen Humphries replied after Roberts moved on. He then turned back to me before saying, "and Minister Roberts doesn't even appear to be too shaken up about the news too much, does he?"

"Stephen, I'm just a fruit inspector, but I think he's too busy trying to launch a gospel group to notice things like that. Nothing will sink in to him as long as he feels he's about to take us out on tour."

People began to flow into the Gospel Network much more rapidly as we chatted. Church members from all over metro Atlanta were filling the tables left and right. The Greater Mt. Zion Unity Choir was the mega-church most heavily represented as they took up over four tables, while New Hope Baptist and Holy St. Phillips

African Methodist Church members streamed in as well. All of their choirs were known to be progressive and spirit filled. All of them anxiously awaited our performance as more people filled the room with good will and brotherly love. Many of them had participated in Gospel Extravaganza's, whereby two or three choirs would perform back to back. Thus, most in attendance had come to know each other, but since we'd never performed in this fashion, we were an oddity. Most didn't know us lyrically or personally, and to say the crowd appeared anxious to get a glimpse of us was an understatement. Out of nowhere Bianca arrived to the table with a glass of water and a napkin in her hand.

"Hi Kyle."

"Hello Bianca, it's good to see you."

"And you also. I wanted to tell you that you guys sounded wonderful at church today. I brought you some water in case you might like a sip, and here's a napkin in case you start sweating like you did at church earlier."

"Thanks for both, but the sweating is alright. It just symbolizes the sweat and pain the Mandingo slaves shed when they sang the gospel back in the day."

Brother Humphries over heard the conversation and whispered to Brother Akins.

"Man, if anybody that fine gave me a napkin I'd wipe the Chattahoochee River up if she asked."

"Then ring it out and catch every bead of sweat before it hit the ground," Akins responded.

"Okay, you just go right ahead and sweat if that's what you like Mr. Mandingo man."

I stared at her momentarily. Touched by the goodwill of her actions I didn't want to refuse her overture.

"Wait a minute Ms. Kincaid. Because of my fondness for you and my respect for your opinion I will defer the need to show my perspiration to the world. We shall re-create the Mandingo man without it after all."

"Good idea black man," Bianca said as she held the napkins out in her hands, ever smiling while I took them.

"Thank you too, black queen."

"You're welcome. Now I'm going to sit down and get ready to enjoy your performance again."

"Sounds great to me, I think you'll like it. I might even sing lead this afternoon."

"What," she asked nervously?

"Just kidding, I'll be back over there later," I said.

Bianca turned around slowly and walked to the adjoining table. I then turned my attention to the doorway as Pastor Jackson and Pastor Bradford walked in. They noticed us instantly and began their slow journey toward our table. Just a few years ago the tall lean Jackson would have converged upon us quickly. Now, his movements had become far more measured as he propelled himself somehow from side to side, like a penguin perhaps. Most of us realized that his public visits were rare, and his presence was well received.

"Good afternoon gentlemen," Pastor Jackson began. "You all sounded so good that I thought I'd come out to witness this again and show you men my support. Fine makeover you all have done, real fine."

"Thank you both for coming," I said as I stood to shake their hands.

"What did you say son," he replied?

"I said thank you for coming," now shouting while Pastor Jackson adjusted the earpiece in his ear. As I welcomed them, I thought about the huge unspoken void left with Pastor Adams absence. We felt empowered by having him playing bass guitar along side of us every week.

"Take my seat, pastor"... "No here, take mine," Brothers Akins and Humphries offered as the two men stood over us gleaming with pride and brotherly love.

"No thanks gentlemen," Pastor Jackson said. "That's kind of you but I think it would be better to let you all bond together while we just grab a seat over there. Maybe that beautiful lady over there will have us at her table," he stated while gazing at Bianca. She gracefully welcomed the men to join her as they walked over, and it pleased me to know she would be in good company. Everything on the surface was seemingly going great until my conscience began to tug at me again while walking back to my table—'You're being called.'

"What I was trying to tell you earlier was the more I get to know you the more respect I seem to have for you," Brother Humphries whispered as I took my seat again.

"What, for not reacting angrily about going back to the third row to sing?"

"That's only a start. More remarkable is the fact that I don't know anybody who drives an old pick up truck like you do who is able to command the attention of a woman like Bianca. She's fine brother, and very classy. That gives you a lot of props in my book."

"Who can find a virtuous woman? For her price is far above rubies," I lamented.

"I don't know, I'm still wondering who can find one that fine," he said.

"Thanks, Brother Humphries, that's awfully prophetic of you. There aren't many brothers like you, either," I confirmed.

"Maybe not, but I'm still a baby in my spiritual walk, believe it or not. You, on the other hand, are teaching me, even when you don't know it. And most of all, you wield phenomenal clout and leadership amongst the brothers. We'd have a rough time finding our best spiritual selves if it weren't for you, you know."

"Oh, y'all would be okay," I confirmed. "You'd step up if you had to."

"Oh you're right, I would," Humphries said. "And I wouldn't know the first thing about what I was doing if I did, either." I smiled before turning my attention to Minister Roberts tuning the piano, then to the new bass player warming up on stage. Minister Roberts had acquired him recently, and where he got him from was anybody's guess, but one thing was sure, he strummed that bass far better than Pastor Adams could ever hope to, but he was no substitute for Pastor Adams. My eyes then turned to Bianca's table. I watched Pastor Jackson as he conversed with Minister Bradford and two deacons from Mt Tabernacle who had just arrived. I thought when this moment came, if it ever came, Pastor Adams would be around to reaffirm and interpret my vision—my calling, but he wasn't here. Scenarios of me walking into his business office on a weekday afternoon, or even strolling out of the sanctuary together after choir practice discussing it under a starlit sky, were those I'd envisioned. As my mind wondered, I heard Stephen Humphries voice competing with my thoughts.

"Just the thought of where we'd be if something happened to Pastor Adams and Pastor Jackson, and Minister Roberts was next in line to take over as head Pastor of the church."
I cringed a bit.

"Say what," I asked?

"Hey man, are you even listening to me?"

"I'm sorry. Excuse me, Stephen, but why don't you hold it down for me for a little while, okay? I'll be back."

I rose up from my table and walked over to Bianca's, shaking hands with well wishers who awaited us to take the stage along the way. Bianca had Pastor Jackson and Pastor Bradford thoroughly enthralled in conversation as I approached them.

"Pastor Jackson," she said, "I can tell you used to be quite the ladies man in your day. That's why I want to see you here with your wife the next time you're out. We can't have you getting into any kind of trouble. Same goes for you Pastor Bradford, because I can also tell you were once as mischievous as he was."

Both ministers would have likely corrected anyone else with a long winded and self righteous defense of their marital fidelity. Instead, Bianca had the two men grinning from ear to ear like innocent schoolboys.

"Excuse me for interrupting you all, but Pastor Jackson, I need to talk to you," I asked. Maybe you should come along too, Minister Bradford, if you don't mind."

"Kyle, is everything alright," Bianca asked?

"It couldn't be better sweetheart. I ordered you a vegetable plate and a glass of tea. Hope you enjoy it, but please excuse us. I'll get your company back to you soon."

"I'll hold you to that," she replied.
The men initially looked puzzled as they accompanied me down the hallway.

"This better be good Kyle," Pastor Jackson warned. "I was getting to enjoy that fine lady of yours."

"I understand Pastor. Everybody does."

"Then that's not good Kyle," cautioned Jackson. "I'm sorry to hear that." I started to explain what I meant until the rich sounds of gospel music began to play softly as we approached the prayer room. I pulled the drapes back and the men stepped inside for their first time.

"Very nice touch," Pastor Jackson remarked before looking over to his colleague.

"What do you think of it Minister Bradford?" I asked.

"Oh, it's a little different 'havin' a prayer room and a restaurant with no sanctuary to speak of, but as long as I can feel the spirit in here I don't reckon I have a problem with it," Minister Bradford replied.

"Well I sure hope you don't, because I'd like you both to join hands with me in prayer for the message you are about to receive. Holy father, may the words I prepare to speak to these men be the words that will help glorify your kingdom...Amen." I calmly arranged three chairs face to face and invited the men to sit.

"Pastor Jackson, Pastor Bradford, I strongly believe that the Holy Spirit is telling me that I'm being called into the ministry." The room grew quiet for a moment.
Pastor Jackson smiled warmly at me while Pastor Bradford stared in a baffling fashion.

"Young man, do you know exactly what it is to minister?" Pastor Bradford asked.

"Yes sir, I believe I do." I replied.

"So tell me what you believe, then." I instantly felt perspiration mounting from my forehead down to the palms of my hands. So sure of God's desire for me to communicate his message I quickly gathered myself. Refusing to be robbed by doubt, or memories of that day on the football field, I looked the men squarely in their eyes as I calmly spoke words echoed by my grandfather to me.

"To minister is to find a need and fill it, or to find a hurt and heal it." Pastor Bradford nodded his head in approving fashion while looking to Pastor Jackson. Pastor Jackson, of course, knew me more intimately, and therefore never wavered in his glowing reaction to my announcement.

"Pastor Bradford, I've known this young man all of his life. I knew his mother, bless her soul, a woman of great faith. I also know his father, a long time deacon at Mt. Tabernacle. I even fondly remember his grandfather, Lazarus Medley, who used to be the head pastor of our church. He knows what he's saying, and most important, I think he knows who's telling him to ask for it. Pastor Adams was right all along."

"Right about what, Pastor Jackson?" I asked. "You mean he knew?"

"Did he know? He's been telling me that he believes you've been called to preach for the last five years or more. Not long after you walked off that football field and traded that fancy corvette in for a pick up truck. He knew God was speaking to you, trying to make you see you have a higher calling. Heck, he heard about you holding Bible study at your job and got tickled pink. He even laughed to me about you taking two of his watermelons. He told me it was probably you who did it, and that you'd admit it eventually— even when nobody had a clue about it."

"Really?"

"Of course. He knows you're no thief, and he figured the *best* of us can sometimes fail. After he laughed about it, he told me he wanted you to teach that New Members class before he asked you. Once you did, he was so pleased to hear you did such a good job that he was tempted to come to you about being a preacher. His better judgment settled in though, because he knew that choice had to come from above, not him—or nobody else—if you were going to do it the right way. That's the problem with so many preachers today. There's no telling who's been called sometimes, and the pulpit shows it."

"Well I've been listening to the Holy Spirit while I prayed about it, and I would like to hear from Pastor Adams himself about my decision, so tell me. Just how sick is he?"

"Deacon Sheffield was the only one who joined him on the trip, and we got just one call from him the day before yesterday. He said the pastor was pretty bad off with a fever, chills and sweating and the like, but stable enough to barely comprehend what's told to him. If you want guidance I'll share enough with you to keep you on track and fortified until his return. Do understand this much, son."

"Yes, what is that, I asked?" Pastor Jackson's facial expression grew more serious.

"As you might be aware, you're going to have to do a little more than give an ordination sermon, no matter how much that I, 'yo' pastor, and the spirit of 'yo' ancestors would like you in the pulpit. Do you understand?"

"I've long known that Mt. Tabernacle wouldn't have it any other way."

"Well I've got my own set of ideas and expectations outlined for you, but I'm sure the pastor would want to have more input into this than anyone. I'll talk with him as soon as he's able. I'm sure he'll have some duties he'd like you to perform for the church. In the mean time, I suggest you set your mind to doing a lot more of what you simply described—just finding that need and filling it, and finding a hurt and healing it. I'll be praying and watching to see if The Holy Spirit is truly walking this walk with you. And remember, everybody who thinks they're called is not necessarily chosen."

"I know, and you can believe I understand Pastor Jackson. Please excuse me. I hear the music of the band starting up so I better hurry back to the stage." Shaking the men's hands I took three steps toward the exit when the vast range of duties and responsibilities of a hopeful pastor raced through my head. Curiosity got the best of me as I stopped in my tracks and turned around. "Do you have a hint of what he'll want from me exactly?" Pastor Jackson pondered a moment before shrugging his shoulders.

"Oh there are a few possibilities now, but it's hard to say. Pastor Adams might just want you going down to Haiti to help him with some unfinished work, or God forbid he might be so sick that he just might want you to help bring him home. Maybe he'll want you right here helping out with the new prison ministry. I've got the perfect assignment for you though."

"Oh yeah, what is it?" I asked.

"I want you to go on and hold that new choir together. That's it. That's enough of a ministry to maintain to begin with. You still its president?"

"Yes sir I am."

"Then that'll be your first assignment, keeping them spirit filled and moving in the right direction for now. I must say I don't know where those new brothers came from all of a sudden, but at least by the sounds of things I'd say you were off to a good start."

"Thank you, sir. I hope you continue to enjoy our performance."

"And I hope you were careful about what you prayed for, just in case you get it," he replied.

I exited the room to find the choir had started singing without me. Nothing matched my eagerness to join them as I hurried toward the stage. I hopped onto the stage knowing that God could beat the devil hands down any day, and just to prove me right I stepped behind a fully working microphone. Watch out now!

If good gospel music were soul food, it would be safe to say we served the Gospel Network crowd up properly. Ed Tyson, Charles Nix, and Keith Terry again highlighted the performance with stirring solos. Stephen Humphries, and Brothers Williams and Daniels vocally roused them as well. Alas, the Mt. Tabernacle congregation was elated in the triumph over the apparent end to our long vocal suffering—and theirs too.

A vast number of the mega-church choirs could easily stir an audience with their thirty plus members. We were doing it with just fourteen men, and their nodding heads of approval confirmed we were the gospel equivalent to 'the little train that could.' Psalms says to praise God with your voice and the harp, and that's correct, but if you're going to showcase good gospel to the world you have to come with it. Even Minister Roberts would often say, good choir singing consisted of great duration, dynamics, tone and note. As obnoxious as he could be, on this subject he was never wrong. We weren't as good as we could be, but we were quickly getting there. It was safe to safe they considered us a sensation, and the talk surrounding us as we ended our performance was at a near fever pitch. As new and exciting as the fanfare became, it quickly reminded me that this 'Born again' man wasn't for it, and I walked straight over to Bianca's table. Bidding good night to the ministers and deacons I asked her to leave with me. I was ever grateful she obliged, and we walked into the night.

TWENTY ONE

My mood was quite relaxed while driving Bianca home that evening. I dared to wonder if the day could have gone any better than it had, actually. The only exception was Pastor Jackson's remark about the possibility of my going to Haiti to help out with the work of Pastor Adams, and it was a big exception. If that was the Lord's will I stood ready, but looking over at Bianca it occurred to me that I might need her close to me, or she could very well need me. Besides, as much as I missed Pastor Adams and genuinely cared for his welfare, the prospect of going to whatever region of Haiti he visited and catching malaria also didn't exactly resonate well.

"You know, to be part of a new gospel sensation you sure do seem to be awfully quiet. Is everything okay, Kyle?"

"Oh sure it is, sweetie, I'm just sorting out a couple of things in my head I guess. Here, let me turn on some gospel music." The sounds of Glory 101.5 filled the front cabin of my truck and added to the existing serenity of a night. We'd enjoyed more quiet reflection than words thus far, at least until Bianca broke the silence.

"Tell me. Why do so many couples play secular music while they date, and once they get married they all of a sudden find themselves listening to gospel?"

"I don't know why Bianca. If that's true, then maybe good marriages are rooted in the words of gospel music, and maybe they evolve. I've never thought about it, but that's a good question."

"How could you know?" she replied. "From your conversation, it doesn't sound like you've ever been close to marrying someone. Besides, you start the dating process off by listening to gospel music. Maybe you'll be just the opposite."

"Meaning?"

"Meaning maybe guys like you start out loving gospel music but wind up listening to gangster rap or something. You'll probably end up singing 'shake it to the left, now shake it to the right,' or 'work that money maker' after you marry. You just never know," she said before calmly awaited my response.

"How do you know I don't already love gangster rap?"

"Because you and gangster rap go together like oil and water, that's how."

"So you think you're getting to know me huh?"

"A few things about you I'm getting to know, a lot more remains to be seen. Tell me, who do you live with? Do you live by yourself?"

"Actually, I live with my father."

"Really? That's interesting. You never told me that."

"I guess it's because you never asked."

"Well, I assumed since you told me all about your grandfather and great grandfathers you might have volunteered something about your Mom and Dad as well."

"That's a reasonable assumption. My Mom died of breast cancer when I was nine years old. She was the anchor of my life and the sweetest and most God fearing woman I ever knew. She was tall with rich, jet black skin, high cheek bones and keen, lovely features. Her innocent looking eyes were also rare. You happen to look a bit like her, you know."

"That's sweet how you talk of her, and nice that you say that, but it sounds like you look more like her than I do."

"And how would you know. You never saw her."

"That's true, but you spoke of her innocent eyes. I can look at your eyes and tell that whatever wrong you've done in your life your eyes apologize for it, and they say you didn't mean to do it too. I'm sorry she's passed on Kyle. What about your Dad—why haven't I met him? Did he play a famous Medley role at Mt. Tabernacle too?"

"He loved that church as much as any of my ancestors, but some people are just cut out of different spiritual cloths."

"Meaning?"

"Meaning Daddy and Pastor Jackson had a big falling out over some issues in the church many years back. Daddy never fully discussed it, but he was awfully disappointed, and I understand. It was once a given he'd be chosen as the next leader of Mt. Tabernacle, and not just because of who his father and grandfather were to the church, but he himself. But during granddaddy's long illness, somehow, Pastor Jackson and Daddy began to have some political differences. Before Daddy knew it, Pastor Jackson had started to sway the Deacon board toward getting a new Pastor from outside the church. It really hurt him that many were convinced by either the lies or exaggerations told by Pastor Jackson, so Daddy decided he didn't ever want to go back there again, and till this day he still hasn't."

"How long has it been?"

"Somewhere close to twelve years now. It still hurts him, but Momma was probably hurt far worse from it than he was. She always told me I was meant more for the calling than he was, though."

"And what do you think?"

"I've been praying about it a lot lately, and asking Him to show me the signs that will confirm my notion that I'm called. I believe he's shown them to me."

"Really Kyle, I think you've been called because I sure envision you as a Preacher, but how do you know if that's what God wants?"

Just before I could answer Bianca, my cell phone began to ring.

"Hey Daddy what's wrong. You say you're feeling sick? Really, okay, I'll be along there shortly. What? Bring you a pound of fried shrimp. You don't need any fried shrimp. You're going to get enough of telling me to shut up, too. Okay, I'm on my way. I may bring my friend, so put some cloths on and be decent, goodbye."

"I trust that was your father; is everything okay?"

"Yeah, he just said he's feeling sick and I need to come home quickly and bring him some fried shrimp, that's all."

"I didn't know fried shrimp had medicinal uses. He sounds like quite a character."

"He is. He lost his leg recently from diabetes and has been playing on my sympathy ever since."

"Well, it sounds to me like you might be a little harsh with him, don't you think?"

"Harsh!...harsh on him? I think I'm the victim, if you want to know the truth. You've just got to meet him one day and see for yourself. In fact, if you're not in any hurry, I was wondering if you don't mind coming over this evening to meet him. Would you mind?"

"Sure I'd like to meet your father."

"That's good, he'd like to meet you too. Now, back to your original question, how do I know if that's what God wants?"

"That's right."

"That's a good question that unfortunately isn't asked enough these days. I think you have to have a relationship with him first off. It starts by talking to Him regularly, just like we're starting to talk regularly for instance. As you dwell on the spirit and the word, you reach a point where you know what actions of yours are in line and consistent with what he wants. You think and pray about it, and then ask him where he wants you to be, but it all starts with that relationship."

"I know you talk to God Kyle. It appears you have a strong relationship with him too."

"That's true, but I'm saying I've been hearing this calling for me to join the ministry for some time now, but the guilt in knowing I've sinned has kept me from hearing God's affirmative answer."

"But what did you do that was so sinful? What could keep you from hearing God's answer?"

"I told you I played college football."

"I know. Were you really as good as they say?"

"I was better than good, but I wasn't great, as some will tell you."

"I'm not understanding you. Why weren't you great?"

"Because, if I were great I wouldn't have paralyzed a young man like me, that's why."

"But you didn't mean to do it."

"That's true, but I didn't mean to not do it either."

"I'm sorry Kyle."

"I am too. Hopefully Reggie knows I'm sorry also, but I did something today that I've wanted to do for a long time, despite that hit and despite the way it's changed my life."

"What did you do?"

"I stepped out on faith. I went forward with my request to be a minister at Mt. Tabernacle today." Bianca's jaw dropped as we pulled up to the driveway of my house. She continued to stare at me in disbelief for more than a few moments.

"What's wrong?" I said "Why are you so quiet? Isn't it everyday you go on a date with an aspiring preacher?"

"I'd like to say of course I do, but." Bianca said before seemingly harnessing the rush of her thoughts. "Oh Kyle, that's so wonderful. I've known it was your calling, even since the day we spoke in the break room the first time. God bless you, she said as she smiled and grabbed my hand."

"I'm going to need a whole lot of prayer," I replied while bringing the truck to a halt. Well, this is my humble home. Allow me to get the door for you."
Bianca glanced at every aspect of the neat and modest brick home as I escorted her out of the truck and toward the steps.

"Your place has lots of character," she said.

"You're being kind. Actually I sold my own place a couple of years ago to take care of my Dad. This is my childhood home."

Our home was a modest brick structure, and I knew Bianca had dated men who resided in far more lavish dwellings than this, but I silently applauded her comment while opening the door and inviting her in. Once inside, I stopped her in the front foyer.

"If its character you like, just hold on a minute," I said before I yelled out to my father.

"Daddy...hey Daddy, I've got somebody here that I want you to meet. Are you presentable?"

"Of course I'm presentable," said the voice from the bedroom down the hall. "But then again, I'm at home, and I can run around looking any way I want. Are they presentable, you mean? And did you bring me my shrimp?"

"You know good and well that I'm not buying you any fried shrimp."

"Darn you boy," came the voice that soon accompanied the sound of his cane hitting the floor slowly and steadily as he grew closer. "I knew I should have whipped your butt more often when you were younger. Then, we'd have a ready made solution to this problem because all you'd need is a flashback. Ooh, I'm sorry young lady," he said after entering the room and noticing Bianca.

"Sorry my foot," I replied. "You knew she was going to be here, and you're just showing off for her because you've gone and got yourself a brand new leg, that's all."

"Now stop that, both of you," Bianca said. "Kyle, I'm surprised to hear you talk so cruelly to your father, you should know better." Bianca walked over toward him and extended her hand.

"I'm Bianca Kincaid, Kyle's friend. How do you do, sir, and what shall I call you?"

Daddy's eyes quickly turned from looking tense to exuding joy and wonderment. They mirrored a heart that was melting like butter. The warmth Bianca transmitted by merely shaking his hand offered a temporary relief from the hideous disease that often put him in a sulky mood lately.

"So this is why you been on the phone so much, talking real low and singing the oldies but goodies, huh? Fredrick Medley is my name girl, but you can call me Papa, and it's too bad I'm not thirty years younger, otherwise you could call me a fine replacement for the company you're now keeping." Papa Medley chuckled while gently hitting me in the leg with his cane. I responded with a big grin in his direction and casually shook my head, certain that Bianca now understood that the two of us had a bond that transcended far beyond the harsh words we exchanged.

"You're still a very handsome man Papa," she replied. "They say the apple doesn't really fall that far from the tree, so who knows, you might have been."

"Oh, you wouldn't waste your time with him Bianca, trust me," I said. "Besides, I'm more like my Momma anyway. He's just delusional."

"Now just you wait a minute, who are you calling delusional?" Daddy asked, subtly preparing for a light hearted dual to display his machismo in front of Bianca. "You're the one who struts around here everyday acting like you can sing, not me. If I'm delusional then you're a lot more like me than you think." He searched Bianca's face to share in his lighthearted giggle until I interrupted on a more serious tone.

"Daddy, lets go sit in the den, I've got something I need to share with you."

"Alright son, but aren't you going to offer Bianca something from the kitchen first? Bianca, are you hungry?"

"No sir."

"Thirsty?"

"I guess I could use a tall glass of water," she replied. She wasn't thirsty but upon sensing his need to be a good host didn't want to offend his hospitality. Papa Medley went to the refrigerator and reached for the same jug of the purified drinking water that I so often urged him to drink more of, and poured her a glass. I waited until her drink was in hand and she had thanked my father before speaking.

"Alright, are you two ready now?"

"Here we come, son. It's this way girl." Papa Medley gestured toward Bianca with his hand in the direction of the wooden kitchen door which led to the den, almost as if the home might be ten times bigger than its size and they had several directions to choose from. He held the swinging door for us to pass through before letting it go and walking in the den to join us. Upon Papa Medleys invitation, Bianca took a seat next to Momma's picture in the den. As the hinges still lightly squeaked from the doors release, she noticed Papa Medleys eyes switch from her to the photograph. The look he gave her compelled her to cast her eyes downward, then over in the direction of the picture also, until her eyes too became fixed on it. Now focused on it, Bianca appeared stunned at what she saw. The resemblance between her and Momma was so striking that it had to be like looking at a slightly older picture of her own self. She wasn't scared or spooked however. A childish woman would have been spooked. Looking at me, she seemed to recount my remark about their physical similarities during our stroll through the park. Hopefully I'd gauged her correctly—that she'd determined weeks ago that she wanted to be something significant to me since, after all, a woman ultimately chooses a man. Bianca Kincaid then sat back in the chair, seemingly pleased at what she saw. Her demeanor suggested pride in carrying a resemblance to someone so beautiful and meaningful. Indeed, she could carry the feminine torch for both of us if Papa Medley didn't stare too hard, I thought. The next words I uttered to Daddy proved to be more than ample enough to divert his attention.

"Daddy, I've told you before that I feel I'm being led to the calling of the ministry, right?"

"Yeah you told me, but you were talking about the Music Ministry, weren't you son?"

"No, not quite. I love music, but God is calling me beyond that. I've told Pastor Jackson today that I want to be a preacher, right there at Mt. Tabernacle." Papa Medley's casual approach to the evening quickly dimmed.

"Kyle, every man and woman must decide what God wants for them. Knowing you the way I do I want to first commend you for doing just that. Now, having said that, do you really think you know what you're asking for?"

"I believe so," I answered.

"You believe so, huh. Listen to me, you better know. Now tell me, of all people to approach about this, why in the...did you pick Pastor Jackson, who just happens to be the biggest snake in the grass..."

"Daddy, just stop," I insisted. "Pastor Jackson is taking Pastor Adams place until he's well enough to return back from Haiti, that's why I went to him. It really doesn't make any difference, does it? He's too old to think about throwing up obstacles for me if he wanted to. I just don't see him doing it, especially the way you said he did you." I tried to let my words trail off softly in reverence to the pain he still harbored when his dreams in the ministry came crashing down without notice or cause. If there was ever a time for a real sensitivity between us, I knew it had to be now. I walked him over to the couch, and as we sat down I placed my arm around the shoulder of this once imposing bear of a man.

"You've got to stop holding on to those old scars and let them heal Daddy. Times have changed quite a bit since you were active in the church. Most folks are too busy lifting The Omnipotent One up nowadays to bother with bringing anyone down." Daddy paused to absorb the weight of my words before rising up from the couch.

"You know there's a difference between optimism and naiveté, and boy, you sound bout as naïve as they come, but I'm tired. It's about my bed time now." He extended his hand to Bianca as he spoke.

"Excuse me Bianca, it was very nice to meet you, sweetie, and I hope you do come again." The subject had to change, and change quickly before his eyes welled with tears, I noticed. Daddy was Christian humble but street tough, and the only time I remembered him crying was when Momma passed, so I escorted him down the hallway toward his bedroom so he could save face. Men like him don't cry in front of other men, and especially women, but I would later discover that Daddy wasn't about to cry at all. The truth was that I annoyed him too much with my optimism, he would later confide.

"Don't think just because you're in the Lord's house that people can't and won't hurt you son, and when they do, it can take a lot out of you, at least if you let it."

"I know Daddy, it's trying me now, but I'm toughening my armor and trying not to let it."

"No, you just think you're being tried, but you ain't seen nothing yet...not until you immerse yourself in the ways, business dealings, and the fickle people in the church, and then add all the politics on top that goes with it, and my, my," he said before drifting off in thought. "Heck, you'll probably deal with it better than I did—but still. Still, you're going to see. By the way, what do they want you to do to fulfill your calling, of course other than your sermon?"

"They just want me to really take charge of and lead that choir of men we got over there now."

"Hold on. You feel good about that," he asked skeptically?

"Course I feel good about it. 'No weapon formed against me shall prosper.' Besides, we're about fourteen strong, and I don't see the devil doing too much in the way of preventing us from getting stronger. Relax. Everything will be okay, alright?" Daddy looked at me with the most guarded "if you say so" look in his eyes I've ever seen, and quietly hobbled back to bed.

Bianca had no wish to rush up the steps when I drove her home tonight. Instead, she paced herself slowly up the stairs, seemingly in no hurry to bring an end to the day. I didn't realize it was Donald's recent phone call that made her do it, and that she couldn't help but compare the two of us. She remembered ending her evenings with Donald by normally thanking him for the generous gifts. An epiphany now made her see that those evenings with him were as empty as they were expensive, and she resented herself for patronizing with the shallow extravagance he spewed upon her for so many years. It was fools gold, she thought, and wondering 'how could I have known' didn't bring her the consolation she'd hoped for when she reflected upon it.

Not so with me, though. Maybe it was too soon to tell me, but hopefully the glow in her smile, and her merciless, slow gait as she bid me goodnight would convey it. She realized during "the walk" that she had inadvertently left her cell phone inside, but on this day she didn't care. She dismissed the oversight like any poet would—knowing that cell phones were mainly for transient strangers anyway. Strangers, transplanted like uprooted plants, they now lived in new places with little family, few friends, and no church homes to fertilize them. Merely acting as if they have plenty of each, these same strangers hugged their cell phones like desperate roots, roots searching to entrench themselves within the fertile soil that will allow fresh water to flow upwards through their souls and spell— life, instead of aimlessly wandering around town with ample minutes, still uprooted. She felt relieved to no longer be in that category as she basked in the mutual affection from me, Papa Medley, and her Mt. Tabernacle family. Slowly, Bianca could feel her roots becoming entrenched again in fertile soil, and it felt good—good to be alive, to be a young woman and to finally feel free. Now, it didn't matter that she'd spent all of her adult life playing down the curves of her sculptured body by wearing loose fitting clothing. It was time for 'the walk'. Why? I wasn't exactly sure, for man really knows. I'd like to believe it was because my eyes weren't quite like the lustful ones of testosterone filled men whose stares she felt most everywhere. I had no idea it had been a while since she had employed it, but 'this walk' was for me. As naughty as it looked, it was, after all, just a walk.

I waved to her while I watched it. Trying to act nonchalant; I pretended I didn't see it. I smoothly accelerated as I continued to wave, but sooner than I'd realized, my pick up truck took flight atop the curb before violently scraping a fire hydrant and crashing back down upon the street. *Good God almighty*, I thought. The devil must be busy tonight, and my eyes would have been better off on the road. Driving off I thought about the beautiful stride Bianca exuded, at least until the fender fell partially off the front end of the truck and began to drag along the street. Whatever attention I didn't draw from hitting the fire hydrant was well compensated for, as the fender dragged along the street with a loud noise accompanied by huge sparks that most had to wait until the 4th of July to see. It would cost me nearly $500.00 to get the damaged fender repaired. But every sin has its price I reasoned, and a little lustful gawking was no different. Until judgment day, I was at peace with it.

TWENTY TWO

The spinning wheels on the Cadillac Escalade again rotated brilliantly as Donald Morton headed south on I-75. He had been driving since 7:30 am and calling her almost every hour on the hour since the day began. It was now almost 8:00 pm and he was now rolling past Chattanooga, Tennessee. "Where could she be all day," he wondered out loud. He pushed the button located just above him to illicit the warm personal greeting.

"Thank you for using our service, how can we assist you Mr. Morton?"

"You added Bianca Kincaid's number to my list earlier didn't you?"

"We sure did Mr. Morton, would you like me to call her again?"

"Yeah, would you?"

"Sure sir, hold on."

****

As her telephone rang inside, Bianca was walking upwards toward the top of the steps and listening to the sound of his pickup scraping the fire hydrant. A little guilt over 'the walk" began to consume her until she dismissed it after resolving that a grown man needs to know how to drive his own car, under any circumstances. She cared for Kyle and hoped the damage wasn't too severe, but her Motor City toughness overcame all sentiments and rendered any man to be responsible for his own actions, even a spiritual man like he. If he were going to be able to handle her, then he would be no different. Unlocking the door she heard the telephone ring vibrantly now. It was probably Momma calling, she thought to herself. It was their ritual to talk on Sunday, even if they chatted every other day of the week. She'll laugh when I tell her about today's experience with Kyle, she thought as she picked up the phone with her trademark smile.

"Haay-ah"! she said sluggishly into the receiver as she picked it up. The greeting was in sheer mockery of how she noticed some black southern women greet each other in the south, contrary to saying hello. "Haay-ah what, Bianca," retorted the man's voice. Where have you been? I've been calling you all day."

"Donald?"

"Of course it's Donald. What's come over you, and why are you talking like that?"

"I thought...I thought you were my mother," she whispered silently.

Bianca knew she owed him no explanation, and even felt angered. The thought of hanging up the phone occurred to her as she wrestled with the fact that it wasn't Momma, but instead Donald calling once again. But she decided to exude calmness while grappling with the reality of hearing his voice. She calmed herself down to see where the conversation would go.

"I've been calling you all day, baby," Donald painfully acknowledged. But a volunteered explanation of her whereabouts was now replaced by silence.

"Bianca?" he asked.

"Yes, I'm here," she replied.

"Baby I miss you so much that I've been going crazy. I hardly eat, and going to sleep often times is impossible when I think about you."

Not too long ago those words would have melted her heart, beckoning her heart to respond with the fervor of a tennis ball hit resoundingly back over a net to its sender. Now, the silence on the other end became even louder. Donald knew the elementary ploy was falling on deaf ears, and thus cut through the chase for an instant reaction.

"I'll be in Atlanta at about 9:30 tonight."

"You'll be here, for what?"

"As I said, I'll be there around 9:30. Now I'm a little tired, and truthfully, between this road and wondering if another man's been holding you all day I'm nearly exhausted."

"Donald you shouldn't do this to yourself. You have a business to run in Detroit, and whatever else you're doing with your life is none of my concern. It's over between us.

"I've got people who *will* run the restaurant. Secondly, I don't think it's over. I've thought about us and even prayed about us, and I know God didn't give me your phone number if he didn't mean for me to have it."

How dare he put God in whatever deceit he used to find me.

"Now I'll be staying at the Piedmont Pavilion for a few days, and I'm looking forward to seeing you soon—like tomorrow."

"Why are you doing this? I can't see you, Donald; I have a job to go to."

"I know you do. Peachtree Motors I believe it's called, located at, let's see, 7125 Juniper Street in East Atlanta. You don't have to give me directions, I'll find it."

"Well, I still won't be able to see you. Why are you coming to my job?"

"For a couple of reasons, sweetheart. For one, my car owners manual says it's time for an oil change, and most importantly God says to name it and claim it. Now those are two good reasons to start, and besides, you know how I feel about you. Maybe we'll get a chance to chat over lunch. Your co-workers won't mind the fact that you know a good looking and highly successful man, now will they?"

"Donald don't!"

"I'll see you tomorrow, now I know you're just a little confused, but trust me, everything will be alright after we talk things out, goodnight, baby."

She held the phone to her ear before glancing at it in disbelief. Slowly, she placed it down on the handset as her mood grew sullen. The euphoria of the day subsided as she thought of how it had been turned upside down with just one single phone call. Her remorse from it all beckoned a spiritual curiosity for which there was no immediate answer. Lord God, what have I done to deserve this? She examined her Christian walk for clues as she asked herself. Was it because I slept with Donald before marriage? Did I see clues that told me how he sustained our lavish lifestyle, but ignored them? Or speaking of my walk Lord, that walk I did for Kyle a little while ago wasn't very Christian at all. Maybe that was just the invitation of sin the devil needed before he used me to help scratch Kyle's truck and send Donald here. What was I thinking? But no God, you are good and merciful, and therefore I ask you for your forgiveness.

Bianca's remorse and fear changed to defiance upon her realization that God has not and would not forsake her, and she spoke aloud. "The nerve of him to threaten my life and just come here like that, thinking we've got a chance at anything. What was I ever thinking when I once loved him. I've got to handle this, but how?" She pondered as she touched the phone again, thinking of Kyle. Grasping the receiver she lifted it up to dial the only number in Atlanta she knew by heart. Kyle would want to help me as a friend, and also as a spiritual guide. But wait, who am I fooling? We both have the potential for something much more than friendship, and any man, especially a strong Christian man, doesn't need a woman with this kind of worldly drama dumped on him at the beginning of a relationship. To ask him—or to even mention it—would be selfish.

Secure in this knowledge she lowered the receiver down and hung it up. I've got to rid myself of Donald on my own, without Kyle getting his hands dirty with this in any way. Attaining a minister's ordination in an old fashioned southern church will be challenging enough for him. She pranced across the floor, praying for the words that would turn Donald around and send him back home as quickly as he arrived.

****

Donald drove the Escalade up Peachtree Street until he reached the trendy 'Buckhead' district of Atlanta, locating the plush Piedmont Pavilion Hotel just before 9:30 p.m. Pulling into the valet parking area he brought the vehicle to a smooth halt. As he stepped out into the night air he yawned, grabbed his luggage from the rear door, and handed the valet attendant his keys. Strolling into the hotel lobby he greeted the staff with a burst of contrived personality and short term energy level most akin to a sprinter. And why not? A long distance runner required stamina and pacing, but the type of con he was about to employ didn't call for long term relationships. It only called for a bunch of short moves that would be difficult for an innocent soul to assess.

"Is this a lighthouse or a grave yard?" he boldly asked as he approached the front desk. As he spoke, he noticed that innocence in the young black-male desk attendant, whose eyes instantly lit up to receive his banter. He was joined by an attractive, middle aged white female as the only hotel clerks on duty tonight. Thank goodness for this, he thought. Donald had no desire to test the racial overtures and good ole boys of the south who might distrust him even if he approached bearing the gifts of Santa Claus. They both smiled at him in welcome amusement, bringing a measure of relief from the nervousness that inwardly consumed him each time he tried his hustle.

"You've just arrived at Atlanta's most premier hotel, the Piedmont Pavilion, where life abounds 24/7," the young man whose name tag read Kirk replied.

"It's so quiet around here I can't tell Kirk."

"Well, a 'baller' like you should arrive earlier in the weekend instead of on a late Sunday night, and then you'll see what I'm talking about." Kirk had barely echoed the last words when his female co-worker cast a frown, displaying her annoyance with their unprofessional, street banter. It didn't matter, because soon she would find him to be as cute as most women saw him, and if she didn't, she didn't matter anyway.

"So what type of room can we accommodate you with," she asked?

Don flashed the photogenic and endearing smile that disarmed women from coast to coast. He looked briefly toward Kirk before turning toward the woman whose name tag read Joann.

"Well first Kirk, I'm doing great, because God is good my brother. But I'm no baller, I'm just blessed and highly favored to be with you both tonight. Let's get the Presidential Suite Joanne," Donald said with assured confidence.

"And how long will you be joining us, Mr..."

"Dilbert, Robert Dilbert is my name, pleased to meet you both."

"Let's just take it week to week for about a month okay? I've got a series of conference seminars I'm planning that can wrap up anytime, know what I mean?"

TWENTY THREE

Minister Roberts paced barefoot across the room's plush white carpet. Already owning seven copies of the New Testament, he clutched one of them firmly in hand while listening to the tape of Manpower's Sunday performance as it softly echoed in the background. The soft sensation of fine wool under the balls of his feet had a way of reaffirming his sense of royalty while harboring him in a comfort zone uniquely his own. Though it was an avid ritual, the 37 year old minister never recognized the physical and pompous phenomenon that his heels never touched the floor when he walked—never! His voice rose to a near fever pitch in mock preparation for next Sunday's sermon on the subject of contentment.

"You see, the vexatious, and carnal spirit of your average homo-sapian beckons with an insatiable and guileless thirst, which pacifies him while simultaneously jeopardizing his very soul and existence." Impressed with his own oratory Minister Roberts stared blankly off through the windows in a daydream. His mind began to fog up with omnipotence as he imagined himself calming the congregation down from their exhilarated shouts of amen and thunderous hand clapping while motioning them back to their seats. He then envisioned the ovations he received as coming from a flock of congregation members whom he had pastured and cultivated in the utopian church of his own. And the choir, he marveled. The Unity Choir, which consisted of dozens of brothers and sisters, would all have angelic voices, all singing in unison at a heavenly pitch without a single member off key. And the Manpower Choir would be the talk of the town with their numbers reaching over seventy strong men of God on any given Sunday morning, hallelujah! They too would sing in perfect harmony, with distinctive sections of bass voices that boomed ever discriminately from their tenors. In a desperate search for validation by most anyone with a pulse he departed from the daydream and turned his head toward the couch to Etta.

"What do you think baby?"

"That's real good beau, but you just can't talk about gay people in the church like that, saying they come to church thirsty to hook up wit somebody. I mean, I knows what you trying to say cause I knows you beau, but somebody else may not take it that way, know what I'm saying?"

"At what point did I talk about gay people Etta?"

"Come on Beau, everybody's 'knowse' what a homo-sapien is nowadays. People just not stupid as you might think they is."

"Yes, Etta, I believe I know what you're saying," Minister Roberts acknowledged while shaking his head in exasperation. Suddenly the phone rang and briefly detached him from his sexual object of the past few months.

"Hello...God bless you too Minister Jackson," Roberts said upon answering. "Yes, I can talk now. Of course I'll be ready for next Sunday's sermon. I want to tell you what an honor it is to address the congregation in Pastor Adams absence...what? You know already? Okay, well, good...what...you have exciting news for me? Okay, I'm listening, and what news is this?"

Minister Roberts braced himself, fully realizing how rare it was for Pastor Jackson to refer to anything as news, but instead as a message from God. It usually began in ways such as "God sent this message through me today to give to you." Or, "through another person or situation yesterday I received a message from God to tell you," and so on and so forth. Thus, this 'news from the pastor was interesting enough to throw him off kilter and delay a textbook Christian response.

"I talked to Pastor Adams today," Pastor Jackson's began, with his words flowing through the receiver in a measured southern droll, "and though he was weak, mighty weak in fact, he affirmed his faith in the power of God. He told me he's in good hands, and he's going to be alright. The doctors want him resting at least another two or three weeks in that Haitian hospital before returning to us, though."

"Well all glory be to God. But tell me, is this the news, Pastor Jackson," Minister Roberts asked?

"You don't listen too well, do you boy? Why no son, that 'dere is yo' Pastor's prophecy from God, and even though it's news worthy, it's his relationship with God and what I'm bout to tell you that makes it the message!"

"I understand, Minister Roberts replied, genuinely pleased to hear of the progress of Pastor Adams yet turning red from feigning humility from someone he deemed beneath him. He tried to suppress his annoyance through his voice as best he could, but the truth was apparent several months ago when he arrived. Minister Roberts Boston roots and Ivy League mentality didn't only come with a healthy disdain for bland gospel singing. Old fashioned country oratory was even further down his list of valued traits. Too bad Kyle Medley and Pastor Jackson epitomized them both! Unfortunately, they'll never complement my vision of a new church leadership. We'll have articulate preaching, with fast moving tongues, fast moving ideas, and fast moving piano keys. And the gospel singing, have mercy. The gospel singing will blow you away long before you even hit your seats on Sunday morning!

"Southern folks not stupid, you know boy!" Pastor Jackson's loud words shocked him, cracking the silence that was Minister Roberts's day dream like a ball of thunder on a quiet night.

"What? Why, heavens no, of course not, sir. Why, my grandmother is from Kansas," Roberts responded in desperation. It was too late though, as Pastor Jackson's snarl resonated throughout the phone line.

"An educated man should know that Kansas isn't in the south. Now's as far as the news," Pastor Jackson continued. "I also told Pastor Adams that Kyle Medley has become a candidate for pastoral ordination, and as sick as he was, he was just tickled pink. You do know Kyle came forward today with his pastoral request don't you," he asked?.

"No, no I didn't know Pastor Jackson."

"You didn't? I thought you knew what kind of spirit was in that boy since he was leading the choir and all."

"I didn't have the slightest idea."

"That just goes to show you. It must be the spiritual message in Kyle, working busier than the news in you, to put a message like that inside of him. That's it! That's just why you didn't know it, because you're looking more for the news than the message—Have Mercy Jesus!"

"That's not so, pastor, but tell me, what about me?"

"What about you? You know you're sounding like a child looking for his fair share in a candy store."

"Did you tell Pastor Adams I was going to preach next Sunday?"

"Who's going to preach...oh...you? Jackson replied. Oh sure, he probably knows. Pastor is always happy when he's got God's disciples stepping up to the plate in his absence, you should already know that Minister Roberts!"

"That's good news."

"That's good what?" A stifling pause followed, but not before
Minister Robert's face turned from medium brown to red.

"I'm going to tell you again, young man. If it's coming from God, it's the message. If it's coming from man, you'll find it in the church bulletin or on the 6 o'clock news. Now, for the last time, which one are you more focused on Minister Roberts?"

"The message sir, the message of course... and sir, exactly what is Kyle's assignment for ordination, may I ask?"

Minister Roberts posed the question hastily, further signifying his ignorance of Mt. Tabernacle's long standing church convention. Truthfully, he was too low on the spiritual ladder to ask it in any fashion. Pastor Jackson was alarmed, for so over-protective of Kyle and distrusting of Roberts was he, that Roberts merely uttering Kyle's name equated him with a jewel thief.

"What did you ask me boy?"

"I said, what is Kyle Medley's spiritual assignment for ordination?"

"That's what I thought. You just hold on a minute boy, cause this ain't Boston."

"Meaning, sir?"

"Meaning certain things we just don't discuss with everybody and you ought to know by now that a man's spiritual assignment at Mt. Tab is one of them. What were they teaching y'all up there in Boston, anyhow?" Minister Roberts looked downward, like a puppy dog being chastised, and the phone fell quiet until Jackson again spoke.

"But then again, on the same token, you could play a role in his success. And if—and only if you will, then you might deserve to know, so maybe...maybe...just in this circumstance I'll tell you anyway."

"Anything I can do to help the brother build his bridge right," Roberts replied, "so please, go ahead."

"It's really simple. Kyle is a fine Christian man 'wit' a long family history of serving and fellowship at Mt. Tabernacle." Pastor Jackson's fondness for Kyle made Roberts more determined to hide his annoyance.

"We've seen the calling he has in him for a long time now, and we just been waiting for him to see it. You know, sometimes you can be too close to something to really see it."

"Yeah, I know—but I thought I was getting close to you," pastor.

"What?"

"Nothing, nothing Pastor Jackson, let's forget it. Please continue."

"I heard that," Jackson muttered. "Well barring any new orders from the pastor upon his return—Kyle simply has to keep those men going in the right direction up until Men's Day Weekend. I picked that assignment for him, you know. Then he's going to give his ordination sermon. After that, Lord willing, he'll be following in his grandfathers and great-grandfathers footsteps. You know it was a pity that his father didn't pastor the church, he sure deserved to, but sometimes things happen when a man lets politics get in the way of his religion…but anyhow, now that we're talking bout that—you planning on conducting yoself ' right with Kyle and those men of Manpower right?"

"Oh, most certainly pastor!"

"Good, then I'm sure you'll do all you can to 'hep' him if he needs it, right?" The deafening silence in the line spoke louder than words.

"Isn't that right?" Pastor Jackson's words echoed again to Minister Roberts once more.

"Of course I'll do my best to help if he needs it, Pastor Jackson, you know that. But he's very proud you know, so I don't think he'll ask…"

"Proud my… I don't think I've ever seen a prideful spirit or bone in that young man's body since I've known him—and I've known him from whence he was a little boy, so maybe you can just hep' him before he even ask. And while you doing it I think you might want to search 'yoself' and yo' spirit too. It somehow sounds a lot like bad news, and not too brotherly."

"I'm sorry, what I meant to say is… Minister Roberts uttered after regrouping, but Jackson cut him off before he could finish.

"Now, you have a blessed night," 'click', went the phone in Minister Robert's ear before he could clean up his revealing banter.

"I'll just be," Minister Roberts fumed—terribly upset that Pastor Jackson seemed to see right through him, particularly at a time when he thought he could convince the old man of most anything.

"What's wrong Beau, you alright?" Etta asked from across the room as she sat up on the couch. Minister Roberts hung up the phone and looked over to her, as if he'd forgotten she was there, because he had. He now noticed that her red skirt was now halfway up her thigh, revealing two shapely legs full of the scars, bumps, and bruises that only an upbringing of life in the ghetto provided women of her caliber, he figured. He was unaware and unconcerned that those marks came from years of sexual abuse by her own uncle.

"It'll be okay Etta," he said.

"No, it won't. Its church business, aint' it? I can tell. When you 'gonna' take me to church wittchu' like you promised, I can help you, you know. You don't think I know how to act around them church folks, but you'd be surprised cause' I do." Etta waited patiently for a heartfelt reaction from Elgin Roberts that was not forthcoming. Feeling bitter with each passing second she gathered her pride and flung her next words like a dagger towards him.

"Every man needs a woman Elgin, especially a 'wannabe' minister like you."
Minister Roberts stared stoically, his eyes growing larger with alarm at the very notion of her going to church with him, a proposal he offered only lately, upon her urging at that, yet one he never truly considered. He dismissed her attack on his pastoral aspirations as easily as he dismissed her.

"Etta, let's go to the bedroom now, okay sweetie? We can always talk about this later." Elgin Roberts walked over to her slowly, all the while looking about her body while carefully avoiding a direct glance in her eyes. He stroked and massaged her arm in hopes of getting her aroused.

"Let go of my hand Elgin," Etta softly told him, but she was never adamant about anything, so Elgin Roberts continued until the tears appeared on her cheeks. She then abruptly shouted. "Get your hands off of me, right now. They feel like a spider. They don't feel like a man who really cares for me like he should...and they never did." He looked intently at the marks on her body for the first time as she sobbed. Unaware that the hideous marks were put there by an uncle who sexually abused her at a young age, he dismissed them to ghetto living. Exiting the room, he grabbed his Bible, turned on his gospel music, and pranced about the floor to practice yet another mock sermon which he dreamed would culminate in being his greatest yet.

TWENTY FOUR

Friday, June 9
8:15 A.M. Peachtree Motors
Atlanta, Ga.

Today would be like few others. I could feel it before opening the service department doors and stepping under the banners and multi colored balloons lining every room. Peachtree Motors had experienced solid growth for the last few years, but nothing compared to the euphoria of the sales manager's announcement that Afro Business Magazine's recent call. They'd informed us that last year's sales figures had placed our company in the top 100 minority dealers in the nation. My steps were deliberate even though I attempted to appear nonchalant while strolling toward Bianca's office. By now, everyone figured we were becoming an item, and I was hardly ashamed. The only thing is when this happens on the job site, the devil gets particularly busy. With lies and truths about Ed swirling, I decided that the devil was busy enough. Rounding the corner I came upon Bianca's office. She was sitting down with her back turned to me, neatly organizing her desk with no knowledge of my presence. An appreciation of the beauty that the Lord made came over me as I paused to marvel at her glistening skin and hair before speaking.

"Good morning Miss Kincaid."

"Kyle, it's you! And good morning to the handsome man of the cloth," she said as she whirled around in the swivel chair, grinning. "How was your day yesterday? I didn't see you after church, and I noticed you didn't call me. Not that I'm complaining mind you. It's just like you to call."

"Well, quite often I have to spend some time with the Word, and with the preparation of a sermon, and with an ailing and obnoxious father. Not to mention a group of men who are finding newfound fame singing for the Lord. But I thought about you hard enough though. I'd kind of be surprised if you told me you couldn't feel it." Bianca blushed like a schoolgirl, her lips glistening before revealing her signature white smile.

"Just listen to you," Bianca replied. "I feel telephone calls Mister Medley, not game. That sounds like game. And you know the last thing the world needs is another preacher with game. So boy, you better watch yourself, because I think you just might have it."

"Naw, I'm just calling it as I see it. You should know that by now."

"I was starting to feel that before you got too cute," she said as she stopped her paper shuffling long enough to look me sincerely in my eyes. It lasted only a moment, but the glance was genuine enough to pacify me. It was also potent enough to make her change the gears of her conversation, as was her way I noticed whenever she caught herself conveying too much affection towards me.

"But we are at work," she responded. "Hey, how's your truck? I thought I heard a little noise when you left the other night. Is everything all right?" she asked.

"Ohh, it's just fine," I said. "I, uh—I just had to swerve a little bit to keep from hitting a stray dog in the road you know? It's just my luck to scrape a water hydrant when I did."

"I see," she said as she turned her head and started giggling while trying not to look me in the face. "I wonder who the owner was for that little animal. They should have had a leash on their puppy, don't you think?" Bianca was now staring down to the floor, still trying not to laugh.

"It was fully grown, by the way," I confirmed.

"Oh I'm sure," she replied while doing her best to adjust her demeanor. Embarrassed, I had no more to say about the matter. Some things are better left unsaid when our mouths begin to take certain paths. Out of nowhere, Ed Tyson approached us.

"Adam and Eve, what's up? You know there's a catered luncheon the owners are having in our honor at 12:00 sharp. So don't you two start eloping so fast you forget," he warned. "And Kyle, I heard there's going to be a special acknowledgement for you too."

"Okay, Ed, we'll be there." He turned to walk off but suddenly halted.

"Excuse me, B3, I mean…Bianca, but Kyle, can I holler at you over here for just a second?" he asked.

"Sure thing, excuse me Bianca." Bianca shook her head as I walked toward Ed, making certain he caught her guarded glance in light of his mischievous comment. Without a doubt he was the one person who could make her squirm.

"Watch out Ed before you start some trouble man, now what is it?"

"I just wanted to say….I wanted to tell you that joining Mt. Tab and the Manpower Choir has been one of the most gratifying things I've ever done, man. I mean, I think it's even starting to change me for the good."

"Really Ed…how so?"

"Well, I had a hot buyer for that used van. You know, the one you guys over in the service department told me was a piece of junk."

"You mean the nicely painted red van with the horrible engine and slipping transmission that came through here two weeks ago, right?"

"Yeah, that's the one. A contractor was ready to give me $7,000 cash for it. He said it was just what he needed for his small business, and that sale was just what I needed for a fat commission. I was just that close to taking it too!" he exclaimed, as his voice rose.

"So what stopped you?" Wait, let me guess. You could hear the Holy Spirit speaking to you, I trust, right?" I asked, trying to pinch hit for him, and bring him to a spiritual home plate.

"Yeah…I think. I really think I could Kyle."

"Amen, Amen…"

"And also, I could also hear Nora's voice in my head. You know, the fine new aspiring minister y'all met a couple of weeks ago. She was telling me that our courtship is over, since the guy I had hustled was her father." He looked at me seriously as he spoke, and I naturally found it more troubling than if he were joking.

"Well, did you hustle her father Ed? Is this a bad dream or is this the truth?"

"I wouldn't call it hustling," Ed responded, "and I'm not really sure it was her father, you know?"

"No I don't know Ed. You never got DNA I see, but is this allegation true is the question?"

"What do you mean?"

"What on green earth have you done, Ed?" He looked at me as if he were trying to tell me, but stopped short.

"Hey, I better get to work now. You both are coming to the luncheon aren't you?"

"Of course we'll be there. I'm excited for this company Ed—you know that—but I'm even more excited for your spiritual walk." He appeared to blush before walking off as quickly as he came. "I mean it Ed," I told him as he walked away.

"Wow, what a heart." Bianca sighed sarcastically. "By the way, does anybody other than that Music Minister of yours not like you?"

"The devil doesn't, and he can be a formidable foe. Just look, he's even got his grip on you by having you all up in my private conversation."

"What do you mean 'all up in it'?" she replied. "When Ed Tyson gets loud and says he was that close to taking something, I think the whole world's ears ought to be on alert."

"Yeah, okay, maybe you have a point. But the Lord is working on him, I can tell these things. It might take a minute or two, sometimes weeks, but I can often see it in a man."

"Really? How so?"

"Because I see it in me, and I know what to look for, lets call it a sixth sense. I just know the Lord is working on him. Anyway, I'll look to see you later at the luncheon okay?"

"Okay Kyle, I'll be in your corner when they honor you," she said. We smiled eye to eye as I looked to see if the coast were clear before reaching for a kiss on her cheek. I was ill prepared for what followed.

"Oh no sir, Momma told me that you don't get your honey where you make your money. Now you sir, make your money over here, while I make my money over there." She pulled her cheek away from me and pointing to my work area. "What's gotten into you anyway? You must be caught up in too many ribbons flying around here this morning, partner." I was becoming as embarrassed as I was entertained, and gathered myself quickly before firmly asserting to her.

"Oh, you can bet I'm fine, just fine. Now, why don't you just share with me what else yo' Momma told you?"

"Alright, I will. She also told me not to bring my personal drama to work. That if I have it, to give it to Him, and any part of it that I'm not wise enough to give to Him, to at least leave it at home." Wow, I thought. She did have two very valid points. What was I thinking?

"You're right, I was being unprofessional, I'm sorry. Look, I better get to work, right over there, right now." Feeling humbled, I pointed in the direction of the service area to show where I intended to go park myself. But as I turned around Bianca grabbed me by the arm and pulled me close to her. Looking around first like a sentry protecting a castle, she planted a soft and succulent kiss on my lips after noticing the coast was clear.

"There, right there. Now don't you go confusing that with honey," she whispered.

I spent a moment savoring the taste of her moist lips as if I were a starved peasant encountering his first luscious meal. Sure it was sin and I was lusting in the flesh, but I was content to leave it to the Gods to do the math on this one.

"If that wasn't honey, then what was it?" I asked in a whisper. Still speaking low she cooed.

"Let's just call it inspiration. Look, you have an admirable spirit young man. I just don't want to kill it, alright? Watching you walk away like a sad pup simply made me think I might, alright?"

"A sad pup?"

"Yeah, a sad pup—not to be confused with the full grown dog you almost hit the other night when you ran into that water hydrant."

"Oh, so you saw that, huh? Well I guess you didn't even see that big dog," I said in macho rebuttal as she coyly smiled. "See you at lunch Bianca," and each and every time my spirit feels low.

180

TWENTY FIVE

Friday, June 9
10:16 A.M.

Today at Peachtree Motors grew more festive for everyone with a pulse. The smell of catered chicken and salmon steaks filled the sales showroom while the Customer Service department was flanked with several red, black, and green banners inscribed with "Welcome Afro Business Magazine." They hovered above an assortment of delicious cakes touting smart, car shaped designs, and together they made the new cars come to a new life of their own.

The white Escalade with the spinning wheels rolled up slowly to the service department. Its driver stepped out of it and was instantly greeted with a professional courtesy which already went above and beyond the call of duty.

"How can we help you today sir?" I eagerly asked him, as he was still several steps before approaching. I normally didn't work the front intake counter, but I greeted the nattily dressed man in the yellow silk shirt with white roses on it anyway. Instead of responding, his eyes gazed around the bay areas of the service department, and then peered through the glass door that led to the sales office, almost as if nothing were ever said to him.

"Again, can I help you, sir?"

"Yeah, I'd like an oil change, and give me your 12 point inspection while you're at it. That ought to take a few minutes, won't it?" Donald asked, as if he wanted the procedure to take more time.

"Only about thirty minutes," I said. "Let me get some information on you and your vehicle and..."

"I don't like a lot of paperwork, alright? How bout I just give you $50.00 cash for the oil change, okay? You can just keep the change."

"We don't do business like that, sir. I'll forego the paperwork since it's just an oil change, but I'll give you your change back. It'll be $35.00, and you can pay when we're done. You want to give me the keys and just have a seat in the waiting room?"

"Alright, here are the keys," Donald said. "Your waiting room looks a little small though."

"There's a lot more room in the sales lobby you know, and you can help yourself to some food and cake while you're in there if you like. We're celebrating being named to the top 100 black auto dealers in the country today. We'll have a luncheon shortly, and by the way, I'm Kyle, the service manager." I held out my hand for him to shake. He looked puzzled before reluctantly grasping my hand and shaking it like a jellyfish.

"That's good for you folks I guess, huh Kyle?" He said before dropping my hand with more enthusiasm than he shook it. I think I'll go inside and look at your new sports cars. By the way, I hope you all got some new models because that big Escalade isn't sleek enough for me anymore, you know?" Before I could reply, he tossed me the keys, turned around and eagerly walked into the sales lobby.

"Arrogant joker," I muttered. "What does it profit a man to gain the world, and lose his soul?" My curiosity for some reason began to get the best of me. Where is this joker from? I wondered as I walked toward the rear of the vehicle. My eyes then searched his rear plate to see if it offered any clue. I knew it wasn't Georgia, even if he lived here now. Michigan, The Great Lakes," it read.

Friday June 9, 2007
10:55 A.M.

Don approached the sales floor with a swagger closely resembling a predator in the forest about to capture his prey. He gazed at the first two offices on the right side of the showroom and saw they were empty. They must hold sales meetings in that room, with their chairs neatly positioned on both sides of the rich, walnut desk. Bianca likely wouldn't be there because she mistrusted glib tongues. She always did. It was fine by him too, at least until the day she realized Donald had the glibbest tongue of all, and fell out of love with him. Reflecting on the days she used to hang onto his every word he found his confidence waning. Where will the magic come from now? It certainly wasn't in the air. No, the magic was now replaced by the indignation of trying to find her—uninvited at that. He turned his attention to the new two-seat sports car in the showroom. He ran his index finger along the top of the maroon convertible. As he did, he reminisced about the boyhood gifts his mother showered upon him when she sensed he felt alone. Unfortunately the sentiment was granted the solitude given to anyone fixated on a showroom vehicle. It didn't take long for Ed Tyson to observe his trance and approach him.

"It goes smoothly from 0- 60 in ten seconds and is loaded with options, like a navigation system and 5 disc CD changer. The best part is that it doesn't have half the price tag of a Porsche. Ed Tyson is my name."

"Donald is mine, good to meet you."

"I've got a blue one parked right outside. Would you like to take a quick spin?"

Donald scanned the nattily dressed Ed Tyson well before answering. The prospect of taking the convertible from 0 to 60 m.p.h. into the cool spring air was intriguing. Maybe a whirlwind of fresh air would rejuvenate his thoughts. Maybe, just maybe, it would infuse him with the sweet talking words to say in his mission to win Bianca back. At the very least it might restore needed vigor to a predator that had suddenly lost it upon finally encountering the cave of his prey.

"It's tempting. I've wanted to drive this one for quite some time now. But I'm going to wait."

"Wait? Wait for what man? It was weight that broke the wagon player. This car here has got your name on it. I know, because I move them all the time. You are sleek and cut, this car is sleek and cut. Nothing to wait for other than the price tag to go up, you know."

"Maybe another time Ed, right now I'm looking for somebody."

"Is it another salesman?" Ed asked, trying to hide the frantic emotion behind his question.

"No, it's not a salesman."

"You must be from the magazine then. Are you from Afro Business Magazine?"

"That's right, I am from Afro Business. How did you guess?"

"Just a feeling, that's all. As the top selling car salesman here at Peachtree Motors I size people up quickly, you know. Of course we're all a team here, and I'm only telling you that just in case it's worth something to your article."

"It may be valuable at that. But tell me, Bianca Kincaid. She is a part of your team here also isn't she?"

"Bianca?" Ed paused a moment, a bit surprised. "B3? Yeah, she is a member of our team alright. A very lovely member at that...but she processes financial paperwork, why in the..."

"The whole is never greater than the sum of its parts, Ed. You're a smart guy, one would think you knew that." Ed retreated with a few ounces of the new-found humility he'd only recently stumbled upon.

"That's true," he said as he began to silently think. And God must have sent you here to talk to her and test me at the same time. "Kyle told me I would be tested more often now—while trying to embrace the Lord—than ever before. To think I'm just realizing it's not all about me now, wow. Of course it's about Bianca too. Just goes to show you." Let me take you to Bianca's office. It's this way."

The two men walked down to the end of the huge sales lobby, bypassing the colorful new vehicles, the food and the huge ornamental banners on their way. As they turned toward the smaller corridor, Ed naturally broke the silence.

"You probably want to meet Kyle Medley, our service manager too, right?"

"For what?"

"For what?" Ed echoed with disbelief as Don sensed surprise.

"That's the guy who's changing my oil right? I've already met him—we talked."

"Then you know he's a good man, a deeply spiritual man who keeps us all balanced around here too," Ed said.

"No I didn't, but maybe he can balance my tires while he's doing all that balancing," Donald replied.

184

Ed cocked his head sideways, peering at the man incredulously while they walked several feet beyond the restrooms and cubicle sized offices. He decided to dismiss the comment as he slowed down and pointed at the nondescript office on the left, just a few feet before their approach.

"It's right up here, the third opening on the left," he pointed out. "I can't wait until we see the look in her eyes when I tell her Afro Business Magazine wants to interview her. I better warn you first, and let you know that she's a gorgeous woman. I mean fine! Ya'll might want to skip the interview and just put her on your next cover. I can see it now, 'Peachtree Motors sales are off the chart with a new B3 model!' No joke, I'd bet that edition would sell out."

"What's a B3 model?" Donald spoke sincerely, clearly not amused. "Listen Ed, I think it's best for me to approach her alone, okay? Just like I approached you and Kyle alone and got your insights, I want to approach Bianca the same way, know what I mean? Now thanks for leading me over here, but I'll just take it from here. Why don't you go back up front and wait patiently until I call you for that test drive. Maybe I'll buy the convertible from you soon, fully loaded, alright?"

"No problem man, sounds like a deal, we only need to know your favorite color before we do the paperwork," Ed said, giving thumbs up to Donald before he headed back to the sales floor. Ed felt happy to do a good deed for someone while also counting his next commission check in advance.

"And get that case of hyperactive disorder checked while you're at it," Don muttered as Ed walked away.

Don turned his attention to the office without the door and crept closer to peer inside. As he approached, he noticed her back turned to him as she sat in the chair, her hairstyle nicely done only much simpler than in times past. Hoping to get a whiff of the exotic perfume she always wore, he quietly stepped a few feet closer, only finding his sense of smell displaced by the sound of papers shuffling while gospel music played from the small radio on her desk. Bianca worked diligently while singing verses reminiscent of the songs she sang as they rode around the parks of Detroit.

185

"You know it's silly to run from Don Morton, and even more foolish to hide."
Bianca heard the voice she had by now associated with Satan himself and instinctively whirled around in the chair, dropping the finance package to the floor and grabbing her chest frantically at the same time.

"Don't be surprised baby, you had to know I was coming. And there's no reason to fear because I'm not here to harm a hair on your head. Here, let me pick these up for you." He knelt down and neatly scraped the white forms back in the yellow envelope right after they spilled like dominoes upon the floor. Donald was always neat and organized with detail and paperwork, she thought. Too bad he could never see himself as a legitimate businessman.

"What do you want Donald?"

"What do I want? Well, first I want to say hello. It's really good to see you. You look more beautiful now than ever before. What do I want?" he repeated. "It would be nice if you to told me you're glad to see me too." Still kneeling on one knee he handed the envelope back to her while looking for an invitation that never came. Bianca gathered herself, composed yet silent as she received it, and determined to not offer any sign of negotiation.

"Enough. What do you really want Donald?" she flatly asked.

"I just want to talk to you Bianca. There's a lot that's been eating at me since you left, and so much I've wanted to say. That's not to mention the things I wish I could take back. It's hard to find the right place to begin, but I've got an idea. Let's go to lunch. I passed a couple of four star restaurants on the way that looked like the kind of spots you would like."

"I don't yearn to eat at four star restaurants anymore, Donald, I'm sorry."

"So it's five star only now, huh? Okay, not a problem, I can handle that."

"No, you don't understand. I have no doubt you can handle it Donald. Listen, we're having a big luncheon here today, and I really..."

"I know, Afro Business Magazine is here."

"How did you know?"

"I met Ed a little while ago, him and a grease monkey named Kyle too. He's changing the oil in the SUV and ought to be done any minute now."

Bianca's eyes instantly squinted with scorn and Donald didn't fail to notice.

"Listen, I must be getting too close to you too soon. I'll just step back during the picture taking. Come and join me afterward for a test drive of that new convertible on the floor, okay?" So help me God knows that won't happen. The last thing I want is for Kyle to see us together. That's out of the question. Test drive huh, well let me test drive you're a-- right out of here.

"Better yet, I'm getting a little hungry. Maybe I can think of the name of this restaurant I saw on Piedmont Road. Let's see, what was the name of that restaurant? Oh forget it, you probably know of better ones. Well, it's 11:20. Just tell me where you want to go and we can be there by noon."

"I don't know if I should leave the job that early, but maybe if..."

"If what baby? Tell me."

"Listen, would you just leave now and promise not to return to my job again, Donald?" Donald was taken back by the remark, but remained cool. He'd known this task wouldn't be easy but just how hard was anyone's guess.

"Actually, I do remember the name of the place now, but there's no need to get testy about it, sweetheart. Join me now for lunch and I'll leave your job completely alone, deal?"

"That sounds like a deal, and I hope you'll stick to it." Bianca said.

"I gave you my word, now I'll go get the SUV and we'll meet out front in say, ten minutes?"

"Ten minutes it is, but you can follow me in my car, now please, go. We'll eat wherever you like, but go," she insisted and paused for a moment to weigh her fears against her hopes before speaking further.

"And by the way Donald, I'm not going to run from you this time."

"Say what?'

"You heard me. This place I work, wherever I live, if you hadn't found that out too, they're both off limits to you unless you're invited. You've been successful at finding my job I see, but push me—threaten me like you did before—and I'll have a protection order served on you that may lead to questions of how you are living." I'll trust you and all ten or so of your identities can also be found in one place, she thought, but she was also wise enough to know she'd said enough and there was no reason to outright provoke him. "Do you understand me?"

"Yes. Yes I understand, now would you just stop? Stop saying that. I'm not here to hurt you dear," Donald repeated emphatically, but it was too late. It didn't matter what his intentions were. Her defiance and her wrath were traits he always dreaded envisioning the day she stopped loving him, and that day appeared to be now. Donald stared at her intently as she checked her watch. In just a few minutes the luncheon would start, and she wouldn't be there. She wouldn't be at Kyle's side when the company introductions were made either. Nor would she be there to beam up at him when he'd lead the company in prayer over the bread they were about to break, or when Afro Business Magazine profiled him—and she'd have to convince him to stop running from the limelight and learn to accept a little recognition for a change. Worst of all, she wouldn't be there when Kyle just looked for her to be there. But this was for a purpose, and if the situation were handled right she would rid herself of Donald without Kyle's help.

"What did you say?" she asked in response to hearing him mutter.

"I said I'm not here to hurt you." Donald stood in the room looking humbled, like a disobedient child in fear of a spanking. Bianca sensed it and displayed no mercy as she barked her last order to him like a drill sergeant speaking to a fresh recruit.

"Pull your truck to the side door there, not to the front of the building as you suggested, and prepare to follow me."

"Okay Bianca," was all he could say before he retreated to the service area to pick up his car from the man he now thought of only as 'that grease monkey'. Just then the phone rang and she looked at the caller ID. It was Kyle, but she couldn't answer. She knew he anticipated seeing her now, and though he was worth knowing more than a lie to explain her absence, he deserved far less than the truth. No, for now the call would have to go to her voicemail until she figured out exactly what to tell him. Heaven help me, she moaned until the phone finally stopped ringing.

TWENTY SIX

Donald tried following her through the parking lot as closely as he could until she found a space. Realizing he had to settle for a parking spot some nine or ten spaces away from hers, he hit the steering wheel in frustration. Making matters worse, Bianca's steps were as quick as any pace he'd ever seen her employ as she exited the car and headed for the front door. He'd soon discover her desire to end the date was even more immediate.

"Allow me to get that for you baby," he said, nearly winded after running to catch up to her as she reached for the door handle of the elegant Japanese restaurant. In earlier times she never would have attempted to open that door herself, but instead given him the honor of being a gentleman. Now she slightly tilted her head sideways, bored and unimpressed, as Donald grabbed the large ornamental handles affixed to the heavy wooden door and flung it open. They walked inside with the shared intimacy of two oppositely dressed strangers at a Halloween costume party, and Donald quickly decided he could tolerate no more of it.

"Hey Bianca, this dimly lit room holds the same ambiance of some of the places we used to visit, don't you think?"

"I guess it does," she replied, recalling with boredom how she'd introduced him to the word 'ambiance' years ago when despite his money he'd never known what it meant.

"You guess it does?" he repeated.

"Well yeah, I figured you'd like it."

"I see."

"Hello, you both dine inside or on patio?" asked the Japanese hostess upon her sudden approach.

"We don't have much time, so I think a booth right over there will do," Bianca said as she pointed to the non-descript wooden tables in the room's corner, but Donald had already fixed his eyes on the beautiful setting of tropical trees and waterfalls that decked the outdoor patio, and cast a small frown away from her as if to display only minor dissatisfaction with her choice.

"I'm in no hurry," he confirmed.

"But I am. I have a job I need to get back to," she retorted.

"I see...Very well. Then let's at least compromise."

"Compromise what?" she asked, looking puzzled.

"I'm only saying, since we only have time for lunch, let's at least do lunch right, that's all I'm saying."

"Meaning?"

"Meaning I'd prefer a setting that's quiet and romantic. Let's do the patio out there, alright?" Bianca looked over to the outdoor patio she'd already noticed before his suggestion. A year ago that setting would have excited her enough to draw Donald's attention to it before he had a chance to notice. Though still in love with water falls, her new found affections for Kyle now caused her to view it with the same excitement as finding available storage space in a basement. She did manage to maintain a good measure of diplomacy, however, knowing she couldn't fake it by attempting to contrive emotions of the old self that had nearly vanished.

"Good choice Donald. It does look like it some of those same diners."

"Very nice, you both enjoy," the hostess replied.

"Yeah, we both enjoy," Bianca muttered as they both walked briskly behind the hostess before settling into a chair that Donald so charmingly pulled out. Still trying to act normal she took a seat, placed her purse on the table and feigned relaxation as the waitress arrived.

"Iced tea for the lady for starters, and me, I'll have water to drink," Donald confirmed while Bianca smiled pleasantly towards her.

"Now this is the way we always rolled," he began. "Lovely day, lovely atmosphere, and now I finally get to see your lovely face again too. Bianca, I can't even pretend. I've really missed you." Dead silence filled the air in place of her anticipated reply. It wasn't a major problem though, since Donald had already decided he wouldn't easily give in to the awkwardness of the moment.

"Listen Bianca, dear, I know I've made a couple of mistakes, I'll admit...but."

"The best of us sometimes do, Donald...but here comes the waitress." Donald was used to being in control, but now looked dumbfounded as another waitress arrived with their drinks and flipped open the menus.

"I bet their grilled salmon and sushi combo is delicious. As I recall, it's your favorite, right Donald? You want to try it? It'll be my treat," she offered.

"Sure, I'll try it, but you don't have to pay. I'll cover it, and whatever you like as well."

"Hello, you both decide what you like to order?" the Asian waitress managed in limited English.

"Let me see...egg rolls along with the egg drop soup will suit me just fine," she said. And I think he's having the grilled salmon and sushi combo."

"Very good, that all, she asked?"

"Yes, that's all, thank you," Bianca said.

"Oh come on Bianca, why aren't you eating?" Donald asked as she walked off.

"I'm really not that hungry, and besides..."

"Besides what?"

"Listen, I know you're about to get sentimental with me, and I understand. We had some great times together, but everybody comes in your life for a reason or for a season."

"Go on."

"No, that's okay, forget it."

"No, please continue," he insisted.

"Well, the time we spent engaged, going to Bishop Searcy's church...I really began to learn the Word for what felt like the first time in my life."

"And you're saying?"

"I'm saying it meant something to me Donald. It meant a lot. The spirit fed me there, even when I didn't know I was hungry, and..."

"I know, I know. Let's just stop right there," Donald begged soothingly, hoping she'd stop, but she wasn't finished.

"And I can't believe I was naïve enough to believe that God, or anything higher than a bogusly earned dollar bill, was feeding you!"

"Now wait a minute Bianca."

192

"And Bishop Searcy was like a father to me, and like a father to you too."

Her voice started breaking as she was becoming emotionally vulnerable, a position she vowed she would never allow Donald or those bad memories to visit her to again. She regrouped nearly as instantly as she fell apart, though. It was a tough trait Donald had always admired in her, namely because it mirrored the inner city Detroit toughness he likened to himself.

"I'm going to the restroom to wash my hands," Bianca said as she abruptly left the table. She hoped Donald didn't see her eyes beginning to water, and in her haste she left her purse behind on the table.

Donald was initially baffled that she'd become so emotional, but wise enough to realize just how devastating her last encounter with him must have been. Maybe I can talk her into coming back home. Come back, get engaged again, and rejoin the church they loved, or better yet, get married here in Atlanta and bring her back as Mrs. Donald Morton. But how, he wondered. Unlike being eight months removed from each other, it seemed more like eight years. The only plan he could think of was to take it slow, for given her emotional state, he had no plan.

Donald looked across the table at her purse and noticed it to be a simple, far cheaper version of the suede Gucci purses he'd purchased for her in times past. Why didn't she still take them with her everywhere she went and above all, where was his ring? Nothing about this scenario was making any sense but he didn't want to mention it. It would be too confrontational, he reasoned. He unconsciously took his index finger and began to slide it across the side of the purse, then slowly made his way around the top and over the church program sticking out of it. A church program, huh? He looked up, hoping she hadn't turned around. What if she looked back and caught him roaming around her purse on her trip to the restroom? He tried not to think about it, but was instantly reminded of the way she conducted herself on their dates in the past. Whenever she excused herself from the table, when walking away she would always turn around and flash that smile. That smile alone spoke volumes, assuring him that if she ever did leave him, she would never leave for long. This time, she never turned around. He now hoped she would delay her return while he continued to run his fingers about it. Shunning embarrassment he took the program out and began to read it:

Mt. Tabernacle Baptist Church, located at 1547 Peachtree Plains Dr. in Stone Mountain, Ga. welcomes all to our Men's Day Celebration Weekend, Sunday, June 17, 2006. The Men's Choir— strong men of God will be featured. Come one, come all, and come as you are, for the hospital is for the sick as the church is for the sinner.

"Hmm, how interesting," he thought. Donald removed his wallet quickly from his hip pocket and took out a random piece of paper. Retrieving a pen from his shirt pocket he began to write down all the pertinent information. Just before finishing he heard the door close from the women's restroom and all of a sudden her face peered across the room at him as if her eyes were taking a final picture. No time to put the program back without her noticing, he thought. He instead firmly placed it underneath his left leg on the seat while casually placing his wallet and pen in his right pants pocket without notice.

"Hope you're feeling better. Is everything okay?" he asked upon her return.

"I'll be alright Donald, she said as the waitress served them their dishes. Donald prayed over and blessed their plates similar to the way he'd always done and then some, and Bianca began eating before he could even say 'Amen'. Donald suggested a familiar topic to strike up a conversation as if he hadn't noticed.

"You know I still have season tickets for our old basketball champs baby."

"I know. I liked their center though, and Detroit traded him," she replied. Surprised at her response, he slowly chewed his food before saying another word.

"It doesn't matter, because I still have season tickets for pro football too."

"Yeah, but they traded the quarterback."

"Okay, so what?"

"So they were both good players, and now they're gone.

"It's been years since that trade...Well, what about the Fox Theatre? Nothing is like the Fox, you love the Fox...and Belle Isle, come on, I know you miss them. You can't tell me you don't miss the Fox, and that view we love from Belle Isle Park?"

"Got a Fox Theatre right here in Atlanta just as nice, and Stone Mountain Park is pretty too."

"Yeah, but it's not Belle Isle and you know it," came his frustrated reply. "I don't understand. Why are you acting like this baby? Come home."

Donald, I must be leaving now. I don't think there's anything more we need to discuss?"

"Oh yes there is, maybe not now, but there are things to discuss," he confirmed. I see you'll need a little time to get used to the idea of 'us' again though, so I won't force it."

"There's nothing to force. I'm sure you'll find somebody else to go to all of those romantic and fun places with you again, but it won't be me. Goodbye Donald. I can walk myself out, and remember our deal. You will not be coming to my job."

"That's right. I won't come to your job again. I'll honor that, so help me." Bianca took forty dollars from her purse and placed it on the table.

"Good, thank you, and I won't be needing your money again either," she promised. "As I said, this meal is on me. Have a safe drive back to Detroit, Donald," she said as she briskly walked away.

TWENTY SEVEN

Friday June 9
7:15 A.M.
Atlanta, Ga.

Charles Nix caught the train to the West End station, transferred to the bus line, and was now walking three blocks toward the single one bedroom apartment building which showcased dirty off white bricks and too many cracked windows about its exterior. So much of his life had fallen apart since he smoked his first vial of crack cocaine. Looking at the bright side of things was all he could do. The gospel songs he'd learned in the prison choir brought him solace and peace when the lights went out. The songs he was now learning in the choir fortified him more and brought pure joy while making it through the day. All of the songs helped him cope with his troubled past and the deceptive promise of what used to be his future, and he began to sing one of his favorites as he walked.

"It's in my heart to serve my Lawd.

"It's in my bones to serve my Lawd.

"I'm telling you that I'll be serving the Lawd.

A broad smile suddenly appeared on his face aimed at nobody in particular. Charles was overcome with the song's simple yet pure meaning. The smile grew even wider when he recalled a recent choir rehearsal. On this particular night Kyle had insisted to Minister Roberts that the word 'Lord' be replaced with the sound of 'Lard'—that is, if we were going to sing the song right. Minister Roberts was livid, deeming the suggestion too phonetically radical and country. Charles attributed it to Roberts upper class Boston roots and dismissed it while silently wondering where black people like him really came from anyway. Walking onward into the night he smiled further, for like a lost tribesman he realized he embraced the same 'ole time religion' ways of Kyle and the rest. His spirit was virtually all he had. Gone were his expensive health club memberships of the past, and due to his long stay at the Atlanta Penitentiary, they were almost forgotten. Gone also was his license to practice pharmacy. The full time job at the car wash would have to do for now. His second job as the night janitor for the soul food restaurant was a blessing, but gone also was the restful sleep he used to enjoy. Still, he gratefully counted his blessings while moving closer to his apartment. The third floor stairs leading to his unit were sometimes a hurdle for many to negotiate, but his thirty six years had been kind to him as he opened the door he trotted up a flight of steps. Not even winded, thanks to prison conditioning, he slowed for a moment upon hearing a heated argument between two men across the hallway. They sounded like they were fighting over liquor. Once upon a time in his professional life he would have been appalled to hear such chaos anywhere near the $350,000 home he shared with Francine and the children. Now, he savored the fact that unlike prison he didn't have to see them, and gladly turned the key to the door and locked it behind him.

Stepping inside his apartment unit, he neatly took his car wash uniform out of the bag and folded it for tomorrows wash. He untied his shoes, discarded his pants and shirt, and instinctively looked at a picture of his girls. Brianna and Chastity were now aged 12 and 13 and Charles Jr., was going on 15. They were beautiful now. They were even more beautiful ten years prior when they believed he was superman, and nothing, but nothing could take away his cape or his power to love and protect them. Francine had sent the picture to him recently. On the surface it seemed like a thoughtful gesture, but like any surface there was more to it. He checked the alarm clock. It was 10:25 a.m. Time to run the shower, take a nap, and prepare for his 4:00pm shift at the car wash. Slumbering to the shower he cut the hot water on high and the cold on low, not because he was so meticulous about that temperature mix but because the water system was as cheaply calibrated as the dwelling that housed it. Slowly he stepped inside the shower, and as the lukewarm water cascaded down upon him he began to enjoy one of the few things in life he could firmly control. At least until three minutes passed and he heard the phone ring. Who could be calling this early on Monday morning? What nerve. Don't they know it's my bedtime? He amused himself with these questions as much as anybody who had few friends could before his curiosity prompted him to jump out of the shower. Grabbing a towel he hurriedly wiped his feet and legs before rushing to answer it, still dripping wet.

"Hello, this is Charles."

"Daddy, Daddy, its Chat."

"Chastity? My Chat—Chat. How's Daddy's big girl, and why aren't you in school today?"

"I'm sick Daddy, I've got a cold, and I miss you Daddy. Mommy said I could stay home from school and I begged her to let me call you just this once though. She said that if you have an extra $500.00 to give her then you could pick me up and take me with you today."

"Your Mommy said that?"

"Uh-huh.... I miss you so Daddy."

"I miss you too baby. Where's your mother Chastity?"

"I'm right here," Francine blared over on the party line, "hang up Chastity."

"No Mommy."

"Why does she have to hang up?" Charles asked.

"I said hang up now Chastity!" Francine was now yelling and Chastity's voice now disappeared.

"All that money you robbed from those banks for over two years, and all you can send me is $400.00 a month?" Francine screamed in her most agitated voice.

"Francine you know I would send you more money if I had it, but I keep telling you I don't. It's been six months since I've been out, and not letting me see the kids is hurting them as much as it's hurting me…, besides, you make…"

"Don't worry about how much money I make. I've got the news article right here.

"Gentleman Bandit throws dye pack back at teller after politely requesting she not insert the dye pack in the bag. Dye pack explodes in her face as 'The Gentleman" nets off with $20,000 dollars."

"Are you saying it's not true?"

"I do recall asking her not to put the dye in, but there was never half that much money..." Charles replied loudly before lowering his voice. It didn't matter because she cut him off again.

"Oh, and I suppose you didn't throw that dye pack back in her face either huh, Mr. Gentleman?"

"Yes I did," Charles said calmly, "but there was never more than $1,800 dollars in that bag. The banks lied!"

"Oh really, and why would the bank lie on a gentleman, is all I want to know?"

"Probably to get more insurance claims than they deserved, I guess... hell, I don't know why...but they lied!" Charles became fueled with the kind of anger and rage that only the devil in the form of Francine could generate.

"Yeah...right. Maybe I should show this article to your precious little babies who think you're all 'that' Charles."

"Please don't do that Francine."

"Bye the way, it sounds like you're used to the price jumping up on you, so be over here in two hours with $1,000.00, or don't bother to see these kids for another six months."

"But I pay child support. I've got rights, Francine."

"You've got a right to get served with a temporary restraining order the next time you threaten me and my children."

"But I've never threatened you, what are you talking about?" he asked innocently.

"I'll give you till 1:00 o'clock, and then I'm going downtown to the courthouse to get the order, that is of course after I show Chastity the article about her sweet Dada," (click)!

Charles looked at the phone with a mixture of disbelief, rage, and sadness rolled into one. It didn't matter to Francine that he was telling the truth. She could well guess that he didn't have a dime more than the $64.38 he kept beneath his mattress, either. He could feel his blood boiling as he paced the floor. Time in prison had made him accustomed to sacrifice, discipline and routine, and those traits had served him well on the outside so far. But his emotions had been as guarded as the jail cell that guarded society from him. He resigned himself to the fact that nobody — not even some his fellow prisoners who teased him when calling him the chemical bandito—could work him like Francine. How does she do it?" He began to wonder aloud.

"With God's help he'd beaten a crack addiction. He'd even traded a 'Buppie' lifestyle for two small time jobs and a monthly bus pass. Where he lived, the way he now dressed, and a fraction of the money he once splurged was now used to make it from paycheck to paycheck. Of course, none of it mattered, for Francine could use every tool in the book to work him like a fiddle.

The children were reduced to human tools, used to drive him crazy and send his emotionality through the roof. That's why she sent the pictures, and it worked. He missed them terribly, and of all the things he had given up, Brianna, Chastity, and Charles Jr. were non-negotiable. He turned the shower up as hot as he could stand it while scrubbing his body down. If he was going to entertain the devil then at least he would be acclimated to the climate, he reasoned. Wiping himself dry he walked over to the closet. Enough of this! Sliding the thin, wooden door to the left, he turned to the one suit, one white shirt, and single black bowtie in the closet. He put the suit on slowly, as if he were about to attend a lavish dinner party. Like an old ritual he patted the miniature Bible on the right side pocket to insure it was still there. He often read the big one on the night stand, and had forgotten he had put the small Bible in the same spot he used to keep it because it carried a trademark he wanted to forget. But they were both still there. The small painted gun was still fitted neatly in the left pocket, exactly the way he had placed it six months ago upon his release, but only as a memento to his past life. He wanted to pray, but reasoned God had nothing to do with his future steps and declined. He then put the thick, fake mustache over his mouth, grabbed his keys, and hurried out the door. Glancing up at the door where the argument over liquor had ensued just an hour earlier, he now heard nothing but silence. He wondered if the men had stopped fussing after fighting to their deaths, or had they merely grown quiet with pity after the thin walls revealed his dilemma with Francine. He was resigned to not pity himself even if they thought the latter while moving briskly down the steps. Checking his watch he noted the time was 8:05 a.m. Perfect, he reasoned, as his impending actions would soon bring him the needed money to reunite him with his girls.

After a twenty minute train ride, Charles Nix found himself casing the outside of First Peachtree National Bank. All of his senses were keenly alive. First, he noticed local traffic was far busier than mornings of years past. No policemen or guards were anywhere in sight, and the bank had been open just over ten minutes. He casually walked inside and over to the narrow desk and began to fill out a deposit coupon. As he did, he painfully avoided speaking to everyone in earshot, even though as a gentleman it had always been his custom. Entering the line he grew slightly nervous. Where have my nerves of steel gone, he wondered? Maybe the nerves were still there. Of course, they were just numbed while his mind was high when 'The Gentleman' first called on the banks years ago. The teller finished serving a customer at her window and smiled as everyone in line moved inches closer. Charles waited. The wait for this moment years ago was always accompanied with random, foggy ideas, an impulsive mood, and a demented sense of euphoria. He now waited with a cleaner mind and purer heart than the man who rode this devilish slide backwards just years ago.

"It's in my heart to serve the Lard, I'll be serving the Lard," he quietly lamented.

The next teller had dismissed her customer and moved him to the front of the line. Wow, what a song, what a meaning, what a responsibility… what on earth am I doing?

"Next customer!" The young black female to his far left smiled as she spoke to him. But Charles didn't move. He couldn't. Beads of sweat that had popped up on his face now trickled down his neck and into his white shirt collar.

"Next customer, she repeated?"

"Young man, they are talking to you, you know," echoed the voice of the elderly man of 75 plus years. He cast a huge smile when Charles turned to look behind him.

"Of course you can step aside if you're blessed with enough money and need me to go ahead of you now, son. I've got a little money to get, but I can't wait on you too long, because I just don't have your kind of time." The old man chuckled at his own words as he spoke, and suddenly Charles wondered if there was anyone that innocent in his midst prior to a robbery.

201

He nodded at him in distant fashion and walked over to the young lady. Looking back he could still see the old man smiling at him while leaning on his cane. Walking coolly towards her he noticed the small silver cross she wore over her gray knitted sweater. Her wrists were thin, like she was, and he surmised that she must be no more than 21 years old and a day. *One must pay attention to everything when robbing a bank,* he thought.

"Good morning. Can I have a withdrawal slip?"

"You certainly can sir," she said with a most chipper grin. "And good morning to you also," she said, and just like that it was a beautiful day in the neighborhood—for her.

Charles began to write when he peered to his right and noticed the old man still looking at him, even as he was being called to the next window. Somehow, another thing caught his attention about the place, something a blind man could see. *Angels were in it.* They were in the teller's beauty and in her innocence. They resided in the old man who, like ultimate destiny, saw something in him. They were in the faith that he couldn't see manifested in the spirit of this old man whose words flowed with the wisdom that only too few could hear. What's more, the song planted in his head wouldn't leave, it couldn't.

"I'll be serving 'the Lord' he repeated over and over until finally understanding Minister Roberts point for not changing its pronunciation. It had a real spiritual meaning associated with it, unlike the phrase used by newly freed slaves to accentuate their Negro kinship. Besides, right now he needed 'the Lord' more than 'the Lawd', a nice sounding term true enough, yet still more akin to a stick of butter. Nope, Charles reasoned he needed 'The Lord 'now! He began to write on the slip of paper as he looked up at her.

"Excuse me. I know this seems a bit odd, but do you have a cell phone?" Charles asked.

"I do, but it's not customary for tellers to hand out their personal cell phone to customers," she replied, and Charles politely ignored her.

"And while you read this note," he said, "would you mind taking this for me also? Please don't be alarmed."

TWENTY EIGHT

Friday, June 9
1:30 P.M. Peachtree Motors

Festivities were cranking up well this morning at Peachtree Motors. Between the pictures taken and the fun and laughter shared between the magazine staff, employees, and patrons, the atmosphere took on the tone of a New Years Eve celebration. Jocelyn Waters, the dealerships single black female owner, was introducing and heaping praise and gratitude upon every soul in the company thus far except for me, and this suited me just fine.

"And I think I'd be remiss if I failed to introduce our service manager and the man who's responsible for so many customers who happily come and go, Mr. Kyle Medley."

Clapping hands and whistles abounded for several seconds until Jocelyn hushed the forty-seven employees down.

"In some ways he's our accountant as well," she continued, "since he's forever making sure that we here at Peachtree Motors keep count of our blessings too!"

"Amen to that—God Bless him—that's right—a good man—please don't let him sing," came more voices from the crowd.

Pleased, yet embarrassed, my eyes scanned the small crowd while smiling in appreciation. Reversing my glances in anticipation of seeing Bianca proved futile as she was nowhere to be found however. *Hmm, that's strange, where could she be?* My attention was diverted when an unknown man wheeled two cases of champagne over to the nearest table and began to unpack them. Jocelyn glanced over at me as the majority of the crowds eyes lit up in approval. I walked over to the microphone and prepared to address them.

"Good afternoon and welcome Afro Business Magazine and all

of my Peachtree Motors family. I'd like to ask that you all gather around in a circle and then clasp hands and join me for prayer." They all huddled closely before I continued.

"In the Bible it says that you must first sow a seed before you can reap a harvest, and long before this celebration was even a vision there came a team of people who believed in treating people in a Godly fashion and doing things right the first time. Our mission has been to release the stigma of a car salesman by glorifying Him first, and through His grace we are doing just that, Amen!"

After the prayer, the majority of the crowd shook their head while contemplating the meaning of my message before promptly eyeing the champagne. I contemplated the challenge of ministering to an audience who couldn't wait to have a drink when my cell phone rang.

"Praise the Lord, this is Kyle," I answered.

"Is this Kyle Medley?" The woman's voice on the other end asked casually.

"Yes it is. Who is this?"

"This is Yvonne, the bank teller at the downtown branch of Atlanta Trust. I'm calling on behalf of Charles Nix. He's down here at the bank asking for some help."

"Help? What kind of help?"

"Well, I noticed he was behaving oddly while standing in line, but that was no big deal. It was when he walked up to my window when someone seemed to recognize him and shouted 'The Gentleman Bandit is in the bank. I've seen this guy before and he's going to rob us.' "As soon as she said this about ten customers came out with their cell phones and started snapping his picture. Strangely enough, he had handed me a note to call you before everything even happened."

"Really? I wonder why he didn't bother to call me himself?"

"I don't know, but I have a feeling it's for a good reason. You know, possibly something deeper than just a guy thing, but anyway, he wants you to come down here and pick him up. I think you better hurry." While speaking to me Yvonne was coolly tucking a toy gun Charles had given her moments ago—with the note—in her purse. Casually snapping the strap she maintained our phone conversation as if she were only tucking in her car keys.

"Let me talk to him," I said.

"Okay, here he is."

"Charles, is that you brother?"

"Yes it's me, Brother Medley."

"What the...never mind, I'm on my way."

As soon as he hung up his cell phone he heard the many greetings well enough to tell that someone special had just entered the room — and then the distinctive voice.

"Kyle? Hey, is everything alright?"

"Yes. Everything is just fine, Bianca. Good to see you finally made it back, but I have to go make a run."

"A run? A run where? Is everything alright? I'm going with you. You're taking me with you, aren't you?"

"I don't think you want to go where I'm going, Bianca. Besides, you've already missed half of the celebration going on here." I hoped she'd share what had suddenly kept her from being in her office for half the morning, but I quickly realized no explanation was forthcoming. Jocelyn then walked up to us and tapped me on the shoulder as Bianca took a couple of steps back.

"I just wanted to thank you for the lovely prayer, Kyle. It was very timely."

"You're welcome Jocelyn. Listen, would you mind if I took the rest of the afternoon off? I know how important this event is but, I...I have to run an errand."

"Of course, take the rest of the day — with pay," she replied.

Bianca had completely turned her head by the time I glanced back over to her. If there was ever a time when it appeared she was uncomfortable with even the appearance of an inter-office relationship, it was now, while in front of Jocelyn. As much as Bianca knew Jocelyn liked her, she still retreated a few steps further as she spoke.

"May I ask why you are being so coy Bianca? Everybody knows you two have a vibe that's on and popping, okay? Now, all I want to know is are you going with him or not, because the both of you look like two fish out of water without the other. Besides, neither one of you drinks alcohol, so there really isn't much for two workaholics to do around a bunch of alcoholics, so relax. Now are you joining him or not." Bianca appeared a little embarrassed, having no idea until now that Jocelyn or anyone else really knew there was more than a pure friendship between us.

She warmly returned the broad smile that Jocelyn cast her way. It was a smile of relief and appreciation that, at least to Jocelyn, she didn't have to hide what was obvious to those who have ever really been fond of someone in a special way. Jocelyn's attitude reinforced the notion that in this new world, she had found one person, other than Kyle, who she trusted—a sister who cheered on her hopes of finding real love, even if she hadn't.

"Of course I'll be joining him," she said, "and I see why so many blessings have come your way, Jocelyn," she added.

"That's funny girl, because I've been saying the same thing about you too," Jocelyn replied. "Having money to buy things is nice, but having a good man is even nicer, trust me."

"I do," she responded.

"Now half of this crowd is waiting for Kyle to leave so they can stop pretending they don't want to drink all the champagne. Now find a nice demo vehicle, say a shameless prayer for us shameless sinners, and get out of here, okay?" she said smiling.

We walked swiftly as we left the sales floor. Once outside in the new car lot I marched passed by my pick up truck and over to the giant SUV.

"Are we going to put out some kind of fire or something?" Bianca asked.

"You could say that. Look, you know I normally drive a pick up, but if you're coming with me we might need a little room."

"A little room can be a good thing." I stopped at the sleek black Denali demo with the alloy wheels.

"You like these?"

"I've sort of gotten used to that little old pick up truck of yours by now, but this will do," Bianca replied sarcastically.

"Good, hop in." I adjusted the seat and mirrors while glancing over at her. Since I'd always gone on God's missions by myself it initially seemed like an oddity for Bianca to join me. But from the very second we whisked away from that sales lot together it felt just right. Driving along I broke the silence in hopes she felt the same.

"You know of course this isn't a date."

"I don't care," she replied, "but I think a good ole fashion southern minister would get a big black Cadillac and wear a large hat if we're going on church business. A car like this falls right in line with a service manager who calls a woman late at night to pray for her car!"

"Very funny, but this is church business actually."

"Really?" Bianca asked. "Then pray tell pastor, what the people 'gonna' say 'bout' you driving around in a big luxury sedan wit' all dey' hard earned money lika' this?"

"They ain't going to say anything I hope. They're going to see their pastor is doing all he can to spiritually uplift them in every way, and they'll probably buy it for me."

"That's a good answer," she said before changing her tone. "And you'll take it right?"

"Probably not...I'll just turn it down and tell them that my pickup is running just fine, and then give it right back." Bianca smirked and shook her head as her teasing subsided.

"Hmm, now I can see that. I don't know why, but I can definitely see that."

"Oh yeah, nobody's going to say Pastor Kyle Medley is pimping his congregation."

"You want to bet?"

"You're right, let's take this back and get something less showy."

"Pastor to be Medley, don't you dare turn around. You're going to drive us around in one nice car on at least one nice day before I scream, okay?"

"Okay, okay I hear you," I chuckled before turning the dial to the AM radio news talk channel just in time to hear the tail end of the announcement.

"And if you're traveling downtown near city hall right now all we have to say is 'don't go there.' The police are detaining some guy they once called "The Gentleman Bandit" in connection with an attempted armed robbery. News crews are everywhere." The other announcer then offered his take on the situation.

"They once had a song about that guy didn't they? I remember it now."

Chucky Nix with the dapper kicks,
Robbed banks to help supply a fix,
One too many times carried in his toy six
Now he's doing 8-10 up there in the sticks

"Wow, that's too bad. Some guys just never learn," the announcer lamented.

"Do you know him Kyle?" she asked.   She didn't ask me that.

"Those AM stations just talk way too much for me. And they're biased, too. We have a couple of tunnels ahead so I'm switching this to FM.

"Is that...Isn't he one of the new members in the choir?" Bianca asked. I paused for a moment, still reluctant to answer. Defending Charles past could be as brutal as defending my own.

"Yeah, that's him, but I don't recall ever introducing you two. How'd you know his name?"

Moments of silence elapsed as I looked over to Bianca, but she was now silent, even after catching my glance.

"You want to tell me what's got your tongue, or do I have to watch this on the mystery channel?" After Bianca didn't respond I pleaded with her, "Oh come on now."

"Alright...alright...I didn't want to tell you."

"Tell me what," I asked? "Why aren't you talking?"

"Because I don't want to seem petty," she answered.   "But, on the other hand, you might want to know what many of the people at Mt. Tabernacle are saying Kyle, and you don't have to listen that hard to hear them either."

"Go ahead."

"They say Charles Nix is, or was a bank robber."

"Is, or was, which one is it? Alright, no need to wonder. He used to rob banks, but he's served his time and repented."

"Hey, I'm just the messenger; remember you asked me, alright? Anyway, they're still wondering if it's right that he be in the choir, singing to the rest of us."

"Ah, that's foolish. He's a good man. How are they going to judge him, whoever they are?" The gentleman bandit my...let me change this station to some gospel music or something. By the way, you can tell me if you'd like me to drop you home first, cause it just so happens that we're riding over to the bank right now to get him, and you might not want to get your hands too dirty. Think about it, what will the people say?"

"If you don't stop it," Bianca replied, clearly not amused. "I'm here with you, okay? I don't mind. After all, this is what you've chosen to do."

"Maybe that's it. Yeah, it's what I've chosen to do, and given what a strange day this has been, I'm kind of wondering what you've chosen to do."

"What do you mean?" Are you mad at me for telling you? Now that makes a lot of sense, just shoot the messenger, right?" Bianca exclaimed.

"That's not it. At least, not all of 'it' anyway," I sighed.

"I have an idea. Suppose you just start with "it", and then we'll move to the rest of 'it'. Either way, tell me what you're talking about."

"Alright, I will. Early this morning, I was in the service department—alone, just straitening up some things, when this strange, cocky kind of guy comes walking in. He appeared to be looking for someone, and he just so happened to be from Michigan. And then you took a banker's kind of lunch. I just had a funny feeling about it, that's all, and basically, what I'm asking is....is there something I need to know?" Silence filled the front cabin as Bianca paused, pondering her words carefully before speaking.

"Yeah, there's something you need to know, Kyle." I put my elbow on the armrest and coolly peered at her, trying to look inside of her.

"Okay, I'm here. Tell me. Tell me right now what I need to know."

"Are you sure you can handle it?"

"Oh I'm sure alright, just go ahead."

"You need to know that this is just one reason why I don't date my co-workers. It can get way too messy. Secondly, shall I continue?"

"Go ahead if you must."

"In spite of these convictions I remain drawn to your friendship now, more than ever. In essence, I'm right here too—with you that is—if you want me to be."

Bianca grabbed my hand as we approached the stop light. I tried to look her in the eyes, but this time I was blinded by the honey on her glistening lips. I placed the SUV in park since the light seemed to stay red forever, then I leaned over towards her. Her head remained stiff, almost frozen, as I softly kissed her lips. They were every bit as tender as I'd imagined, with her tongue sweeter than the taste of fresh watermelon. Before either one of us realized it, the sound of car horns began to blare behind us.

"They've got a lot of nerve, interrupting us like that." I blurted.

"Let's just drive Denzel," Bianca quipped. "We're both in the wrong, on many levels at that."

"You're right. A minister shouldn't hold up traffic kissing a woman in the middle of the street and looking like he's in Training Day or something."

"A single minister kissing a woman at that," Bianca countered.

"You're right. I see your point. A single minister shouldn't kiss 'his woman' in the middle of the street."

"Stop being silly now Kyle," Bianca replied with a smile. "You know that's not what I mean."

"I know, but maybe…maybe it might be a good idea if we both stop worrying about how things look sometimes. Especially since they're not always what they seem."

"Agreed," said Bianca.

"I put the SUV in gear and turned the radio back up as I pulled off from the light.

Snarling traffic engulfed us as we approached the First Peachtree National Bank on Mitchell Street. Three police cars lined the left side of the street, while news crews from several major television stations lined the right. Dozens of nosy bystanders added to the hoopla by gathering about and gossiping while trying to get a peak at what all the fuss was about.

"For God's sake, what a mess," I said. "Listen baby, I want you to stay in the car and wait until I come out."

"Yes sir." Bianca replied.

I jumped out the SUV and scurried past the crowd as I headed to the front door of the bank.

"Sir, you can't come in here right now. Look closely and you can see this bank is temporarily closed," the policeman barked.

"Just who are you, anyway?"

"I'm Kyle. Kyle Medley, and I'm here to pick up Mr. Nix," I stated.

"Certainly, we've got orders to let you come in Mr. Medley, follow me."

The officer unlocked the door and led me through the bank lobby and inside the branch manager's office where Charles sat. Immediately his eyes lit up when he saw me.

"Thank goodness you're here Kyle."

"I'm glad to see you too, but not under these circumstances, man. What's going on here anyway? The branch manager eyed me up and down before walking over to us to speak.

"I'm David Baxter, the branch manager here at First Peachtree National Bank. We have a rather embarrassing situation here. By the way, are you his lawyer?"

"Don't you dare insult that man like that, you hear me?" Charles ranted. "That's the President of the Men's Gospel Choir of Mt. Tabernacle Missionary Church and soon to be it's next Minister."

"Are you kidding me?" Mr. Baxter muttered while exchanging mocking glances with the police officers who surrounded the conversation.

"Not on your life am I kidding you," Charles responded. "Besides, I haven't done anything wrong to need no lawyer. I got God representing me this time around in your bank, and its different now. I'm different now, you understand?"

"Maybe you might want to cool it down a bit Charles." I beckoned. "Please continue Mr. Baxter, now again, what's the situation here?" Mr. Baxter began to speak sheepishly.

"Mr. Medley, some of our bank customers recognized Mr. Nix when he walked in here today. Apparently they...we have never forgotten him since years ago when he achieved his....ah... notoriety, from visiting our bank. Customers alerted us and we alerted the police on the notion that Mr. Nix came in here to rob it. But it appears he was just trying to make a legitimate transaction. Needless to say, things got a little out of hand."

"So he's free to go," I asked?

"Yes he is, Mr. Medley. It appears that Mr. Nix is only guilty of his past reputation, and since it was us who jumped the gun here we thought we'd make him comfortable until you arrived—especially since he insisted on leaving the bank with a man of God. On behalf of First Peachtree we'd like to offer you both our most sincere apologies. Now if it's alright with you, we won't say anything more to the media other than the fact that this was just a case of say.... mistaken identity. I trust you both feel the same way." He extended his hand to shake to Charles, then me. I grasped his firmly, only to feel the conviction of a jellyfish in his grip. I then walked over to Charles as he eagerly jumped up and shook my hand with the firmness of vice grip pliers.

"Kyle, again I'm so glad you came man, now let's get out of here."

"Okay Brother, just slow down, I'll take you home, come on." Charles spotted the teller, 'Yvonne', and as he walked over to her, he whispered, "I'll never know how to thank you."

"You're welcome Mr. Nix," she said as she held the small golden cross up from her neck. "Actually, you already have. I heard you over there. Just keep lifting Him up, and hold on to your faith in case you ever get that feeling that brought you in here again." "I will, sister," Charles replied. Minutes later Charles and I walked out of the bank together as the news cameras resumed snapping our picture. Charles opened the front door of the SUV a little surprised to see Bianca in the back seat. "Would you like to sit up front?" he began.

"No its okay, I'm fine back here. This looks pretty serious gentlemen. Anything I can do to be of help?"

"Charles would probably like to keep this matter private Bianca, but thanks."

"I see. It's a guy thing huh? Okay, I'll stay out of it. I only hope you guys don't mind me catching it on the news along with the rest of Atlanta tonight," she quipped.
Charles and I looked at each other in dumbfounded fashion. There were more than enough news crews present for a bank that didn't want to leak a story.

"I wasn't asking to be nosy, Charles. I really would like to help if I could. Never underestimate the power of a woman, gentlemen."

"It's my kids. My ex won't let me see my kids and it's driving me crazy," Charles blurted."

"You have a right to see your kids Charles," Bianca replied.

"I know that, but who's going to tell her?"

"The police will tell her," I added.

"The police? Let me tell you about the police, man. Half the police will lock you up for nothing when they come out to your house. And don't let your lady be fine, then they'll try and punk you out and get her phone number first, and then they'll lock you up."

"Well, in that case you can get you an attorney," I said.

"An attorney, huh? Most attorneys will promise you utopia if you give them a $1,000.00 retainer, then one way or another, they'll leave you high and dry in court. Nobody cares. I work two jobs, eight days a week, just to give her $650.00 a month. Nobody cares if I see my kids or not, but let a man miss a few weeks of child support and see what happens to him."

"Unfortunately he's right Kyle," Bianca shared. I've known women who've raked a good brother or two through the coals using the system." As they finished speaking a song began to play on my cell.

Praise ye the Lord, yeah, praise ye the Lord, praise him for his mightiness….praise him in the firmament of his power.
Charles looked bewildered. "Is that your cell phone Kyle?"

"It most certainly is…praise the Lord, this is Kyle,"

"He's got gospel music on his cell phone Bianca, Charles asked?"

"He sure does, doesn't everybody?" Bianca said as I tuned them out to answer it.

"And roof- ruff to you too Brother Humphries…yeah, I heard the news about Brother Nix. It's going to be all right though. What do you mean? You're not talking about Brother Nix? Brother Terry… what about him? He did what? The casino…what were you two doing in the casino? Right, he won $20,000. Okay, well good, maybe he'll give the Lord 10%. He just wouldn't leave? What do you mean he just wouldn't leave? He lost it back. Look Stephen, I don't, and God doesn't have anything to do with that. He mortgaged his house, and that's just one reason God doesn't have nothing to do with it. You're scared he's going to do what? Wait a minute, you were there, why didn't you talk to him? And what will make him listen to me then? I'm sorry. I'm not a fireman Brother Humphries. I'm not going down to any Underground Casino to put that one out! Right, don't hold your breath...Good bye Brother Humphries." I flipped my cell phone down quickly before looking at their faces. "Why are you two looking at me like that? I'm not starting my ministry in a casino, I'm sorry."

"We aren't looking at you any particular way Kyle. Charles, are you looking at Kyle 'like that'?"

"No...not 'like that' Charles answered.

"I don't think I am either. Charles, have you tried using a sister?"

"Look, you're a sister, and you already know most sisters don't want a man with a bunch of Baby Momma drama to begin with, so they're not going out on a limb to talk to my ex."

"Kyle," Bianca began, "why don't you take Charles and I back to my car. We're going to visit his ex wife while you go to the casino."

"Are you sure Bianca? Wait a minute. I said I'm not starting my ministry in a casino."

"You didn't start your ministry in a casino, you officially started it at First Peachtree National Bank when you came to get me, so rest easy," Charles responded.

"That's true Kyle," Bianca added. "We'll make sure your tombstone will never read, 'This man started his ministry in a casino,' right Charles?"

"Absolutely, and by the way, Brother Terry likes the Blackjack tables when the slot machines aren't going his way."

"He does? And how would you know that Charles?"

"Oh, I just heard him talking about it, you know?"

"Yeah...right. Okay, I'll drop you both off. But be careful Bianca, and call me when you're done, okay? And Charles, don't let nothing happen to her."

"Like what?"

"Like if your girl goes berserk or something, whatever. Just don't let anything happen to her, alright?"

TWENTY NINE

I surveyed the scene before entering feeling like a cautious astronaut circling a foreign planet before landing. The city had voted to allow casino gambling over three years ago, and that decision brought changes. Visitors weren't the energetic teenagers and sight seeing tourist of yesteryear. They'd been replaced by older, hardened looking adults who carried a somewhat ragged and lost look on their faces. Some who weren't lost were visibly agitated or down right mad, with a hurried look on their faces. Others were cursing to themselves out loud. Conversely, many walked briskly to enter, as if attending a carnival or worlds fair.

Still plotting an approach, I decided to follow the couple holding hands together for my entry. The inadvertent tour guides lead me inside the gothic structure and toward the huge, dimly lit room. As my approach grew near my senses came alive with animated sounds and visual spectacles everywhere. Glancing about the room my eyes were first struck by the dimly lighted designs. All the workers were dressed very neatly too. If I didn't know better, I'd think I was either in heaven or on the Titanic. I moved over to the crap tables where I found several men and women gathered around, some on one knee, waiting for the dice to fall their way. Without spotting Keith Terry anywhere, I strolled about the various tables. Lets see, poker, war, that's wasn't it, no…it was blackjack Bro. Nix said. Looking at the second blackjack table my eyes quickly spotted Keith. The petite female dealer facing him had just delivered two cards to him— one showing a 7 of diamonds and the other a 3 of spades. Keith's initial wager was $200.00, and she quickly moved around the table of five. As she did, she obeyed their wishes to further hit or hold, while immediately relieving money from two whose fate it was to be in excess of 21. Moving with the quickness of a cat she was terribly efficient, making her round in less than 30 seconds before coming back to Keith. She focused on him for roughly six seconds, yet her eyes awaited his prolonged decision to hit or pass as if he'd taken hours to make up his mind. Keith agonized before nervously addressing her, obviously unsure of his decision. She showed a Queen of hearts, which didn't mean she had a heart, and a 6 of clubs, which by the looks in the player's faces she had already beat them with many of. Hands trembling, Keith placed an additional $200.00 up to the circle of the table.

"Double down"! he said half heartedly "and come on ten."

Most of the dealer's eyes at the other tables only remotely acknowledged the self inflicting wounds gamblers had endured throughout the day, but the demeanor of Keith's dealer had taken on the role of a boxing referee and a social worker. She pitifully caste her eyes on the badly beaten opponent in hopes he'd realize he'd had enough. But Keith wouldn't lick his wounds and go home.

"Are you sure you want to double this bet, sir?" Keith looked back at her, himself struck by a sympathy that most dealers would never convey

"Yes, I'm sure," he feigned.

"Alright, good luck!"

The dealer 'hit' Keith with another card, a 3 of diamonds, bringing his grand total to 13 against her 16.

"Doggone it! He exclaimed, but he had no choice. He had to hit it again, but not before the three onlookers who stood next to me began to prophesize.

"Poor sucker, he could have left with thousands, now he's down to what, about $600.00?" said one.

"He could have had twenty grand to be exact...all that money!" another lamented.

"He's a fool who needs his butt whipped," echoed another.

"No my brothers, he needs Jesus!" I shouted.

"Then Jesus better bring him an 8 wit' the other hand," another bystander barked. Keith had ignored them thus far and this would be no exception, but my comment must have seemed eerily familiar since it caused him to cock his head ever so slightly. Unfortunately, it didn't cause him to turn around and miss his wager on the next hand.

"Hit me again!"

"Okay...God luck."

She quickly delivered his fate, serving the next card in the deck to him in the form of a 9 of spades. The CPA added up the 9 with his hand in about a millisecond, about as fast as others with far less training with numbers could do. That 9 of spades brought him a grand total of 22, and just like that he was busted.

Keith looked on in agony and promptly put his head down on the table in disbelief while the dealer shook her head. Without hesitation she began confiscating over $400.00 worth of chips, one stack at a time. Keith brought his head back up while she took the last stack.

"No... no way... not this time," he countered as he violently grabbed her small wrist with his hand. This is a gimmick, a set up. You all set me up!"

The dealer, obviously used to drama, calmly and coolly looked him in the eyes before speaking. "Sir, I told you to leave this place over two hours ago, I almost begged you, but you wouldn't. Nope, instead of leaving, you go and hand the casino the deed to your house. Now, unless you want things to get worse and have your butt put in jail, I suggest you let go of my wrist, or I'm calling security."

"I can't believe I came in here, I'm sorry, lady. You're right, you told me," he stated calmly while releasing her wrist. "Are you alright?"

"I'm fine, but you need to leave before you spend your whole mortgage up in here— right now."

"You're right, it's time to leave alright," he said softly. Slowly, Keith lowered his right hand and released her wrist downward to the table, and for a few moments normalcy was restored. Seconds later the same hand rose back up above the table, this time gripping a small derringer pistol that he held to the side of his head without hesitation." The dealer was going about her routine of dealing new cards to begin another round when she abruptly noticed the scene unfolding. Her coolness had disappeared, and now her eyes popped wide open.

"Sir, what are you doing? Please...please don't do that," she screamed. Players and dealers at surrounding tables who were absorbed in their own dogfights abruptly stopped their games to catch the action, all with varied reactions.

"Please forgive me," Keith cried out in anguish." A well dressed man who happened to be one of the luckier players at his table coolly surveyed the situation and decided to comment.

"You'll blow your brains all over my nice outfit the way you're holding that pistol if you pull that trigger, and I for one won't forgive you. Just take $50.00 of my chips and put that pistol up man."

"Go ahead and let that fool kill himself," begged another. "He might as well be dead if he can't keep a dollar to his name to save his life anyway."

"Your luck just ran out at a bad time man, it'll get better next time, just remember the game's not over until you pull that trigger," the well dressed man reassured him.

"God forgive me!" Keith pleaded, and it was time for him to hear my voice again.

"He won't. It won't happen. God will never forgive you if you pull that trigger Keith." I calmly echoed. "Your soul will spend eternity in hell. This brother here won't forgive you. What's worse, your wife and your kids won't forgive you either. Not even the clean up crews they'll send to mop your brains off the floor will forgive you brother."

"I know that voice." Keith turned his body around to catch my face. Looking surprised he stared at me while lowering the gun down.

"Brother Medley! What are you doing here? I can't believe you're in here man. Are you starting a casino ministry?"

"Maybe in the future Keith. Right now, I can't believe I came in here myself, so let's go!"

"This is awful Brother Medley, I'm ashamed."

"You should be, but I'm praying I can deliver you from this, Brother Terry. Now what are you going to do?"

"He's about to go to jail for grabbing me and sneaking a weapon in the casino," the petite dealer interrupted. "They must have seen you do it on the camera floor upstairs, because I see two officers coming to arrest you over there to my left. You two better get to stepping fast."

"I think you should leave, like the lady says, Keith."

"I'd try that exit door over there to the right if I were you," she advised. I'll try to tell them I'm okay when they get here. I don't believe you wanted to hurt me or yourself. Luckily, so far you haven't, but I can't give you any guarantees, so go—now!" Keith grabbed his two remaining chips and frantically turned to me.

"I'm parked way up on the third deck, where are you Brother Medley?"

"I'm on the main floor. Go to my car, its closer. I'm driving a black SUV with alloy wheels, but don't as much as say my name again in this casino."

"Okay, okay. We better hurry."

"We? I'm not hurrying anywhere, you are. If you're not caught by the time I get there, the best I'll do is take you home." Keith scrambled away as I thanked the lady for her kindness. The goons were fast approaching, and though I was innocent of any wrong doing, I had no wish to face them either, so I turned and briskly walked away. Curiosity caused me to turn around and see her calling the officers to her table. One stopped to talk, but the other didn't. Hopefully he didn't know I was with Keith. I coolly walked out to the first floor deck the way I came in. As I approached the vehicle I heard Keith's voice as he was crouching down near the passenger door, trying to remain out of sight.

"Brother Medley, is that you? I hope that it's you."

"It's me."

"Where's your pick up truck? What did you do with the pick up truck?"

"It's at the dealer where I work, but you're not in a position to worry about where my pick up truck is are you? Just get in." I took off with Keith lying down in his seat reclined fully back. Exiting the parking structure he pulled the seat up.

"I guess you want to know why I do it, huh?"

"Only if you want to tell me," I replied before he fell silent. "Listen Keith, I'm in no mood to pull teeth out of you. For starters, I guess you got a bad habit. A disciplined CPA shouldn't have to gamble for his money, and a man of God should have the faith to know he'll receive it."

"I know it. I have a bad habit, and I need prayer brother. You know, my wife told me if I can keep a stable savings account for a year she'll let me come back home to her and the kids. Unfortunately as bad as I want to do it, I can't. I tried to quit many times. It lasted four months this time around. Four months! But that's not why gamblers like me do it. Hey, I heard that you're going to be a preacher. Is it a preacher or a pastor?

"God willing I hope to be a pastor, but why do you ask, as if you know the difference or something?"

"I think I do," Keith said.

"Oh yeah? How's that? Do they teach it to you in gambling 101? Or did you learn the difference right on the casino floor next to blackjack and poker?"

"Very funny, you got a few jokes don't you, assassin?" I quickly pulled the car over to the side of the road. Visibly agitated by his words I threw my arm behind the seat and turned to face him. "What did you call me?"

"Hey man, relax. I was playing ball over at "The House" when you were at Tech. I used to see you slamming people to the turf after you tackled them, just for the heck of it. I know about your nickname and I know about the boy you paralyzed, alright? Listen man, I'm not trying to make you feel bad, or anything like that. It just seems like you might have to be reminded that your walk in the Lord hasn't always been so straight and narrow either, alright?" I put my head down and sighed while taking the keys out of the ignition.

"I'm sorry Keith. You're right. You're so right. Go ahead man."

"As I was about to say, a preacher only needs to know how to preach a good sermon. He doesn't even have to know the Bible that well, as long as he can get folks electrified and riled up for their money. But as you and I know, a pastor should be different."

"True...you want to keep going?" I asked.

"A good preacher needs to know the Bible," Keith said, "but neither one of them are scared of money. I know because I do their taxes. A good pastor though, he needs to know God and the Bible, and just as importantly, he needs to understand why I gamble. Kyle, you care, but you don't understand." I brought my head back up with amusement after listening to his words. "Tell me why I do it Brother Medley," he continued. I paused for a moment to ponder his words before speaking.

"Keith, I can't tell you why you do it," I said. I can definitely tell you why you shouldn't do it, though. That place is the devils den. You walk in a casino and you don't see any windows for starters. It's dark, with no clocks to remind you of the time."

"That's not always a bad thing you know," Keith suggested.

"You're right, except for one thing. His Holiness doesn't want you walking in the dark, my brother. He doesn't want you getting comfortable when you and your family's livelihood are on the line. And the only people who don't need to know the time are the old and the rich, and even they need to know the signs of rapture in time. Even the people I noticed who won big don't see it's time to leave. They get free alcohol so they can get drunk and give the money right back. Sort of reminds me how the settlers offered the Indians liquor for their land.

"You may be right, except rapture's not coming to the casino."

"Look man. Rapture is coming straight through the casino, and everywhere else."

The two of us stared at each other for a few moments until Keith nodded his head and turned away. Looking out of the passenger window as the rain started falling Keith began to reflect.

"As I was about say, they do it for the rush Kyle. It's that moment when a gambler doesn't know what's on the other side of that card— or the number that's in the last roll of the dice while it's tumbling. It's just the rush. What you noticed was accurate. Sometimes the money itself is secondary. But it's that rush from wondering man."

"Is that right? I'll take your word for it, and thanks for the lesson. Still, that's what the Indians said Keith, what a rush, now look what happened to them. They went from a rush to a reservation. You keep up this gambling habit and you'll go from rush to hell, both here on earth and through eternity. You see there isn't any peace in it, even if you win, right?"

"Yeah man, yeah I know," Keith answered.

"Listen, our Men's Day celebration is next Sunday, and choir rehearsal is still this Thursday night. Now if the choir and the church do anything for your soul, I'd like you to be there Keith."

"Man that's an issue you'll have to take up with my wife."

"What's a weak answer like that supposed to mean?"

"It just means that she is the one that suggested I join the church and the choir in the first place, that's all."

"Well I can't say that I'm surprised, since I like all her suggestions so far. She wants you to save your money for the needs of your family while bringing you closer to the Him. Sounds like a good game plan to me. But please brother, give me something better than that. What do you think about it?"

"I love that church, man. I'm starting to love singing for the Lord, too, but I still haven't heard any voices from God, Kyle, if you want to know the truth." I looked at Keith feeling unsurprised by his words, yet cautioned myself from showing too much frustration with him.

"And you're not going to. You see, between the clicking sounds in that roulette wheel coupled with the sound of those slots, it's impossible to hear God. It's just not going to happen. First, you have to hear the *voice of redemption*."

"How do I hear that voice? Where will it come from?" he asked desperately.

"You'll know it," I assured him. "It'll be the voice that tells you that you're not living right, even if others think you are. It's the voice that tells you that you want to live right, even if you have to travel the straight and narrow path to do it. It's God's voice spoken through the words of the songs that we sing in our Iron sharpening Iron Men's choir, too. Take the time to think about them. Talk to him. Pray, and keep on praying in a place where he can hear you. Listen to His voice until it becomes yours. You see, everyone has their stock and trade my brother. A gambler has to wager money before winning like a saint has got to pray and show faith before he's blessed. Now you're good at putting your money down, stay with God. Learn more about the faith game and gamble on him. Do it Keith, and I promise you, you won't need to be a C.P.A. to start counting your blessings, and you'll have the contentment from hearing from him a lot." Water welled up in Keith's eyes, but pride wouldn't allow him to cry.

"I'll try a little harder man. Wow, I never thought I'd get this far gone."

"Just remember you can come home, brother." I held out my hand for Keith to shake. He reached out and grabbed it in a heartfelt way as my cell phone rang with my favorite gospel chime.

"Whatever you do Dear Lord, please don't take your song from me. Whatever you do Lord, don't take your blessings from me…"

"You got gospel music on your cell phone man? I've never seen…"

"Yes I do, doesn't everybody? But hey, we'll talk again later. Don't forget about practice this Thursday. Until then, stay out of the casino, okay? I'll be praying for you, and holding on to your gun too. Now go on, go get your ride out that parking lot and go on home. Thanks for the lesson too, I know that a rush is for real cause I feel it in my heart for Jesus."

"I'll look forward to feeling that rush one day too my brother, goodnight."

The song played again as Bianca was now calling. I hesitated to answer, opting to enjoy the value in watching the confidence in Keith's body language as he hopped out the car and turned up his collar.

"Hey man, that's my hat you have on. You could have asked me for it," I shouted.

"Let's just call it spiritual covering for the rain man. Just pawn the gun and give me the difference later. You do owe me, you know." I smiled as I thought, Lord give me wisdom in teaching and leading this black man to Christ, and finally answered the call.

"Sweetheart, how are you? Is everything okay?" I asked.

"I'd frankly be much happier if my friend didn't have to let a gospel song play eight times for all of mankind to hear before he answered the phone. Especially when he knows it's me on the other line."

"I'm so sorry. It wasn't quite like that, but I'll make that up to you anyway. How did everything go?"

"Well, Charles is on his way to the park with his wife and two kids."

"Say what? How in the world did you do that?"

"I didn't do much, other than have a long talk with her while Charles sat in the car. Through our conversation I realized she still loved Charles, she just didn't want him to have the emotional energy for anybody else."

"Poor lady," I said sarcastically. "And what about all the money she wanted?"

"Knucklehead, I'm trying to tell you, she just wanted the man."

"How do you know these things?"

"Because I'm a woman, and I know a woman."

"That's scary…really scary. Well, since you know so much, tell me. Will they live happily ever after or what?"

"I'm not sure about that. She took him through a lot, so there's a good chance that he'll reunite with his kids through her, but then dump her after finding another woman who has maternal instincts. He'll then go out and try to get custody of his kids, and if that doesn't work he'll get a cash hustle where he doesn't have to report and pay too much of his income to her for child support purposes."

"How poetic! It sounds like a really ghetto happily ever after scene."

"No, silly. I just wanted you to know how the devil works in real life. Kyle, if you're going to be a minister you'll have to stop being so naïve and understand how the devil works."

"Where have I heard this before? Okay, I hear you. Now, would you mind telling me how this all happened?"

"It's simple. After I broke the ice between them once again they asked me for a little privacy. After that they must have talked like old friends for maybe an hour while I waited in the car."

"Really, that's wonderful. I wonder what they talked about."

"Now, Kyle! You know I wasn't about to get nosey, that's none of your business."

"I'm sorry. You're right, it really isn't. I was just a little curious how it all worked out, that's all."

"I believe you're being nosey Kyle."

"In the name of the Lord I got a right to be a little nosey when it comes to my flock, alright?"

"I suppose you're right. Charles and Francine want you to know anyway, especially if you're teaching this Saturday's new members class. Are you?"

"I am, but what does New Members class have to do with it? Tell me, what's going on?"

"Okay. They both rejoiced over kicking their drug habits through faith, prayer, and discipline. Then they talked and laughed like old friends who hadn't seen each other in years.

"Really?"

"Yep, and before I knew it she'd looked him in the eyes and asked him if he could possibly forgive her for the way she's treated him."

"Wow, and what did he say?"

"He took a minute to think about it before saying he'd forgive her, but only on one condition only."

"And that condition is?"

"If she'd renew their wedding vows and never bring up the darkness of their past, then he'd forgive her.

"And then what?"

"She tearfully agreed, and told him she's prepared to follow him anywhere as he follows Christ. She wants the whole family to join the church. They're so excited that they can't wait."

"Seriously?"

"Yep, and he's hoping you're teaching Saturday's new members Bible study so you can teach them all. Isn't God good Kyle?"

"Yes sweetheart, God is so good, all the time. Now how soon will I see you again?"

"How soon would you like to see me?"

"Tonight, if possible," I said. "I know you've had to bend your ears a lot today in order to know so much about their business, so you're probably tired."

"Forget you boy, you just make sure you're teaching that class Saturday. I'll call you later."

THIRTY

Stephen Humphries didn't get the sick call until 7:00 a.m., long after he'd already departed from schedule by sorting and loaded up the freight for the other three employees of Ebony Courier before watching them leave the building. Now, at 8:22, he'd barely enough time to prepare to run the most challenging route of all, and time was of the essence as the business owner prepared to deliver the overnight mail personally. After sorting stops 1-27, he loaded it all in the eight year old mini-van that he'd recently paid cash for since he couldn't qualify for a small business loan and dashed out of the warehouse hoping to make the delivery commitment of 10:30 a.m.

After turning the ignition twice he started the engine and accelerated fast, and in a matter of seconds he was roaring past the gates of his small warehouse only to abruptly stop and jump out of the vehicle to lock them. Jumping back in the mini-van and speeding off again he noticed by chance that he was driving 55 mph in a 35 mph lane. It wasn't something he relished, but at it justified a means to an end. His brash nature and confident attitude dictated he would do whatever it took to get the job done. Stress was a mere after thought, for the spiritual neophyte dreamed of competing with the likes of the big courier companies one day, and his faith offered him the promise that he would. Joining the Mt. Tabernacle Choir recently was a perfect way of keeping him in touch with other strong men who, like him, wanted to control their own destinies too. He'd first discovered several of the men already appearing to do so, before later realizing that those that did were wise enough to understand that success was more attributed to the blessings of Christ than any tactical decision they'd made to get there.

In his haste to beat the clock, he barely slowed at the stop sign. Unfortunately, he should have stopped. The lady in the red mustang convertible had just pulled off ahead of him. She appeared to over accelerate, thus rolling through the stop sign behind her seemed harmless until suddenly a basketball bounced in front of her car with a young boy in hot pursuit of it, forcing her to violently apply her breaks in the middle of the intersection. The front bumper of Stephen's min-van plowed into the back of the mustang, creating the kind of commotion that makes everyone nearby either highly concerned or glad it simply wasn't them.

"I'll just be," Stephen shouted while hitting the steering wheel with his fist in frustration. While following the woman's car as it pulled over to the side of the road, he reminisced how just a few years ago he would have probably driven away in attempts to avoid an accident report and the fact that he was probably riding dirty. Thankful that he now lived clean, he now lamented how the incident might raise his insurance costs. The right thing to do is to pull over still, he reminded himself, and as he did, the petite young woman from Pakistan exited her car. She checked the rear of her car as he got out and checked the front of his. Surprisingly, her vehicle barely revealed a scratch, and his vehicle revealed only a minor dent in the middle. She sighed with relief upon seeing her car still intact.

"I'm sorry, are you alright?" Stephen asked. He was genuinely concerned about her health, despite the fact that his schedule was now thrown completely off and he stood no chance of profiting from many 'late' delivery packages which were now to be delivered well beyond their delivery commitment time.

"I'm fine, the lady responded with a smile. My father just bought me this car, and I'd hate for him to think somebody wrecked it, and thanks to Allah you didn't. You can hardly tell anything really ever happened."

"Well, do you feel the need to make a police report?" Stephen asked.

"No, it would be a waste of time."

"Okay, if you don't see why, then I sure don't," he rationalized, "and if you don't mind, I've got a schedule to keep, so I've got to keep it moving."

"You are a nice man. I'm okay, you go ahead now," the lady reassured him.

"Thank you. You take care now," Stephen replied as he hopped back in his van and waved goodbye to her. Driving along he let out a sigh of relief as he noticed her in the rearview mirror still waving goodbye, as if they were eternally connected for life.

"Somebody up there likes me," he muttered to himself before blowing the horn and embarking again on the job at hand.

THIRTY ONE

The name that used to make me proud at the end of the day now haunted me...Assassin! Keith said it, but he'd only been the latest to open up an old wound and pour peroxide in it. It was unfair, although disturbing me further was the fact that it had been seven years, and I could count the times on one hand that I'd called Reggie. I glanced at the telephone, but found the mail accumulated over the last couple of days to be a friendlier diversion. Mail is important, I reasoned, so I sat down at the living room table and sifted through the letters. Discovering each letter less important than the last I tossed them all them back down on the table. I then glanced back at the phone and pondered whether his phone number was still the same. How many people keep the same number for seven years anyway?

It didn't matter since I deemed it a pitiful question, one conveniently posed rather than trying to overcome a fateful flaw which lay within me. For many it would be a simple phone call to make but for me it was a huge mountain to climb. I picked up the phone and dialed the number anyway. It rang several times before someone finally picked it up, and by that time so much anxiety had built up within me that I'd run up half that mountain before he answered. A decent bit of fumbling could be heard through the receiver for several moments, and alas the raspy voice on the other end began to speak. When it did, the sounds of sandpaper rubbing bark could be heard coming from his vocal chords, giving his words a blue-collar clarity while confirming the seven year old number was indeed still the same.

"Kyle Medley. Even with caller ID, I don't believe this man," he said. Silence prevailed for some time because I was speechless, wondering what to say while falling back down the mountain.

"Is this Kyle?" he asked.

"Yes Reggie, this is me. How are you my brother?"

"I'm alright, I guess. I can use my right arm after all these years, even though not much else works."

"Praise Him...Praise Him. So all things considered, you are doing alright?" I awkwardly confirmed far more than I'd asked.

"Some days are better than others you know, but I'm still trying to adjust. I guess I'm trying to accept the things I can't change, change what I can, and simply lay here and stay pissed off when I don't know the difference. That saying does go something like that, doesn't it?"

"Actually it's 'God grant me the wisdom to'..." I started to correct him, but closed my eyes in agony at mid sentence, hoping to avoid the potential expense of being 'right'.

"Yeah, I understand, that's pretty much how it goes."

"You sure about that, or are you just patronizing me?

"Patronizing you, patronizing you how? I asked.

"You know what I mean, making me feel good while you're really blowing smoke up my ..."

"Man, oh man. Reggie, I'm so sorry for all of this, so sorry for what I did to you, you just don't know. If I had one chance to rewrite history, I'd do it. But I don't, and though I've told you I'm sorry before, I need you to forgive me, man. Truth is, I need you to say it. I've asked Our Redeemer already, but now I'm asking you." Another deadening silence filled the line before Reggie said another word.

"You know, every day I sit here motionless and think about, what if? I was so close to a young man's dream man, playing professional football, so close, and now look at me. Just take a good look at me. Heck, why am I telling you? You don't care."

"Don't say that," I begged. "Yes I do Reggie."

"No you don't. You don't even stop by to say hello from time to time. I guess you're busy though, right? Now you call me out of the blue and just up and want me to forgive you? I see, you must want that microwave forgiveness, right?"

"It's not like that at all," I said.

"Sure it is. Or better yet, maybe we should just add water and stir you some forgiveness like a quick drink, right?"

"Okay, okay. I see your point. You're right man. I haven't really called or come around. But trust me, it's not for the reasons you think. Listen, I got an idea. Do you have a relationship with God, Reggie?"

"I try to keep the faith man, if that's what you mean. In spite of wondering how he could let this happen to me, I try. Is that good enough?"

"I hate to tell you this, but I don't think so, Reggie."

"Then come and take a look at me, and then you can ask yourself if I look like a good candidate for a relationship with him to you?" He'd left me speechless before he continued.

"I'm sorry," Reggie said. "Maybe that was a little too strong."

"That's alright Reggie, I understand."

"Good. Since you went there you might need to understand it's really more of a love-hate thing, if that makes any sense to you."

"I know what you mean...I understand. But listen, I've been called into the ministry, and from time to time I teach the new members orientation and Bible study at 10:00 o'clock on Saturday mornings at Mt. Tabernacle. I'll be teaching it tomorrow, and I'd like you to come."

"The assassin, called to the ministry, darn, what's next. So that's why you want forgiveness, huh?"

"I've always wanted your forgiveness Reggie..."

"Is that right? Well, at least I know you're not doing it for the money. Tell me, why didn't you play pro? Me, I had no choice. But you, I heard you passed up a ton of money, and you didn't even work out for the teams. Rumors floated around saying you didn't even want it. Even then, nobody believed it. I didn't. "

"You may as well believe it now. I didn't want the chance to hurt anybody else, ever. I just wanted to fade from the map. Funny thing though, while trying to fade away I found something bigger than the pro's man."

"Are you for real?"

"Yes, I'm for real. I found Jesus years ago, but guilt has had me more crippled than you in a sense. That's the main reason I haven't called or stopped by. But now, it's about you. So much about me and what has held me back. Will you come out tomorrow? I can pick you up if you'd like me to."

"Alright, I'll come out, if it'll make you feel better. You can come pick me up. I'll be ready first thing in the morning, but don't try to keep me in church all day on a Saturday. I may be paralyzed, but I just ain't ready for that now. Besides, you know Tennessee is playing."

"I got you Reggie. See you at 9:00 brother," click.
I breathed a sigh of relief. I finally made the call. Feeling a little better it was now time to focus on my father, who hadn't had my attention as much as he used to lately.

"Daddy, I'm home. Hey you old coot, where you at? Daddy?" There was still no answer. Oh well, he's probably sleep.

"We're in the den, but hush up boy, will you? This girl has got my king, and I'm going to need to concentrate to get it back."

"This girl...What girl are you talking about?" Bessie Simmons is the only woman that's asked about him in over a year and we know what happened the last time she came over.

"I know what you're thinking. It isn't Bessie Simmons. You know I ran her off on accounting that she talks way too much. She'll take a man out his game because she never puts a period on a sentence, so heaven help her. This girl I got in here now, I haven't known her too long, but she doesn't seem to run her mouth at all. Her checker moves are killer lightning fast, and she's a lot more pleasing to the eye than Bessie, too."

"Oh really, now this I gotta' see. You mind if I just come on in and meet her Daddy?"

"Hold on a second." Papa Medley could be heard talking loudly on the other side of the doors. "I'm going to introduce you to my son, baby. The truth is, they just say he's mine. Sometimes I'm not so sure, know what I mean?"

"Daddy I heard that. You ain't right for that and you know it."

"Alright son. Stick your neck in for a moment, but be sure not to stay too long, alright? We're sort of enjoying having this quiet time to ourselves."

"Very funny Daddy...so be it. I'm coming through the door now."

Trying desperately to harness my curiosity, I swung the wooden doors open as nonchalantly as possible, only to find Daddy and Bianca. Both were sitting on opposite sides of the checker board, grinning from ear to ear.

"Surprise Kyle," Bianca gushed.

"Hey, this is a nice surprise."

"I'll say, it's got to be," Daddy added, "because you've never seen a lovely lady like her waiting for you to come home—shy of your mother anyway. See I know, because I've seen a couple of his past girlfriends, and I'm telling you girl..."

"Daddy, that's enough, thanks, now don't you have something to do?" Daddy looked uncharacteristically sheepish as he apologetically answered.

"Well, I've read my Bible, and watched about as much TV as anybody else could today."

"Why don't you go read that new book I bought you last week about the diabetic diet, then."

"Kyle, don't make him leave," Bianca sweetly asked.

"That's right son, don't make your old papa leave," he replied in his best tone to mimic Bianca's. "Besides, I flipped the pages of that book and didn't see no fried shrimp so I closed the thing right back up."

"Well, open it again alright, or I'll call Bessie Simmons and tell her you're lonely tonight."

"Bessie? Alright son, you win," Daddy conceded. "I know you'll do it—he is that low down to do it too, you know," he confirmed to Bianca. "Heaven help me, anything but that woman. I'll find something to do around here, trust me. Bianca, it's been such a pleasure."

"Indeed, Papa Medley. You've got quite a game, sir."

"I saved my best game, just to make you feel welcome tonight dear. But next time, you'll have to work a lot harder than that to get my king girl, understand?"

"I'm sure I will, Papa Medley."

Daddy grabbed his cane and had begun to lumber off when he stopped short to make his final announcement.

"Oh, I almost forgot. Pastor Jackson called the house tonight looking for you. Doesn't he have your cell phone number?"

"Yeah, he has it."

"That's what I thought."

"He probably wants to talk to you then Daddy. Sometimes men can carry a lot around on their heart without knowing how to get it off."

"Well, that makes sense. I don't think I'd know how to unload that much garbage if it were in my heart either."

"Yes you would Daddy, because you know the power of forgiveness, and how to give man's sins to the Lord. What did he say?"

"He just said that several people called and said they were coming to New Member's class tomorrow. He wanted to know if you'd still teach it, so he wants you to give him a call, that's all."

"That's all?"

"Oh yeah, he also asked—kind of by the way like—if that was you and one of the choir members on the TV news channel today."

"What did you tell him?"

"I told him I didn't know, but then he told me it was about a bank robbery and casino holdup or something, and then I told him no way. Ain't' no son of mine going to get caught up in no mess like that, right?"

"No way, never, you know it," I confirmed.

"I know. He's lucky the spirit kept me from cussing him out, truth be told."

"Lighten up. You don't curse anyway. He probably wants to ask you to forgive him, but is either embarrassed or doesn't know how. Remember, forgiveness heals."

"Excuse me, but how would you know?"

"What do you mean, how would I know?"

"Meaning who have you asked to forgive you lately, is all I'm asking."

"Let me see. Well, I find myself asking Momma all the time now, even though I didn't have the sense to do it when she was alive."

"Your Momma would understand son. She would, rest assured. Now why don't you come a little better than that?"

"Alright, I called Reggie tonight." Daddy's eyes instantly grew bigger.

"Reggie! You talking bout' Reggie Pittman?"

"I sure am."

"Well I'll be darn. What did he say? On second thought we can take it up later if you like, when your company is gone."

"It's okay. I'm taking him to new member's Bible study tomorrow."

"Well I'll be. You know, I'll give you a couple of points for that one. Yes I will, because that isn't anything but the Holy Spirit working. Still, don't think you're cute enough to preach the gospel to me though. Just keep me posted on how things go."

"I will. There's a spot for you tomorrow too, you know." "Like I said, just keep me posted, okay? Now, goodnight." Papa Medley labored on to his room, but not before stopping and turning around to give me a glowing look of approval. It was the same look I'd grown accustomed to seeing whenever he witnessed me applying spiritual doctrine to a situation. I attributed his silence to his unique spiritual fabric somewhat torn by his unfortunate history with the church. Though he spoke contrary to it, I interpreted those eyes to secretly convey the hope that I would one day take on the leadership of the church without the pain he saw, and on a good day that look said enough.

"Bianca, it's been a very long day, how about you and me just cuddling on the couch for a little while?" I asked her as soon as Daddy closed his door.

"You're right, it's been a long day for me too, but you've been mannish enough for one day, and I'm not cuddling on your couch. I'll let you just hold me for a little while though."

"Oh hug, hold, snuggle, tomato, tommotto', why? Just, why do women do that?"

"Do what?"

"Make things complicated when everything else is going just fine. See, that'll kill a good relationship before it starts—right there."

"Kyle. I'm sorry, but lets be fair. I believe running around all day helping your black a..., excuse me, helping you with your ministry is a bit more like minimizing your complications as opposed to starting them, don't you? I'm sorry, excuse me. I don't know where that came from," she confirmed.

"It came all the way from Detroit, as far as I can tell. But hey, you got a good point. I was only kidding baby. Thank you, black queen, for your deeds today. You didn't have to, and I can't say how thoughtful it was and how much I appreciated it. Truthfully, I was really in awe of the mere suggestion of your support, and needless to say I'm sure God loved it. I guess I'm going to be hushing my mouth and just holding you for a while tonight."

"Good, in that case, I'm all yours." Bianca replied as she walked to the couch and fell into my waiting arms. It was clear she knew the value of submission, but only when the time is right.

THIRTY TWO

Saturday, June 10
9:05 A.M.

I looked over at him as if he were a long lost friend who'd just arrived home. When he looked over to notice me, my eyes quickly darted back to the wheel. Both of us were fairly quiet throughout the ride with neither wanting to say much. Too many words between us would easily volunteer the fact that we knew so little about each other, other than our mutual tragedy, and too few words would keep us locked in a dead heat of boredom. At last, Reggie broke the silence, starting with his body language as he turned his head to peer at me with every few blocks we drove.

"You know, I don't believe this," he said subtly, before turning his head quickly away.

"Oh yeah, what's so hard to believe, Reggie?"

"I never thought I'd ever hear from you again, that's all, and if I ever saw you again, I figured it would be on cable T.V., during a pro game one Sunday afternoon. I had the channel flipped time and time again so I could just see you hit somebody and cause the fumble that would lead to your teams winning touchdown. I envisioned how I would curse you out as I watched you—with the words put together and everything—before I even saw you."

"I understand how you felt, Reggie. Like I said, that's a big reason why I turned down the offers when they called. I didn't even try out, and Atlanta still drafted me in the first round. But, I don't think God wanted me to potentially hurt someone else the way I hurt you. Now I've told you this from my heart, so what do you want from me?"

"What do I want? What do I want, you ask?"

"That's right. I mean, I've told you last night on the phone how bad I felt. I'm even telling you now and you're still talking about how bad you wanted to cuss me out. So just tell me, what do you want me to do?"

"Hey man, be for real, just let it go."

"What?"

"You heard me Kyle. You asked me and I've told you. I just want you to let it go. Your spirit seems broken worse than my spine. Listen man, I'm suppose to sound a little bitter, because that's how idle time and being disabled can train your mind to think. Wanting to cuss you out if I saw you on T.V. is one thing. Not ever wanting to see you go on and play pro football is completely another. See, one thing you gotta' realize is that I've come pretty far from the 'why me' stage of my injury."

"Really, that's surprising, but good. You mind telling me how you got there? Was it your faith? I hope I'm not being too personal."

"Naw', it ain't that personal. I'll tell you why. Truth is, I think God sets some people up who have egos the size of mine, or maybe they set their own selves up. See, very few guys were fast enough to catch me with a football, and if they did, most weren't strong enough to bring me down. But he sets a lot of guys up like me, guys who think they're going to make it big and have all the cars and all the fans and all the sex—and as soon as they do, as soon as they think they've gotten over, then bam. Something screwed up happens, and they get crippled emotionally, physically, or financially. I was one of those people, except all three things happened to me. This is just payback, that's all. I've got to pay the piper, plain and simple. It's not your fault, either. God just used you to do this. Now, you need to just let it go and move on."

"You're being way too hard on yourself Reggie. You didn't even get to dance to the music first."

"Oh yeah I did, I danced. It wasn't on the biggest stage I planned to dance on, but I danced, and I couldn't see myself ever turning the music off either, especially if it were on football Sunday, when it would be time to put my cleat in someone's face. But you, you on the other hand never had that kind of cockiness. You did what you did. You hit black and white boys alike—hard and fast, but oddly enough, before me I never saw or even heard of you trying to really hurt nobody."

"Well, your rationale is a tough one and not entirely true, but if it works for you, so be it. The thing is, you're wrong. I might have been color blind, but there was something inside of me that did want to hurt people. I haven't got over it either, at least not completely. Haven't even felt worthy enough to receive my calling to the ministry, to tell you the truth."

"That's my point. You might as well since you can't change the past. Listen, you're telling me that consciously you didn't mean to hurt me right?" I sat up in my seat a little before answering.

"No. Of course not."

"That's what I know. You didn't even give any interviews after that either, so I knew you felt guilt."

"There you go, you got it."

"But you 'wanna' know what?"

"What?"

"Guilt is bull crap, that's all it is. It don't serve no purpose, other than to let Our Maker know that we know who he is, kind of like we got his phone number in case we decide to call, that's it. And all the while we're feeling guilty we serve the devil by staying forever stuck at some place in our lives."

"Reggie, I hear you. There might even be some truth in what you're saying too, but as for me, I've decided to call, and if I want Him to hear me, I have to repent. Without remorse for my sins, I can't spiritually pass go, and you can't either."

"I've felt remorse," Reggie explained as if it were an alien emotion. "Once, when a big game was on the line, I felt it in me to take the ball to the left side of the field. I usually listened to my instincts too, but instead I faked to the left and ran straight up field. I got tackled, gaining three yards when we needed eight, and just like that, we lost the game. I felt remorse, letting my team down, but never guilt.

"If that's the best example you can give, then you definitely need prayer."

"Alright. Maybe you can pray for me. But if you're going to

let guilt beat you up, then you may need prayer more me. Listen man, you seem to know a lot about this church thing, I'll give you that, but is a little kitten a bad word to use on Saturday morning?"

"Not if you're really referring to a kitten, it's not."

"Very well then," Reggie said, "because I have to tell you the best way I know how. All of these years you've been feeling guilty and turning down the pro's, feeling guilty and not calling me or coming to see me; feeling unworthy to hear your call to the ministry ....you've been acting like a, a great...big.... Kitten, if you know what I mean." Reggie raised his head up to face me eye to eye.

"You trying to call me the name I'm thinking you're trying to call me?" I asked.

"That's right, if the shoe fits. Now, 'what are you gonna' do about it? Beat up a guy that you've already paralyzed or what?"

"No, I'm not going to beat you up Reggie."

"That's good news. Now, since you aren't, may I continue?"

"Yes, you may Reggie." "The nerve of this joker, 'may I'.... so much for breaking the ice with him— somebody's about to fall through it!"

"Now tell me," Reggie demanded.

"Tell you what?"

"What would you do if you became a minister?"

"I'll help the poor, and the sick. I'll also protect my flock, save souls, and even help you, whatever I have to do to fulfill my calling and wherever God leads me."

"Help me? Help me, did you say? Tell me, do you belong to one of Atlanta's mega churches? You know, one that's got the big congregation and big money everywhere?"

"Not exactly, see we're not quite there yet, but we're growing fast. Take a look for yourself though, because we're here." I pulled the vehicle into the parking lot and brought it to a stop. As I did, Reggie tried in vain to adjust his body and view more of the modest structure that was Mt. Tabernacle. He frowned when he did get a full view of it, and didn't try to conceal it.

"Don't judge a book by its cover now, even though we just got a new roof put on last year. We've got the best pastor and the best men's choir this side of the Mississippi."

"Yeah, yeah....that's wonderful man, just great. Y'all also got a cemetery in the back yard too, what's that all about?"

"Those are my ancestors back there, but I'll explain later. Listen Reggie, your language is one thing, but it'll also help if you brought an open mind to God's house, you know."

"Fair enough, but let's make a deal first, you release the guilt and I'll try."

"I'll think about it," I promised as I walked to the back of the big SUV and slid the wheelchair out. Wheeling it around to the passenger door I popped the lock as Reggie opened the door with his good arm. I then reached for Reggie's limp body. With all of my strength I pulled him out of the seat and placed the withered 180 pounds of him in the chair.

"Damn, I mean for goodness sake, man. You still working out or something?" Reggie asked.

"You bet." I rolled him toward the church sanctuary, lifting him and the wheelchair up and over the large curb.

"Sorry about that, but I'll shave these outdated sidewalks down if I became a Minister here. They'll accommodate the physically challenged. I'm a little embarrassed, I want you to know."

"There you go again," Reggie said mockingly. "Excuse my manners, but I'm a little embarrassed too, because I really don't give a squat about the sidewalk. Like I asked you, are you still working out?" I was caught off guard at Reggie's steadfast inquiry of my physical prowess and complete disregard for the sidewalks.

"I do a little, about four times a week to be exact."

"Good, so you still taking care of yourself, still running you mean."

"Of course. You know I've got to take care of this temple. Haven't drank alcohol to this day, never smoked either."

"Good for you. Do you want a medal or a dog biscuit?

"What did...?"

"Never mind, how fast are you in the forty?"

"I don't time myself any more, but I'm probably just under a 4.8 in the 40 yard dash now-a-days, why?"

"Release the guilt man. You're going to need to bring that down to a 4.3."

"A 4.3 for what? Oh no. No way! You can just forget about it, now come on in here to new members Bible study. You see, this is the kind of thing I gear up for these days."

"Okay, if you say so Kyle," Reggie replied casually.

We walked past the sanctuary as I opened the doors to display it to Reggie. "This is where we hold church on Sunday. Bible study is on Wednesdays. We do our Manpower's Choir rehearsal here every Thursday night at 7:30 too. Can you sing?"

"Sing. Sing for what? Nig..., please! Does this voice sound like it can sing?"

"What did you just call me? That's it! I'm wheeling you out of here. You can just sit in the car until we're done."

"Wait man, I was saying Negro, hey, what did you think I said?" Just as I turned him around, Lauren, the church administrator, walked out of her office.

"Hi Kyle, guess you're getting ready for your big day next weekend huh? Just wanted you to know I'm looking forward to the Men's Day Celebration. We've been getting a lot of calls about the choir, too. I've been referring them to Pastor Jackson. Off the record, I think he may want to talk to you. And for what it's worth, I love hearing you guys sing, and I believe in supporting our men. Also, the Gospel Network called and wants to know if you all want to give an impromptu performance tonight. I told them I'd have to ask you first. And lets see, you have a new member already waiting for you in the classroom and, hey, wait a minute. Is that? That's Reggie Pittman sitting right here isn't it?"

Reggie's head had been down since I had threatened to wheel him back to the car, but newfound attention from Lauren breathed new life into him and sparked memories from years past. His head shot up and he now cast a broad smile from ear to ear at her.

"Yes, Reggie Pittman, that would be me dear, how do you do?"

"Reggie Pittman, wow. I remember watching you play, ever since we were at Dunbar High School. Well, I was a ninth grader while you were in the eleventh, so you probably never noticed me, but I always knew who you were. And Kyle, of course everybody knew you were the star at Westview High. I went to a lot of both of your games in high school and college, and…wait a minute. I'm so sorry. I didn't realize."

Lauren looked sadly upon the two men as her heart and mind digested the gravity of their relationship. When she did, water filled her eyes, with some spilling over on her cheek.

"Welcome to Mt. Tabernacle Reggie." She then leaned over to my ear and whispered softly. "Oh Kyle, God bless you. I want you to know that I believe in the men of Manpower, no matter what anybody says." Lauren walked briskly down the hallway wiping the tears out of her eyes. As she did, Reggie proudly looked up at me.

"You see that? She remembered me. She remembered Reggie Pittman! Ain't that something? Okay man, I'm sorry, I shouldn't have said that. I'll watch my mouth for sure from now on. Just give me another chance. Hey, let's go on in. There's a chance I might like this."

"Very well then," I answered, while I replayed Lauren's last phrase in my head, "no matter what anybody says?"

"Yeah, she remembered 'ole' Reggie Pittman," he beamed. "Oh, and she remembered you too man."

"What?"

"I said she remembered you too." Reggie repeated.

"Yeah, yeah. Okay, she knows me Reggie. I'm sure she probably remembers me when I played, but we don't talk about football around here, not around me I guess."

"What kind of church is this that doesn't discuss football?" Reggie asked earnestly.

I backed him through the door of the new member's Bible study room ever so carefully, with Reggie in the wheelchair in front of me. I was quickly greeted by Bianca's warm and familiar voice before he could turn around.

"Minister Medley, would you like some help?"

"Bianca. Hey sweetheart. I'm not a minister yet, remember. Almost, but not yet."

"I see you claim what you want to claim, don't you?" I didn't answer. "Well, don't you?" I smiled and shook my head, knowing full well she was referring to me claiming her as my woman.

"Why didn't you tell me you were coming?" I asked.

"Because there's no need for a public announcement when I want to hear the Word."

While listening to Bianca I turned Reggie's wheelchair around to face her for an impending introduction. His neck was nearly ready to break from the sharp angle he'd been gawking at her thus far, and upon a full view his eyes sparked with even more life.

"I see." I replied.

"And please, do not refer to me as sweetheart while we're here in church, you should know better!"

"Sounds like you'll have to check yourself too, now that you're in church like me brother." Reggie chided.

"That's true Reggie. There are no perfect men, only God is perfect."

"Really? Reggie coolly asked. "Well, from the way you've been checking me today brother, I sure can't tell."

THIRTY THREE

"Reggie Pittman, meet Ms. Bianca Kincaid. Bianca, this is Reggie."

"It's quite a pleasure, Mr. Pittman," Bianca said, welcome to Mt. Tabernacle."

"Call me Reggie, please."

"Okay, Reggie. Minister Medley, I know we only have ten minutes before we start. Is there anything I can do to help you set up?"

"I'm okay Sister Kincaid, no...wait. On second thought, you do a great job of welcoming people and making them feel comfortable. Welcome our new class members as they come in, please?"

"Of course, Minister Medley," she beamed.

"Tell me, Bianca, how do you and Kyle know each other?" Reggie asked.

"Well, he and I happened to have met at work several months ago. I like him, as a man. I believe in him and I trust him. It's probably fair to say he's helped change my life, and we've become very good friends in Christ ever since."

"I see. That's great. Kyle does appear to be a very good man," Reggie said.

"Appears to be? Tell me, how do you know Kyle?"

"Well, Kyle and I kind of met by accident a few years back. It's fair to say he's been the vessel that has changed my life too, you see." I was diligently placing Christian handouts on the tables until Reggie's comment found me silently applauding a grace in him that surprised me.

"He thinks a little spiritual exposure might do me good," Reggie continued, "and there's a chance he might be right. But honestly, I just came to stick my toe in the water. I'm not trying to get too wet, you know?"

"That's okay too, Reggie," Bianca responded. "There are a bunch of good spiritual swimmers out there who started out with just their toe in the water." I overheard her prophetic words and naturally became excited.

"Amen to that," I shouted, "and if they're blessed, then like Jesus they'll soon be wading in that same water too," I said before singing the popular spiritual.

"Y'all let him do that around here? Can you? Are you supposed to do sing like that?" Reggie asked, appearing quite serious. Bianca cast a discerning look at Reggie, one that let him know that his comment lacked nobility. The look served its purpose well, and instantly sobered the expression on his face. Bianca turned her attention to the opening door as Charles and Francine Nix walked in arm in arm.

"Good morning you two," she warmly greeted. "We're so glad to see that you both could make it out this morning, together."

"Girl, what are you talking about?" Francine replied. "God is laying his hands on this family again, so you know I have to be here with my man."

"Alright then girl, you just go now," Bianca feigned in her best attempt to sound like the girl next door. "You both can have a seat anywhere you like. We'll be starting shortly." I beamed at my gracious hostess before greeting Charles in a manly, bear hug of a handshake. As I did I whispered in his ear.

"Man, forgiveness is next to Godliness, so you know you're my hero, right?"

"Well, I do love her, but let's just hope there isn't too much water under the bridge that I can't forget, okay? See, even though I haven't been a saint Kyle, I need to learn to forgive, and even more, to forget," he confessed to me.

"Just keep repeating that to yourself, and you'll forgive her. Years of love and faith to come will help you forget," I whispered.

"Alright, but know that you're my hero man, you and Bianca, for caring enough about a brother's plight to make a difference."

Charles greeted Reggie while joining Francine for their seats. As they did, the door opened once more, and a woman of about 5'5 walked in and abruptly stopped just two steps in her tracks. She wore a bright orange dress with a matching hat and high heeled shoes. Her orange belt gripped her small waistline, and her waistline supported a curvaceous figure that made her look much like a version of an old fashioned soft drink bottle. Her legs were shapely as well, but revealed dark marks underneath the white, fish net hosiery that failed miserably to cover them. She was ghetto sexy for sure, yet far from glamorous.

"Heys y'all," she said in a thick southern accent while waving awkwardly at everyone. "My name is Etta." Bianca sensed her awkwardness before anyone else and scurried over to greet her with a smile. As she greeted her, Etta took off the right hand of her matching white chiffon gloves and shook her hand, leaving the left glove on to clutch the small Bible she cuffed smartly in her arm.

"Is I in the right place?" Etta asked as she shook Bianca's hand many times over without letting go. "I mean, this is the new member's Bible study or church orientation and all, ain't it?"

"It sure is." Bianca replied in a heartfelt manner. She would have broken a noun or a verb, anything to make Etta more comfortable, but hoped another opportunity would present itself.

"I'm Bianca Kincaid. Welcome Etta, we're glad you could come. I guess you've met Minister Medley already." I glanced at her in a curious fashion, knowing it was the first time I'd ever laid eyes on her.

"Good morning. I'm Kyle Medley Etta and I don't remember what service I met you in before. Was it last week, or was it some time before that?" I waited for a response from her that would offer a clue, but instead of answering Etta stood mute. By now I was even more curious but I reserved my questions, not wanting to add to her further discomfort. It was too late, for Etta seemed to feel my eyes and possibly every other eye in the world upon her.

"Peoples, I really shouldn't be here at all y'all, cause' I wasn't even invited. Not really, and I's' feelin' real funny bout' this, so you nice folk scuse' me. I'm gonna' leave now, just go back home and let y'all be until..."

Etta turned around sadly. Slowly, she opened the door and walked out. Bianca looked over to me and shook her head as I nodded, knowing what she was about to do. Bianca quickly rose up and hurried out right behind Etta in hopes of catching her before she went too far. Everyone sat speechless while I excused myself to check on them. When I did, Reggie seized the opportunity to break the silence.

"I think a lot of proper talking, high society folks makes Etta feel uncomfortable. Matter of fact, I think she's so removed from the right noun or verb that she even gets uncomfortable when she uses too many of them—but that's just me, Reggie Pittman talking." As Charles and Francine consulted each other, trying to make sense of what they'd just witnessed in spite of Reggie's declaration, I walked back in the room.

"Alright, I'll leave you two alone if you wish," I called out to Bianca and Etta while closing the door back behind me. Gathering my notes and my nerves before me I addressed the class while attempting to exude all the Medley confidence I could muster.

"Somehow I thought there would be a few more people here today, but I was wrong. One thing is certain though. After today, you all can go out and tell everyone, everywhere, that they're all welcome here at Mt. Tabernacle."

Charles and Francine clapped wildly while Reggie discreetly turned his right hand over and back to suggest his indifference. Bianca returned through the doorway with her arms around Etta and they too joined in the applause while warming up to each other like sisters.

"Remember Etta, you have God's invitation to be here so you don't need anyone else's, so please feel free to have a seat."

"That's what I'm talking bout'," I followed. "If He put it on your heart to come to church, then you're in the right place, Etta." Etta took her seat, and the door opened again. This time, a black man in his early 30's walked through it. He stood about 6'3 and carried at least 290 pounds of baby fat about his body. His black leather pants and matching vest hugged his massive frame as he switched swiftly about— taking steps nearly as small as his apparent attention span. Stopping to pause, he looked about the room with one hand on his hip and his stomach poked out. He didn't speak, at least not initially, but walked briskly out the door, cracking it open and holding it with a foot that revealed the clean penny loafer shoes he wore. He looked above the door and re-inspected the room number, as if it was only him that was alarmed. Returning to the room he looked intently at me, then at Charles before asking.

"Is this the New Member's Bible study?" he asked in a voiced laced with honey suckle femininity.

"Oh, 'hell naw'!" Reggie blurted out. I looked sternly at Reggie before speaking.

"Reggie, what did you promise me? Just what was our oath regarding this house?"

Reggie cocked his head back and closed his eyes, as if he were suddenly knocked asleep. I then looked earnestly upon the man as Charles and Bianca dropped their mouths. Francine had a look of rage in her eyes, once when he stepped in and also as he left out. On the contrary, if Etta passed judgment, her face didn't show it.

"Yes, this is Mt. Tabernacle's new member's Bible study, and we're about to begin, but I don't think we've had the chance to meet. My name is Kyle, Kyle Medley. Who might you be?" Somehow I felt the man wouldn't run out the door like Etta, and thank goodness I was right.

"My name is Ramario. Ramario Raytron Baxter. Friends call me R square. Good friends call me R square to the B."

"Ramario will work just fine," I assured him. "Now tell me, where are you from? I haven't seen you here at this church before, so help me out a bit, okay?"

"Before I answer your questions, I have to know if you ask all your guests these questions."

"Fair enough," I said, until Etta interrupted me.

"They sholl' do Ramario, he asked me the same thang'. And you don't have to worry bout' notin', not even being a homosapien like you is, not if God called you're here."

"Oh honey!" Ramario gasped. "Put a lid on it, please," he begged. "Alright folks, I'm here visiting Mt. Tabernacle for the first time, okay? And in case you're wondering, I'm going to the Pride Festival down at the park this afternoon with a friend, okay?"

"You mean the Gay Pride Festival down at the park?" I asked.

"We just call it The Pride now, just The Pride."

"We see, and what are y'all so proud of?" snapped Francine.

"We're proud to be just who we are baby, free of the fish for starters!" Ramario snapped back before looking over to me. "Do you want me to answer more questions from the peanut gallery too, or am I done?"

"Now you both stop it. Just stop this right now," I ordered.

"This isn't the setting for judgment. Judgment comes when we meet The Almighty One at the gates of Heaven. But one things for sure Ramario, you come prancing in the house of God—an old fashioned church at that—dressing, talking, and walking like an abomination of his image. Now as I always say, I'm just a fruit inspector, but I'm a heck of a fruit inspector, and this is not a forum for you. This house, this room, these people, we...we are not a harvest for your type of fruit!" Ramario looked at me in an unwavering fashion before speaking again.

"Before you go any further, allow me to ask you a question preacher, fruit Inspector, or whatever you happen to be."

"Medley, the name is Kyle Medley," I said. "and your sarcasm is not appreciated."

"And your attitude is not appreciated," Ramario responded. "You don't like what you see, is that right?" he continued.

"That's an understatement. You are a mistake of nature," I told him.

"But hold on a moment. You're leaving something out aren't you?" he asked.

"Like what?" I replied.

"Like the fact that I am one of God's children, just like you and every other man who attends this church."

"Really? And....what makes you think that?" I asked.

"Because, one of your choir members—and I can't say who— says so for starters. He's the one that invited me here, by the way, and he's a gay man, just like me."

"No way," someone shouted.

"Way," Ramario confirmed. "And do you want to know what else?" I was caught off guard by the allegation as much as everyone else, and found myself trying to digest his words at half the pace in which he spewed them.

"What?" I sluggishly responded.

"God don't make any mistakes, now does he?" I sat motionless for a moment before answering. When I did speak, I chose my words carefully, speaking slowly and measuring each one while my temper flared within me.

"It is an insult, Ramario, that you bring this 'act' before this church, to one of my first Bible study lessons at that. My eyes bulged and I felt my nostrils expand as I stood up from my chair and walked towards him. Though unaware of it, I was clinching my right fist while holding the Bible in my left hand. Reggie was the only one in the room who had seen that look in my eyes before, and he cried out to me in desperation.

"Kyle don't. It ain't worth it man. Don't do it!"

"Oh, you're too late Reggie. He deserves it. Truth is, he deserves it far more than you did." Bianca looked on and held her Bible while covering her mouth. "Oh no," she whispered, and the room where peace recently abounded became filled with tension.

"Now that's a real man," Francine shouted. "Handle him, Kyle! Handle him like I wish my man would have." Charles looked at Francine sternly as she mildly recanted.

"I'm sorry baby, I shouldn't have said that. Forgive me, but someone needs to lay some heavy hands on that boy."

"Someone else needs to understand why we're here." Charles replied before Reggie yelled out from across the room.

"Kyle no, I'm begging you," Reggie pleaded. "Ramario covered his head with his hands, grimacing more with every step that brought me closer. "God, have mercy. I done walked up in the wrong place today!" he cried out.

I moved ever closer to him before stopping and staring at him for a moment, then I loudly proclaimed, "Ramario, the voice of God has commanded me to deal with you. You came in here a sinner, and though you're hardly the first, do you want to know what's worse?"

"No...What?" Ramario asked through a panicked filled voice.

"You want church folks to call you R square to the B, which is a strict violation of man law!"

"What?" Ramario asked in disbelief.

"And you know what's even worse than that? I asked.

"No I don't, but I know you gonna' tell me," he answered.

"You didn't even bring your Bible! Here, take mine. You're

going to need it if I'm going to teach you what the scripture says."

"What it says about what?" asked Ramario, halfway relieved.

"About everything," I answered, "and Reggie, stop acting like a kid in an amusement park, because you didn't bring your Bible either. Bianca, would you get another Bible for Reggie please?" Reggie let out a sigh as the door swung open with one last visitor. The stranger happened to be a slender, nattily dressed black male in his early thirties. He stopped in mid step as Bianca replied.

"Yes dear, I think we have another one in the drawer here. I'll go get it."

The stranger stood there for a moment as if frozen, but he quickly thawed out after a ten second survey revealed all he needed to know.

"And dear, would you check to see if there might be one more for me?" he asked. Hearing the familiar voice caught Bianca completely off guard. Her fingers trembled as she pulled the drawers out from the desk while searching for the Bibles. Courageously she tried to ignore the assault on her senses, but only in a blur did she observe that there were indeed two Bibles left. Grabbing them both she raised her hand up to offer one of them to Reggie, who couldn't easily get to it, while looking over to the doorway. Her worst nightmare was now confirmed. It was Donald Morton!

THIRTY FOUR

Pastor Jackson seemed happy. Happy to not only let me teach the new members class, but to also have me cut my teeth on any other pastoral function he could offer me. After all, helping me assume a pastoral role at Mt. Tabernacle made sense in several ways. For starters, the aging Minister could finally atone for the painful rift between himself and my father, Papa Medley, years ago. Another reason is that it might alleviate the rush to sanction Minister Roberts, whose musical talents he admired but whose pompous leadership he utterly distrusted. Last but not least was the fact that Pastor Adams would be tickled pink, even if he never quite said it. Still, keeping the pastoral rituals of Mt. Tabernacle consistent called for nothing ambiguous.

Every aspiring minister had to be called by God, not by man. And every one of them not only had to have an assignment, but see it through until its completion before ordination. Thus, giving me the task of keeping the Manpower Choir intact brought Pastor Jackson peaceful comfort for several reasons. The men were now the talk of the whole local church community, and my love of singing His praises came naturally, even if my vocal talents didn't. It was the easiest assignment imaginable and needed no second guessing, at least until Bessie Simmons, former female companion of Daddy's and the official church gossiper, called Pastor Jackson at home last night. He recalled the conversation as if it were a nightmare, particularly since the very second he picked up the phone, it was.

"Praise the Lord, Pastor Jackson," Bessie greeted.

"Praise the L…" he tried repeating before being cut off.

"Pastor Jackson, did you see the 6:00 o'clock news tonight? Oh I'm sorry, this is Sister Bessie Simmons," she finally acknowledged.

"No I haven't, Sister Simmons, why? What's the problem with the news?" he asked.

"Oh, the problem isn't with the news, Pastor Jackson. But you might want to brace yoself' though. Are you sitting down?"

"Sister Simmons, I'm laying down in bed. Is that good enough for you?"

"That'll do," she answered. "Now, first off, you know I don't like to gossip. And you know I don't like to be the bearer of bad news, especially if it's got anything to do with Mt. Tabernacle, now don't you Pastor?"

"Of course you don't, Sister Simmons. Now please, will you just get to the point?"

"Alright then...but since it's already all over the news it ain't really gossip, now is it?"

"Maybe not. For all practical purposes we'll say it isn't, alright?"

"Good. Well Pastor Jackson, there's a really, really big problem. And it's with the men of the Mt. Tabernacle Manpower Choir, Jesus help me."

"Jesus is with you, Sister Simmons, now go ahead."

"Well, I turn on the news today—you know I got to watch my 6:00 o'clock news on Channel 15 because they got my lottery result. I mean, they often times speak about our church community, you know, with the new property taxes and zoning issues and such."

"Of course, now would you just go on?" Pastor Jackson pleaded.

"Well, okay. I'm watching the news today and they got our own Kyle Medley, big as day, going to the First Peachtree Bank to pick up a man they think was robbing the bank. And it looks like the man they think was robbing the bank is a member of our Men's Choir too. They call him the Gentleman Bandito, yeah, The Gentleman Bandito, that's his name. He'd rob the bank in a suit and bowtie, always carrying a toy gun in one pocket and a Bible in the other."

"What you talking about now girl?"

"Wait a minute now, that ain't all. I'm not finished yet."

"Oh would you just finish then?" Pastor Jackson beckoned while sitting upright in his bed.

"Alright. I'm still watching, cause' they still hadn't posted the... you know they still hadn't talked bout the zoning issue, and the next thing I see is a picture of Kyle Medley, again. This time he was down in the casino with a man who they think was pointing a gun at a lady after losing his money. They both then ran out the door. And, I took a good look at the man he was with, and I'm almost sure that he's in the choir too! I didn't believe it. But there his picture was, again, just as big as day."

"Sister Simmons, are you positive about this? I mean, you didn't have a fit when yo' number didn't hit last night and catch a fever or anything like that, now did you girl?"

"I beg your pardon, Pastor Jackson. You and I both know that gambling is a sin."

"Yeah it is, but that don't mean...anyway, all I'm asking you is.... are you sure?"

"I'm as sure as sure can get. The only thing I'm not sure about was whether a third man I saw on the news whose' wanted by the law belongs to that choir of ours. He looked like one of the new ones though, and guesses what they accusing him of?"

"It's a little too late for guessing, so please, why don't you just tell me?" Jackson pleaded.

"Sure you don't want to guess?" she asked excitedly.

"Sister Simmons, no offense, but I really want to hang up this phone."

"Okay then. He's wanted for hit and run and leaving the scene of an accident." Just watch the news, or call Kyle and ask him where he's been today."

"It's late, and I won't do no such thang'. Besides, I think I know that boy a bit better than that. You just go on to sleep, and trust I'll get to the bottom of it, okay?"

"Well let me finish. Did you know that Kyle Medley paralyzed a boy on the football field some seven years ago? You see, most of us didn't. One thing for sure is that the news sure made everybody know it when they showed him."

"I've known that for years, but that was an accident..."

"Well, you better know it. And you better make some calls and find out what's going on right away. You see, I called most of the Deacons wives right afterward, and most of em' saw the same thing I did. And with Men's Day coming up next week, we aren't none too keen on bringing no bandits or no gamblers or no hit and run drivers or no cheap shot hitters on to represent Mt. Tab next week. And we done already told our husbands to not accept it."

"Well, I'm sorry to inform you Sister Simmons, but the Deacons don't run Mt. Tabernacle, and who is 'we'? Meaning no disrespect, but you're not even married, are you Sister Simmons?"

"You don't have to be a smart aleck now, cause I speak for the Deacon's wives whether I'm married or not, and you best remember that hell has no fury like a Deacon's wife scorned. Now God Bless you, Pastor Jackson, and good night," she said in a most polite manner before hanging up the phone.

****

Bianca stared at Don while attempting to register the sudden shock and disbelief of the moment. She clutched the two Bibles and held them closer to her bosom, while slowly turning around to face me. She then walked ever so slowly—almost deliberately toward me.

"Here. Here are the two Bibles you asked for, Minister Medley," she said while placing them in my hands. She then walked toward the new members, as if to join them, but instead turned around, looked back at Donald, and took a seat next to the desk where I now stood. Observing her sudden, pensive demeanor, I also turned toward the man in the doorway.

"Good morning. Won't you come in and join us Mr..."

"Morton. Donald Morton." Donald replied, as my eyes squinted just a bit while viewing him.

"Mr. Morton. I've heard of you. We've even met somewhere before, it was..."

"At the dealership," Donald replied.

"That's right. At Peachtree Motors, not Mt. Tabernacle, right?"

'That's right."

"So tell me, you've never been to Mt. Tabernacle?" Donald looked around, appearing only slightly uncomfortable before answering.

"That's right, I haven't."

"I didn't think so," I continued. "So, just what is your purpose for coming here today, Mr. Morton?" Donald heard the question but gave no answer. Instead, he calmly walked past the first row of chairs, as every eye in the room, especially mine, followed him. He stopped at this chair; a chair which his demeanor suggested was seemingly reserved for him. The chair happened to be placed behind a table directly across from Bianca. Ever so casually, Donald removed his designer sweater and draped it over the back of the seat. Never taking his eyes off her, he slowly, meticulously sat down. In fluid motion, he then unzipped the Bible case with the initials D.M. handsomely embroidered on it, and placed it on the table in front of him. He then crossed one leg over the other, methodically flashing his brand new two tone alligator shoes before speaking.

"Is this a courtroom or a new member's class? You see, I've joined a church before, and I didn't know a cross examination was necessary," Donald blurted defiantly.

"It isn't," I countered, "but I'm embarking on a real ministry here. It's a ministry that's founded with people who already love the Lord or people who sincerely want to get to know him."

"Then it sounds like I'm in the right place." Donald responded confidently. Now tell me, have you asked these wonderful people that same question?" Nearly everyone in the room responded almost in unison.

"He sho' did" Etta began. "Uh-hmm,' yes Lord he did too," responded Ramario.

"Yes he did," echoed Charles and Francine. Reggie flipped his good hand over again to further signify his indifference, as three more prospective members walked through the door.

"Well bless all of you if that's something you need, but I don't care to be nterrogated," Donald said.

"They were merely asked a simple question, Mr. Morton, not interrogated. But you know, as I think about it, I can now understand why you'd even use that word—interrogated." I retorted. "It must fit your lifestyle." Donald flinched at the remark and peered at Bianca, who briefly glanced back at him before lowering her head. Donald then looked back at me and frowned, while Reggie surveyed the situation and suddenly appeared very interested, again.

"Please excuse me, but we'll have to table this for later Mr. Morton. It's time to welcome our genuine and authentic new members and get them seated."

I modestly raised my voice to begin the announcement.

"On behalf of Mt. Tabernacle, I want to welcome everyone who's come out today, and I truly thank God for motivating your decision to do so. Open your Bibles to Genesis, where we'll get a good understanding of the beginning." Most Bible pages could be heard flipping briefly as I continued. "You know, I had originally planned to lead you all in a general direction of the Bible from here, but upon surveying the needs of this particular flock, I've decided to take you all where my new ministry will go. And that is to man's biblical map toward living a full gospel life while surrounded by present day, worldly temptations." All heads in the room nodded with keen interest and unified approval as I looked about them.

"I guess I'll take that extra Bible since it looks like this Morton dude already has one," Reggie suggested. I walked the Bible over to Reggie and noticed his eyes beaming with genuine gladness. Upon receiving it, Reggie desperately flipped toward the rear of the Bible in search of Genesis. Leaning over him, I helped Reggie turn to the front of the book, until we located Genesis. With my right hand placed on Reggie's shoulder, I again addressed them. "I'll ask that everyone stand and hold hands for prayer before we begin." Just as everyone stood and held hands there came more knocks on the door.

"Feel free to come right in, you're just in time for opening prayer," I yelled out. The door knob turned slowly, and the image of a large gut well hidden under a gold and red dashiki flashed in the opening before anything concrete could be seen. In no time, the rest of the person joined it as he walked in and caused my smile to dim. It was Minister Roberts! Stepping deliberately with his Bible in hand, he eerily exhibited that trademark walk, balls of his feet down first with heels suspended in air, never touching the floor. He looked over the circle of worshippers like a Roman gladiator inspecting a garrison of soldiers.

"Are you here to join us, Minister Roberts?" I asked innocently.

"Not quite, but I'm here to teach them for sure," he stated.

"What do you mean?" I asked.

"Pastor Jackson is in the business office, and he wishes to see you right away."

"You mean after I'm done with new member's class, don't you?"

"No, I'm afraid he'd like to see you right now," he confirmed.

"Now? Could it be that serious?"

"Yes, right now. He requested I temporarily relieve you."

"Relieve me? Relieve me for what?'

"He needs to address a situation with you, its urgent. I'll lead them in prayer and study until your return."

"Urgent? Sorry, everybody, but I'll be right back," I announced. By God, what could he want at a time like this? "I was going to start at Genesis 6 verses 4-8, Minister Roberts. If you'll begin there I'll probably return before you finish."

"No need for you to hurry," Minister Roberts replied, "I happen to know those passages quite well." I headed for the door, but before turning the knob, I turned around and looked at my flock. I was glad I did, for all of their faces—with the exception of Donald Morton— displayed a look suggesting they wanted me to shepherd them.

THIRTY FIVE

Saturday, 10:45 A.M.

"Come on in Kyle." Pastor Jackson had finally acknowledged me after only twelve knocks at the door. Entering the small, cluttered office for the first time I noticed the aging man holding the phone receiver close to his right ear. Rumor had it that Pastor Jackson clipped the hair out of his right ear regularly to clear a path for the auditory jungle. I don't know if that's true, but anybody close to him knew that if you wanted to have a meaningful conversation with him, it had to go through his right ear. Otherwise, he'd quickly become annoyed and patronize you for the sake of diplomacy. I fidgeted a bit while waiting for him to finish his conversation, anxious to get the meeting over with and return to what might become my new flock. In an attempt to kill time I turned my attention to the old Civil Rights photos taken during the 1960's on his wall. Daddy always said that Pastor Jackson lied about being at the great marches and demonstrations along side the great black leaders of those times, but so help me, out of over ten pictures of the most memorable events ever displayed, I couldn't recognize a younger version of Pastor Jackson's face anywhere. I still reserved judgment while I waited.

"I guess he's a good man, but frankly I don't know Pastor," Jackson said to the party on the other end of the line. "Well if he sings in the Mt. Tabernacle Men's Choir then....well.... well, what's his name again? Fred Tyson? Oh, Ed Tyson you say? Sorry, I never heard of him!" The Pastor then covered up the receiver with his hand.

"Kyle, do you know a Ed Tyson?" Why is he asking about Ed? I wondered, yet I nodded affirmatively.

"Is he a good Christian man?"

"I believe so," I said. Pastor Jackson then removed his hand and turned his full attention back toward the caller.

"You say you've heard he does what? And you buying how many? Have mercy, that's a lot of money. Well I don't know, but if you're that worried about it just don't buy anything from him. Yes, I do remember yo' daughter Nora, a beautiful red bone girl she is. Says you think she's in love wit him and you don't want to hurt her feelings huh? Well Pastor, I'm sitting here with a fine fella' that happens to work with him, and he just told me 'I betcha no', when I asked if he was a good Christian man. So, I'm going to leave that one alone and let you and the Lord work it out. Okay, I hope to see some of your flock from the Faith Hill congregation at our Men's Day Celebration service this Sunday. God Bless you too Pastor Johnson, goodbye." He hung up the phone and for the first time since I'd entered the room Pastor Jackson looked me directly in my eyes.

"Thank goodness that's over. Give me the strength!" he sighed.

"Give you the strength to do what, Pastor Jackson?" I asked. "By the way, I told you 'I believe so' when you just asked me about Ed Tyson being a good Christian man, not 'I betcha' no.'

"If you say so, son, but frankly speaking, we've got bigger fires to put out, far worse than that one, although a choir member who's a crooked car salesman and wooing the socks off the beloved daughter of the respected pastor of our sister church don't help thangs' none."

"I've seen changes in Ed Tyson from years ago to the man he is now. I believe the Holy Spirit is working on that man. But, what do you mean pastor? What bigger fires are you talking about?" My heart dropped from sensing something was terribly wrong.

"Son, I don't know where to start. Before I begin, let me see. Do you know the fancy way to pull up Friday night's news report on the computer? See, I've been watching it on T.V. since early this morning, and what I've watched—and heard about you and those men in the choir—has made this the strangest and the saddest day in my ministry. But we can't wait here all day for the news to come on again, so just tell me, do you know how to get that there 'action news' on the computer?"

"Sure. It's not hard, Pastor Jackson," I said as my mind raced to yesterday's events.

"Then do it, you can use this one here." I went to the desktop computer and pulled up Friday's Metro Times newscast.

"Where do you want me to look Pastor Jackson?"

"You can go looking for most anybody that looks familiar to you to start with, including yourself." You just might be on Me Tube," he said.

"You mean You Tube," sir.

"I said it right, cause I ain't' on nobody's tube, but you are," he confirmed.

"Me?" I looked up with surprise while scrolling down the page to the various headlines. Seeing my own face along with Brother Nix jarred me, and I immediately stopped and read the caption aloud.

Gentleman Bandit Strikes Again!

Charles Nix, alias 'The Gentleman Bandit', having stayed out of sight for several years, resurfaced at the seen of his very last bank robbery Friday morning. Ironically, he was wearing the same trademark tuxedo and bowtie that made him famous years ago. In what police believe was a heist gone bad, a man believed to be down on his luck Southern Tech star Kyle Medley, arrived to rescue and provide an alibi for him. Both men were detained several hours before their release, as police credit quick response time and alert customers with thwarting the attempt. Kyle, known as 'the Assassin', left football for good after paralyzing Reggie Pittman in an SCC title game, and rumors about his mental health have abounded over the years.

"But Pastor, this isn't true. I just went over to the bank after he called me and asked me to pick him up. He was just upset over some personal matters with his ex-wife. You see, it was all a misunderstanding....and down on what luck? I've never been better. Everybody knows the sporting community penned the name 'assassin', on me, not me. I even asked them to stop calling me that long before that incident, but they wouldn't. And detained? I wasn't detained... and who are they calling crazy?" I was infuriated, but still held on to my cool.

"Now just calm down son, and tell me. Isn't this here Gentleman Bandit one of the newer members of our beloved Manpower Choir?"

"He sure is. But we call him Brother Nix of course, not the Gentleman Bandit. The man paid his debt to society, now can't they let him move on?"

"Far as I'm concerned, if he's moving on in Christ, then yes he can, but if he's moving on in the world, then that's another story. Go ahead and read on, and speak up a little louder."

"Yes pastor, I dutifully replied, as it occurred to on me how Minister Roberts always understood Bianca's words, and every other female's voice who spoke anywhere near him, without ever asking them to repeat themselves. Only the men had to shout to be understood. Shoo devil, shoo now, I told myself, as I shook my head and read a little louder.

Driver Injures Woman Before Leaving Accident Scene

A hit and run driver slammed into the rear bumper of a car driven by a young woman today in West Atlanta, injuring her badly before telling her he had no time to fill out an accident report. The woman was escorted to the emergency room in tears by nearby residents. While filming her son's basketball game on video camera, one witness heard the crash and briefly captured the man's face and license number. She rendered this photo to action news. He is believed to be Stephen Humphries, owner of Ebony Courier Service. He is wanted by Atlanta police for questioning, and anyone who has knowledge of his whereabouts is urged to call police immediately.

"But this doesn't sound like the Stephen Humphries I know." I stated while looking up at Pastor Jackson.

"So you do know him?" he asked.

"Know him? I know him well enough to know he yearns to understand how to lead a good Christian life. You probably know him too." But Pastor Jackson just shook his head.

"I thought he looked familiar, that's about it. And is he one of the new members of that choir too?"

263

"Yeah, he's not the most recent, but he's one of the newer members of the choir too, I solemnly responded. "Wait pastor, now where are you going with this?"

"Question is not where I'm going, but where all of you are going if you keep playing with Your Father and the church.

"But pastor..."

"Read on son, I don't think you're finished yet."

Man Risks Life Saving Three
Children In House Fire

"I don't believe you all got anything to do with that one now, do you son?" Pastor Jackson asked.

"I'm afraid not," I sadly replied.

"Would have been nice, but somehow I kind of figured that. Now read on some more, just a little louder please.

Gambler Bets On Six Shooter When Game Fails

An unknown gunman threatened a casino blackjack dealer yesterday afternoon and demanded she return several thousand dollars he'd won earlier before he ultimately gambled it back and lost it. Upon her refusal, the gunman turned the gun on her in an attempt to recoup his losses. At this time his identity is unknown, but police have made a positive ID on his accomplice. He is believed to be Kyle Medley, the ex-collegiate All-American football star who wasted Atlanta's first round pick after confirming his intention to enter the draft some seven years ago. News reports are just in confirming that Kyle had been questioned in a unrelated bank robbery attempt gone bad just hours before. Casino cameras revealed Kyle arriving within 15 minutes of the attempted robbery, but leaving empty handed with the suspect as he drove the getaway car. Both men are presumed to be armed and dangerous, and bank executives interviewed earlier suggested Kyle's mental state as being highly questionable. If you see either suspect, call the police immediately. Do not try and apprehend them. Talk about things going from good to bad to worse."

"What, I'm supposed to be a crazed lunatic who'swanted by the law now?" I asked. The look on Pastor Jackson's face confirmed that his once highly regarded spiritual protégé needn't ask a question to which the answer was so painfully obvious.

"Kyle, let's you and I just cut through this here chase, as they say. I've called the police a little while ago."

"You did what? You of all people called the police, and now what?"

"I told them I was your spiritual father, and I told them that whatever has happened that you'd have nothing to hide. I also told them you'd be there at the downtown precinct by 12 noon."

"Well that was thoughtful. Now please only tell me you don't believe a word of this."

"I believe two things. One of which is that often times the devil gets busier when a man tries to grow closer to his Redeemer, and secondly, that the police are indeed looking for you. That is what I believe, so my suggestion is entirely appropriate. Furthermore, they said they were coming on over here this morning to arrest you during yo' new member's class, and that's the last thing you or the church needs. I couldn't let that happen' son."

"I understand Pastor Jackson."

"Oh, and I told them you'd bring that gambling fellar' the Humphries fellar', and the bank robber wit' you too." I was still in shock, yet tried to gather myself.

"I see. Well pastor, I better get going then."

"Alright, son. Oh, and one more thing."

"What's that pastor?"

"That great big ole she-boy in the leather pants. The one that stopped by my office a little earlier looking for today's Bible study, you couldn't miss him. Is that.....meanin' you know, is he?"

"Is he what pastor? Is he a friend of mine? Or you want to know is he in the choir too?"

"All of the above, son."

"Pastor, I've never even seen that man before today. For that matter I've never really seen a couple of other folks in there before either, but we still have to spread the word to reach him, right?" Pastor Jackson let out a sigh and shook his head again before speaking.

"Kyle, sure we have to reach him—and many others too, but I have to tell you. I'm tired, and I just don't have the energy to address these things any more. In fact I was about to announce my retirement just before Pastor Adams left. In other words, I'm praying for you son.

"Wonderful pastor. I hope you'll allow me in the leadership fold. I want to be a vessel for change, and I've got the will and the energy for it, even if you don't." I thought my words were inspiring. They were at least sincere, but Pastor Jackson looked at me with the sadness that conveyed no words were eloquent enough to matter.

"Kyle, I've been looking forward to the day when you would want to step in your forefather's footsteps and lead Mt. Tabernacle. I already prayed that you would. But I'm sorry; the way things seem to be going so fast down hill I'm tended to think that it's best to just disband this Manpower Choir." My neck went back as my eyes opened wider in an effort to absorb the news.

"What do you mean disband it? We're not a rock and roll group, you know. We sing from our hearts, pastor, you know that! Besides, we're already scheduled to sing for the Men's Day Celebration next week."

"No, I'm afraid you won't. Not next week, or next month, or the months after. Not at least for a while, until after this phone stops ringing and you all are no longer the bad talk of the town, and that's all to it. Well, almost all."

"Almost all? What else?" I asked, feeling so numb I was nearly immune to more bad news. "Pastor Jackson, what else?" I repeated.

"I don't."

"You don't what?"

"I don't think it's your time to be an ordained minister Kyle, that's what. You see, as much as I know the devil gets busy when good things are about to happen, he seems to be working overtime with you. Besides, I gave you one assignment and an easy assignment at that. You do remember what it was, don't you?"

"To keep this choir going in the right direction," I replied. "I know. I guess I haven't done a very good job of it—at least by the way things appear anyway."

"That's right, I'm afraid you haven't. As a man I didn't ask you for much, I couldn't, since I felt you were already legitimately called. Now, I don't know who's calling you. I just know right now nearly everybody seems to be calling me. We need to wait. It may or may not ever come. But we need to wait, and also pray, so we can be sure. Until then..."

"I'll wait pastor. I'll pray. I'll do whatever God asks. But my men not singing, or even being a part of our Men's Day Celebration?" I shook my head, nearly lost for words.

"This too shall pass son, this too shall pass," Pastor Jackson confirmed. "Now you just go on now, and make things right with the law. After that, well, keep praying fervently, and understand that Our Savior has a place and a time for you. While you're at it, remember that you can minister to lost souls in many other ways other than as a preacher at Mt. Tabernacle too." Pondering his words I turned to walk away, but quickly felt compelled to address him as I thought of my father, Frederick "Pappa" Medley.

"You know. I know that's true. I minister to people everywhere already. But my problem pastor...my biggest problem is that this sounds just like what you and some of the deacons told my father years ago."

The aging pastor hung his head down, as if ashamed, before responding. "God spoke then, and that's what God is saying now."

"No pastor. I was young then, and didn't know any better, but now I do. It was man who spoke in my father's case. And just like then, its man who's speaking now!"

THIRTY SIX

Saturday, 11:15 A.M.

Lauren's words resonated with more meaning now. Since she fielded all the church's calls, she must have known something was wrong all along. As for me, never in my wildest dreams did I envision leaving new members class headed to the police station. Taking Bianca to the park, or to dinner possibly, but not to the police station. Why not go back to Bible study and let them all know that this was all a big misunderstanding. Let's see, I'll explain it to Bianca-she'll have a million questions. Then, I'll politely ask Minister Roberts to go back to Boston, since his arrival and zeal for gospel excellence seemed to start all of this trouble to begin with. And Donald, he can't hold a candle to me, no explanation warranted there. I passed the small counter where the Metro section of today's paper neatly rested. Folded upward it displayed my picture alongside Keith Terry's. Disgusted, I walked on. My ministry hadn't begun, nor lasted long enough to suffer this kind of embarrassment, yet here I was. I stopped short before wallowing in pity. More than enough spiritual leaders are trying to explain themselves and ask for forgiveness lately. Just keep walking, let them sort it out. In my haste I suddenly thought of Reggie. I'd forgotten about him, and of all the people I had to leave, there was no excuse for having him depend on anyone but me for a ride home. I turned around and made my way back, only to hear Bianca's voice before turning the corner in the hallway to see her with that man.

"You've got a lot of nerve, coming down here to a place of worship," she began.

"I've got a lot of nerve, huh? You should see the way you look at that man. It's as if we never had anything. We've had three years together Bianca, three whole years, and you're ready to throw it all away just like that? You hardly know this man. You couldn't." I remained still while listening to what the love of my life could possibly be saying to the man that had to be her ex-fiancé.

"I think I know him better than I know you, or any one of the many names you go by."

"Bianca listen, I'm sorry, but I'm here today for a reason."

"And that reason is?" she asked.

"To tell you something important, something you need to know."

"Look, I'm past the impressionable stage Donald. So what can you tell me now that I don't already know?"

"That I'm prepared to give up everything, for starters. Every illegal thing I've done or ever planned to do. I just want you to come back home with me and marry me. We'll run the restaurant and the restaurant only. I swear this to you inside this church right here and right now."

"Donald don't, please don't do this," Bianca's begged, her voice beginning to break as she spoke. But Donald wasn't finished.

"And if you don't come, then I won't leave. I'll stay here as long as I have to. I'll even sell the restaurant and join Mt. Tabernacle if you want to make this your, our home," he said sincerely, almost in tears.

"Donald, listen. You join the church and stop living in sin in order to be close to God, not a woman. You do those things because he is calling you."

"And who is to say it's not God that's calling me to repent, huh? Who can tell you better than me that its His voice talking to me?"

A strange silence fell upon them both. Only God did know if he was being truthful, although the fruit inspector in me smelled a lie bigger than his vanity. My own carnal concerns now beckoned me. Was she kissing him? Hugging him? I had to know, so I stepped from around the corner, prepared for the worst with no understanding of what—short of Bianca slapping him and saying goodbye—could have been best.

"Hi Bianca, are you alright?" I asked. Before she could answer Donald stepped into my path with his chest out, wagging his finger in my face in macho fashion as he spoke.

"Yeah she's alright. Why wouldn't she be?"

"Excuse me, but I was talking to her, not you, and you might want to be more careful," I said while lowering his finger downward with my hand.

"Stop it, both of you," Bianca demanded. Yes Kyle, I'm fine. Thanks for asking. Where have you been?"

"I'm sorry, sweetheart, I've been in a rush, but I'll tell you later."

"Sweetheart," Donald mocked, "Hey Kyle, I hear Mt. Tabernacle might be interested in some more men's choir members, when is choir rehearsal, I might be stopping by."

"The choir is not expanding its membership at this time. We're in a transition."

"A transition huh? So in other words I can't come to the next meeting?" he asked.

"The church is open to all, so is the choir, but I don't see any meetings in the near future either. Believe me, I'd tell you if it were, even if I didn't want to see your face, and I don't."

"Then maybe just you and I can meet then. I think we really need to talk," Don insisted.

"Is that right? Talk about what?" I asked.

"We need to talk, man to man about Bianca, that's what."

"Don't be silly," Bianca interrupted. "Donald, I can speak for myself, you just need to listen, both of you," Bianca said.

"Both of us?" I repeated. I was stunned and confused, yet turned my attention back to Donald.

"Alright, why don't you meet me about 6:30 next Saturday morning at Stone Mountain Park, just you and me, if that's what you'd like?"

"Yeah, that's exactly what I'd like. But you didn't ask me to bring my Bible, preacher man."

"You can bring whatever you feel sustains you for life, a Bible or boxing gloves, it's alright with me."

"Kyle and Donald," Bianca called out. "You both are taking this way too far. I'm disappointed in both of you."

"Both of us?" I asked. "You've heard him. He wants to meet with me. Maybe he needs me to minister to him the best way I know how, so we'll meet."

"Not before you both meet me with me then."

"What?" We both replied simultaneously.

"You heard me gentlemen, I'll be giving you both further instructions soon."

****

Fifteen minutes later I was pulling out of the parking lot at 11:20A.M. Reggie was in the passenger seat, hanging on to my every word as I spoke via cell phone to Keith.

"Okay, so it was a toy gun after all, alright, I'm with you man. So maybe you can get the blackjack dealer to tell everyone that you didn't point it at her after all, but just be there at noon, alright? Goodbye." I then dialed Stephen Humphries as Reggie intently looked on. "Hey Stephen, you know you have to get down to the police station right? You didn't? Then trust me, you do? Then twelve noon it is. I know, I know. Yeah, I know the black man is misunderstood. Yeah, I know. At this rate he will one day wind up on the endangered species list, but just meet me there at noon, okay? Yeah, that's very true. Yeah, often times the devil does get busier when you give your life to God—that's so true. Oh, you said you're too busy with life and your business today to give the cops a nod? Listen man, just be there at twelve, alright?" I ended the call and looked over at Reggie, who, despite his physical limitations, couldn't have appeared more animated if he tried.

"I'm sorry things wound up the way they did, Reggie. I know you're probably disappointed too."

"Disappointed? Who's disappointed? Man, in my wildest dreams I never would have guessed a church class could be that far off the chain. Y'all had the real Gentleman Bandit there, a cool city slicker, a flaming gay dude, and most of all, you should have seen that country girl named Etta go off on Minister Roberts right after he walked in. I mean his eyeballs almost fell out when he saw her. He stuttered when he told her she might want to go to the meeting room up the hall instead. And why'd he do that? She let him have it, telling everything, and I mean everything. Looked to me like an Ivy League boy been kicking it wit a 'Bankhead hoochie' on the low—and it all came to light today. Hey, man, why did you leave? Folks in there weren't even feeling that Roberts brother at all. Where did you go? And why are we going to the police station all of a sudden?"

"We're not going anywhere. I'm going to the police station. Now I can drop you off at home on the way there, but that's where I'm going," alright?

"Naw. It's not alright," Reggie stated. "I don't want to be dropped off anywhere. You took seven years to call me, now you want to drop me off as soon as things get interesting. I don't think so. Don't take me home Kyle, at least I'm asking you not to, okay?"

"But I thought you wanted to get back home and watch college football."

"College football can wait. Besides, I learned to partly wean myself off of it during baseball season anyway. No, life is calling now, I can feel it, and I don't get that feeling too much any more. Listen, you contacted Reggie Pittman and started the day with Reggie Pittman, so end the day with Reggie Pittman." I glanced appreciatively at the man with lifeless legs but whose spirit was far from castrated and suddenly realized that me and Reggie were indeed on the same team. It was the team of life, a partnership of two young men running side be side after their train had been derailed. Reggie was far from finished, however, because he grew cockier with every mile I drove away from his house.

"Let me guess. You called me to make a peace with me that you needed before you could make a peace with yourself, right?"

"Wouldn't most anybody?"

"Probably so. They just wouldn't wait seven years, that's all. But let's forget about that for now. Let's put this picture together. You're about to become a Minister of your great granddaddy's church and you either need some closure or some easy souls to save so you call me—I can dig it."

"Okay."

"You also looked poised to lead everybody in that room to heaven today, even me, and I'm really feeling that, man, I really am."

"Good, Sherlock."

"Alright, then. It also looks like you had the table set to make Bianca—the finest honey on this side of the Mississippi by the way, yo' first church lady while you were at it, is that right?"

"That's not a given now," I replied.

"Look man, don't dance with me. I didn't just get off the boat and further more I'd think you'd be crazy not too, especially since she seemed to be feeling you too."

"You think so? Alright, go ahead."

"Thank you. Now, from what I see, you got a couple of problems. I've never been a true member of the God squad; I guess you can easily tell that. But even I know that you don't go from teaching a new members Bible class to rushing to the police station in the same morning—so this gotta be serious."

"Oh yeah, it's serious alright."

"And if you want to set things straight, you got to deal with it, right?"

"You're batting three hundred Reggie."

"I hate baseball Kyle, I told you that. I hate it. Tell me I'm shaking and baking with the pigskin and ready to run it down their..."

"Okay, okay, you're shaking and baking with the pigskin, now would you just finish?"

"I'll finish alright, but first you have to stop playing with me and tell me what's got you rushing to the police station."

"Just forget it, its a little personal. I can handle it."

Stopping at a red traffic light that wouldn't turn green until rapture, our attention was drawn to the voice of the loud street evangelist on the corner. He was dressed in an old and weathered beige suit that was only visible from the chest up. A plywood banner that read 'Jesus Saves', cloaked the front and back of his torso. Citing passages from the Bible at random, the middle aged black man shook a small bell feverishly in the direction of anyone within roughly a half mile of him. Reggie turned his head from the stranger back to me.

"I bet he's only hoping folks will fill that empty bucket near his foot with money, what do you think?"

"I'm sure money wouldn't hurt him, but he'd probably be just as happy to hear most anybody say 'Amen' now and then."

"What a rosy view of mankind. I think I'm going to puke. Well anyway, keep your secrets if you have to, 'Mr. Handle It'. This street corner's gonna' need someone like you to take it over and replace him in a few years, either when he gets too old or somebody jacks him and hurts him for his money. You're a prime candidate you know."

"Anyone ever told you that you can say the nicest things sometimes Reggie? Okay. You win, I'll tell you."

"I struck a nerve didn't I?" Reggie asked.

"Not really. You're beginning to annoy me, and I'm trying my best not to take you home, that's all."

"That's real."

"Anyway, everything was going fine until a few days ago, when I get a call from a couple of the members of the Manpower Choir."

I relayed the strange turn of events, sharing with him the news articles. Since he'd asked, I explained as best I could why Bianca must have walked out of Bible study with Donald, as if I really knew for sure. I even told him how we'd nearly come to blows before planning 'the meeting'. All Reggie did was intently read and listen, like a masterful football coach weighing all the options while plotting strategy. Remarkably he said nothing until we approached the police station.

"It's clearer now," he muttered just before I got out of the car.

"What do you mean? It's clearer now?"

"It's much clearer to me. What I was trying to tell you earlier was right, so here." Reggie's good hand labored to go down in his pocket. After the Herculean physical feat, he announced, "I have the answer to most of your problems right here."

"What?" I asked in disbelief. He then placed an object in the palm of my hand. "A stop watch? Come on now."

"Just take it in there for good luck," Reggie said, "okay?"

"You can move over and hand me my Bible for good luck, how's that?" I replied.

"Okay, take em' both, the stop watch too. You may need it in case they lock you up for a long time. Then you'll dream that you've got someplace to go in a hurry, and with this you won't be late."

"Got jokes huh? Well let's just see how fast 911 take's you home if I don't hurry out," I promised.

"Hey man." Reggie said slowly. "I'm praying for you." He'd

caught me off guard.

"That's awfully decent of you. Prayer for me is going around a bit lately. I'm praying for me too."

"Oh you'll be alright. I'm praying in another way, though."

"Oh yeah, and what way is that?"

"I'm praying you'll play again, this time in the Pro's and not just for God, but for you and me." Staring at him I felt bewildered, yet somewhat touched.

"Listen Reggie, if I ever played again, it wouldn't be for anyone but God, and with my mean streak I don't see it. Now tell me, how would my playing be for you?"

"Because God knows I deserve a chance to walk again."

"Yeah, but how do you figure?" I asked in earnest surprise of his comment.

"I'll explain later, just take this, okay? Take it for good luck, just take it for me," Reggie lamented. I grasped the stop watch he offered and placed it in my pocket, unable to say no thanks to something he held so dear.

"Now don't be late, its 12:00 o'clock already—so get on in there," Reggie ordered with the swagger and confidence of a major league coach.

"Right."

****

I walked into the police station, certainly an atmosphere vastly different from the one I'd just left. There was a stench in the air, jail cells with their crusty charcoal bars. The mood changed quickly when a sergeant took me to a room where twelve choir members waited. They'd come to lend their support, as word of my cancelled ordination had spread quickly among them. Less than an hour later we were being escorted out of the station by the police captain and that same sergeant. They'd bought my explanation of the week's events with guarded skepticism. Charles Nix was asked to not return to that bank as part of his parole, and agreed. Video footage clearly showed Keith Terry had a toy gun pointed at himself and was given a warning. The bystander who shot the video footage of Brother Humphries accident had kindly sent it to the police to prove his innocence. They'd painstakingly refrained from cuffing and jailing Humphries. He was defiant at the mere accusation he'd never stopped. Still, it was a hand's down victory, and topping it off they surprised me. They were football fans, and they asked for my autograph while patting me on my back. Three of the officers then confided in me how they wished they had a patrol partner as loyal to them as we were to each other.

Our celebration spilled over into the police station parking lot. We deserved acknowledgement, if only from each other. Brother Akins then launched into the song 'Stand', and who could refuse it? We sang it with depth, harmony, and feeling, as officers and passer by's alike either smiled or sang along. We'd ended the song with most of us shaking our heads, overcome with the spirit. Akins then beamed.

"Man, the congregation is going to be so pleased when we sing that one for them tomorrow."

"What are we going to wear Kyle," asked another?

"Yeah, are we going with our black suits or our purple and gold robes next weekend?"

"I hope Minister Roberts doesn't make us rehearse all Thursday night because you know we've got these songs down pact, right Kyle?"

My God, they don't know the whole story. I waited a few moments, as if living a bad dream. But there was no escaping it, so I lowered the same boom that hit me earlier.

"Brothers I have some unfortunate news to share with all of you. As nice as it is to be vindicated by the police for all this, in the eyes of the church we still stand accused."

"Accused! Accused of what? I was cleared!" said Brother Humphries.

"Me too, I've done my time, and I'll go to an ATM or check cashier before I will a bank," followed Brother Nix.

"They acknowledged no harm in how I lost my money and pointed a toy gun at myself?" said Brother Keith Terry.

"Nobody said anything bad about me, did they? Well did they?" Brother Ed Tyson asked as if he knew he were guilty before we answered.

The men of Manpower reacted as differently as their voices.

Two were visibly mad, and announced they were quitting. Four more were stunned and speechless. The majority of them wallowed in disbelief. Of course, Brother Humphries was more vocal than anybody. All were hurt. All felt cheated, and all looked to me for answers—answers that even now I couldn't give.

"Brothers, most of the church has the notion that we we're all just a huge bunch of sinners in one way or another, or simply not living right, including me—especially me."

"Including you?" Humphries asked. But aren't you way too boring for that rep man?"

"Thanks a lot Stephen, but yeah....especially me. And because of this rumor—maybe this fact, we will not be participating in any Men's Day Weekend ceremonies next Saturday or Sunday."

"But I thought you were going to be a Pastor at Mt. Tabernacle," said Brother Nix.

"I thought so too, but I'm not going to be anything. You see, I paralyzed a man seven years ago. Many of you have already heard about it by now, well it's true." The men grew quiet and solemn.

"We ought to get our own church," Brother Humphries said. "I know that's right," others repeated.

"So where are we going to rehearse?" asked Brother Akins." "Yeah, we need to pick a place where a man can be a man, that's for sure," echoed another. I liked the spark I was hearing, and therefore sought to make fire.

"There is a place where we can hold our Men's Day Celebration gentlemen. The acoustics are good, and it may be the closest thing to heaven on earth for us yet."

"Don't kid me and say the shower man, because I'm serious," said Brother Williams.

"We're going to meet at the West Gate at Stone Mountain at 7:00 A.M. next Saturday morning. I hope you all are in shape, because we're climbing up that mountain. Our Men's Day retreat will begin once we reach the top, any questions?" The men stood quiet while their minds processed the notion.

"I'm cool with that. Sounds like the right call, your Honorable Pastor Negro," said Humphries.

"Thank you Stephen. And I want everyone there, including

Ramario and the one that invited him." Somehow I think all of the men had something to look forward to. At least I did.

THIRTY SEVEN

5:30 am; Wednesday prior to
Men's Day Weekend

I ran the trail at Stone Mountain Park like a machine. Painful thoughts of a failed ministry and a love at the crossroads consumed me, but Reggie's stop watch came in handy. My first mile clocked in at 11 minutes. That was slow by old standards, yet awesome in that it was accompanied by more of the 'hurts so good' pain any athlete worth his salt appreciates. Bianca didn't come to work Monday or Tuesday and hadn't returned my calls. Now I know why Forrest ran. Small beads of sweat now oozed from my pores as my internal engine warmed up. So it happened that a piece of her I'd grown accustomed to having to myself from 9-5 was absent. Still, I counted it a blessing. After all, Bianca was a self actualized woman. The last two days I'd reminded myself of that—how she might instinctively need to take time for emotional upheaval. Spiritually mature men, and even carnal men almost twice a woman's age, appreciate the value of it. Knowing I needed that same time to reflect wasn't enough though. I had to do what worked for me. Pace yourself, four miles to go, run. Run until the pain subsides. Run, run like the sparkling stream over to the right that leads to the river.

Ask God, run faster, harder. Jogging past the two mile marker I checked the stop watch-11 minutes-reset. Prayer and a work out are all a good man needs. Run, run until the sun peaks through the clouds again and finds its way through the leaves. Beads of sweat that appeared a mile earlier had now become droplets of steam as I approached mile three—reset. Feeling that old twinge in my right knee haunted me and reminded me of earlier battles, but at 28 my body was new engine only slightly out of tune. Speak to my heart Lord; bring my mind and body new life. Keep going!

I hadn't told Dad, I couldn't. It would hurt or anger him, maybe alienate him more from the church, if that were possible. Worse was the fact that I'd have to listen to months of 'I told you so'. But he was right. Church folks have a strange habit of allowing politics and ego to interfere with God's business. Yeah, you told me so, but the Medley name will carry on, even if neither you nor I become Pastors at Mt. Tabernacle. Mile number four — 13 minutes — reset. Just don't react like the other men either. I'd told them I wouldn't be ordained, thinking it would ease their blow, but The Brothers somehow rested their hopes in me and were even more outdone than I. If Dad's pain were anything like theirs, I'd be better off joining a monastery and becoming a monk instead of telling him. I'm tired and winded. I want to stop. Don't stop, keep running! They felt cheated because they believed in me, a complement far worthier than the drunken fans who used to hold signs and chant my name on Saturday afternoons. It's a race for God, therefore, you can't stop. One mile to go! I'd kept my promise to Momma, hadn't I ? She was right, at least by the voices who really counted. Half a mile to go, and soon I'll need to sprint. Anything left?

If I could just fill this minute, with 60 seconds worth ...
Oh God, it hurts, almost there-keep going, and hope she didn't go back to Detroit with him. Run faster, harder. Keep running, run like the creek, which leads to the stream. I did it. I'd come full circle around the mountain and stopped at the gate. The same gate I asked Donald to meet me at. Stop the watch. I'd run five miles in fifty six minutes. Since I'm a man, just what would I allow myself to do to him if he came for war? It was now 6:15A.M. , and the morning dawn was fully upon me. I feel to my knees for prayer and wisdom, and after a few minutes of heavy panting I turned my attention to the top of the mountain. Perfect, that's it. Thank You, God. Donald and I both deserve company this Saturday morning. Let it be a day of reckoning. What better way for Men's Day to begin? My cell phone was ringing another favorite song of mine now, 'after I've done all I can'. I stood up and answered it. It was my woman!

"Hey baby, I've been thinking about you."

"I've been thinking of you too."

"Are you still in Atlanta?"

"I am."

"Listen, sweetheart. I know it's been tough on you lately. I'll get another job else where if you need your space."

"That's nice of you, but I'd never ask you to do that."

"Okay, you're acting strange. You mind telling me what's going on?"

"I've been on interviews all day both Monday and Tuesday with the Atlanta News Network. I'm praying they'll hire me as a journalist Kyle. The only problem is they are interviewing over twenty others for this job. "

"Good. You'll stand out better among twenty others. Now let's claim it. So, you're staying in Atlanta after all?"

"Maybe."

"Oh, I see."

"Listen, Kyle. I told you I'd be giving you more details. I want you to come down to the Spoken Word tonight. I'll be reading."

"Great, what time do you want to meet?"

"Sorry. We won't be meeting. If anything, you will be meeting Donald. I've asked him to come also."

"You what?"

"Just trust me, and if you care for me you'll do this for me. Now it's at 7:30. Are you coming or not."

"Yeah, I'll be there, but..."

"Good, because I've got a message for the both of you."

"Should Donald and I hold hands and sit together or what?"

"You don't have to go that far, but I do want you both behaving properly."

"I've always behaved prop...Okay baby, I won't miss it."

"Good, see you tonight."

"You know you're scaring me."

"Not like the two of you are scaring me, goodbye, Kyle."

****

As fate would have it, Donald and I arrived at the front door of the Spoken Word Café at the same time. Neither of us acknowledged the other as we approached the door. Once inside, we both searched for seats at opposite ends of the room. None were available, except the two chairs that sat empty at the first table on the left, close to the stage. I walked over and grabbed one, pulled it up, and sat down. Reluctantly, he came over and followed suit. I spoke to him as he sat.

"Good evening, Donald."

"Good evening, what's your name?"

"My name is Kyle, Kyle Medley." As if he didn't know by now. I extended my hand, and just like before, Donald grabbed it for a heartfelt two seconds before letting go.

"This is just crazy," he said before sitting down. "You know, I think you make her nervous."

"Me? Really? Remember, she left you, and thus far I don't see her packing her bags and leaving me, so there's the proof showing who makes her nervous. You need to just give it up."

"Is that right? Well guess what. I don't give up easily when I want something," Donald replied.

"Maybe that's your problem. You never recognized she's somebody, and not something."

"Hey man, when I need a social worker I'll tell you. In the mean time, just remember. I'm the real love of her life, and she invited me here for a reason, so chew on that in case you think you've got it like that so soon."

"I see." He did make at least one good point. She must have had a reason to invite him that was beyond my understanding.

"So, did she invite you to her readings when you two were in Detroit?" I asked.

"Sure she did, all the time." His answer made me wonder if I really wanted to know more.

"And did you go?"

"No, I didn't. I was usually too busy running the restaurant," he answered remorsefully.

"That figures." Now ring the bell Kyle.

"Go change my oil boy," Donald pompously muttered, ending our back and forth banter for good.

Piano music began to softly play as my thoughts turned to how easily I could whip him all over the stage right about now. But I'd made God and Bianca a promise to behave myself, even though one way or another he had it coming.

"If you only knew how fast...I could kick your jive city ..." I thought.

"Our peaceful civil rights leaders' were special," I muttered under my breath. The lights dimmed in the audience as Bianca graced the stage. Wearing a lavender sun dress and matching turban over her head, she couldn't have looked more elegant. She smiled warmly, almost shyly at the audience. Scanning the crowd and spotting us she nodded coolly, like a drill sergeant taking roll call, then grabbed the microphone like she owned it, like we needed to have anything more in common.

"Good evening. I'm Bianca Kincaid. I've written a poem about the personal choices you make in life and in love. It's dedicated to two special men in my life, both whose friendship I'll never forget. It's entitled 'Don't look for me.' I hope you enjoy it, since it bears my heart." Why on earth is she saying 'never forget'? No wonder she's acting so strange, Donald's about to run her away from the both of us!

Don't Look For Me

"I've spent so many countless days, lost inside myself
Chasing love like rainbows while I put God on the shelf
Now I've got two men in life, who say they love me true
While standing at the crossroads I have wondered what to do

Well I've known love like I've known time
Seen both vanish like morning dew
Once had a solid grip on them
Resting snugly in the arms of you

So easy I was pacified, not thinking all things through
But now I will be sanctified, and seek God's message to,
Tell you both don't look for me, in claiming your life prize
Though thankful, yes I'm humble still
But I now wait to please his eyes

For he will guide me, through the storm
Don't look for me you two
May find him also guiding you
The path to follow true,

So pull your anchor, rid your traps, your bait as well won't feed
My appetite for a Godly man, see I've prayed and planted seed
And if it's you he'll tell me, if it's you I will be led
To you by him to you for him
You see pray and wait for he's glorious!
Then maybe to you I will be led."

"Wow," I muttered.

"Umph," echoed Don. We both sat speechless, sneering at one another while the crowd feverishly snapped their fingers in approval. Donald then broke the silence between us as the noise subsided.

"So, now you've heard for yourself. She's told you flat out not to look for her."

"What? I don't have to look for her," I firmly replied. "She normally makes herself easy and available for me to find." He winced at my words but sat quietly. Ten minutes later found us still sitting around and scratching our foreheads. We were both unaware that Bianca had left the building, and more ignorant to the fact that many in the crowd were now watching us. All that was certain was the scowl on our faces each time our eyes met while scanning the room for her. Realizing our search was fruitless, I broke the ice.

"Man to man, I don't blame you for trying to win her back, even if you had to come over 600 miles to do it."

"Oh, so you're telling me you'd do the same thing I see."

"I don't carry myself like you, but yeah, as special as she is, I'd probably do more. The difference is, I'd show a bit more 'spiritual sensitivity' as I did it."

"And what do you mean by 'spiritual sensitivity,' he asked in mocking fashion?"

"I mean an understanding of God's presence in this church—an understanding of his presence in Bianca, his presence in me, and most of all in you Donald—if he's there."

"That's funny. And you don't think I already understand these things."

"No I don't, and it's not funny, because you don't act like you do."

"You're right, it's not funny—it's hysterical. How easy it is for people in the church to judge a man. Oh yeah, Bianca's told you some things about me I'm sure. And you assume that because of my old lifestyle that I never knew God. Did Bianca also tell you I grew up in the church with a single mother who died when I was 12 years old?"

"No, she didn't...but my own mother..."

"Maybe she also left out the part that I had no father, and practically raised myself."

"I'm sorry, I lost my mother at a very young age also, but don't confuse the issue. That's no reason to not be a strong man of God."

"No, brother. *You've* confused the issue. Just because you *claim* to be a man of God doesn't mean you're going to get Bianca, my woman, on a silver plate. In fact, you might want to try and convince the media you're a man of God first. See, I've read the papers this week, and I don't think they know. Secondly, I hope you listened to her tonight, and if you did, you won't confuse another issue.

"Which is?"

"That her affection might not be handed to you period, that's what. And expect no affection coming from me for trying to take what's mine and has been mine. Wake up. To get a woman like Bianca takes work, and you're out of your league, choir boy, trust me. Now Saturday morning I'm going to welcome you to my world, where there are no silver plates. I'll see you at 6:30 sharp. I hope you can afford a good watch because I don't want you late.

"Right," I confirmed before allowing the devil to get me seething. "What you don't want is for me to be on time," I muttered.

****

Donald left the table abruptly and headed back to his new hotel, the Economy Inn. The Economy Inn was located on the West End of town, a good distance from the Deluxe Hilton he'd checked into over a week ago both in miles and in luxury. The lone night clerk greeted Donald as he approached the desk. "Good evening Mr. Morton, what can I do for you."

"How about a 5:00 A.M wake up call, Orlando?"

"You got it Mr. Morton. I hope you parked that nice ride in the lighted area where I told you to, because I'd hate to see it stolen?"

"It's just a car Orlando...just a car," Donald assured him.

THIRTY EIGHT

Friday Morning
Peachtree Motors

Bianca hadn't shown up all week. Everything, from the words to her poem to her not returning my calls, was slowly conditioning me for the worst. It would take more spiritual reserve to get through the day, I knew that. I went through all the usual routines this morning. Like a robot I was as productive as ever and just as void of emotion. Where could she be? I wondered. That's when I heard Jocelyn's footsteps. Now there's somebody with some answers about Bianca's whereabouts. The only problem was my vow to give her what she wants—don't look for her. Yeah, right. Still tallying the logs, her footsteps grew closer.

"Good morning, Kyle, how's everything?"

"It's great Jocelyn....just great, and you?"

"Good, thanks. There's something I meant to tell you by the way."

"Really, what's that?" I eagerly asked?

"Well the car—the demo SUV you've been using?"

"Yeah?"

"It's a wee bit overdue, and it may be time to service it also. You mind checking it back in?"

"No. Sure don't."

Of course we've got to get it ready to use as a loaner vehicle next week."

"Sure, no problem." After all, that's what Cinder-fellars do after the big dance, right?

"What did you say Kyle?"

"Nothing."

"You know filling Bianca's shoes isn't going to be easy. We'll all miss her. I'm sure you're going to miss her too."

"Yeah, I'll miss her, but the show must go on, you know."

"That's right, the show must go on," she confirmed as we both stared at each other blankly. Okay that does it," Jocelyn said. "Do you need some time off Kyle?"

"Time off for what?"

"Time off to heal a little from all of this, that's what. Hey, I read the newspapers. You've got a lot of drama going on, way too much drama for a man who's about to become a minister. And by the way, how come I was the last person to know you were a number one draft pick a few years ago?"

"Because you don't even like sports, how's that for starters."

"Maybe not, but still, I know what being number one means."

"Yeah, I guess you do. Hey, since you do, you must also know that being number one can also mean that you're just Mr. or Ms. Irrelevant turned upside down too, right."

"This has to be a tough week for you."

"You don't know the half of it Jocelyn."

"Then do it—take some time off for a change. You never do, and you deserve it."

"Listen, I'll be just fine Jocelyn, trust me."

"I know, for the time being you will." Jocelyn then looked at her watch. "It's nine-thirty, she's on her way over here now, you know." For no reason other than my own anticipation, I looked at my watch too.

"Nine-thirty huh?"

"Give or take a few minutes, yeah."

Jocelyn meant well even while toying with me, like I'd fly through the ceiling at the mention of Bianca's name. I dismissed it though, knowing she was too lonely, to help herself; a textbook result of what dozens of 70 hour weeks could do to a woman. The door buzzer sounded and more footsteps approached. It was Bianca. Deep down I was as happy to see her as anyone who wasn't supposed to be looking for someone else could get. Still, I harnessed my amusement as she spoke.

"Hello Kyle, hey Jocelyn," Bianca cheerfully greeted.

"Hello Bianca." I replied, barely looking up from my manifest logs of the day.

"Have you told him, Bianca?"

"No, not yet, I'm about to though."

"In that case, I'll just let you two be. After this, my policy will be no inter-office relationships. It just takes too much out of me." Jocelyn walked off as Bianca came towards me. I kept my head down, seemingly more focused on the manifests than on her.

"Are you going to look at me, Kyle?"

"Excuse you, maybe later."

"Excuse me?"

"Yeah, excuse you. See, everything seemed to be going just fine, until all of a sudden your ex comes to town, to my church, to our church. And then, as if the week wasn't hectic enough, I get invited out by you, to join your ex, to hear you tell me, us, or whoever not to look for you. That was all I needed to top things off. No, wait, there's more. After that, I don't get a call returned the all week. So do excuse you for asking me to look at you. I'm thinking I might be better off staying in 'don't look for you' mode."

"Baby, I'm sorry, but please, look at me," she innocently repeated. I was genuinely upset, and keeping my head down and doing most anything helped me to not confuse her beauty and sweetness with the principle of it.

"I'm listening." I replied.

"I asked you to trust me, and you promised me you would, didn't you?" She was right about that part, but only right enough for me to bring my head up until our eyes met.

"Yeah, I promised to trust you. But still, how do you justify inviting me out to listen to a poem I thought only Donald needed to hear? Don't look for me. That's real cute. Why couldn't you just tell him that in a telephone message and leave it at that?"

"Because, Kyle, Donald won't stop when he's competing for something, especially a woman. I think it had something to do with him growing up without a father, and almost motherless since she died so young. I think it did something to him. He'll try his best to win before accepting the alternative, you see it's too second rate. For him, to lose a woman, particularly me, is out of the question."

"It's a trait in him you still admire, right?"

"It's just a trait in him I know about, okay? Look, I know what

289

you're thinking, and the answer is yes. Yes, it used to impress me when he pursued me the first time. Every woman likes a man who knows what he wants and pursues it. And don't try to convict me or him, because in many ways you're just like him."

"Oh, I don't think so!"

"Oh really! You're relentless too, just in a quieter way. You were a relentless football player, and you don't find many people who believe in the redemptive virtues of men like you do. "

"What do you want me to say?"

"And you probably would be a pastor at Mt. Tabernacle by now if it wasn't for your guilt. See, that's the only real difference between you two. Donald doesn't let the world judge him, but you do. You embrace guilt and give it a home. For him, discarding guilt is like a casualty of war."

"I don't see how you make that comparison so easily. While you're at it though, add in a conscience and a sense of morals. When you do, you'll see. The man has little in common with me."

"If you say so. Anyway, this is now, and that's all that's important. The traits I admire now are those of a Christian man, who goes all out for what God wants. You know it's funny, but I believe my values began to change after sitting in Christian counseling in Detroit with Bishop Searcy, even while Donald sat right next to me."

"That's the beauty in it. God can speak to you most anywhere, anytime."

"So true. And pleasing Him can include a man listening to his woman when she tells him what she needs, you know. To trust her, like she trusts him, and then faithfully see where that trusts leads."

"Alright, I understand. So you thought you'd neutralize him by having both of us meet together, and both listen as you tell us you don't want to be bothered with either one of us, huh? Then maybe, just maybe, he'll walk away right?"

"That's right. Except it wasn't merely a ploy. It's actually how I feel."

"Good. Well I listened. I think I displayed enough trust by faithfully showing up, too. Don and I even walked in together, looking like the odd couple at that. You saw me at the same table with him I'm sure too."

"I did."

"That was a nice poem, by the way."

"Thanks."

"But it backfired. The whole thing backfired."

"What? What do you mean it backfired? Backfired how?"

"You see, him and I have planned to meet at 6:30 in the morning. He seems to be obsessed with coming face to face with me. I'm supposed to know that you won't come to me on a silver plate."

"That sounds just like him. Let him be obsessed, just don't go meet him. You don't have anything to prove to him."

"Nope, I gotta' go. You see, tomorrow is the start of Men's Day at Stone Mountain."

"And how does that have anything to do with Men's Day at Stone Mountain? You never mentioned anything about Men's Day starting at the mountain. Men's Day is supposed to be at the church."

"It's going to be spiritual retreat for Manpower on Men's Day. I called for it because the church doesn't want the Manpower Choir participating in theirs."

"Are you serious?"

"I won't be giving any ordination sermons either."

"Says who?"

"Says Pastor Jackson, the deacon's wives, and over half the church from what I hear."

"Kyle, I'm sorry, that's terrible news. Let's start your own church then."

"No, I'm a Medley, and Mt. Tabernacle is my own church. I've come to realize that in spite of a scarred past, I'm still a leader, and a worthy one at that. I think God has used you, the Manpower Choir, and even Reggie as a vessel to reveal that. I'm not going to start a new church only to find that people are basically the same wherever you go. Besides, I've got strong men of God behind me no matter what people say."

"Okay. That's fine, if that's your wish. If that's what he's calling you to do, then do it. But please, don't meet with Donald."

"I trusted you, so trust me this time, Bianca. Mt. Tabernacle is too small a church for the three of us, at least for the way he's acting. Plus, you're a lot of woman, but you don't divide by two easily. Now,

I'll reconcile whatever I need to with Donald at 6:30 in the morning."

"I don't like that. You two don't need to meet like that."

"We're going to try it God's way."

"God's way? My way is God's way! All you have to do is walk away, he'll have nothing to face."

"Nothing to face tomorrow, you mean. That'll do nothing to insure the day after. You've walked away already, and look what good it's done. Now I'm going, and that's it." Bianca put her head down, seemingly hurt by my words. Now, I'm no expert on women, but I know that being "right" doesn't matter as much when the woman you care for looks like that.

"I'm sorry, Bianca. That's not completely true. I never would have met you if you hadn't walked away and come here…"

"I agree. I never would have met you either. Still, I wanted to handle this on my own, without bringing you into it."

"I know. I can tell, and truthfully you did. Your way didn't backfire so badly. The only thing that really backfired is the extent to which I thought I needed you. Don't feel guilty—I chose to come into this. I won't regret it either, no matter what happens. Now you suggested he's relentless. That means we'll never have any peace if I don't go. By the way, where are you going?"

"You know, with so much happening I forgot to tell you. I got the job with the Atlanta News Network. I thought we'd celebrate, but right now, I'm not feeling it. Kyle, promise me you'll handle it like a Christian man."

"I will, I promise. Congratulations! We'll celebrate when the dust clears."

"Sounds good, of course you know I don't like too much dust, right?"

"What do you mean by that?"

"You just think about it. What time are the men coming?"

"The choir brothers arrive at 7:00 o'clock, why? Where are you going?"

"I'm going home. Say goodbye to Jocelyn for me. Tell her I'll be in touch."

"Anybody else?"

"Yeah. Tell everybody else; all the service techs, the salesmen who still call me B3, even Ed. His type, they don't stay in church too long, but give him my regards anyway. Whatever you do, don't say goodbye to the Christian man I care so deeply for. See, he's the man I was talking about in that poem."

"I know baby."

"Do you really? I think if you did, you'd have nothing to prove."

"Just trust me, alright?"

"Goodbye, Kyle."

****

My cell phone had been inundated with so many calls this evening that it sounded more like a scratched gospel recording playing every five minutes. The calls were mostly from the Manpower Choir members, all clamoring with excitement.

"Yes, Brother Akins, dress as you wish but wear flexible shoes. That's right, 7:00 o'clock . No, we're going to walk the mountain, not climb it."

Then the phone rang again. "Yes, Minister Roberts. Minister Roberts? Why didn't I tell you about it? I guess I thought you'd be more than happy to preach at church without me this Saturday, that's why I didn't invite you. What's that? You'd hate for us to do anything without you? That's good. Okay, then come on. Yeah, we're all going to walk up the mountain. That's right, but don't worry. I'm sure that Tofu diet has prepared you just fine." I hung up the phone and said, "You probably weren't asked to preach tomorrow, anyway."

The phone rang a third time. "Praise the Lord. Oh, hi Ramario... Ramario, who gave you my number? I'm sorry. Yes it's true—I want you to come out. How do I know you're not already out? Look, I'm talking about out to the mountain, that's all. Yeah, of course they're going to judge you, you want me to lie? But that's the reason for the meeting anyway. We're judging ourselves for a change. You know how to get there? Then who's bringing you? Okay, we won't worry about that right now, see ya."

When it rang a fourth time I felt like a promoter. "Brother Humphries, my main man. Yeah...me too. I'd rather be on top of the mountain than sitting with all those judgmental folks in church tomorrow myself. Good, I'm excited too. Yeah, I played ball for a minute. No, I won't race you up the mountain—not tomorrow anyway. We're walking up together for God. Alright my Brother, see you then."

Then Reggie called, and I knew it was God's doing. "Hey, Reggie," I nearly shouted, "I'm sorry I haven't called you lately, but I've had a lot...what? I'm not a woman so don't worry about it, okay. Yeah, I'm still going to meet Donald in the morning. No, I'm not going to bring anything but a Bible with me, I've already told you that. You want to come? Why? Listen, we're going to walk to the top of that mountain. You can't roll up the mountain in that wheelchair on your own, that's impossible. Look, what about your classic football games reruns? No, I'm not trying to play you. No, I won't make that bet with you. Okay I'll come and get you, be ready early. How on earth will I get him up the mountain?

The phone rang one final time, from guess who?

"Hey Daddy, I'll get it on the way home, don't worry. You heard about what? You're right, I wasn't going to tell you, who did? Yeah, that sounds just like Bessie. Alright, I know you're going to tell me I told you so, so just go ahead. If it's alright with you I don't even want to hear it when I come home. You're what? Oh, really? I'm proud of you too Daddy, thanks. I'll see you soon."

THIRTY NINE

Saturday Morning
Day 1 of Men's Day;   5:00 A.M.

I prayed for half an hour this morning. Real men do pray you know. Upon hearing Daddy moving about in his room as I finished I decided to check on him.

"Hey old man, you awake in there?" I asked before gently pushing the door open to find him getting dressed. "What are you doing? Today's Saturday, you don't have to go to the doctor today." He was moving slowly about the room, pausing only briefly before answering me.

"That's right. And guess what?"

"What?"

"I already know it."

"Okay. Then why are you up so early?"

"Because I figured you'd be leaving out of here early without telling me, just like you're doing, that's why."

"Come on. Don't start getting sensitive on me all of a sudden, it doesn't become you. It wouldn't be the first time I left early, would it? After all, a bull like you doesn't need a baby sitter you know."

"No son. Not yet I don't, anyway. Listen, I've got something I want to give you before you go. Something that both me and your Momma wanted you to have."

"Really? After all these years, why are you giving me something from Momma now?"

"Because she wanted me to wait 'till' today, that's why." Daddy rose up slowly and walked over to the closet. Grunting mildly from the pain, he then perched himself up, nearly tip toeing on his one natural leg. Reaching far back on the shelf he fumbled about before pulling out what appeared to be a large box wrapped in old, yellowed towels. As he turned around it was obvious he'd developed a slight limp from the feat. Still, he managed to escort the box slowly, methodically—with the esteem of a Gladiator wielding an Olympic trophy—back over to the bed. Slightly panting he then propped the box, then himself, down on it. Patiently, he took his time unwrapping small, yellowed towels of the box's outer shell before peeling away layers of what was once bright new cellophane, now turned old, gray and brittle. A Bible appeared, its beautiful condition signifying the rudimentary wrapping had served its purpose well over the years, though asking it for more time would be pushing it. The procedure happened in such ritualistic fashion I'd gotten the feeling he'd rehearsed it before, if nowhere else but in his mind. After removing the last piece he spoke, which was good, since I'd been rendered speechless.

"This is the Bible your mother wanted you to use for your first sermon."

"Are you serious?" I asked, even while realizing Daddy wouldn't dare make this up.

I ran my left hand gently about its smooth, lavender finish. I then ran my right hand across the engraved insignia at the bottom corner that read, 'Pastor Derrick Medley, Preacher of The Gospel'.

"Momma did this? That's unbelievable. To God be the glory! It's beautiful, very beautiful. But I told you yesterday, Bessie even told you, I'm not an ordained pastor. They don't even plan on making me one. And don't let this hurt you Daddy, but I'm not even due to participate in the Men's Day service at Mt. Tabernacle." I hated to deliver this dagger to him, knowing he'd lived a life of hope through me for so long, but his reaction to the news was much better than I'd imagined.

"And you may never be much at Mt. Tabernacle."

"But..."

"But you've got a flock of men coming to meet with you soon. They're looking to you and you only for spiritual nourishment. How many men in a flock can a Pastor effectively minister to?"

"Seventeen or less." I quickly answered, thinking of Pastor Adams sermons.

"That's right. And you're not meeting them in a man made church either. You're meeting them on a mountain top. God gave Moses the Ten Commandments on a mountain. I like that. If I were a younger man I'd leave with you and join you for worship up there myself." Daddy made me happy to feel this news wasn't heartbreaking for him.

"Really...Daddy?"

"You bet. You see, you don't climb a mountain to judge folks anymore. Folks in white sheets will even tell you that. No, you can do that right here on the ground. You go up to the mountain to feel closer to God, and judge yourself if anything. You take this now, and go preach the gospel son." I kissed him on the forehead and gently brushed his steely gray and peppered black hair back with my hand. After that I made my way out the door.

FORTY

I'll just be....why are you driving this old raggedy truck Kyle, where's your SUV, in the shop?"

"No, I don't an SUV, I own this pickup truck."

"For real?"

"For real, Reggie!"

"So this is what you drive?"

"That's right, this is what I drive."

"Then I'll just be....do you mind if I say it—just this one time?"

"Yes, I do. Can't you find another way of saying it?"

"Okay. No wonder you won't be leading a church no time soon; just look at your ride!"

"What's wrong with my pickup? Listen, my ministry won't glorify materialism, Reggie, and a lot of your comments—the size of our church, my car—they're making me believe you think otherwise. And furthermore, how will my playing pro football make you walk again?"

"Because," Reggie replied.

"Because what, I replied back?"

"Because Kyle, there's a pricey operation I want, that I need. It's new, or at least I just heard about it, and it costs over thirty thousand dollars. There's no guarantee that afterwards I'll have any movement in my legs again either, but there's a chance. I can't get a loan for it, because I don't have any credit or remaining clout to speak of."

"I see, and you want me to play pro ball again so I'll have the money to help you. Is that what you're asking?"

"Yeah, that's right. That's what I'm asking of you, because if you do, it would mean even more to me than my forgiveness could ever mean to, man."

"Whew, you did have to put it to me like that, huh? And you didn't want me to feel guilty right?"

"That's right, and I still don't want you feeling guilty. It's like I said before, who cares if you got God's phone number if you ain't' gonna' call?"

"Oh, but I call on him Reggie."

"Well alright then. Do you still love the game?"

"Yes Reggie, I do."

"Then if you call on him why can't you play? Why can't you muster your faith, trust yourself, and just do it?"

"Because I don't want another man crippled when he should be walking, that's why. You picked a fine time to ask me about all of this, do you know that?" I asked.

"Good, because you picked a fine time to call me, and we couldn't pick a better time for you to stop playing with his number and either crap or get off the pot." Reggie shot back.

"But you don't understand. Even if we put my feelings aside, I'm older now and I've slowed down, a lot. Making matters worse, the world thought I was crazy then, and they're only sure I'm crazier now."

"I understand because they're right, I do too. Well, you did turn down a lot of money, and for the life of me I don't see why you want to deal with all of this church drama. But all that doesn't matter. I've contacted three teams this past week about you."

"You did what?"

"They happen to be the three of the teams that were once interested in me once upon a time, Atlanta, Baltimore and Chicago. They want to have you at their next football camps to work out— those are in six weeks, by the way."

"Wait a minute! Hold on! You've just gone and wasted your time, brother. It isn't that simple. By the way, I didn't know you were my agent."

"Well, now you do. Actually, I think I'm pretty good at it, too. And it is that simple—as simple as ABC, baby. Besides, I've got some time to waste, you don't. I guess we're getting a bit closer, huh?"

"Yeah, we're almost at the mountain," I said while looking at Reggie as if he'd lost his mind.

"I know that. I mean closer as friends; you know, the way we think, even spiritually."

"Oh, that kind of close. Well, I'm definitely your brother, but close in terms in the way we think? I'd say we're about right here," I responded while briefly taking my hands off the wheel to spread them as far apart as possible.

"Take a day or two and think about it, and remember who's asking you to do it. I am, Reggie Pittman, and you can pray about it too." Reggie Pittman's telling me I can pray about something? "In the meantime, I know it's not always all about me."

"Do you?"

"Oh yeah, lets talk about you now. What cha' gonna do if this dude brings a gun?"

"I don't think he'll do that at all."

"Why wouldn't he?"

"I just don't think he wants to win that way, that's why."

"Since you got it all figured out, do you mind telling me how he wants to win?"

"I can't say. He seems to be big on mind games, so I'll expect that."

"Is that all you'll expect? Here, take this with you in case he tries to blow your mind." Reggie went into his right pocket and came out with a 9millimeter hand gun. I looked at the big, black object with shock.

"Where did you get that? I told you not to bring that thing, no guns…gimme' that," I demanded as I snatched the 9mm out of his one good hand. "Too many black men feel a gun is the answer to their problems already. Now that's it. If you're coming to this retreat with me, you'll have to commit yourself to learning the ways of a spiritual man, Reggie. Otherwise, after today, these 'entertainment sessions' are officially over for you. And like I told you before, if I even think about playing pro football, it would be for God."

"For God? I never saw God promote a football game or sell anything during the commercials, so what do you mean, playing for God?"

"It would be to glorify him and for the uplifting of my own spirit and others, which I don't see a need to do with a gun or with a football."

"Then there you go. It sounds like *that's* where I'd fit in."

"You think so, huh? Well a spiritual man doesn't uplift himself by resorting to violence of any kind."

"Hold on. I was talking about the need to be uplifted. Tell me. A spiritually saved man doesn't abandon common sense, does he?"

"No, he doesn't. A spiritually saved man knows that common sense isn't all that common, so he trusts God more than he leans to his own understanding."

"Man, it might take me a minute to get to where you are, but you 'wanna' know what would be nicer?"

"Yeah, tell me."

"I hope I wouldn't be as boring as you if I ever did. Really, I hope you know what you're doing. As far as the football goes, well, the Lord knows your playing could uplift me and you know it. Hey, look, there's a man over there. Isn't that him? That sure looks like him," Reggie confirmed.

It was now 6:20 A.M, and we were still under the cover of darkness as we drove closer to the man in the parking lot. Our headlights revealed it was indeed Donald. He was dressed down in blue jeans, gym shoes, and a white shirt, and he was casually leaning against his white SUV with his legs crossed as if he already had the situation under control. He glanced at us briefly before turning his head away, as if to say he was unfazed by our arrival.

"Yeah, that's him. I'm going to park. Stay in the car, no matter what happens, just stay here," I told Reggie.

"I don't have much of a choice you know. Just turn your truck and park where I can see the both of you, alright?"

"Okay, here....keep my cell phone." I parked and faced Reggie as he suggested. As awkward as it looked it made sense. Getting out of the vehicle, I took a few steps towards Donald while deeply inhaling the cool morning air.

"I see you brought two men to do what should only be a one man job. It figures. I should have known that the choir boy would be a little scared," Donald boasted.

"I hope you don't believe yourself nearly as much as you want everyone else to. Never mind him, he can't even walk, and he won't have anything to do with this."

"Good. I don't have all day, and as you know, this is personal. There's bad blood between me and you, but you already know that right?"

"No I don't. I know about the blood Jesus shed for you and I, but not about bad blood between you and I."

"Alright, just tell him to hit those headlights."

"Reggie, cut those headlights back off." I shouted. "I never told him to turn them on."

"I'm sure you didn't. Listen, Kyle. You probably are a good man. Hey, we never got properly acquainted. I'm Donald Morton."

"Alright, I'm Kyle Medley." To my surprise we shook hands again, only this time more firmly.

"Kyle, we're from two different worlds, by now you must know that. I've pretty much been on my own for the most part, you know, raising myself ever since I lost my mother. You say you know what it's like to lose your mother when you're still a kid?"

"Yeah, I know all too well what it's like."

"Really? Did you have a father?"

"Yeah, still do, and he's a good one at that."

"Well, I didn't have a father, and nobody else that counted— nobody to point me in a direction and tell me what it was to be a man. Not a blueprint, no map, nothing, you understand what I'm saying?"

"I understand."

"Good. Then you know what it feels like to feel lost."

"Like an African slave separated from the motherland, I understand."

"Well put. Then you can also understand how I could make some mistakes in life just trying to find my way, right?"

"Sure, the devils busier under better circumstances."

"That's true. You see, Bianca doesn't understand that, and I need her to. But hey, that's not your problem."

"No, it's not. Sorry Donald."

"Maybe not, but you do understand. That's a start. You see, I want you to think of Bianca as my sister, and Detroit as my... our motherland. That's how I feel, and I have to take her back."

"You have to take her back Donald? You merely have to stay black and die," I told him as I stepped forward with my arms folded.

"You're not interested. That's what I figured, but that's alright. I've got something in my truck for you." Donald motioned to his SUV and stared briefly at me before turning around and walking toward it. Oh no, what on earth was this man going to his truck to get? Reggie's suggestion to bring a gun now raced through my head. What was I thinking? I stood firm with my legs planted wide while Donald opened his rear truck gate. Out of it flashed what appeared to be a suitcase. Grabbing it with one hand and meticulously closing the door with the other, he walked back towards me and placed it down on a nearby bench. To say the least, he now had my full attention. Looking up at me as if he had me in his grasp, he popped the suitcase open while maintaining a cocky, self assured glow. The look assured me that the suitcase's contents held the type of surprise that could make either one of us happy, but probably not me. My mind now raced even further. No way was I going to let him assemble a gun and shoot me, so I walked closer to him.

"You can come even closer than that if you want."

"Okay. I think I will."

"Yeah, I want you to see this before I give it to you." I walked closer, visualizing no less than three ways I was going to disable him if he made any quick moves.

"Kyle, I know Bianca told you everything about my old life as a hustler, but it's only half true. I'm going back home and giving it all up for Jesus."

Whew!

"Congratulations Donald," I replied while wanting to wipe the perspiration that formed on my forehead. I don't know how you're going to spiritually go from 0-100, but I'm happy for you."

"50 to 100 is more like it."

"Alright, excuse me then, 50-100. So what's with the case?"

"Not much, other than the fact that it contains fifteen thousand dollars of your money, free and clear."

"My money? I haven't done anything to earn fifteen thousand dollars."

"Not yet, but you will. See, I want you to leave Bianca alone, completely alone, and just take the money."

"What on earth makes you think I need fifteen thousand dollars so much that I'd leave Bianca alone?" I asked.

"So you could give it to me for starters man, that's what," Reggie shouted from the truck, obviously eaves dropping on our conversation.

"Roll up that window right now and mind your business Reggie!" I shouted back.

"I can't. You should have rolled it up if you wanted it rolled up. But forget about this window, just take the money," Reggie ordered.

"So that's Reggie, huh?" Donald echoed. "You know, I read the papers about you this week. Thanks to you, I almost look like a choir boy."

"Oh, I doubt that seriously."

"Oh really? The papers crushed your reputation. They say you're crazy. And everybody in that room seemed to realize you weren't going to be teaching any New Members classes after Minister Roberts came in. On top of that, you're what, almost thirty years old? Let's be real. You're nothing more than a glorified grease monkey at your job. Yeah, I remember you. At one time you could have made it big. Pro football scouts now wouldn't waste a draft pick on you for anything. So let's face it, maybe it's time you went someplace else and started your own ministry. If you do, a little money won't hurt you at all, now would it?

"I'll be alright."

"Good. That's really good for you man, I really hope so. Me? I'm squaring myself back up. Hopefully, you'll tell Bianca that."

"And why would I tell her that? You tell her, its not my business."

"It is your business now, because that's what I'm paying you for. Take it, and don't as much as talk to her again. I'm taking her back to Detroit. I'm running my restaurant and rejoining the church, that's it. Look at it like this. You get to land on fifteen grand after having a fiasco of a week. Sounds like you can help yourself and maybe that poor guy you paralyzed in that truck over there too. Take it. It'll help erase the past and give you a fresh start somewhere. There will always be other women too, you know that."

"You sound pretty sincere Donald. I think you'll turn your life around also. God bless you man, but I'm not taking this money and telling Bianca anything. Like I said, I'll be okay. So will you, and so will she."

"Listen man, take this money and stop playing games with me," he demanded before grabbing me tightly by the arm. I looked him in his eyes and saw true desperation before knocking his hand away as hard as I could.

"I'm not playing any games with you, and don't handle me like that again, you understand?"

"Yeah, I understand. I should have handled you like this!" Donald said before solidly hitting me in the mouth with his right fist. The sting of the blow as it landed ignited my senses like a crackling bolt of thunder.

"Oh you done it now," Reggie shouted as my bottom lip went numb and swelled instantly. A trickle of blood oozed out of it and traveled down my chin and I wiped it away with my fingers, surprised by its redness. The act infuriated and pained me, and I found it nearly impossible to not react with the violence of yesteryear.

"I've had a fiasco of a week, but you're about to have one fiasco of a morning if you don't listen to me. I'm going to give you a chance to erase this, like that punch never even happened, by leaving and going home—I mean to Detroit, right now. I'm going to forgive you. Trust me too when I tell you there will always be other women." I said, pulling out my front shirt from my pants to wipe even more blood that was now flowing like a river from my lip. Suddenly, Donald back handed me across my face with his left hand, only this time striking me more disrespectfully than painfully. I wallowed in disbelief for a moment before vividly picturing five ways to dismantle him. But thoughts of the blood of Jesus, blood shed for me and for him, entered my mind. Those thoughts beckoned me to walk back to my truck.

"Where do you think you're going?" Donald asked in disbelief, but I continued walking; ignoring him, trying to blot him out completely, but it didn't matter. Before I knew it Donald jumped on my back—about 225 pounds of him. I stumbled from his weight a few moments before regaining my balance. Convinced I didn't want to further encounter the element of surprise, it was on now. Instinctively, I spun him around twice before grabbing him with both hands and hurling him down. After hitting the ground Donald let out an incomprehensible, undefineable and primitive wailing sound full of agony, but I wasn't finished. Revisiting number 44's trademark maneuver, I placed one hand on his chest and the other on his waist. My blood now boiled as I raised his torso to the air with both hands. It had never been this personal before, and slamming him down violently could never have felt better. But I knew I wouldn't, I couldn't. All of a sudden my trucks headlights reappeared, and a familiar voice yelled out from its direction.

"Don't do it, Kyle. Listen to me now. You've changed. God's redeemed you. You took the time to call didn't you? Now set him down. You have to set him down, now!" Reggie demanded. I was semi-lucid and breathing heavily, almost unaware of myself and so caught up in the moment that I hadn't noticed several cars carrying all thirteen men of the Manpower Choir and more—had pulled up alongside my pickup. One by one, their car doors slammed, all sounding like out of tune African drum beats. In a sense, that's what they were, oddly rhythmic, yet purposeful. Brother Nix ran over to me first, with Brothers Humphries and Lange following closely behind. Two cars blew their horns as others ran toward us.

"For God's sake Kyle, set him down," Nix begged.   Still panting, I ignored them while I looked up at Donald. If they and the rest of the world thought I was some kind of monster, it was time for my actions to now speak otherwise.

"Are you alright?" I asked him while looking in two eyes that rightfully revealed nothing but fear. I set him down on his feet and began brushing dirt off his arms and legs. He raised his hand up to block my actions and signal me to stop. The brothers gathered around us to listen to our dialogue. Some looked worried but all were intrigued.

"Your lip is as big as a grapefruit, and you want to know if I'm alright? Donald said. You got lucky and caught me off balance, but I'll be alright." I noticed his hand bleeding and sensed he was in pain.

"Listen, Donald. Being a Christian doesn't make a man a punk or a sell out, you know."

"For your information, I also already know that," came his exhausted reply as he wobbled to keep his balance as if he were on a tight rope.

"Then know that nothings changed," I confirmed to him. "I'm not taking that money. I will do you a favor though. I will invite you to our Manpower retreat. We're aiming to be better men of God and to come full circle with ourselves. Now, if you want to do that—if it's really time, and your body can make it up the mountain, then you're welcome to come."

"I'll come; I think I'd like that," he said, still puffing. "But still, I'm not leaving here without Bianca. And furthermore, something has changed."

"What?"

"That fifteen thousand dollar offer," he labored to say, "is now off the table. Bianca will surprise you, and leave with me anyway. Then, you'll have nothing. But yeah, I'll come," Donald confirmed before promptly falling flat on his back.

FORTY ONE

Daylight was breaking as the crispness of the cool morning air invading our senses. We were clearly in God's backyard as all the men of Manpower, along with Reggie, Donald, Ramario, and Minister Roberts, banded together at the foot of the mountain and prayed. Wasting no time we began our climb up the steep mountain, spread apart, yet banded together and more invigorated by the exertion of each step. The men's stamina and their teamwork were admirable, especially as we found ourselves confronted with the yeomen's task of rotating three men at a time to carry Reggie—and his wheel chair—toward the top. Initially overprotective of Reggie, I quickly relaxed after seeing how responsible the men were, and Donald surprisingly extended as much care to him as any of us. Passing the mountain's halfway point, the drudgery of the walk began to show its effects on some of us, but we tirelessly forged on. Gradually, the beauty of the landscape below revealed itself more as we approached the mountain's peak.

"Has everyone seen this before?" I asked before reaching the top. Nearly half answered yes.

"Oh yeah? What about that? I pointed out far in the distance. They all turned their heads to witness the terrain I'd pointed to. Off to our right were several miles of vast green landscape which blended beautifully in with the sky. Although massive buildings and other tools of man were perched about them; they now appeared small enough to be plucked by our fingers

Minutes later we arrived at the top. The physical aspect of the retreat was now behind us, and each man seemed to claim a personal victory over the climb in his own different way. Most of us neared exhaustion as we silently dispersed in every direction upon the narrow peak. Nobody brought a camera, so we all took a mental snapshot of the view to insure it would never disappear.

"Nothing like the power and beauty of God," one of the brothers said as we walked. Some said Amen, while others raised their hands up to echo the same. I gave them a little more time to bask and reflect before speaking.

"Brothers, let us gather around in a circle. We're going to begin to have our own Men's Day Service right here, right now."

"Well all right," announced one, while others gathered.

"Brothers, I've called this retreat here today for several reasons. First of all, it's no secret that there's been a lot of negative talk about us going around the church lately."

"You mean around the whole city don't you?" Brother Humphries asked.

"Around the church, the city, heck, if you listen, people question the way we live all over the world. But if the world were an apple, as your spiritual leader I want to talk about its core. Because at the core, at its root, is where you'll find us."

"Alright now."

"See our reputation, and the way people view us is important, very important. But there's one thing more important than other folk's opinions of our Christian walk. Other than God's opinion, what matters most is our own opinion of our walk." The brothers grew quiet as they all seemed to reflect on themselves. "Well? Anybody want to speak up?" Brother Akins broke the silence.

"As the senior member here I'll begin, if that's alright."

"Oh it's alright," the brothers lamented.

"I happen to be a good family man—a hard working, God fearing man at that. And through God's grace and my entrepreneurial efforts, I have left an inheritance for even my children's children. I also humbly say that with all the women in Atlanta, I've never stepped out on my wife."

"Amen" "Amen to that." Good man." "Really?" asked someone who sounded like Ed Tyson. Brother Nix then followed with more self righteous testimony.

"The man they called the Gentleman Bandit years ago never pointed a real gun on anybody, even when he was lost and on drugs. And guess who helped start the prison ministry when he was locked up? It was me, Charles Nix," he volunteered.

Added Brother Tyson, "Well, let's say out loud that I know what a lot of people are thinking. I never cheated anybody in a car sale — they always got what they paid for, okay? And many people think I'm just a player of pretty women, but I never did a sister wrong to this day."

"My brothers," Minister Roberts began. "I don't know how this whole thing went astray, but that's why I came out today, to bring some leadership. Like I've always said, God commanded me to make you a better sounding choir, to prepare you for Men's Day. I've been earnestly charged with this task, and....hey, why are you all looking at me like that?" Most of the men were so annoyed with Minister Roberts they looked beyond him. Their eyes now rested on the intriguing stranger who stormed into Bible study recently.

"What. I know what a lot of 'y'all are thinking. Let me tell you that even though this air up here seems clear, I want to clear it a little bit more. I am not gay, alright? I am a metro-sexual, thank you very much. Most of all, I'm not even a member of your choir — so don't blame me for your problems, okay?" The men deemed him to be at least half way right — why blame Ramario? Their eyes quickly moved down the row.

"Well I'm good to my wife too, and you'll only catch me at a club every now and then," added Brother Williams. Surprised he spoke no more, it dawned on me that if words were money, Brother Williams would be a tight-wad. I wanted to bring up how I once saw him at the park hugging on Brother Daniels, but I'm glad I didn't. Come to find out they were first cousins who happened to be that close. With the aggression gone from their faces, the field was now open up to brave volunteers.

"I don't know about y'all, but I'm on defense, brothers, Brother Lange confirmed. I'm just a tired truck driver, trying hard to not cross too many white lines when he gets sleepy. I may need prayer and therapy when I come off the road though, cause my wife is tripping hard and I'm thinking about stepping out for my own sanity." The men all responded as self righteously as they could and then some, bringing the obvious disgust of both me and Reggie. Brother Humphries shook his head in disapproval too, even though to this day he'd done a good job of keeping his sinful vices to himself.

"I want you all to know that it was through watching my Momma play bingo at church when I was only about six years old that I got my first exposure to gambling," said Brother Terry.

"Come on", "give it a break", "no he didn't, Negro please," the men shouted, and now I knew I'd heard enough.

"I've never heard such a crock of self righteous crap in my whole life! Just stop it, all of you," I said. "Maybe in a small way everyone here is right, but we're bigger than this. We're much bigger than this. Deep down in our hearts we know that this isn't what we've gone out of our way for? As for me, I know this isn't why I woke up and tugged up this mountain. The truth is hard at times. Just like this steep mountain walk, it's a road not traveled by everyone. But I have to tell you, I sin. And when I'm not sinning I'm often thinking about sinning. Yeah, accident or not, I paralyzed this man right here seven years ago, but that's not all. I'm sure I've physically hurt several others too, and I can't say it was the nature of the game, because it was the nature of me. You see, that's our problem. We as black men have to stop charging it to 'the game' you understand? Wait a minute, what's that noise I hear?"

To our rear the conveyor belts to the sky lifts started moving. The sky lift transported people up and down the mountain via cable, and though it wasn't as vast a ride as the Appalachian Mountains, it spared them the walk and enhanced the view.

"Isn't it too early for the park to transport people up? Who on earth is that?"

"Well if it isn't too early for us," Brother Akins yelled as he walked over to the incoming sky lift, "it isn't too early for what looks to be Papa Medley, Bianca, and another gentleman I've never seen before coming up."

"That doesn't sound likely, are you sure about that," I yelled?

"Yeah he's sure, Daddy yelled in response as the cabin stopped. Daddy, Bianca, and another black man were now in view. The unknown man was about 5'11. Distinguished looking, he appeared to be in good condition, looking 63 years old even if he was 72. Like my father, he was dressed casually, wearing beige slacks, a light blue sweater and beige hush puppies. Also like Daddy, you could dress him up in rags, yet still see the presence of a regal man of the cloth beneath them. Bianca waved and descended back down as both men exited the sky lift.

"Don't look so surprised, son," Daddy said while walking toward us. "Like I said this morning, I figured you'd be expecting at least 17 flock. So now, you have me and another man of God to help you minister to the rest, alright?"

"That's fine Daddy, welcome aboard."

"What happened to your lip, son?"

"Oh, it was kind of an accident. Tell me, who is this other man of God?"

"He's Bishop Searcy, my pastor from Detroit," Donald responded. "Hello Bishop," Donald beamed.

"Hello Donald. And hello men of Mt. Tabernacle."

"Welcome to Manpower's retreat Bishop Searcy." I said. "But how did you know about it?"

"Our mutual friend, Bianca called and invited me a few days ago, Bishop Searcy explained. "She told me that strong men of God were coming full circle with themselves this morning, and that she'd hoped Donald might be here."

"Oh, I see." I replied, now certain I could know Bianca for years and not know what she might be up to or how to ever measure her value.

"Needless to say, I didn't want to miss it," Bishop Searcy acknowledged. "Has anyone given their testimony already?" he asked.

"I'd just begun, but you're more than welcome to continue Bishop Searcy."

"Bless you. Well brothers, some of you may not know me, but many will say I'm one of the most popular ministers you'll find in Detroit and across this country, but that doesn't matter. I'm Bishop Cameron Searcy. I started my ministry with a small congregation of eight people. One of my first church members was Donald's mother, a young woman who believed in me half as much as she believed in God Almighty. I met her when she was a young girl, and unfortunately God took her while she was just a young woman. Before she went to glory, she asked me to look out for her Donald, here. I promised her I would, but I fell woefully short of the task. My ministry grew, but as I focused so much on the urgent, I forgot about the important. Donald, you were the important, and I was so busy I became blind. And now, if you will, I've come south to this mountain, to ask you and God for forgiveness. God forgive me." He beseeched the sky before turning to Donald.

"Would you forgive me also, Donald?"

"I'm fine Bishop. I could have come out better, maybe walked a more straight and narrow path if I had someone like you in my life, but I'm okay. I know what that path is now though and I'm prepared to walk it. Yes, I forgive you."

"Good, thank you. Now listen to me. I'd like to escort you back to Detroit with me, son. And when we get there, I'd like to give back to you a generous gift. No offense, but I owe you too much to receive a gift like that from you."

"That's fine, but not so fast Bishop Searcy, I'm bringing Bianca back with me too." Bishop Searcy paused, wanting to speak, yet even amid an atmosphere of truth and disclosure he knew certain things weren't privy to everyone.

"Excuse me gentlemen." He walked over to Donald, grabbed his arm gently, and while leading him a few steps away whispered in his ear.

"Donald. Bianca called me here, but it wasn't only for this retreat, understand?"

"You're telling me...?" he asked somberly.

"That's right. She appreciates what you two shared, but now she's wants to move in another direction, and you have to accept it."

"And she asked you, my pastor, to intervene?" he whispered back.

"I'm her pastor too you know, and yes she did. Let it go. Come back home with me. You'll find out who God has meant for you, and when you do, you'll know she's for you, trust me."

"Alright, I see. I hear you, whew. Give me a minute Bishop, I need to process this whole thing; maybe get lost in this retreat, if that's makes sense."

"It makes great sense, but instead of getting lost, get found in it. You see, there's a spiritual component to love—that love between you, your brother, your sister, and especially your woman. Take your time. Absorb the fact that real love among them all will never disappear." Daddy dutifully waited for the men to return before offering his testimony.

"Well as the senior member here, its probably fitting I go next," he announced.

"Well alright. Let's go. Amen," the men chirped.

"You know, pride is indeed a sin," Daddy began. "I know. For years I've carried too much of it. I've refused to come to church and fellowship with you and my church family, all because I had differences with a couple of church members and wasn't picked to be the next Pastor of Mt. Tabernacle. I was embarrassed. At first I felt like a shoe in, only to later feel like I was kicked out. Notice I said 'feel', because in reality, I was neither. God recently revealed to me that I didn't let go and let him work it out before turning my back on the church. I've lied to myself and everyone else, pretending that I don't miss this fellowship, too. I've lived all of my life for it. I'm now asking God for forgiveness on this mountain where we stand."

"God bless him, forgive him Lord. Yes, yes."

"Now those are real voices of redemption talking. Thank you, Bishop Searcy and Pastor Medley for keeping it real. That's how you come full circle and repent brothers. Anyone else?"

"I'll go next, since I was the first choir member to make the news," Brother Nix said. "I might have paid my debt to society for masquerading as the gentleman bandit while on drugs several years ago. But I won't really know until judgment day if God's going to forgive me."

"Oh come on now, he'll forgive you, he's a forgiving God," I assured him.

"That's right, Amen, Lord help us. Kyle is right."

"Well, I'll try and believe that. I do believe in an angel in the form of a bank teller last week. You know, if it weren't for her I would have let hopelessness, despair, and the thought of not seeing my kids push me to robbing that bank again. It's amazing what the devil can do with you if your faith isn't strong."

"Well."

"My family is back together now, and it's better than ever. For once I believe I have the power to keep things right. Yeah. I've got another chance to make it right because the Lord used the bank teller, Bianca, and Kyle to save me from myself. I hate to say it, but

314

from the looks of things, Kyle had to pay a much bigger price than I did, however."

"What are you talking about, Brother Nix? You're not to blame for anything." I said.

"I thought we were keeping it real." Brother Terry responded.

"We are."

"Then it's true. I've been going out squandering money for years now. How much? I don't know. I add up the numbers right for everyone else, but my own finances I'm too embarrassed to even think about. It was supposed to be one more night that I lost control, only this time it was with a toy gun. Kyle was there to save me from getting shot or arrested. It should have been a bad night for me alone. Instead, it was bad for Kyle. I've got a choice to either quit now like a true man of God, or keep gambling until it kills me, but Kyle should be an ordained minister. Instead, he gets the prize of listening to us cry out to the clouds, because that's all we're doing."

"I disagree. I don't think that's what we're doing here at all," Ramario said.

"That's right, Amen. What, huh? Ramario? Manpower's voices echoed again.

"I don't know if it's my turn or not, but I got to tell you all, this whole experience might heal me after all. See I lied, I am gay."

"Just tell me when we get to the surprise," Brother Humphries quipped. "Now are you telling us that walking up the mountain has cured you—like, healed you from being gay?" he asked.

"No, I'm gay, as gay as it gets, and I don't think I can be healed that way, because this is me. In a way I belong here and in a way I don't."

"I know that's right!"

"Hold on a minute Ramario. You care to tell us what you're talking about?" I asked.

"Okay I will. See, I really live in Oakland, California where I rarely ever dress or talk this way, but I want to. I love the Lord, I love being black, and I don't know if I can be healed at all, because I love being gay. The only thing I'd love more is being a woman. The real problem is the black church would rather reject me or sweep me under a rug."

"That doesn't add up man." "Too much for me." "I didn't bargain on this," echoed the brothers.

"Trust me, I know it's hard to justify. I came here to Atlanta for a Gay Festival, trying to build up my nerves, and I'm sorry. This experience wound up being very real somehow, but I intended for it to be only a practice run. I want to go back home and come out."

"Wait a minute. You're saying you were just going through the motions, right?" I asked.

"At first I was, yeah."

"Brother. You picked the wrong place and the wrong retreat. Even I know that," Reggie said.

"That's right. Sure did," echoed many of the men.

"Did he really?" I asked them. "Is Ramario's lifestyle...are his sins any better than ours brothers?" Many pondered but nobody spoke up. "Are they? Don't fool yourselves, because the answer is no. This isn't the military. The church has to do more than simply say we'll just gossip, but you better not tell. Too many of us consider being strong men of God to be just 'practice' anyway. No, we're too scared to 'come out' like the sinners that we are, no matter what the sin of choice. Go ahead Ramario."

"That's basically it. I leave here to fly back home tonight. I've been building up the nerve to do it, to 'come out' to a black church. I've even dreamed of this.

"But coming out to us or any church is a sin, and that's your dream?" Brother Humphries asked. "That doesn't make any sense."

"Then I've been dreaming of coming out with the right church-one that might appreciate me for being honest. One that'll appreciate me for not transmitting Aids to females in the black community or for not running around on the down low."

"What do you want, a medal? Or would you rather have a dog biscuit for not doing something you know you shouldn't do anyway? And you call this a dream?" Reggie asked.

"No, I'm not saying it like that. All I'm saying is, I want what all of you want—a church home that won't judge me so much that I can't get my praise on while trying to find my way, that's all." The men grew speechless, pondering his words further. "Thanks for reminding me how I should bring my bible to church too, Kyle."

"You're welcome, Ramario. I want you to read it and come back here the next time you're in Atlanta. We'll discuss scriptures that good ministers in Oakland, California and all over the world love to share."

"Okay. I'll read it."

"Good, and while you're at it, try and leave out the phrase "good friends put the R to the B" when you introduce yourself back in Oakland, alright? Things might go over a little better without that."

"Good call, son." Bishop Searcy said. "And here's my card Ramario." Come visit us at Greater Hope if you're ever in Detroit, too." We definitely won't sweep you under a rug."

"Thank you, Bishop."

"Who's next?"

"I'd like to speak again, if I may," Minister Roberts added. "I admit that, through all my frustration with your singing, what's happened this past week was my fault. Truth is, almost everything I touch turns sour. I know I'm too often motivated by my ego, maybe my dreams. I pray fervently for a Godly woman, an anointed choir, and real position in the church—all of that, but whenever I receive any degree of it, it's never good enough. I taint it all, and bring it misery."

And that's the way the morning went. Everyone came full circle about something, and at times everything. Even Ed admitted using Nora to get close to her father only to make a sale. It was too bad, because he discovered he really cared for her, but by that time it was too late and the damage had been done. It was all a beautiful, healing experience, but what moved me most was Donald addressing me before leaving with Bishop Searcy.

"Kyle, I apologize for being a thorn in your side and hitting you in the lip. You could have really hurt me back there. Even though you got lucky, I owe you."

"No you don't. You don't owe me anything."

"Yes I do. At least I owe you an apology. I was wrong about something else too."

"What's that?"

"You'll have Bianca to yourself now. She's your woman, and you are a rich man."

"I'm blessed in many ways, but so are you Donald. You have a strong spiritual father in Bishop Searcy, I like him."

"Isn't that the truth? He came along late, but he did come, didn't he?" he boasted.

"Yeah he did. I feel the same way about my own father."

"I'm going to enjoy bonding with him again," Donald said. Hey, 'um', I can tell you and Reggie are close. He really wanted you to take that money I offered earlier too."

"True to that," Reggie spoke up.

"But like I said, the offer to you Kyle is over." Reggie sighed a little. "But Bishop Searcy said he was going to make an announcement to the church to support my restaurant even though it's surrounded by casinos. That ought to make a difference. Maybe help me pay off a few people I owe one day."

"Okay, that's good."

"What I really want to say is this gathering, this retreat did something good for my soul. After this, I'd feel bad knowing I came and did nothing but strike a good man. Hey Reggie, yo Reggie," Donald called.

"Yeah, man, I'm right here," Reggie answered.

"Could you use fifteen grand?"

"Yes I could my brother. I need a thirty thousand dollar operation."

"Well, here's half of it. The other half is on you."

"Man, you a real....I mean God bless you man," Reggie said. "And to think I would have busted a cap in you earlier when you went to your trunk?"

"Really?"

"Oh, sure. Lucky for you, I can't aim. Besides, Kyle threw the gun in the lake anyway.

"What gun?"

"Don't pay him any mind, Donald."

"I thought we were all being honest today, Kyle?"

"Anyway, Donald, I misjudged you and I'm sorry. Before we all leave, I'd like for you and every man here to gather and join in for a song."

"A song? Okay, but what about tomorrow?" Brother Gonzalez

asked. "Tomorrow's Sunday, the last day of Men's Day Weekend. What are we going to do?"

"Yeah, we haven't got to that. What are we going to do about it?" they asked.

"Listen up everybody. We're going to participate in the final day of Men's Day anyway, even if we don't do anything but show up, direct traffic, and hold the doors for people. Our debt's been paid by the blood of Jesus—that's right. He's already paid the price for our sins. Now let's rejoice and become a living part of this huge rock we're standing on, no matter what tomorrow brings. Now, in honor of Pastor Adams, let's gather around in a circle and say a prayer for him. Someone pick a favorite scripture to read, and afterwards we'll sing 'Eyes Toward the Heavens.'

As the men gathered I noticed many didn't even look the same. Donald seemed humbled, as if willing to let go and let God take over for the first time in his life. Minister Roberts self righteousness was no match for the wrath of God either. He never said another word until we all departed. Ramario on the other hand was totally enthralled and in no hurry to catch a departing flight from Hartsfield Airport just two hours away. Papa Medley gleamed at me, silently saying all the things his lips didn't have to, while Bishop Searcy voiced deep appreciation for a worship service like few he'd ever taken part in. Hopefully it was a bonus after connecting with Donald again. Reggie looked as confused *and* enlightened as a man could ever get, and asked me to hold onto the briefcase of money indefinitely while I escorted him and Daddy down the sky lift. Thanking me for bringing him along, he still eyed it closely. Who could blame him? It contained half the key to half of the life he had yesterday.

FORTY TWO

7:00 A.M
Mt. Tabernacle Church

Ordinary morning drizzle met the sunrise on the horizon as I walked from the truck to the church door, but not much else was ordinary. Sure a huge, colorful Men's Day banner covered the church lawn, but Mt. Tabernacle had always been proud to advertise the few, dedicated men that represented it. That was the first oddity, because Greater New Mt. Zion—the second biggest Men's Choir in Atlanta, was already here. Three yellow church buses carrying fifty or more men lined our tiny parking lot. Many more buses from other churches would follow. Also different, I was no longer alone and at my own pace. Little did I know I would hardly ever be. Daddy, with his cane flanking my left, made it necessary to push Reggie's wheelchair so slow that he couldn't stand it. I was beginning to love Reggie like a brother, but he was spoiled. His advice about releasing guilt must have been sticking though, as it dawned on me that there was nothing more annoying than pushing a spoiled ex-athlete like him around, even if I'd paralyzed him.

We walked inside the sanctuary in enough time to get a seat at the front. As we did, Pastor Jackson appeared from the rear door of the sanctuary. He was happy to see me, but elated to see Daddy. Something about him also appeared sad, as if his most favorite meal in whole in the world were being served cold.

"Praise God, Fredrick, you came back," he exclaimed. "It's so good to see you, and you came back for Men's Day at that!" Daddy was uncommonly gracious while shaking his hand.

"It's good to see you too, Brother Jackson, you too. I guess I've been gone long enough."

"Much too long, and you know it. Well I'll be. Hey, a couple of visiting pastors are addressing the congregation today, but its only right to honor you and the Medley name by allowing you to address the Men's Day congregation first." Daddy glanced down at the floor before bringing his head up to respond.

"You know, there was a time when that would have meant a lot, Pastor Jackson, but that window is now closed. Thank you, but I don't need that courtesy anymore."

"What would you say if I told you that *I* need you to address them then?" Daddy looked surprised as Pastor Jackson continued.

"Frederick, more than anything, I'm sorry for my role in driving you away years ago. It was innocent, but ignorant. Inviting you to speak I'd suppose is a fitting way to bring you back."

"Your apology is accepted, but things happen for a reason. God has his plan. I just want to enjoy the service now, and show my support for the church, my son, and these men."

"Alright," Jackson conceded, "but Fredrick, Kyle, speaking of His plan, I just got the call fifteen minutes ago."

"What call," Daddy asked? "What are you talking about Jackson?"

"The call was from Deacon Sheffield, who's been by his side the whole time during the Haitian mission. Pastor Troy Adams has died."

"God no!" Daddy cried out.

"But pastor, I can't believe that," I said. "I thought he was improving. Have mercy."

"I can't believe it either, gentlemen, but it's true. I'm in shock, just like you. A part of me wants to go on with the service like nothings happened—like he's going to walk through that door right after our praise and worship celebration and revive this house with a stirring Men's Day sermon. You know, one that will encourage us all to be better men."

"I wanted to see him," Papa Medley said. Oh why did I wait so long, Lord?" Daddy asked, shaking his head and rocking his cane back and forth. "Jackson. Say, Brother Jackson."

"You say something Fredrick?"

"Yeah I did. Why don't you let Kyle address the congregation and tell them?" Pastor Jackson paused.

"No...no...God No! In light of everything that's gone on, it would be awkward. It would be suicide. I'm sorry Fredrick, but the people aren't ready for that either—not from Kyle, especially now."

"You haven't changed a bit, Jackson. The people need leadership. They don't run the church, and even they know it."

"You haven't changed much yourself Fredrick, still jumping to conclusions. See it's not just about the people. Have you thought about Kyle, Fredrick?"

"Of course I have, he's my son!"

"Then realize there's no telling how they'll react to your son, especially after getting the news about Pastor Adams passing. Kyle's been tested and convicted enough this week already. Fredrick, I'm warning both of you. It won't be a nice reception." Pastor Jackson then looked to me. "Kyle, you understand what I'm saying, right?" Dad and I fell silent. I weighed the wisdom of his words tempered with the image of an old man who had little strength for battle, while Daddy looked at him as if witnessing déjà vu all over again.

"Pastor Jackson," I said, "I appreciate your concern, but please, let me do it." Pastor Jackson seemed shocked.

"What? Think about that. Take a minute and really think about that," he advised. "Are you sure you want to try that?"

"Pastor Adams wanted leaders to step up in his absence, didn't he? He talked about it a lot lately. It's almost prophetic, like he knew this day was coming soon. Yeah, I'll do it, don't worry." The aging pastor's face revealed the stress of contemplating too many ordeals over too many years to count, and unceremoniously handed me some very short reigns.

"Alright. Go ahead, Kyle. Just be careful. The congregation doesn't want you talking like you're running things, understand? The men aren't going to sing or anything, either, right?"

"Just let me handle it pastor, I'll know what to say. I'll speak what's been put on my heart."

"Very well. By the way, what on earth happened to your lip, son?"

MEN'S DAY

Brothers who weren't directing traffic outside held doors for members and guests. Other's positioned themselves in the aisles, ushering people to their seats until the mid-sized sanctuary filled up. Manpower members were dignified in their black suits, holding their heads high like men should do on any occasion, especially Men's Day. The smiling deacons and their wives preceded everyone in the front rows across from us. Men were proud, though the restaurants around town were emptier than Fathers Day.

Behind us flowed dozens of people arriving early for this coveted service, and of course there was Bessie Simmons. Bessie waltzed in wearing a fire engine red dress and matching hat measuring half the size of Georgia. After smiling at those who tolerated her, she cast a stiff frown when Ed Tyson approached and attempted to escort her to her seat. If I didn't have a clue before to what Pastor Jackson tried to warn me about, I did now. Ignoring Ed, Bessie scanned the sanctuary and finally focused on the three of us. Her face conveyed a sneering look of betrayal after seeing Daddy and I in close proximity to Pastor Jackson. Maybe she simmered because Daddy, unable to withstand her mouth anymore, had put some distance between their friendships. Or maybe after years of jumping and shouting in the third row, she now needed a purpose and in our inequities had found one. Whatever the cause, she was visibly adamant about pursuing it after yanking her elbow from Ed and negotiated her way to her seat.

She rested herself and promptly rocked her animated body back and forth, then side to side. It first appeared to be a childish, futile attempt to get the attention of one or all of the deacon's wives, who all sat in front of her and out of view. Too bad she couldn't use her cell phone to gossip in church, I thought, but then again, she didn't need a cell phone. The finest football defense was actually no match for these ladies, for three of the wives instinctively turned around to acknowledge her. Two more quickly followed suit, and suddenly it was scarier than anything I'd ever seen on a football field. Unknown musicians came to the stage followed one by one by nearly fifty men of Mt. Zion, all dressed in beige suits and burgundy ties. They spilled over into the sanctuary as if they were crossing the border, but they weren't aliens. They were our brothers, just stopping by to offer their brand of gospel nourishment for a grand occasion. My eyes found Bianca graciously allowing Charles Nix to escort her to her seat. She looked up and smiled broadly at me as the musicians began their instrumental brand of "Praise and Worship."

I smiled and winked back to her while rich music suddenly filled the spacious room. It was a stirring, rhythmic gospel sound, filling the air with the kind of soul, pain, and heartfelt beauty that invigorates our soul and reminds us why we live in case we've forgotten. The piano played like an old friend, stopping by for a heartwarming visit. The drums like an injection of fuel to get the blood pumping. The bass guitar carried the groove with the strength of a backbone that would never give, while the lead guitar told everyone to wake up and hug someone if they hadn't already done so. The saxophone spoke to our hearts and made some smile, but the clarinet revealed our souls and boldly moved others to more than a few tears.

When the instruments arguably could say little more than they had, a relatively short, older man in his early 70's approached the microphone. He carried a pronounced limp while hauling a nearly crooked body, a body that denoted a life full of blue collar battles which nearly got the best of him, in fact. But his voice. It was his voice! Slowly, he grabbed the microphone from the stand and lifted it humbly to his mouth. His choir brothers smiled, clearly excited about the vocal treat we were promised to receive. Someone shouted "Alright Grady," and we *knew* he was destined to leave his mark on this song. He sang about the life of a man—a strong man trying to serve his God, his family, and his job, along with the added weight of this world on his shoulders. His words were

poetic, but that silky quality in his voice was moving, mes-
merizing; possessing a uniqueness that harbored and engulfed our
fathers, our brothers, and our sons all rolled into one on this day.
Somehow, somewhere during the song, Grady's old, worn body
was transformed into a classic car. Like the beauty in a classic car
often justifies an ancient exhaust system, Grady's voice restored
and brought beauty to his aging, weathered body. He finished the
song, no thanks to our shouting and clapping, and along came a
much younger, agile man from their ranks to sing a new one. The
two men were noticeably different, yet both shared the same vocal
DNA. And it went this way for over forty minutes. The train had
run quite smoothly without a conductor thus far, but a new track
needed negotiating. It was now time to speak. It was time to speak
for Pastor Adams, Pastor Jackson, and Bishop Searcy. It was time
to speak for Papa Medley, for Reggie, and for me. It was time to
speak for the Men of Manpower, for Donald, and even Ramario.
Last but not least, it was time to speak because their music minister
advised the men they'd only sing four songs, and no longer was
there the presence of Pastor Adams to request and be granted a fifth.

Their organist retreated to softly tapping the white and black
keys. I glanced at Daddy, who nodded towards me as I looked
over to Pastor Jackson, who held the wrist of Pastor Bradford for
stability before rising from his chair.

"You've earned this Kyle so don't forget, it's either here or that
street corner," Reggie promised before aiming his head down in
hopes his words offered no embarrassment.

"I don't know Reggie, that street corner's not looking so bad right
now," I responded. Lifting up my Bible I grabbed his listless arm.

"Thanks, Reggie," I said, and firmly grabbed Daddy's arm
also before leaving them both.

"I believe in you, son," Daddy confirmed.

"I always knew you did, thanks."

I walked along the front of the sanctuary before turning to walk up
the middle stairs. Reaching the podium I nodded to all of the
visiting pastors before grabbing the microphone, but as I stared
across a sea of faces I observed nearly half appeared resentful

and annoyed, to say the least. Bessie and her cohorts frowned while contorting their faces in the most unimaginable way, but it didn't matter. I felt God's love in the house anyway, and seeing Bianca, Jocelyn, Etta, and Manpower members everywhere only fortified my feelings of favor.

"Good morning Mt. Tabernacle," I began.

"**Um-hum, yeah, yeah, alright,**" many disapprovingly responded as others loudly exhaled in frustration.

"We've been blessed by the Men of Gospel Standards of Greater Mt. Zion Church of God and Christ this morning, and on behalf of Pastor Adams and our Manpower Choir we extend a hearty thanks to them for coming out for Men's Day."

"AMEN" shouted the majority of the congregation while standing and rendering a rousing round of applause.

"This is the day the Lord has made, Mt. Tabernacle. I'm Kyle Medley, and Men's Day is a glorious day indeed. Before I begin, I want to let the church know that I serve as only a messenger today. I'm not here to try and replace Pastor Adams. Nobody can replace Pastor Adams. "Amen to that." But on that note I do have a sad message to deliver." The backs of dozens straightened up in their seats, instinctively bracing for the worst. "Pastor Troy Adams has succumbed to Malaria, and passed on to glory early this morning."

"No, Oh God no!" they shouted. "Jesus help us please!" If their heads didn't go downward their hands rose up to the heavens. Grief engulfed the whole church, filling it as prevalently as the music which preceded it. Women wailed, the strongest of men cried, children frowned with sadness, and Bessie legitimately passed out.

"Yes it's true, and it is with great sadness that I, like you, must share the cruel reality of his passing. As we grieve, as we mourn, let us not be angry however. I want to remind you of the reality that Troy Adams belonged to God and eternity all along, and not us, as we tend to think. Let's cry if we have to, but through our tears let's remember we have been blessed to borrow him for as long as we have before his release back to eternity. Sure, we can cry, but we can also rejoice because his soul was prepared. Will the congregation bow their heads, grab hands, and share with me in a moment of prayer?

"Dear Lord, we come to you in grave sadness over the passing of Pastor Troy Adams, yet we come to you also for spiritual contentment, contentment in the knowledge of the faithful that his soul, his spirit, couldn't be more alive. We thank you for where Pastor Adams has taken our souls, and we trust it was for a reason that you took him Lord Jesus. Sooner or later you had to take Pastor Adams, and for all who knew him, there will be sorrow. In our carnal understanding there should be sorrow. We miss him already, but I ask, what better day than Men's Day to do it? We pray that his loss and this day forever reminds us that he's made us better men, since he was a great man serving a greater God indeed... Thank you. Now as I said earlier, I'm just a messenger today. Though I stand proudly before you, claiming the Kingdom as a child of God, I realize there are a great many among you that have contrary sentiments in that regard, and that's okay, too. It's okay because I don't want to tarnish this day with 'he say, she say', or remotely entertain opinions of right or wrong. In recognition of Men's Day and to honor our beloved Pastor Troy Adams, I'd like to shift our focus to a few other messengers in our midst. Will the boys of the Mt. Tabernacle Boy's Choir step forward to sing please?"

"What did he say? He wants the boy's choir! For what?" Fourteen boys, all between the ages of 8 — 12 years of age and dressed in their Sunday best, looked to their parents for approval upon the impromptu request. Bewildered and pensive, their mothers hastily straightened their ties, buttoned their suits, and patted them on the back before sending them forward to the podium to join me. As they did, I put them in a circle formation with their best singer, Christopher in the middle.

"Jesus loves me," I remarked to their Music Minister. "Can you all play that?"

The musicians briefly conferred with each other before answering.

"Oh yeah, sure," they responded.

"Tell me Christopher and the rest of you, are you all ready?"

"For Jesus we'll rock it steady," Chris replied, speaking for them all.

The boys sang the song vibrantly and slightly off key, but it wasn't their words or voices that impressed as much as the intensity in their faces, conveying they understood fully what they sang about. The children's youthful voices suspended the member's grief and propelled them to their feet. With tear filled eyes, the congregation sang along with the boys until the song's end. They then clapped feverishly for the boy's innocence. They clapped feverishly for their own pain. They clapped loudly in hopes that God would not forsake them during this time of loss. They clapped and they clapped. They clapped until the second I approached the microphone too.

"Those are the messengers of our future Mt. Tabernacle. They appreciate your rousing applause, and we so love them, don't we?"

"Yes, oh yes we do love them," they responded.

"We thank God for them too, don't we?"

"Oh yes, yes."

"I know you do love them Mt. Tabernacle, but let me ask you a question, do they know?" The clapping ceased and the room grew quiet as several displayed angry and confused stares.

"Do they really know you love them? Tell me, as you judge me and the men of Manpower. How many of you have committed yourselves to be a mentor in the lives of a young boy? You all are awfully quiet...I'm waiting." The room was silent now. "It's my fault, though. Maybe I should rephrase the question. How many of you are serving as templates for a boy to understand what it's like to one day become a man?"

Bessie had come alive again, and now hung onto my every word with tears in her eyes.

"To navigate through the maze of violence, drugs, poor morals and social perversions he will encounter almost daily in his quest to be a man? I see seven out of a thousand hands, but oh, we can judge, now can't we."

"Stop it Kyle," Bessie pleaded from her seat.

"We can judge our products well, but we cannot employ are available hands to help shape them, right? We just love em' more when they turn out right, is that it?"

"Stop it right now!" she yelled out in agony.

"This is my message, ladies and gentleman, and this is the last time I will address this congregation, because from this day forward my message will go to the streets. If you are looking for Kyle Medley and the men of Manpower, that's where you'll find us."
Reggie shook his head in shock, his lips said, "You are so blowing it." I grabbed my Bible and hastily began my descent down from the podium toward the pews.

"Stop it, please," Bessie cried out again in agony. "I was wrong. We were wrong to judge you, Kyle."

"Please, stay right there and don't go anywhere," the deacons along with their wives joined in to plead to my amazement.

"We need you Kyle, we're sorry," they shouted.

"That's right, we need a real leader," said another. An old man rose up waving his hand for attention, "I don't think we'll ever replace Troy Adams, but I say we shouldn't look any further. I'll take a Medley man any day." Daddy then stood, followed by the men of Manpower, Pastor Jackson, Pastor Bradford, and the 'Voices of Standards'. Bianca and Jocelyn wept, and Etta and Francine called my name like cheerleaders of yesteryear. Reggie's head didn't know which way to turn next, but he managed to motion me back towards the microphone somehow. Pastor Jackson walked over to it first and made it official. "Kyle Medley, would you mind returning to the podium young man?"

I heard them all, but my mind was truly resolved to serving a street ministry before I even spoke. Between my heart and mind weighing their angry stares and gestures earlier, coupled with Daddy's warnings about dealing with church folks, I was armed with Momma's Bible and on my way. But thoughts of following in my fore-fathers footsteps compelled me and ordered me back. Could I do it in my own way? If so, I could still serve the people in the streets. I could enjoy good gospel music too, and maybe I wouldn't have to push Reggie around in the cold if by some miracle he'd ever join me, I thought.

"I hear your calls Mt. Tabernacle, and I'm humbled indeed. Even though I'm grateful for this opportunity however, I stand on principle, and I must inform you now. If I am to be your next pastor, I'm changing the bylaws of this church. Kyle Medley's going to have the final say so here at Mt. Tabernacle, and I won't be removed or judged on hearsay."

"Well all right," "yes pastor," "fine with us," they shouted.

"And the men of Manpower come with my ministry, and they'll not be judged on hearsay during bad times or even by the quality of their voices alone during good. Judge their spirit. Judge their efforts to show a young man the way. That will be the foundation of my ministry."

"Yes Pastor." "Amen"

"And another thing, if I'm going to be the Senior Pastor at Mt. Tabernacle, then my father, Fredrick Medley, will have to serve as one of my assistant pastors—that is, if he'll accept."

"Okay Pastor Medley," "Thank God for that," they seconded. All of us, especially me, grew quiet while awaiting his reaction. Daddy rose up and looked about, completely overtaken with emotion after scanning the congregation with eyes of wonderment. The sea of familiar faces he'd known many years ago were gone, but in their place were younger, newer faces who'd heard of his legacy and longed to see him fulfill it in most any fashion.

"I'm older these days," he began, "but I'll serve a ministry over the sick and shut in. Maybe I'll see a few old friends while I get to know the rest of you, but I'll serve."

"Very well, Pastor Medley," I said, and a modest smile came about his face as he sat.
The congregation shouted 'Amen' and clapped even more until I interrupted.

"But Mt. Tabernacle, there is one issue we need to address before I lead you. I'm a single man, and all of the pastors over this church have traditionally been married."

"Sorry pastor, we can't help you there, but its okay," someone shouted.

"I know you can't help me there, but I should have a first lady, and there's a first lady that I need—that Mt. Tabernacle needs."

"Where is she Kyle?" somebody shouted.

"Oh, she's out there among you." I said, and looked at her face. With tears in her eyes Bianca smiled at me, glowed at me, and it was all I needed to go forward.

"I won't say her name, because I don't want to embarrass the both of us should she refuse, but she knows who she is. If you'll be my wife, will you come forward?" I innocently asked.

Suddenly, at least twelve relatively unknown women rushed out of their seats and dashed towards the podium, each striking a photogenic pose upon their arrival to cement their worth and prove they all belonged. One even demanded a visiting pastor relinquish his seat for a photo, but they all created an awkward moment at best.

"I'm sorry ladies. I thank you all for coming forward, but unfortunately I'm referring to someone else. Would you all please, please take your seats?" After they scurried back to take their seats I rephrased the question.

"Looks like I can't do it any other way. Bianca Kincaid, I love you. Would you please be my wife?" I asked.

Bianca rose from her seat and slowly made her way towards the aisle. Like a queen who needed no crown she gracefully strode up the aisle in regal fashion as the congregation embraced her with smiles and nods of love.

"Funny how prayers can come true Bianca, because we sure prayed for you," came voices from a couple she'd almost passed on the way. Curiously glancing back to see who knew her so intimately, she was surprised to find it none other than Barry and Josephine. Josephine held up the ring Bianca had given her and blew a kiss. Arriving to join me at the podium she attempted to wipe all of her many tears of joy away, but she couldn't, for the tears flowed faster than the pace of her hands. I handed her a napkin and grabbed both of her hands gently as she spoke.

"Yes Kyle, I will certainly be your wife," she assured, and we hugged each other tightly as the church erupted in applause.

"Mt. Tabernacle, meet your next first lady, Bianca Kincaid." They clapped on further and the two of us embraced again for several moments. Looking out of the corner of my eye I noticed Reggie holding up a stop watch as best he could, desperately trying to get my attention.

"Excuse me a moment Bianca, but I hope you'll be comfortable joining me up here sometimes," I said.

"I think I could get used to it," she replied.

"That's great," I said, and I escorted her to a chair next to mine before walking over to Reggie's outstretched arms. I didn't hesitate to hug him, and upon my embrace Reggie looked up with a serious expression on his face.

"You left Donald in one piece," he noted.

"Yeah, I guess that was a little unusual," I replied.

"It wasn't that unusual, at least not for the redeemed Kyle I've gotten to know," he responded. "Maybe you're ready to play for all of us now, huh?" I looked at the stopwatch and exhaled a bit. He was right. The answer hadn't been in doubt for a while now.

"If you're ready, then take this stop watch here in my hand. It's even better than the last one," he insisted, "but I'm going to need a 4.3, and I won't ask you again if you tell me no," he warned. I took the stop watch out of his hand and smiled.

"I doubt that, but I don't need to be sold anymore, Reggie."

"Really?" he asked before giving me a 'thumbs up' sign. I returned it before starting the stop watch. Standing next to Reggie and watching time elapse faster than an hour glass ironically made me think of the time that had also stood still for the last seven years. I imagine Daddy better prepare a few sermons for the Sunday afternoons I'll be away. After all, like me, he's not out of time; he's just long overdue.

"Let everything that has breath, praise the Lord." Psalm 150:6

Author Notes:

The motivation to write Voices of Redemption came naturally. While singing in a metro Atlanta choir many years ago, I not only contemplated the worthiness of myself, but pondered the inner motivations of what I'd noticed were several men who sang in the choir. I grew impressed with my observations of men of diverse spiritual maturity. Many had fallen down in life in various ways. Many more candidly admitted falling, got back up, and sought the bonding, healing, and redemption that only wise and strong brothers of every race and persuasion can. Their songs on Sunday morning are stirring, and yet they bear only a scant reflection of the powerful phenomena whirling and brewing within their souls. Thus, I felt a story needed to be told, and in an attempt to capture it properly, it needed to me told by a man who shared in the fun, triumphs and tears of this iron sharpening experience.

LaVergne, TN USA
18 January 2010
170364LV00003B/4/P